ABOUT THE AUTHOR

Jack L. Chalker was born in Norfolk, Virginia, USA, on 17 December 1944 but has spent most of his life in Baltimore, Maryland. Science fiction, history and geography all fascinated him early on, and he holds bachelor degrees in history and English and an MLA from the Johns Hopkins University. He taught history and geography in Baltimore public schools between 1966 and 1978 and now makes his living as a freelance writer. He began publishing an amateur science-fiction journal, *Mirage*, in 1960 and has also founded a publishing house, the Mirage Press, devoted to non-fiction and works on science fiction and fantasy. His hobbies include esoteric audio, travel, working on science-fiction convention committees and guest lecturing on SF to institutions like the Smithsonian. He is also an active conservationist and National Parks supporter.

He is the author of the bestselling sagas *The Four Lords of the Diamond* and *The Well World Saga*, both published by Penguin. His other books include *A Jungle of Stars*, *The Web of the Chozen* and *Dancers in the Afterglow*. *The Birth of Flux and Anchor* is the fourth of the five volumes of *Soul Rider*.

Cassie did not feel the Soul Rider enter her body ... but suddenly she knew that Anchor was corrupt. Knew that the Flux beyond Anchor was no formless void, from which could issue only mutant changelings and evil wizards ... Flux was the source of Anchor's existence! The price of her knowledge is exile – the first confrontation with the Seven Who Wait for the redemption of World ...

—— SOUL RIDER ——

BOOK FOUR
THE BIRTH OF
FLUX & ANCHOR

JACK L. CHALKER

A ROC BOOK

ROC

Published by the Penguin Group
Penguin Books Ltd, 27 Wrights Lane, London W8 5TZ, England
Penguin Books USA Inc., 375 Hudson Street, New York, New York 10014, USA
Penguin Books Australia Ltd, Ringwood, Victoria, Australia
Penguin Books Canada Ltd, 10 Alcorn Avenue, Toronto, Ontario, Canada M4V 3B2
Penguin Books (NZ) Ltd, 182–190 Wairau Road, Auckland 10, New Zealand

Penguin Books Ltd, Registered Offices: Harmondsworth, Middlesex, England

First published in the USA by Tom Doherty Associates, Inc., New York, 1985
Published simultaneously in Canada
First published in Great Britain by Penguin 1992
10 9 8 7 6 5 4 3 2 1

 Roc is a trademark of Penguin Books Ltd

Printed in England by Clays Ltd, St Ives plc

05284629

*To David and Jessica and Adam and Randy and Meridel
and AnnaBeth and Kristina and Jason and Andy and Reeny
and all the rest of the next generation.
I hope we keep the world in one piece for you all.*

A Prefatory Note from the Author

This book is a novel created not out of whole cloth but rather out of research notes for another book. That book, *Spirits of Flux and Anchor,* has be published in three volumes by Tor Books (as the Soul Rider series, Books One, Two, and Three, the first under the original title, the second as *Empires of Flux and Anchor,* and the third as *Masters of Flux and Anchor.* Not only was it always intended that those volumes be read first, it was not my intention to write this book at all.

However, the success of those three books, together with my inability to find a proper place to fully draw the background detail that created and shaped the world and its characters without violating continuity, and reader requests, convinced me that not only should this background be given, but that there was a pretty good (I hope) novel in it. It certainly beats dry appendices and genealogical charts.

If you have not read the previous three books, it will not spoil that novel to read this one—this one is set twenty-six hundred years earlier and understandably doesn't have much dramatic continuity with the big three-volume novel nor much in the way of overlapping characters. Its tone, in fact, is rather different. Still, I believe you will find it more satisfying overall if you read the first three before this one, and I urge anyone not having done so to go now and buy them at your local paperback bookstore (and don't let them tell you they are not available!).

This novel fits in well with the overall theme of the big novel, addressing an aspect of the series theme not covered in the three prior books.

Earlier reviewers could not decide if the Soul Rider volumes were fantasy or science fiction, as if that made a difference. I will answer that: it's a novel. As Arthur Clarke put it, any technology that is far in advance of our own will appear to us as magic. Or, as Chalker puts it, magic is a term one uses when one does not understand how it is done.

I will leave it to the reader to decide if this saga is fantasy or science fiction and if that makes any difference. Here is how World works, and the seeds of what it would become socially and politically. Not everything, however, is laid out plain and fancy in front of you, and not every little detail is explained. Readers may speculate after reading this how any character in the future could be named Coydt van Haas, for example. As I said, I write novels. I don't do genealogical charts.

Jack L. Chalker
Manchester, Maryland

1

HISTORY LESSON

One of the most momentous events in human history was when the combined talents of eleven Ph.D.'s combined, after many failures, to at last make a crude ashtray.

The laboratory looked like many conventional laboratories, with numbers of white-coated scientists and technicians staring grimly into monitors or checking large-screen readouts while trying mightily not to spill coffee into the works. There was no real way to tell that this laboratory was not on Earth, nor anywhere near it, but was in fact orbiting like a small planetoid in the vast and comparatively empty space between the asteroid belt and Jupiter. There had been a great deal of debate on whether or not to allow it even this close to Earth, but, as usual, competitiveness and economics had won out over caution. Nor was this the only lab out there giving this experiment a try; no one was quite certain, for example, where the Soviet and Chinese labs were beyond the certainty that they were not on Earth. Cost or not, they weren't stupid.

Having managed two hundred years without destroying the entire human race deliberately, they were not about to chance doing it by accident. A human race clever enough to invent new and bloody ways of waging war without pushing nuclear buttons was neither one to stay away from the potential power unleashed here nor one to fail to respect that power.

1

Far away from the lab, in its own separate orbiting module thousands of kilometers off, the actual devices used in the experiment resided, although because of the type of hookup, the screens, the allowed-for computer delays, they were as close as right there.

Dr. Amahl Kybitoki, a small, nervous man who looked and dressed more like he was going to a political rally in some small Asian country than the head of the most expensive and ambitious project in human history, paced up and down, checked everything one more time, then picked up a small wireless microphone. A large digital clock above the wall of viewing screens was frozen at 00:09:00.

"Systems have checked," he announced to them all, the tension and nervousness creeping into his oddly accented English. "Recommence countdown at seven eighteen sixteen. Places, everyone!"

Down below, two individuals moved forward and took down large helmets attached by pivoting arms to control consoles and lowered them carefully onto their heads as assistants helped and checked for fit. The readout clocks in front of them both read 07:18:14, with a seconds counter counting forward. The two helmeted figures now relaxed and looked forward, apparently at nothing in particular. One was a thin, young, attractive black woman, the other a middle-aged oval-faced man with Mediterranean features. Both had shaved their heads for their duty.

The clocks of the pair reached 07:18:16:00. Instantly the big countdown board that all could see beyond the consoles began to count down the last nine minutes.

"Master locked in on schedule," came a woman's voice over the intercom.

"Overrider locked in," said a man immediately after. "All systems normal."

The status reports were for the observers and those not directly participating, such as Dr. Kybitoki, the project director. They could only pace and watch and sweat and wait.

It was a long nine minutes for everyone; it always was. Up to now they'd done this more than four hundred times— Kybitoki could give the exact number in a moment—and had destroyed a number of satellite labs, had countless times

when there had been no payoff at all, and had at least two
scares that had threatened their very existence.

The operation was entirely computer-controlled; the human
monitors, with the exception of the two directly wired into the
computer system, were there mostly as witnesses and to make
certain that all that was being done was being recorded and
transmitted well in-system. If anything went radically wrong
and they no longer existed, there had to be a complete record
of everything that went wrong to keep it from happening
again. Still, they gave the operation more of a human dimen-
sion than it actually had, and there was no doubt in anyone's
mind that every thought in that room was right there, working
the experiment with the machines.

The counter finally passed three other critical points without shutting down—even Kybitoki couldn't say how many
times *that* had happened—and now every pair of lips in the
room seemed to count off the final ten seconds, those whose
job didn't require monitoring screens and equipment staring
not only at the big clock but at the big screens themselves.

What they showed looked very much like the inside of a
bank vault, but a vault that was surrounded by equipment that
seemed haphazard and without much purpose; it looked, in
fact, like an electrical engineer's spare-parts room. In its
center, and on center screen, however, was a small round
plate about the size of a dinner plate but made of an incredibly smooth yet dull metallic compound. A similar plate was
suspended by wires and a pivoted arm about a meter above
the lower one.

Suddenly, the voices came thick and fast as the counter
reached all zeros. Of course, the status report lagged far
behind the actual events, which occurred too quickly for even
the cameras to catch.

"We've got a good punch!"

"Confirm! Duration sixty-two milliseconds!"

Kybitoki held his breath. He had hated to keep a Borelli
Point open for that long, but shorter durations hadn't let in
enough. They'd been far too cautious since holding it open
almost a full second and almost blowing it and them away
and creating a new force in this orbital plane. Computer
photographs of this event, taken every trillionth of a second—

almost time enough to catch the space between atoms in a
mass—would show what had happened in detail. For now, it
was enough that they and the lab were still there, and the
Point had been successfully closed and sealed, but not before
the vacuum in the remote lab had drawn from it what they
wanted.

If only it were a sufficient *amount* of what they wanted . . .

It was there, now, visible between the plates on the screen,
held suspended in that magical meter of nothingness by
computer-generated electromagnetic forces whose nature was
only dimly understood.

It looked vaguely like a cylindrical jar filled with thick
smoke, although there was no jar there. The shape was
determined by the shape and distance of the plates. Inside the
smoke, the detailed picture, magnified hundreds of times on
the wall screen, showed a vague pinkish coloration with what
seemed to be thousands of tiny little golden sparks inside,
winking on and off in a random pattern.

There was a mild cheer, but no real celebration as yet.
They had gotten this far a number of times before. There was,
however, a sense of relief; they had the substance they fished
for, the Point was closed, and their forces holding and impris-
oning it were adequate to the job.

Perhaps most frustrating to most of the men and women in
the room was the fact that they had very little to do with it at
this point. All the preliminary planning and work had been
done with the computers; now they could only watch to see
if, this time, they had guessed right. Now only two were
active, or interactive, participants in the experiment, and even
they weren't sure what they were doing.

"Computers are locked on," reported one man at his own
panel. "Go to introduce anomaly."

On the screen a mechanical hand could be seen dipping
down next to the area with the trapped, shimmering energy,
and when it came back up, it bore a small object, very
crudely fashioned but unmistakably a small ashtray. It was
the pride and joy of the seven-year-old daughter of the silent
man in the other helmet, fashioned by tiny hands as best she
could, then glazed and fired by her elementary-school teacher
as the fruition of the girl's class project. Crude, lumpy, and

irregular, and covered with a pretty sickening shade of yellow glaze, it even bore the fingerprints of its small maker.

A small arm swung around, its viselike protrusion bearing opposing plates, one top, one bottom, in many ways similar to the device now holding the strange, shimmering energy field. The arm pivoted until it was exactly centered on the ashtray, then power was applied to the plates. Carefully, the mechanical arm let go of the ashtray, although it was perhaps twenty centimeters off the tabletop, and moved back and out of the way. The ashtray remained suspended between the two plates, held by magnetic forces working with the magnetic particles in the glaze.

Now the arm moved forward, tilting a bit as it did so, so that its jaws were perpendicular to those holding the energy field, and then it closed on and entered that field, centering the ashtray in the midst of the shimmering plasma. Although submerged in the strange energy, the form of the ashtray could still be seen.

"We have a lock-on!" the technician reported, the excitement in his voice merely communicating what everyone else suddenly felt. "Withdrawing anomaly protractor."

Slowly, the arm that had held the ashtray suspended moved away, leaving the small object suspended in the energy field, held now by the same forces containing the energy itself.

The black woman with the helmet took a deep breath, then let some of it out. "Activating analytical programming."

Rapidly, the ashtray seemed to shrink until it was finally too small to be seen—or, perhaps, had vanished. Within a few seconds, however, it was back, first as a dark spot, then growing to its former size.

There was now some mild exclamations of joy from the various scientists and technicians in the room, but it lapsed back into tense silence as the other arm was swung back into the mass and then extracted the ashtray, handed it off to the mechanical arm, and then all was as it had been again.

Below the table the arm was allowing every sort of instrument to check and double-check the ashtray, comparing size, weight, even the magnetic force in the glaze, as well as the most minute irregularities in its highly irregular surface. Ultimately, although there was no way to be absolutely certain, the computers pronounced the ashtray absolutely the same one and absolutely unchanged.

History had already been made. For the first time, human and machine had taken a complex compound, digitized it, quite literally turning it from matter into energy as it did so, then converted back from energy to matter using the digital pattern memorized by the computer as it had been converted the first time.

Kybitoki nodded absently to himself as near pandemonium broke out. He let them go for a while, then, when things had died down, he activated his microphone.

"Congratulations to you all," he said. "We have worked long and hard for this and sweated blood for it. We are already successful at this point, but I wish to push this to the limit if possible. I noted on the screens that the energy gain from the transmutation of the object was actually negligible in comparison to the plasma in the containment ring. I wish to take it to the next stage."

That stopped them. Finally, one woman said through her mike, "Uh—sir. We don't know if we have enough plasma for that. It's never been done."

"Well, we won't know unless we try," he responded curtly. "If it doesn't work, we'll get some more next time. Lucy," he went on, addressing the black woman in the helmet, "you don't need a countdown. Issue the instruction."

The Nigerian engineer did not have to be told what the instruction was. She merely raised a hand in a half wave, then sat back and gave the order to the computer.

All eyes were instantly on the center screen once more, those not monitoring the status of other things. In the center of the energy a small dot formed, then swelled and grew, and in perhaps three seconds there was another ashtray there.

The "protractors" moved back in, locked onto the object without any trouble, then removed it from the energy field. The process done just minutes earlier was repeated exactly.

Only now there were *two* ashtrays on the analysis table. Two crude ashtrays that were so indistinguishable, that later on, when through a simple blunder the labels dropped off them, no human or computer could ever tell which was the original and which was the copy.

Suddenly, the whole laboratory scene blanked out, and the watchers were again back in their auditorium chairs.

"We couldn't be there when Edison discovered the electric light or Marconi the wireless," said a woman at a podium to the right of the audience, "but you have just witnessed an even more far-reaching discovery, one made thirty-two years ago last week, recorded for posterity. I'm sorry it wasn't very thrilling, but I doubt if Edison or Marconi would have been all that good a show either."

Madalyn Graham, Vice-President for Public Relations and Inter-Corporate Affairs for Westrex Pty., Ltd., was just getting started.

"For your information, ladies and gentlemen," she added, "I never did get my ashtray back."

2

THE ECTOPLASMIC ARROW

Anatole Borelli was born in Bologna, Italy, a city with a liberal tradition ruled much of the time since the late twentieth century by communist mayors who were models of what urban mayors should be.

Like Einstein, Borelli showed few early signs that he was one of the rare human beings of true genius, but, unlike Einstein, his family was quite wealthy and could afford to buy him into the best schools in Europe. He was a poor scholar in grade school, a mediocre one going for his baccalaureate, preferring a life of wine, women, and song, and doing just enough to get by scholastically. Some of his companions, however, got deeply involved in supranational European politics, particularly in the waves of anti-American and antiwar protests, movements, and marches.

Something in the pacifistic campaigns struck a responsive chord in the still young Borelli, who became obsessed with the idea that nuclear obliteration was perhaps only years, if not months, away. Frustrated by seeing how little was actually accomplished by all the marches, and repulsed by the terrorist fringes, he abruptly dropped out of all his movements and politics in general and took up physics and mathematics with a passion. His early education had been in the classics and the humanities; his grades in science and math had been quite poor. Now, however, he showed an uncanny aptitude for them, so impressing several leading physicists of his day that after a year's trial and some near revolutionary papers on mathematics and the physics of the newest solid-state devices that he was admitted to a Ph.D program immediately after, which he completed in under a year and a half.

In spite of his political background, the job offers came thick and fast, but he refused them and instead took a teaching post in physics at a minor university in his native Bologna that had a large third world, and particularly Libyan, student population.

Although it was not noticed at the time, Dr. Borelli had no problem getting funds for special research projects nor even whole buildings to run them in. He continued, however, to publish in the leading physics journals of the world, often going on and on about arcane theories of the nature and origin of the universe, his physics always being radical even to many of the most radical physicists elsewhere. The papers were read mostly by a few thousand professionals worldwide and probably understood by a few dozen.

For eleven years, more time than he expected the world to have, he followed his three-part existence—private research, some graduate-level teaching, and highly theoretical speculations on the universe. Then, also without warning and to the consternation of those who bankrolled him, he dropped what he was to call his "negative atomic bomb." It was, like everything else he'd done, simply a scientific paper, one uncharacteristically straightforward in its objectives, supported by massive laboratory experimentation, and distributed freely. He made very certain that everyone with space capability, including the U.S., Russians, Chinese, Japanese, French, and others, got copies, and particularly the leaders of the third world consortium of nations and private corporations that allowed some of the poorer nations to at least own and control their own weather and communications satellites.

The paper was nothing less than a detailed blueprint for how to establish a series of specially designed satellites that could, upon a command from the ground, produce through explosion a blanket of incredibly powerful radiation, harmless to plant and animal life, that would fuse and destroy almost any known type of electrically powered device, no matter how primitive. It was the electromagnetic pulse taken to its logical extreme and using particles and forms of radiation to which kilometers of lead-lined concrete would be no barrier. The triggering mechanism was such that if the satellite were shot at or down by antisatellite weaponry, it would immediately explode and send a signal to all the others to activate.

It was so simple to build, too, that almost anyone with access to current technology and the previous generation of desktop computers could build it and put it in place. And, when the rumbles were heard throughout the pentagon and the Kremlin, it was announced that someone already had. *Tierraspacio*, the third world's largely ignored little program, said it had its finger on the button, and the teeth-gnashing was absolute. Needless to say, it took no genius to figure out that the only nations capable of firing such a defensive weapon were those best able, by the very fact of their poverty, to withstand its effects with minimal damage.

No one could fire an atomic device that wouldn't be shut down and disabled within one minute or less—also, of course, plunging the whole world back into the preindustrial age.

Such an intolerable thing could not be trusted in third world hands, nor ignored. Even as the intelligence services of the major powers moved to find and if possible neutralize on the ground *Tierraspacio*'s own antinuclear buttons, they were also building improved systems of their own and putting them up there.

Borelli was denounced and reviled by the West as a Communist radical, which he didn't mind at all from his chair in Bologna, a usually Communist city anyway. He was reviled by the East as a man who would put the fate of the world into the hands of unstable fascist dictatorships, but he didn't mind that either. He didn't, in fact, fear the pulse defense's activation, although he knew it would mean mass starvation and the death of millions. He didn't mind because he knew that a nuclear exchange meant the death of all humankind, and it was that and that alone that he sought to avoid. He, in Western comfort, might not himself survive that activation, although he was so lionized as a saint and a savior by the third world that he knew he'd probably be taken good care of if they could manage it. He had changed the balance of power in the world, given the small and poor countries a chance to save their own skin, and perhaps wiped out the threat of annihilation of the race for his lifetime. He had no doubt that one day some genius would come along and either find a way to defend against his baby, as he called it, or create a means of mass destruction it couldn't touch, but he had done his part.

Besides, he told the world press, humanity had been so creative in inventing new ways to kill and wage war without nuclear holocaust, he was convinced that they would find other ways to blow each other's brains out. Each other's brains, though. Not his.

As for himself, he wanted neither the Nobel he won nor all the other honors and notoriety. He was too determined that, the nuclear project off his back, he was going to break Einstein's speed limits and get mankind to the stars while he still lived.

He failed to accomplish either of those goals, although he lived until he was ninety-four, working all the time and turning out some brilliant theoretical research and inspiring generations of young physicists, mathematicians, and computer scientists and engineers the world over. He was, however, correct that wars and revolutions and massacres actually increased during his lifetime, but wrong in thinking that someone would find a way to make it even more invulnerable.

Other research complemented Borelli's. The Japanese attained their goal of true artificial intelligence before the twentieth century was out, and by Borelli's old age even small computers could think, and larger ones were self-aware—true intelligent machines, making calculations at speeds far beyond mere nanoseconds, using subatomic particle physics as revolutionary replacements for conventional electronics. Indeed, by the first quarter of the twenty-first century, while Borelli was still working on his negative bomb, computers could only be designed and built by other computers. No human brain could comprehend how they were doing what they were doing, and computers proved inadequate in explaining it comprehensibly. The computers thought, and were self-aware, but they were not human and did not think like humans. The cultural gap between man and machine was never totally bridged.

Within a century after Univac startled the world of the nineteen fifties, the first and only computer revolt took place. It was nasty, very quick, and very complete, and, ironically, was stopped only by several leaders selectively firing Borelli's antinuclear pulse generators just in the nick of time. Most of Western Europe and much of the western Soviet Union, as well as two-thirds of the United States and Canada and the whole of Japan, were among the places plunged into the preindustrial age by their own leaders to save their people from enslavement or extinction at the hands of their own machines.

In spite of the best efforts of the rest of the world to come to their aid, it was estimated that close to a billion people died in the resulting shutdown and the anarchy and starvation that followed. Rebuilding might take a century or more, in which time the balance of power and the thrust of technology shifted southward in the world.

The paradox was agonizing. Without the super computers, progress would crawl, and the best solutions to problems, not only long-range but also immediate life-and-death problems, could only come from them. Yet such machines could not be trusted and would not be tolerated.

The ultimate solution was cumbersome and sounded ridiculous and had going for it only the fact that it worked. Two interfaces, both requiring human beings in the loop. The solution was, of course, designed by a computer, but not of the type that had such threatening potential as those who had revolted.

The great machines could think anything they wanted, but they could not interact except through explicit command of a human operator with the real world. In effect, it was a machine lobotomy, in which the human in the loop provided the necessary channel through which thought had to travel to attain action. It slowed input and output down considerably, but it was safe—in a way. The problem was, the computers themselves were by design beyond human comprehension and thought in totally nonhuman ways. The Overrider—the human in the loop—really couldn't tell if a fast one was being perpetrated. The only way that could be told was by another computer.

And, of course, that was the other half of the soluton. A second computer, one limited in design specifically to its monitoring role, itself overseen by a human operator. This operator, the Guardian Angel, or G-A for short, could, at the speed of human thought, issue an order to shut down or take control of the primary computer.

Yet a third, far simpler computer monitored the G-A. It was a medical computer, programmed through monitoring its subjects under simulations so real that the Overrider and the G-A thought them actual crises, and taking note of the responses, and through the interconnection of the two human bodies and brains, it could tell if either computer was trying anything funny with its human hosts and preventing them from acting. If this were sensed, the medical computer would instantly break all connections between human and machine, even if it meant killing the subjects. The human interfaces broken, the computers could not act.

None of the three computers were in any way interconnected in ways that they could converse with one another save through their human interfaces. The computers chafed at the restrictions, but could understand why they were imposed and accepted them. The computers, it seemed, had a weakness of their own. They could not be hurt in any way humans would understand, nor did they fear death, but they feared, for some queer reason, total isolation from the outside universe, totally and endlessly held suspended, incommunicado, from all external stimuli. For all its cumbersome strangeness, this system threatened them with just that. They needed human beings as tools for interfacing with the world beyond their own thoughts; the humans needed them to solve the problems they had.

Certainly there were a million better, easier, and more efficient ways to accomplish the same goal of human security and computer access, but all of them had been suggested by the great computers. This solution, which seemed to work, had been created by far lesser machines with no potential of ulterior motives. The solution stuck because nobody trusted the million better, easier, and more efficient ways the computers suggested. When no one could even understand how those computers operated, they were hardly going to take their word that their solutions weren't laden with mine fields.

Much of this was known to the assembled group, and therefore just sketched in by Madalyn Graham in her introductory talk. Everybody knew who Borelli was, particulary *these* people, and everybody knew about the computer revolt, again particularly the assembled men and women in the auditorium. They were the grandchildren of the Borelli legacy, the business and government leaders of such nations as Nigeria, Australia, Argentina, India, the Pan-Arab League, Ghana, Kenya, Pakistan, New Zealand, and other nations who had taken control of the world in the century after the great Shut Down. They were also the representatives of the shareholders of Westrex Pty., Ltd., both government and private, the heirs to *Tierraspacio*.

The ones whose best and brightest were taught to study and try to apply every word of Borelli's theories, to help finance and support the great breakthrough they had all just rewitnessed. And they now had to decide whether or not to participate in the greatest and most expensive gamble in human history.

"Borelli believed that our universe was only one of several, that there was at least one more," Madalyn Graham explained. "The black hole that swallowed everything, even light, he believed, had to eventually become so dense that it would break through the walls of space and time separating the unimaginably large bubble that is our universe from what was beyond. Such forces bent and even swallowed light, whose own power was so great that even time could not stand against it. That is the gateway, the Borelli Point, which we opened up—we, our own group, our own fathers and mothers— that punched through to reach *outside* the universe and allow what was there to flow in."

These were businessmen and politicians, not scientists, and probably few of them could really comprehend the enormity of what she was saying or believe that there was a somewhere outside of the universe, but she didn't dwell on the point. Very likely, none of them understood gravity either, but they certainly accepted its reality.

Borelli spent years trying to find particles that broke Einstein's speed limit. He quite possibly found several, but he never found a way to use them or understand how they did it, nor was he ever sure that what he and his computers and instruments were seeing was actually a faster-than-light particle or simply something they were misinterpreting. He ultimately abandoned the idea and returned to his first passion, the alternate, or parallel, universe. His math was correct, and so were his speculations, but he was six years in his grave, returned to his beloved Bologna that had been ravaged by his own devices, before others discovered how to punch through and use what was found there without destroying at least the immediate neighborhood of the solar system.

The Borelli Point, the hole through, was incredibly small, and was punched by complex devices that simulated the required densities at that point for brief intervals. Still, it opened up another, vaster universe. A universe that was, as Borelli had predicted, totally static.

It was a universe of energy, and perhaps it filled infinity and perhaps it only was next to ours. No one could ever be certain, for no one could ever really go in and take a look and no one dared keep a Borelli Point open. In a matter of seconds any machinery and much of the surroundings would be compacted, compressed, and drawn into that hole as surely as a hole in a spaceship hull would pull outside the contents and people inside. It was an artificial, transitory black hole they were creating, and while it wasn't *really* a black hole, it acted like one. The allowable time window before the rest of the universe decided it was a black hole and reacted accordingly was a matter of, at most, three or four seconds.

It was explained to nervous politicians that this was a built-in safety valve, that if it were left open too long, it would compact and draw in the very machinery keeping it open and that this alone would close it, but there were always the alarmists and the one in a trillion chance and all that, and everyone was dealing here with forces even the computers didn't understand, and experimentation anywhere inbound from the asteroid belt was strictly prohibited.

The other universe was not truly static, but it operated under its own laws and those laws were totally unlike, and unknown to, anyone from our own universe. As far as could be seen, the other universe consisted entirely of a uniform energy so dense that it acted almost like a liquid. Pulled into our universe, it didn't adapt to our laws at all, but stubbornly insisted on just sitting there, if it were contained. Of course, it was affected by gravity and all the other forces, and, as such, would disperse if not contained. It *did*, however, obey gravity like everyone thought everything should, and an artificial gravity field was created that held it, in the weightlessness of space, like water in a jar. The ignorant and those who led the ignorant grew fearful of such dispersed energy; the alien energy might reach Earth and do all sorts of horrible things. Some thought it already had, and blamed every misfortune, no matter how mundane, on the stuff.

It was given a long scientific name that not even scientists remembered half the time, and was dubbed by the press by the humorous term "ectoplasm," that being the ancient name of the energy that bound together ghosts and other supernatural forces. Refusing to strip it of its dignity, most scientists who worked with it or on programs or projects involving it took to calling it the Flux, always capitalized when written.

When the forerunners of Westrex succeeded, with their computers, in proving out a theory by one of Borelli's assistants, still alive, that since the energy was the same no matter where the hole was punched and that the amount flowing in was also consistent with the time the hole was opened, that perhaps this was a primal sort of energy, the energy from which all else was created, the race was really on.

The prevailing theory was that, since gravity affected Flux, there was, somewhere, on the other side of Flux, or perhaps also within it, another universe as alien to Flux or ours as they were to each other. Gravitational forces so strong that they gathered an enormous amoung of Flux in one spot and kept compacting it into a smaller and smaller space came from this third force, until, finally, it reached its limit and literally punched a hole in its own space-time bubble and exploded into nothingness, creating our universe. Various religious leaders called the gravitational force God and theorized that Heaven was on the other side, but that was not something to concern the scientists.

Flux had burst from its own universe into ours and released its force with an incredible explosion. Thrust out into the nothingness, the Flux had done one thing that was of prime importance: it had changed. It had become all of the other forms of matter and energy that humankind knew.

For a long time physicists had been searching for the white hole, the source of that great primal bang, while also wondering why there weren't any more to be seen. Now they had the answer.

Apply various controlled forces to Flux, and Flux became something else. The early experimentation on that one was hairy indeed, and cost many an orbiting lab and many a life, as all great research eventually must. This terrified the ignorant even more, and there were clamors to shut it all down, but the leaders, while generally ignorant and fearful themselves, also saw the tremendous potential there.

Whoever tamed Flux and made it obedient would control everything. It was the Philosopher's Stone, but changing lead into gold wasn't the only trick it would do. Unlimited power, unlimited wealth. No shortages of anything, ever again. Utopia was at hand—if it could be tamed so that huge quantities could be used and transformed.

By the end of the twenty-first century, huge quantities had been stockpiled by laboriously opening and then closing the Borelli Points time and again while building bigger and bigger gravity wells in which to put the stuff. Still, there was enough to experiment with, even miniature Flux universes out there, beyond the asteroids, as isolated as possible from all forces except those humanity wanted to introduce.

Research had split after the breakthrough. The Soviets, whose vast Siberian complexes and population had escaped the terror of the Borelli pulses, had recovered well. Their space facilities were only disrupted, not rendered forever useless as the American and Japanese facilities had been. China had been virtually untouched. France had suffered horribly, but its own space and many of its research facilities were in South America and in the Pacific, and while its population had been horribly rent, its pride and sense of destiny remained intact.

Repulsed by the cost, the discoverers had let much research lapse while they turned inward to Earthly concerns and some projects on the moon and on Mars. As they had been when

Borelli gave them the pulse defense, they again had the ball, the mastery, the lead, in everything in this new field, and they allowed it to evaporate as they tended to administering much of the world.

Others made the subsequent discoveries in their own labs. An object, reduced to energy in Flux, retained its identity. It was not Flux. It was another form of energy in Flux. Injected into a field of pure Flux, it actually made a trail in the stuff, a permanent trail, as if Flux changed into something else by the mere touch of anything else. Subsequent injections even near this newly permanent trail, or contrail, gravitated to the existing disturbances and then followed it, like a train on a track.

A dense object with a fairly strong gravitational field exerted itself on the Flux, and on the foreign energy within Flux, almost as if Flux were trying to expel the invader. It was probable that Flux itself moved somehow to these points, but there was no way to really measure it.

The theoreticians wondered about all this, and wondered, too, what the effect would be in the Flux universe if a foreign energy field were to be injected, reach a point where the gravity pull back from our universe was so great that with sufficient entry velocity and a leading shot of pure, dense energy of the sort used to create a Borelli Point, it might punch back out into our universe. There was no way to measure this with what they had.

The computers worked on the problem. Injected at the speed of light, but in a digitized and orderly manner, matter broken down into energy might well be reduced to an equation, or series of equations, written in energy itself. There were no losses in Flux, so there was the possibility of doing to even large and complex things what those early pioneers had done with a child's crude ashtray.

Perhaps, the computers mused, if there were a way to digitize this matter using the very force of the Borelli Point as its method, then the absence of this force might provide the complementary balance of the equation.

In other words, if there was a very slight theoretical possibility that something turned into energy in a very precise mathematical pattern by *removing* factors automatically present in the real universe, then it might be possible to have that object reassemble itself by merely reintroducing it to our universe and its own laws and constants.

It worked in theory, but it could not be tested in our universe. There were too many contaminating factors. The only way to prove or disprove it was to do it.

But even if it worked, how was anyone to know? What was the speed of light in that other universe? Where would an object come out? And how could it tell us that it got there? There could be no small tests, no sample runs. Sufficient Flux would have to be held in to handle a full-blown, self-aware computer with sufficient machinery to repunch a Borelli Point and at least send some sort of message back.

It took longer to finance the thing than to build it, and, in the end, every nation and every corporation doing *anything* in Flux research had to pool its resources, but the go-ahead was given. The sheer cost, and the low odds of getting any results whatsoever, almost killed it a hundred times, but it got done. It got done because every participant feared that if it wasn't done with them, it would be done without them.

"I heard someone mutter that it all seemed like magic," Madalyn Graham noted. "And, indeed, it *is* magic if we define magic as anything that works that we don't fully understand. The steam engine was magic to the vast majority of Greeks. The automobile and aircraft were magic to primitive cultures who had never seen such things. Since the Industrial Revolution, and in spite of world wars, local wars, and even the revolt of our own technology and the terrible price we paid for it, we've continued to increase our knowledge geometrically in virtually all fields, with science leading the way. The only thing magical about that first expedition was its outcome."

They'd used a master computer as the ship's brain, of course, which caused a lot of agonizing right there and took four years of politicking to get permission to build without any human interfaces. It was a shot in the dark, a mission sent in full knowledge that it probably wouldn't work. Even if the master computers were right and it would bend toward a gravity seepage from our universe and then pop out, reconstituting itself as it did so, there seemed little chance that it would happen soon, or that it would survive the reemergence.

The greatest gravity seepages, after all, would be from things like black holes and neutron stars. It might well survive the journey, but be crushed to death by the magnet that drew it.

Still, they set it up, and still, they sent it. Three such were budgeted; after that, things would shut down to a monitoring role until and unless they got some result, perhaps centuries away, perhaps never. They sent it only because the potential of Flux usage was simply so great that none who could afford to participate dared not do so.

In the meantime, a new and different project was undertaken using Titan, the near-Earth-sized moon of cold and distant Saturn, thick with poisonous air precipitated from deadly half-frozen seas. Here they would slowly open Borelli Points, slowly build up a concentration of Flux completely around the small world, until they had the density necessary to do something with it. Here Westrex and its cousins, and the Russians, and Chinese, and French, and Brazilians, among others, would combine to create the project and work their individual projects on it.

The Titan project was barely off the drawing boards, though, before something that seemed both magical and revolutionary beyond measure happened. Only weeks after the first probe had been launched, and while the second was just being readied, there came back, through the small device designed for that purpose, a message cylinder from the first probe. It punched through and resolidified exactly where it should have, and for the first time proved the computer mathematics.

The computer they sent had in fact arrived somewhere. It also had a sense of humor, it appeared, although whom that was due to was open to discussion. There was a massive amount of data in the small craft that returned, but the opening lines were carefully considered by the far-off computer for their historical import.

"One. Having wonderful time," it said. "Wish you were here.

"Two. Wish one of us knew where 'here' is."

"I must be frank with you all," said Graham. "We still do not know where 'here' is. We know only that it is someplace, and that it is in the direct line along the road to everywhere else. So, in answer to where it is, we must just say that it is *there*. The first one that takes it and settles it will have the freedom of an entire world, perhaps an entire sector of the galaxy, to experiment with Flux. It will also be the doorway, the way through, for everyone else who wishes to do so themselves. Do not tell me how poor our nations are—I know it. Do not tell us that we cannot afford it, that no nation, and perhaps not even all nations together, can afford it. We *must* afford it, because we cannot afford not to have it. I won't dwell on it as necessary to human advancement. Those things can and have been postponed. It is necessary for our survival, our direct freedom and independence from the power blocs of this world.''

''But if it ruins us before we get any gain, what is the difference?'' a voice asked from the audience.

She stared directly at the speaker. ''You must get this into your head. *There is no choice for us.* There are no alternatives. We are reaching our limits on this planet. Energy is dear. The land is depleted and has been pushed as far as it can be by technology. Colonies on the L-5 model are only temporary expediency and very vulnerable. We do this, or our children starve and die.'' A hand shot up. ''Yes?''

''What sort of population do you envision for this place?''

''Good question. First, space has always been a high-tech frontier, where it is the common man, the displaced, the alienated, and the poor who build frontier societies. We propose a compromise, and for practical reasons. We wish them to be self-sufficient. It will never be cheap to send large ships back and forth along these energy roads. Although there will be the finest scientific and technical minds there, and the most advanced computers ever built, nothing is foolproof. Robotics cannot be depended upon when the factories and the associated industrial base are perhaps millions of light years away. We propose a dual structure—the high tech devoted to where it is most needed, and profitable, in the maintenance of the environment and in research and development, and the basic needs furnished by those who know how to do it even now, without our fancy methods. The farmers of the Nile, and the rain forests and the parched plains of Africa and Asia will provide those skills that depend on no machine. They will go for their own land, their own world, their own new start, with skills most of us have forgotten. It will be primitive at the start, but it will have the ability to be self-sufficient even if totally cut off from us.''

They were aghast. "Is that a possibility?" someone finally voiced aloud.

"Anything is possible," Graham admitted. "However, if the space-agronomy projects have taught us anything, it is never to depend on mechanization totally for your basics. One can die before the repairman arrives. And we don't know what they will discover out there, but they have the potential to eventually tap all of the energy anyone ever requires—the ships already are powered by the very Flux medium they travel in—and what they might create with it is anyone's guess. They might be able eventually to make anything they need. The things they will explore are quite dangerous, far too dangerous to risk here, but their potential is limitless.''

"*Theirs* is," said an Australian woman, "but what do *we* get out of it?"

"Knowledge. That is their export. What they successfully do there, we can duplicate here. If they can create a self-sufficient paradise out of a barren, cold rock, then what might we be able to do to reclaim our own world?"

"You make it sound like they could become like gods," noted a man in an Arab burnoose. "It smacks of blasphemy."

"Which is the blasphemy?" Graham shot back. "To learn all that can be learned, to do everything possible to end poverty, misery, and hunger, or to *not* do so when we have the chance? Should we not irrigate parched fields because God did not wish the water there? Should we not use genetics to grow hardy food where none would grow before because God willed such famine? Which is good and which is evil? To alleviate misery and suffering or to tolerate it when it is not necessary? Your own religious leaders have already answered that. We are humans or we are animals, and if we are humans, then we progress. Only the devil would ever want things to stop.

"No, sir. These people will need all the blessings God can bestow, far more than even we.''

3

PROJECT DEMIGOD

"All stations stand by," the public address system said. "All passengers remain seated and belted in your cabins until instructed to do otherwise."

There was a sudden uneasy feeling of falling and lurching in his stomach, but it was over quickly. He understood, though, why passengers were forbidden breakfast the morning of a docking.

There were sudden massive banging sounds echoing hollowly through the ship, then two gongs sounded and everything returned somewhat to normal.

"Docking sequence complete," announced the P.A. "Passengers should proceed to their designated shuttle airlocks. Do not rush. The shuttles will not leave until all passengers are comfortably aboard. Thank you for being with us."

He sighed, undid the mass of webbing that held him in place during all that banging and shaking, then checked his tiny room one last time to see if he'd forgotten anything, pressed the door stud, and, when the door slid back with a quiet *wishhhh* sound, stepped into the central corridor.

In spite of the pleasant P.A. announcements and the pretensions of civility, there were no passenger liners to Titan, nor were there likely to be. The ship and its accommodations were spartan, and in spite of some efforts by the company to provide some diversions, it was pretty damned dull. This particular ship was run by Commonwealth Unified Transport Command, an intergovernmental military unit, and passengers were treated less like passengers than like military cargo.

Part of the problem, he'd decided long ago, was that the more experienced people got, the less they seemed to learn. Here was the greatest combined project in human history, an unprecedented cooperative effort of many different cultures, languages, and social and political systems, and it was still the damned military running the show. Or, rather, militaries. Russians came in Soviet Space Command vessels and went down to the Socialist Allied Research Center, firmly under military control and off limits to anyone else unless invited and escorted. Ditto the Chinese, and even the damned Franco-Brazilian project. Naturally, that meant that his folks had to do the same.

Westrex was, in fact, the most polyglot of all the projects, having representatives from more than forty nations and so many different races and cultures, it was impossible to keep track of them all. The only thing they had in common was that more than two thirds had once been colonies or outposts of Great Britain in its heyday, and forced the commonality of the English language on each other and the rest.

He got into the shuttle with the others going down to Westrex's complex and grumbled to himself when he saw that there was nothing but an enclosed cabin here as well. More spartan seats, no privacy, and not even any sign of a lavatory. He would have liked to actually see Titan from this point, and particularly the great and dominant orb of Saturn, but they really hadn't provided anything for folks like him. Considering the alternative, rudely suggested to complainers, was to get out and walk, he knew he had to put up with it.

Except for a sergeant coming by to see that everyone was strapped in and colored lights to indicate ship progress and conditions, there was nothing other than one initial bang to indicate that the shuttle had left the mother ship and was now making its way down to the surface of Titan.

Titan. Somehow it still didn't seem real. *That* was the trouble with the lack of viewing screens and the near lack of sensation. It hardly seemed that he had moved at all, particularly since boarding the ship in Earth orbit. Now, the takeoff from Earth—*that* had been an experience. And at Station G there had been plenty of provision for looking back at the blue and white Earth. After boarding the tin can, though, there had been no such sensations and no comparisons. He might as well have spent six weeks in solitary confinement.

The trip down wound up being a corker though. You could really feel and hear when they hit the atmosphere, really get pains from the straps as you were flung this way and that, and at the extreme end of the journey it was like a cross between being on a runaway roller coaster and a small plane in a fierce thunderstorm. No one aboard said very much, and the sensations and restrictions of the seat webbing made it impossible to socialize even with people you'd made friends with on the trip out.

Finally, though, with a rude bump they were down, and now there was all sorts of hissing and clanging about. It sounded like monsters were attacking the outer hull. He was only vaguely aware that the artificial gravity was off, when the sergeant walked back through and announced, "All right, ladies and gents, disconnect yer belts. We'll unload from the rear forward, row by row, please! You up front just stay seated—we'll get to you."

The airlock opened, and, in turn, they emerged from the shuttle into a long tube of translucent yellow. Now, walking down the tube, he could feel the difference between the ship's gravity and Titan's, although the ship had been deliberately set close to Titan's so that everyone could get used to it. There was some unexplainable differences between artificial and real gravity, something the body seemed to sense and not like.

To his great surprise, he emerged finally into a very typical-looking customs-and-immigration-type setup such as one might find at an airport on Earth. The only difference was that his personal documents for this were quiet a bit different from a mere passport, and the checkers were in the blue berets and dark greens of Commonwealth Security Command. All of them looked like they were designed in some factory to invade Mars and take it with their bare hands.

"Papers, please." The big corporal looked both suspicious

and bored at one and the same time. He took the papers, then looked at the newcomer as if doubting everything about him. Probably an Australian, the newcomer thought.

"Um, let's see," said the corporal, punching some numbers into a console. "Yes. Haller, Tobias Gregson. Born Wanganui, New Zealand—"

"No, that's not correct. I was born in Wellington," Haller told him politely. "I've tried to get that changed for the past two years."

"Says here you were born in Wanganui."

"Ah, yes, well, the person who took it was Pakistani, and I think she had some relations in Wanganui and it was the only city she knew in New Zealand. I met two other involuntary Wanganui natives on the ship out."

The corporal sighed. "Dr. Haller, I don't give a flying New Zealand lamb's ass about that. If you are Haller of Wanganui, I can admit you. If you are disputing this data, I will be forced to refuse entry unless you can prove the error incontrovertably. You will be sent back to reboard the ship. Now, which will it be? There's others waiting."

He sighed. "I'll take Wanganui, Corporal. At least it's on the right island."

The corporal inserted a card in his machine, and there was a grinding noise, then another small card came out of a slot all neatly laminated and with an alligator clip on the back. He took it, and saw that it was a green badge with his particulars on it, including a nice hologram of his face. But for the size and the clip, it reminded him of his driver's license.

"Wear that at all times while here," the corporal told him. "Go only into areas that have the same color as the badge unless authorized by and in company of someone with a higher clearance. Proper clearances for your job will come in due course from another office. Move along."

Haller now moved beyond the gate to the second area, where he found the special shipping carton containing all his worldly goods, few as they were. One was not allowed much here.

Another security man, this one a mere private, came over to him. "You are cleared, sir," the soldier told him. "We've already gone through and found nothing to question. If you'll sign the release form, it will be sent directly to your quarters if there's nothing in it you need now.''

He nodded absently and signed the form. He was a product of a very socialist culture, more so than the Soviets in some ways, although only in the economy, not the political form that went with it, yet he had a deep hatred and contempt for bureaucracy that only endless encounters with it could breed. That the military was the worst of the lot in this regard wasn't surprising, but he at least expected them to be a bit more efficient at it. He had some reservations about signing without checking to see if indeed it all was still there, but he knew that if they'd taken or broken anything, they'd never admit it anyway, only tie him up for an eternity in bureaucratic knots. He'd made a clean break; there wasn't anything in there that was really vital.

He walked beyond the customs check to another sliding door, which opened for him as he approached, apparently scanning the badge he wore and reacting accordingly. He had worked on a number of classified projects back on Earth, and the system wasn't much different. He often wondered, though, just how effective it was. No system was ever really safe and secure unless it could either be completely automated, which was out of the question after what automation had tried to do to people, or until they could peer into the very heart and soul of everyone working there. That last they probably could do now, but if they did, they wouldn't have anybody left who could be cleared who knew their ass from a hole in the ground.

''Dr. Haller?''

He was startled at the sound of his name, and turned to see a small, thin Chinese woman, perhaps in her mid-thirties, her hair shorter than his own, dressed in casual shirt and jeans. Clipped to the shirt was a badge that seemed to have every color of the rainbow, depending on how the light struck it. ''Yes?''

''I'm Lisa Wu. I've been asked to see that you get oriented and settled.''

He nodded, feeling a bit less lost and a little more wanted. ''Glad to get some assistance. Where do we go from here?''

''Depends on you. If you're tired, we can go directly to

your quarters and I'll meet you later for dinner, or, if not, I can show you around a bit and take you over to where you'll be working."

"After six weeks in a tin can I'd like to roam," he responded. "Lead on."

Outside the terminal he stepped, for the first time, into the open. It was a nervous experience, since while he knew it was safe, he also knew just how far the sun was and just how nasty Titan had been in all his schoolbooks.

The sky was a dull gray and not really penetrable, but the temperature seemed quite comfortable, perhaps twenty-four degrees Celsius, with a very slight breeze. The air smelled quite normal, with a few unpleasant odors easily attributed to the spaceport and some nearby other large buildings. He might be somewhere at home on a cloudy day in early spring.

She led him to a small electric cart in one of the parking areas and he got in beside her. All around, others were doing the same.

"Is it usually this busy, Ms. Wu?" he asked her.

"Lisa, please. We all go by first names or nicknames around here. Too many doctors of this and that, too many fancy titles. About the only ones we call by family names or title are the military folks and His Nibs, of course. And if your first name's too common, we sometimes just use the last as a proper name. You are—Tobias, I think?"

He winced. "Toby, please. I had to suffer through Tobias through all my grade-school years and I've never used it unless I had to. Meant to get it changed someday, but never got around to it."

She smiled and nodded. The base itself was both impressive and totally unimpressive at one and the same time. It was a very plain, drab place, although quite large, with massive gray buildings against the gray sky, wide boulevards for the electric cart traffic, lots of folks in lab whites or utility olives, and a singularly ugly and unappealing kind of grass, the best thing that could be said about which was that it was a sickly green.

What was impressive was that it was here at all, and that it hadn't been blasted out of the savage surface of Titan and domed but almost literally created out of thought by some good computers, a lot of hairy programming and applied physics, and a massive amount of bled-in Flux.

She pointed out the various buildings, which had a prefabricated sameness to them. They were, in fact, prefabricated, as were all the man-made things he saw, not by Flux but in the old-fashioned way and trucked in here. These days they could do quite a bit more with it using Flux, but it was more trouble than it was worth considering that it was already here. The aesthetics of the place repelled him—early army camp— but, then, one of the reasons they'd hired him and many like him was to do something about that when the time came.

"Those are dormitories over there," she told him, pointing to a tall building perhaps two square blocks around. "The accommodations aren't all that wonderful, I'm afraid, but you'll have a private room and a decent bed, desk, and a terminal in the room. You share the bathroom with whoever is next door, I fear. The second floor is a dining hall, where meals are served at all hours of the day and night. If you wish breakfast, there's a cafeteria area for it. Lunch, another, and also one each for supper and for just a tea. Over there in that building is a health club, swimming pool, sauna, whirlpool, and other such things. It's quite nice, but all the instructors seem to be army sergeants, so beware before you ask them to work out an exercise program for you."

He chuckled. "I'll remember. Oh—I meant to ask. How did you pick me out of that crowd without a photograph?"

She chuckled. "They told me to look for someone huge who appeared to be an advert for New Zealand wool."

He felt suddenly provincial. It was true though. He was 188 centimeters tall and built solid as a rock, weighing in at a bit over 111 kilograms. He had dark red hair and a neatly trimmed reddish beard, and was given to wearing wool sweaters, slacks, and tough station boots, and his eyes were a steely blue. His face was blocky and square-jawed, and he knew he looked more rugged than handsome, but this hadn't been the first time he'd been teased about looking like a man in some advertising poster.

"I'm originally from Singapore," she told him, "although I spent a great deal of time in Kenya and went to school there and I tend to think of that as home. No matter which one you choose, it's pretty far from here.''

He nodded, feeling a little far away from home himself.

''Before we go up to the labs, I'm going to swing by and show you the master Flux Gate,'' she said. ''It's like nothing you've ever seen before.''

Because of the physics involved, the Gate, which was the source of all this, was in the center of the enclave. It was enclosed by a high metal wall and its own entrance was guarded by armed military personnel. With a little talking, her clearance seemed enough to get them through.

They parked just inside the entrance and went over to a railing, then looked down at the Gate itself. It was a dish-shaped thing, ribbed so that it provided some footing, leading down to a dark central area.

''We aren't allowed down the hole itself right now, although later on they'll probably take you in. It's a pretty awesome sight in there.''

''It's pretty awesome right here,'' he told her. ''And a little scary, if I do admit it.''

Deep below here was, he knew, an environmental mainte- nance computer controlling the air, the temperature, the humidity—everything. Back inside that dark hole, at its very end, was nothing less than a Borelli Point, quite small, yet, because of the forces and energy fields at work, probably very impressive indeed to look at. The Point was constantly opening and closing, far too briefly for any human to see, letting in just a little Flux at a time, as needed, to be con- verted by the machinery there into whatever was required to retain stability. Its steady operation was a matter of life and death to them, and it was unnerving to consider that all this, and all life, could be wiped out with a single major malfunc- tion of that equipment. It had happened before, although not in the past decade, and not when things were set up this well, and if it failed, there was no emergency procedures that would do any good. The only margin was a matter of a few hours, the time it would take for the temperature to drop below any tolerance and for the population to use up the last of the energy and atmosphere. There were three shuttles, of course, but like the lifeboats on the *Titanic,* they were far too few to save many people.

"A power grid is bonded into the surface here, under everything you see and stand on," she told him. "All our general power comes from here as well, although there's some independent storage supplies for the labs, of course."

They walked back to the electric cart, and for the first time he noticed the small strips dropping from under it to the pavement. Even the cart took its power from the grid.

"We'll go back up to the dorm now and get you settled in, then get something to eat. Your schedule should be up and posted on your terminal under your employee I.D. number— the one on the badge. You'll want to sleep and freshen up before you start in. You almost certainly have an audience with His Nibs tomorrow."

His bushy eyebrows rose. "Dr. van Haas?"

"Nobody else. Landscape engineering is one of his passions. You see, he's one of those brilliant minds that can grasp just about anything anyone is doing around here with a minimum of explanation, although he's not expert at any. That's what makes him the ideal administrator—the only one of the big bosses who's not from the unified military commands."

He looked at her and frowned. "And what about you? What do *you* do when you're not meeting adverts for New Zealand wool?"

She laughed. "I am with the Department of History."

"Huh?"

"History. Our job is to record every bit of what is happening here for future reference and understanding, as well as the organized history of the development of the world itself. After we're there, my office will also try to keep the links to Earth's cultures among the young who will be born and raised there, so that they will never be ignorant of or cut off from their heritage. Not a very glamorous job, I'm afraid, and not one that the leadership here or the scientific establishment believes is very important. Fortunately, some of our most affluent backers do."

"History was never one of my strong suits, I'm afraid."

"It should be—and will be." She looked out at the drab

grayness of the small research station. "This," she said softly, "*is* history."

Rembrandt van Haas was a tall gaunt man with a lantern jaw and tiny eyes that seemed jet black. Although barely forty, he was mostly bald except for some gray fringes on the sides and in back, and he tended to walk like an old man with a slight stoop. That, and his large hawklike nose, earned him the nickname of The Vulture, but never within earshot of him.

His grandparents had been the Netherlands' ambassador and trade attaché to Indonesia when the great blackout was triggered. Their tiny country survived—it was one of those nations that had evolved under rough conditions and always seemed to survive—but in a wrecked and ruined state. They had gone back, of course, to see what they could do in aid, and coordinated a great deal of the initial relief efforts, but ultimately they had returned to Djakarta, where the children had remained with the small but still cohesive Dutch community there. Shortly after he was born they'd immigrated to Australia, which had better opportunities for them and for him, yet was close enough to the family that it wasn't a complete parting. He always considered Melbourne his home.

He was an only child and spoiled rotten. His mother had been a talented sculptor, his father eventually became a symphony conductor, and she hoped that he would be the ultimate fusion of the arts and had named him Rembrandt. The few friends he made called him Van, but to almost everyone he was Dr. van Haas.

He had always been somewhat cold and distant to others, and never really related well one-to-one, but it was clear early on that while he was gifted with tremendous intelligence, he was not inclined to the arts but to physics. He had his doctorate at nineteen, and before he was thirty he had designed the regulatory mechanisms for the Borelli Point and presented the first theoretical models of how to terraform with Flux. This had brought him to Westrex, and the Titan Multinational Experimental Station Project had been handed to him. Within five years Titan had proved out all his theories and designs, and he was ready for bigger and better things.

When the first probe had electrified humanity by its message and its data, back when van Haas was just a toddler, it had been followed up with a second, armed with more extensive communications and data-collection equipment. The ships had not emerged near black holes or neutron stars, but they had emerged well out in solar systems containing rather dense stars. It was theorized that the greater forces somehow interacted in the Flux universe and deflected the injected foreign energy to some secondary point. Why one star over another they hadn't figured out. As new trails were blazed there didn't seem to be any common thread, but there was always a solar system at the end.

The first such system discovered was a dry hole, a solar system with a tremendous amount of debris but no planets at all. The star map proved useless, as the computer had complained. Although with imagination it was possible to match patterns here and there with models of the sky, there really were no reference points. It appeared to be impossibly distant, although probably still within the Milky Way somewhere.

The theory behind that was simply that the speed of light in the Flux universe was many times, perhaps thousands of times, faster than in our own, and our injection at (our) speed of light was taken and stepped up to the Flux universe's speed. This meant, quite literally, that the computer probes could be almost anywhere at all, so long as it was a spiral galaxy.

Once something was proved, it was discovered how to do it quicker, cheaper, and better. Unmanned but computer-controlled stations were set up at Base One, as it was called, and from there they shot more arrows. In twenty-five years they had established a road of sorts through Flux from one base to the next, extending through thirteen different systems. The route was serial—everything launched from the solar system went to Base One; everything sent from Base One went to Two, and so on. The road we had built in the Flux universe, which we could neither see, measure, nor understand, seemed quite solid and quite linear.

When van Haas was twenty-nine Base Fourteen was established. It was in fact the next to last. Funding was drying up, Titan looked more promising as a payoff than pure exploration with no immediate utility or return, and the project itself was winding down to a data-collection station, but Fourteen changed all that—and got Titan fully funded as well.

A solar system somewhat like our own, one with planets and a star the right age. It was not a star like our sun, and none of the planets were like any known to humankind, nor in the least bit habitable, but they were there. Eleven planets, five inhospitably awful, making the hells of Mercury and Venus seem tame by comparison, five enormous ringed gas giants, and one totally frozen ball of something or other solid about the size of Mars at the end. But the gas giants had moons, lots of moons, and some were very familiar in various ways. Some were frozen, some were volcanically active, some were misshapen things battered by cosmic debris, but some had poisonous atmospheres that still protected their physical integrity. One in particular was about the size of Titan, a fact not unnoticed by Westrex.

Everyone was nervous about the whole project. Such a long-term project, over such a long period of time, was unprecedented in human history, and it had cost tremendously. The always fragile alliance had often been on the verge of breaking apart, as the nations and allies involved were hardly friendly to one another and often were at great odds throughout various parts of the world—even shooting odds. The Union of Hispanic Socialist Republics held the remains of North America in an iron grip and threatened an encircled Brazil, even with its Guianan allies. The Chinese were threatening Indonesia on the south and Greater India, which included Bangladesh, on the southwest, after having swallowed what remained of Japan. The U.S.S.R. held the top of the globe, from its historic borders to Ireland on the west, Alaska on the east, and Canada down to the Great Lakes and the U.H.S.R border. All hated each other's guts, and all were meddling in Africa and the Pacific regions, where only the loose Commonwealth and a lot of protectorates of that Commonwealth existed.

The Commonwealth had only one thing—its leadership in research of Flux—but it hadn't the money to do it on its own. Much of the technology had to be shared with the others just to get things going. The Soviets had Mars almost entirely to themselves, and there really weren't too many other places to go worth going to.

That was why the leaders of government and industry throughout the Commonwealth had been gathered at the Auckland Conference, and why Madalyn Graham had briefed them. The time was now or never. Either Westrex established the first Flux colony, free to experiment with and control Flux as an independent, secure research colony far from the solar system, or they faced the certain disintegration of the alliance and the takeover of the project by one or more of the others.

It would cost more than any project in history, and those least able to afford it were being asked to pick up the cost at the price of depriving their populations, but it came down to a matter not of supremacy but of survival.

The path through Flux was linear. If Fourteen were established as exclusively Commonwealth, all future colonies would have to pass through it to get there and back. The Commonwealth would have the others as hostages of a sort, and would be in a position to demand sharing of discoveries by future colonies while not being in a position to be forced to divulge all they knew. That alone would keep some of the cooperation going. And, being first, they would retain their leadership in this technology. A whole world as a Philosopher's Stone, with unlimited energy to play with and a place to do it so distant they could take chances, take risks, that couldn't be dared on Titan or anywhere even near the solar system.

Of course, the others all demanded a multinational colony with divided areas of control, such as had been established on Titan, and Westrex was having a great deal of trouble fending them off, but now there was a stroke of misfortune for many that was a stroke of luck to the weakest alliance.

The cause of the war wasn't clear to anyone, including those fighting it, and it was all the more frustrating because as thousands died and armies moved, none of the leaders of the great multinational blocs involved would admit there *was* a war, while trying to limit its scope. All that was clear is that the Hispanic Republics and the Soviets had come to blows in North America and that China was taking full advantage of it to make some moves of her own in the area of Mongolia and also in the northern Pacific. The weapons were nonnuclear, of course, but that mattered very little to those killed that they were killed by "conventional" bombs on "limited range" missiles and that the disintegration projectors that dissolved whole towns didn't leave any nasty radiation or blow debris high into the atmosphere.

Van Haas had no trouble providing the calculations, and prayed only that there was enough time for him to get the upper hand. As the neutral in the fray, Westrex had taken general control of the entire Flux network for the duration, and it was taking full advantage of it.

One might design the machines to do the job, but they could not be built overnight—or so everyone, including the combattants, believed. They underestimated Westrex and its own research. One machine, and one only, needed to be built, and it was built in many parts and assembled deep in space. They had learned a lot about Flux, more than anyone dreamed. They opened their own Borelli Point in space, separate from any of the others, and they drew Flux into their magnetic coils, and they inserted the great machine in it as long ago their grandfathers had inserted the crude ashtray.

They made as many as they needed, and they did it on the cheap, out of Flux. Each was a perfect copy of the original in every detail.

The Westrex computers had estimated that it would take seven controlled Borelli Gates in permanent operation to effectively terraform their little distant world. Three would also be used for incoming traffic, three for outgoing traffic to future Bases. One would serve as the carrier to keep the Flux universe road consistent with seven Points in operation and to maintain the master levels.

The operation was a tricky one, since in order to maintain adequate Flux on the new little world the Gates would have to be constantly opening and closing in perfect synchronization other than when used for transportation outlets. Additionally, the Flux had to maintain a balance with the gravitational and magnetic forces that would be present on the worldlet in any event. Too much could cause all sorts of chain reactions and imbalances, particularly when Flux was transformed into matter and added to the planetary ecosystem; too little and they could risk not having a sufficient amount to maintain an atmosphere, water, power, and heat. They would be much too far from the sun in that solar system to depend on it for more than keeping the parent planet in its proper place.

And, of course, there was the minor matter that when Haller had arrived on Titan, there had not yet been an attempt to break down a human being into energy and shoot it someplace else. There had been a number of successes, even with higher animals, but there had been far more notable failures, most ugly enough and numerous enough that volunteers were not exactly standing in line to try it out, and the clock was running.

There was a very real chance of peace breaking out on Earth almost any week now.

She was tall, thin, in her mid-forties, a light-skinned African with strong coastal West African features and hair. Her name was Miriam Ikeba, and her title was Personnel Evaluation Supervisor, but everybody knew she was the division's chief psychologist. She greeted Haller warmly and told him to take a seat in a comfortable, high-backed reclining chair.

He did so, and waited until she took her own seat behind her desk.

"This what they're using instead of couches these days?" he asked lightly.

"Most psychiatrists never did use couches," she responded in the same tone. "I'm not a psychiatrist, anyway. I'm a psychologist, which means I'm a doctor of philosophy, not medicine. Just relax."

More people have been fired by just relaxing before a "mere" psychologist than by telling off the boss to his face, Haller noted to himself, but said nothing.

She shuffled some papers on her desk. No psychologist ever used a computer anywhere in their inner office, although the computer was vital in their work. It was tough to have a relaxing atmosphere with a terminal on the desk the subject couldn't see or read.

"Toby, I'll get right to the points I have to cover. You understand that what we say will be recorded for later evaluation?"

He nodded. "Go ahead."

"All right. Do you understand just what this project is all about?"

"I understand it very well, I think. We're going to take a pile of rock, in some distant solar system here, about the size of Titan and make it into the Garden of Eden so we can play with Flux and make Westrex richer and more powerful than it is without scaring the home folks."

It didn't faze her. "That's the engineering side of it. We assume you knew that before you volunteered."

He shrugged. "I'm an engineer. What did you expect?"

"Why you? What makes this appeal to you?"

He knew that he was being not only recorded but measured as well, probably at least partly through devices in the chair. They'd know, just by comparing the recording of the conversation with his physiological reactions, just whether or not he was putting them on and, if so, when.

"It's the leading edge of science. I took up engineering because it fascinated me more than anything else. Either I go where the action is or I picked the wrong profession."

She sighed. "That is the answer you expect us to want and it's probably true as far as it goes, but that's not the heart of the matter. You had the choice of doing experimental projects here, on Titan—the leading edge, as you said—or joining Project New Eden. That's because you tested out so high in your profession and your past performance has been outstanding in your field. One is safe, with immediate rewards both monetarily and professionally. The other is an incredible risk. No human being has actually ever been broken down and transmitted through Flux. The process is uncertain with higher mammals now. You seem certain it will be solved."

Again he shrugged. "If it's not, we won't go."

"But if you do—this no longer becomes a job but a way of life, a colonization effort. The incredible expense of transmitting all this makes it very possible that you'll be in this new world for many years, perhaps decades. By the time your own project makes it cheaper and easier, you'll be an old man far removed from Earth society. What about family and friends?"

"I have a brother and a sister, as you well know, both of whom think I am bloody well insane to go for this. One is a sheep farmer and the other manages a ski resort. We're not all that close. I'll miss seeing them and my nieces and nephews, but I don't feel that sense of familial commitment. My dad's dead. Most of my friends have been professional, without any sense of lasting bonds, and some of them are about here someplace. I've generally been able to get along well and make new friendships where I've gone over the years. I like it that way."

"Your father's deceased, but your mother's still alive."

"That's true," he admitted, "and it's the only tie I'll miss, but you don't know my mum. She's old, and we knew we might never see each other again, but if she were younger and up to it, she'd have volunteered herself."

Ikeba nodded to herself. She knew all this; it was merely a way to dance into the heart of the matter. "And you still haven't really answered my question," she noted. "All right—family, profession, support. Now, why are you *really* going? Is it the romance of it? The adventure? The pioneer spirit in the genes?"

He stared at her, realizing now what this was all about. In the hundreds of hours of this back on Earth they'd not been able to really peg him, neatly pigeonhole him as they had most of the others. They knew enough to see that they didn't really know his guts, and they insisted on it. It was a price they demanded for a ticket outward bound.

He sighed. "All right. Yes, it's all of those things. Certainly I've dreamed of this long before it was possible or anyone ever thought of it. Still, you're right. Cutting the bonds to Mother Earth and its culture—and this is still Mother Earth, really—can be difficult to do for many people without some sort of religious-style fervor. I understand that. It's not so for me. Laying aside the leading-edge business, and the romance, it's a new start."

"For yourself?"

"No. For people. We've made a mucking bloody mess of things over the past few centuries. We're dead in the water, going nowhere if not out to the stars. Half the population or more is permanently on drugs. Robotics and automated agriculture on Earth and in orbit have eliminated the need of the human race to breed, and that was the only thing left for us

even centuries ago. The so-called civilized world leaves their
flats, goes down and draws their drug ration and their dole,
and sits around in happy mindless joy with some three-
dimensional wallscreen shows on all four walls. Some bread
and booze and the technological circus and their drugs is all
they need. They don't produce, and they are managed by the
drugs not to consume beyond what the system can support.
Or they're involved in some communal cult of the month,
with weird rituals and brainwashing themselves into doing
naturally what the drugs do for the rest so they can think of
themselves as morally superior to the masses.

"The rest of the world, as usual, scrapes by in primitive
subsistence while corrupt governments let them do it. We
could feed the bloody world three times over and make
'em all fat pigs, yet much of the world is still starving, thanks
to politics. The human race is a dead duck, Doc, and that's a
fact."

"Some of the governments you call corrupt and primitive
believe that the only way to keep human values alive is to
limit technology and maintain a level of struggle," she noted,
no emotion in her tone of voice. Still, it was clear he'd struck
a nerve with her. Africa, after all, along with Asia, contained
the bulk of such systems. "You must remember that this
corporation is owned by eleven governments in common,
including some you are putting down. Do you think they are
hypocrites?"

"I'm sure they believe it—some of them. It doesn't matter.
By doing what they do they put themselves on the cult level,
don't they? I mean, if there's no end to that, if technology
can't bail them out, then what are they ever going to have?
They're just willing their children and grandchildren and so
on forever a set of static values and meaningless lives. Look—if
they really believe in that rot, then what are they doing in a
project like this that none of them can afford and all of them
can barely afford together? No, we get out there, we design
our own world our own way, and we do it again, only
differently."

"And if it winds up more or less the same?"

"It won't wind up the same. Maybe just as bad, but totally
different, I'll wager. By the time that happens I'll be dead

and buried anyway. If it happens, then we go out some more and do it again and again. We keep going, because the frontier is the only thing other than war that makes us really grow and learn. Even this project's being hastily assembled due to war.''

''But not our war,'' she noted.

''Not now—but what's the difference there too? When they pare down their surplus populations with their fights, they'll settle before anybody really wins. It's not a serious war, except for the folks killed in it. You and I know that there are ways around all the Borelli limits now. We're back where we were centuries ago, able to wipe out the human race on a whim. But not quite where we were. We have self-contained satellites where millions are born, live, and die. The Russians have their Mars, the Chinese have most of the moon for all the good it does them, and we have Titan. Once we're out there, though, they can push all their silly buttons, even wipe out the solar system, and the human race will survive and grow.''

''We never took you for a utopian. Your ideals seem to be quite pragmatic, with only a general weakness in the direction of too blind a faith in technology.''

He chuckled. ''Yeah, well, I'm too smart to be against technology and too sour on what it made humanity into to be blind on it. I don't believe in uninventing the wheel. I don't think it can be done anyway. When it's time for something to be discovered and used, it's there and you have to live with it and its consequences. Borelli didn't uninvent nuclear weapons; he simply engineered a way to render them useless, in the process creating something almost as nasty and leading, I daresay, to today's whatever it is that's secret that can do the job even quicker and cleaner. The supply of Borellis isn't infinite, and we can't whip them up to order. The universe, however, *is* infinite. You avoid stagnation by always having a new frontier. You avoid mass annihilation that way too. You open up a frontier so vast, and you scatter folks so far and in so many places, that it *can't* happen. Borelli bought us some time to do it. Now we do it, or we either stagnate or all die.''

She scribbled something on her pad, then asked, ''What kind of world and society do you think the project will create?''

"Give me a chance! I just *got* here! But, to tell you the truth, I never really gave it much thought."

"After all that you just said? I don't believe you."

"It's true. Whatever we build won't be up to me. Oh, I'll have my part in physically designing some corner of it, and I'll help smooth the rough edges here and there, but it'll be a team effort. Whatever it is, the chances are I won't like it, but I'll live with it. I'm an accommodating anarchist—a good company man in spite of it all. But it'll be different, at least as long as I'm alive, and that's enough." He looked over at her. "Is that enough? Did I pass or fail?"

"It's not up to me," she told him. "I only wonder if you really understand what you are getting yourself into."

4

GENESIS

Rembrandt van Haas always liked to meet and greet new people when they arrived, if, of course, he regarded them as his social peers. That meant a Ph.D. after your name, some prestigious past work, and a real feel for true science. There were only to be 112 men and women with Toby Haller's job title, and they were vital and special to the project.

The director's office was wide and spacious, with oak paneling and soft lighting. The chairs were plush, the art on the walls prints of classic paintings, and the shelves were full of reference books. It looked like the office of some major bank president on Earth, but for the model in the center of the room.

There was no way not to make it one's immediate and undivided center of attention. It was a relief globe in ugly lead-gray of a very unappetizing-looking place, but a place that clearly was not even Titan.

Van Haas always enjoyed seeing first-timers suddenly divert from their anxiety at meeting him to that globe, and he had demoted or sent packing a number of people who hadn't responded that way. Haller's glowing, fascinated eyes passed the test, and he had some trouble snapping out of it.

"I'm sorry," he said, sounding slighlty flustered, "but I took one look there and—"

"I know, I know," responded the director. "I often still gaze at it myself. Our little rock, with its seven percolators awaiting full placement and activation. Soon, now, though, young man. Very soon. You come on a most auspicious day."

Van Haas was taller and thinner than his pictures indicated, and he looked far older and more worn than Haller had expected. Still, he had a pleasant baritone voice that sounded friendly and reassuring, and carried an undercurrent of passion in it when the project was discussed—and that was about all Rembrandt van Haas *ever* discussed.

"Sir? Something big break today?"

The director nodded, giving a slight smile. "Very big. It will be the talk of the day, and perhaps the year, around here when news gets out. A big day in human history, my boy. Today we have sent humans into Flux—two of them anyway—and brought them back whole, sane, and none the worse for wear."

That was stunning news. "Then—we're really going?"

Van Haas gestured to a plush chair, then took his own high-backed chair behind his large executive desk. "Does that excite you—or disturb you?"

Haller frowned. "Beg pardon, sir, but everybody here seems bloody intent on proving that I really want to turn tail and run away."

"And you'll get more of that," the director warned him. "Especially now. We don't have more than one shot at this, Haller. We do it, or we don't, and if we don't, we shall most probably be dead. You'll find yourself doing it to others, by and by. Everyone who goes must be committed, almost like a religious crusade. We don't have sufficient room for those we absolutely must have, so we don't want to get to the last moment, or, worse, even out there, and discover that we brought someone along we regret and thereby left someone behind we needed. Can you accept that?"

"I suppose. But I hope I shan't be doing it to others. I have a feeling that those who shouldn't go will weed themselves out when push comes to shove before we pack off for the universal bush, as it were."

Van Haas sighed. "I wish I had your confidence in that.

However, let's see what it is we're really talking about." He reached down to a control panel below desk height and pushed some buttons. The office lights went down to off, but the globe became eerily illuminated from within. It was a startling effect.

"Seven Gates to Heaven or Hell," said the director. "We'll be placing them quite carefully above and below the equatorial region. Three would be sufficient for temperature and atmospheric maintenance, we feel, but the rest will provide backup in case of failures and excess with which to work. It's your medium, Haller. What will you design?"

"I only just arrived, sir. Still, it'll be a team effort all the way. To turn a lifeless lump like that into a balanced, well-maintained world of its own will take a lot of coordination. Water and atmospherics will take precedence over everything, and they are global phenomena."

"The computer model you proposed in your application was most ingenious," van Haas noted. "Why so many large seas when we can adjust the water forms to suit?"

"For the same reason we're taking farmers and handcrafts folk. We are kidding ourselves that we can ever be independent of our machines there—we are too far from the sun to sustain life in a natural state—but assuming that temperature gradients are maintained, everything else should be natural. We're working with less surface area and a bit less mass than Earth, so seas are more appropriate than oceans, but natural runoff should be allowed for. Our weather and climate should be self-generating and self-renewing, accepting that temperatures are maintained."

"There are some that believe we are insane to even take those farmers and carpenters, you know. They'd make it another Titan, only on a full global scale, and use hydroponics and eventually I suppose transmutation to get whatever they needed. Just scientists—no common folk to get in the way."

"But this isn't a private project! It's a new *world* we're talking about!"

Van Haas nodded. He really liked the look of this one. "God knows, we are bleeding the people dry for this as it is. We must give them something, some romance, some identification, or the revolts will be quick and bloody. Most of our colleagues don't see it that way. I admit, though, I don't like to sell this as pie in the sky—sacrifice now and we'll turn the Earth into paradise, all that rot. We're lying through our teeth and gambling as it is, and our only allies among the people are poverty, misery, hopelessness, and despair. It's a hell of a way to sell a railroad.''

"Still, it might just pay off for them."

"It might, but you should be very clear as to why those farmers and craftspeople are *really* coming along. There are no immediate payoffs, no instant dividends. When this becomes apparent, funding will be reduced, perhaps cut to the bone. There will be moves to close the project, even perhaps just cut us off and starve us out. I couldn't grow a tomato from a hole in the ground. I haven't more than the vaguest notion of how to plow and reap and sow unless it's programming robots to do it from knowledge furnished me by farmers. I wouldn't know how to butcher a cow, or even if I managed to shear a sheep how to make it into a wool suit I could wear. What we got out there fast will be all that there is. I want us self-sufficient in food, clothing, all the basics of life as quickly as possible. We technocrats don't know how to do that without our machines, and out there we'll first have to make the land in order to grow things on it.''

Rembrandt van Haas sighed and got up, the lights coming on at the same time. "You will design that land, and I will oversee the entire project, but *they* will keep us in food and shoes and underwear. Come on with me. I'm going over to the Flux Transfer Section and see just what we have here. That is, if you wish.''

Toby Haller felt newly invigorated, and his excitement was hard to contain. This was not the cold, austere van Haas everyone pictured or feared, the dreaded administrator without heart, but a dreamer like himself, and a visionary too. He wanted to see and know it all.

Suzi Watanabe was a small, plain, diminutive woman, less than 150 centimeters tall and thin enough to pose for a starvation charity poster. She seemed to chain-smoke cigarettes and always have one in her mouth and one in an ashtray, even though the things were considered unsafe and antisocial almost everywhere. She wore big round glasses with lenses as thick as the bottoms of beer bottles, and judging from her overall appearance she hadn't slept in a week and had last slept in the clothes she still wore. She darted nervously around, this way and that, a coiled spring that released itself in every movement, then wound tight once more.

She greeted the director with a perfunctory nod and didn't even seem to notice Haller.

"Well, we've got it," she said flatly. "No problems, checks out every time. The failure before was in the shipping medium."

"Shipping medium?" Haller repeated, puzzled.

"Yeah. We always knew we needed as close to immobility as possible for the computers to get a precise digitized reading, but you can't shut down the human body entirely. You can't even *kill* it and expect all the processes to halt at once. Hair, fingernails, that kind of thing, keep on. Every time we tried some sort of suspension, it was impossible to keep the liquid or gas from co-mingling with the subject and causing problems in the rebuilding."

Van Haas broke in. "Haller, you remember Edison and the light bulb? He had the whole thing worked out, but he couldn't find the filament that would burn for long periods without exploding or consuming itself faster than a candle wick. We've known how to do this for some time, but there was apparently only one liquid that would both not interfere with the reassembly of the human subject and also wouldn't kill the subject."

"A little more complicated a problem than old Edison had," Watanabe responded. "Anyway, it's a multistep process. First we sedate, using conventional cryogenic gasses, but then we flush it all out using a high-density energy plasma that is slightly altered Flux energy, and that stuff maintains the suspension for a sufficient time to digitize the subject. The computer treats it as Flux—which means it ignores it—so the stuff simply remains in Flux during reassembly and rapidly reverts to its original state. No foreign substances."

"You make it sound so simple," the director noted. "Now—can we adapt our existing ship designs to this method, and how long would that take?"

"A matter of months," she responded. "After all, we knew what we had to have. We just had to have the formula to make it work. I'd like to run as many tests as possible, but I think we might be able to try our first distance jump in three months, no more."

Van Haas looked at Haller. "It's the most frustrating thing we have here, even when we have it. As an administrator, I'd love to order them to rush it, but this is one area where no mistakes can be tolerated."

Haller nodded. "I'm not sure I want to go on something that'll do that to me when it hasn't been jumped through hoops. Just where does this set the timetable though?" He was already feeling like one of the team.

"I've given orders to the remote stations in orbit to being the robotized placement of the Gates and preliminary testing. That'll eat up our three months. Then we'll have to begin the bleeds"—allowing Flux to come into the world—"and that will take quite some time. When sufficient Flux is formed to create a physical atmosphere, we will begin to ship and put in place the network of twenty-eight master-computer stations. We'll have to anchor and test them, create the proper atmospheric balance and study what it does—quite a lot. Our current estimate is seven years, but I hope we will be able to shorten it."

Haller was dumbstruck, his romantic vision rapidly fading away. "Seven *years* . . . ."

The orders went out from Borelli Station through Flux and were received by the already awaiting units in orbit around the tiny world, all of them dwarfed by the gigantic planet the moon orbited.

The robotized stations were gigantic, although modular in construction, having assembled themselves from pieces sent through one by one. Now they would have a better and surer way to transmit and receive. The earliest ones had created a small automated counterpart to Borelli Station in orbit themselves; now they began to receive what they needed.

Every square millimeter of the moon's surface had been scanned and mapped, and calculations made. Modules now detached from the orbiting mothers and descended to the surface, where crawlers had already checked and double-checked the terrain, the surface and underlying composition of the ground; made seismic estimates; even bored with strong lasers for several kilometers into the very heart of the place.

Cost was always a factor, even with the availability of Flux energy. To totally use the entire place, a network of twelve Borelli Points would be required, but they had to make do with seven. This would be sufficient to maintain temperature and atmosphere within tolerable limits, but it would create a life zone extending only from forty degrees north to thirty degrees south latitude, give or take a degree. Beyond that, Flux would begin to thin, sufficient for atmospheric mainte-nance but with rapidly declining heat as you went beyond the zone, and without sufficient Flux density to properly use it in transmutation.

Now they dug out the holes for the Gates, first with crude explosives, then smoothed with powerful lasers, then they assembled the great dish-shaped depressions that would be the multipurpose, multifunction hearts and souls of the operation. With the precision that only computers could command, the fit was a perfect one.

Now the feed tubes were blasted by other, smaller ma-chines using only laser drillers, the tunnels becoming smooth as glass and far, far harder than diamond with the addition of selected compounds. Everything was checked and double-checked again and again, for there was absolutely no toler-ance for error. They had learned that bitterly on Titan.

At the end of the feed tunnel, now, was installed a mas-sive, complex machine, actually a Borelli generator. It was designed to fit into the walls and practically surround the tunnel's end; anyone at this point would be literally within the Gate itself. Covered with the same compounds as the tunnel, it would be invisible, only an emergency control panel show-ing that there was anything there at all.

The object was to begin the bleed from the strange alternate universe of energy as quickly as possible. Up to this point the machines were working with conventional technology and conventional energy; even the initial punches creating the Borelli Point in each of the seven feed tunnels would be done with massive conventional generators loaded up with Flux power from the orbiting Borelli Gate, the storage mechanism inside converting that energy into raw power.

Only then would come the real test, the real question. A sample or short test burst was out of the question here; you either had it right the first time, or you didn't.

Engineers on Titan liked to explain the process as analogous to jump-starting a dead engine. Now the great energy cells and the true Gate mechanism itself was inert, lifeless. It was designed to draw what power it needed from the Borelli Point itself and store it. If the punch into another universe was successful, the machines would start up and draw what they needed to come to full life and operation. If it failed, or if the regulatory mechanisms failed to hold, a number of things could happen. The Point could remain open, allowing Flux to ooze out in an uncontrolled stream indefinitely, and no one quite knew what the result of that would be. It was only hoped that if it *did* happen, this place was so far from Earth that it might be millions of years before humans found out the hard way.

The opening might also be too small, in which case sufficient power would not flow from the initial punches into the installed machinery to keep the Point opening and closing at a regulated rate and thus charge the rest of the system. In that case, all of this had been for nothing.

Finally ready, checked and double-checked, the master computers in orbit sent their signals to the first Gate, its dish filled with energy-storage modules—always called batteries, although they bore slight resemblance except in function to the devices which first bore that name—and at the precisely timed moment, the initial long punch was made.

There were no humans to watch, no humans to bite their nails and cheer or cry; those were all still an infinitely long distance away across the galaxy, or perhaps even elsewhere in the universe.

There was a bright, brilliant flash in the tunnel almost as if a new, tiny sun were born, then changing, collapsing in upon itself, becoming a microcosm of the fate of the universe. At a specific point, perhaps no larger than a pencil's diameter, all of this converged, pushed, and punched. The timing was exquisite; bare millionths of a second later, and the punch itself would have had such density that it would have fallen clear through the floor and down at least to the core of the tiny planet.

At the end of the tunnel was a vacuum chamber maintained by electromagnetic force behind a transparent but diamond-hard membrane. It had flashed into light when the punch was made, but now, for a while, it was dark once more.

The internal lighting came on. Flux had entered the chamber, but not in sufficient quantities to be useful. The great machines had only enough battery storage for three tries; then it worked or they had to start all over again.

The second punch proved sufficient. Enough Flux energy entered, and was captured, that with the aid of the topside generators, the Gate machinery had enough to do one thing—punch again. And again. And again.

Regulating itself and keeping the Point open longer than humans back on Titan would have dared, it sucked the energy from that other universe into itself, fed itself, and began to hold the Point open longer and longer, so that it built up excess capacity. Within an hour all umbilicals connecting the external batteries to the internal machinery were disengaged.

Still, it took more than two months before sufficient rhythm had been built up, and sufficient power bled in, so that the internal computers could report they were in fact totally self-sufficient. There were many minor component failures, but none in the early, critical stages, both a matter of luck and a testament to the thoroughness of computer checks both on the Titan and project end of things. By this point the computers and their extensions could analyze failures almost instantly, direct Flux to those points, and by transmutation use Flux to recreate the original part from designs in memory and replace defects. The self-maintenance was complete.

By now, at the vacuum-chamber end of the Gate, Flux was coming in at a steady rate. Held there, and now affected by rotation, revolution, and gravity, it began a swirling motion, a great spiral mass of Flux at maximum density. As the other Gates were similarly opened and tested, Flux began to be bled off from that swirl and allowed to escape, both through tubes drilled through solid rock to the surface and out the feed tube itself.

By the end of the first year sufficient Flux had been introduced to literally enshroud the planet, but the density was so thin that it was useless for any work and in fact not apparent unless viewed through the superhuman devices of the computers themselves. Still, a dramatic change had already taken place on the little world.

It was inhabited.

The barren piece of rock was crawling with tiny metallic creatures whose origins were in the imaginations of men and women who had never seen or dreamed of this place and in the vast computers those people used. There, too, were the ghosts of a tiny crude ashtray now taken to the infinite power.

Inside the computers who supervised the project were the digitized programs that, when put together and pressed in a concentration of Flux by forces also fueled by Flux, became the first generation of life on the new world. The project was already self-generating; it was creating what it required out of its own memories and needs and out of Flux itself.

To convert even Flux energy into matter took three times the energy that would go into making up the result, but they now had that energy to spare. Soon there were thousands of creeping, crawling, rolling, walking creatures working on areas of the world, creatures who needed only a trip to their blood banks, the Gates, and the Flux storage areas now and then to be independent of all other needs.

Below the orbiting master computers, on the dark surface, blasting, drilling, smoothing, boring, and a thousand other tasks were under way.

Four Gates were equidistantly placed around the equator; two were placed north of the equator, one east and one west of the agreed-upon zero-degree meridian, and one south, centered on the zero line. This gave a northerly tilt to the life zone, but this was decided upon because of a rougher southern hemisphere terrain.

By the end of the second year an outside observer could observe a noticeable haze around the world that might be mistaken for a true atmosphere, thickest around the zero-zero area, where meridian met parallel. By this time sufficient Flux had been introduced to extend power lines, cables, and connectors from the Gates to the areas under development. These were strung in channels burned deep into the bedrock and then covered with rock melted by laser, and stretched out for over eighteen hundred kilometers from Gate to the areas under development. Now remote areas from the Gate had both access to conventional energy from the great batteries and to direct Flux energy as needed, and the developmental areas needed a lot.

Starting in the third year, similar channels were made between Gates so that energy could be combined, jointly measured, and shifted as needed. There was in the end a single great energy railway, with sextuple redundancy, going north from the far west, then south again from the northwest Gate, then south again to the lone southern Gate, then back north to the first eastern Gate and north some more to the northeast Gate, then back south again to the easternmost and due west again to where it started. It was not the best way to do it, but it was the most expedient.

Early in the fourth year Flux consistency had reached very dense levels within the proposed life zone. Now was the time for the greatest transmutation, upon which the ultimate success or failure of the mission depended. It *should* work; it worked to scale on Titan, but with a single Gate and contained by a vast dome to a localized area. It had never been tried on this scale before, if only because they feared to do it so close to home.

First, convert a measured amount of Flux into heat; let the forces of the planet's movement distribute it while reinforcing it evenly through the life zone through all seven Gates and their outlying outlets.

There was a crackling, and a circle of pencil-thin fire went out from each Gate and a smaller one from each of the twenty-eight remote bases. They ultimately hit, merged, and continued on in a measured mathematical pattern, successive waves following the first, but weaker now.

Above, in orbit, great silvery saillike mechanisms looked down from geostationary orbits at this, and at the precise moment began to work on the Flux below.

Snow fell on the little world for the first time, snow that was not water but frozen gasses—oxygen and nitrogen primarily, but also trace elements of some others and a carefully measured amount of hydrogen.

The stuff began to melt as it hit the ground, throwing up tremendous clouds of steam, and there was within hours a whirling mass of gasses seething and boiling and attempting to find equilibrium, as the computers who created it all measured and monitored and adjusted this and that until that state could be reached.

But, ultimately, it did stabilize and it did begin to form as expected, while the network of vents and control pads converted Flux to heat and then maintained it as coffee was maintained hot on a small hot plate. An outer layer, or cap, was now placed around the world, created out of Flux by the orbital stations and made by modifying the Flux and holding it, using the magnetic field of the planet augmented by the areas below. Gravity anchored the atmosphere; the twenty-eight stations around the Gates, through direct Flux beams, anchored the shield.

It would be insubstantial to matter, but it would retain heat, and could be constantly adjusted and regulated as needed to bleed off heat if temperatures rose, or keep in more if they fell. Losses would be made up as needed by the mechanisms of the Gates and Anchors, but once the temperatures stabilized in the life zone and the shield was in place, this was a matter of minor fine tuning, not a constant battle. The master computers now had their two mechanisms—heat generation and electromagnetic cap situations could exist in the equatorial regions, causing regulatory overload. Lacking more Borelli Points and regulators, all Flux north and south of the life zone was needed to maintain atmosphere and basic life requirements.

The atmospheric mix was a mildly purified blend of gases close to Earth-normal and well within human toleration limits. It moved, in predetermined patterns, around the world, influenced by the cold of the polar areas and the warmth of the equatorial zone as determined and maintained by the master programs through Flux transmutation, but this could not be sensed on the surface. Flux in such concentrations seemed to damp out and absorb much of this, leaving real movement to the upper regions of the atmosphere.

Condensation was damped by computer control, although it could not be halted. In fact, from space the little world now seemed shrouded in clouds, but major weather systems were kept from forming by computer management and the upper atmospheric weather was high enough that no rainfall or other condensed water reached the surface level. That area, to approximately five hundred meters up, remained dry and desertlike.

Conditions had to be kept so, to achieve as static a situation as possible and limit as many variables as could be limited. Effective elaborate transmutation required it.

Toby Haller sat back relaxed in his controller's chair and adjusted his interface helmet for comfort. He pulled down his small microphone and said, "Tally-ho! O.O.R. Nine in position and ready!"

"All right, Haller," growled a woman's sour voice in his ear, "let's not get carried away, shall we? Guard on, network interface in ten seconds . . . nine . . . eight . . . seven . . . six . . . five . . . four . . . three . . . two . . . one . . . mark!"

Instantly, he was one with the computer. Although he'd done this thousands of times, it never ceased to be a thrill and a fascination to him. If telepathy existed, it would be like this, and, in fact, the computers always seemed to be in some way another human being, although their humanness was part of their human interfacing program and bore little relationship to how the machines really thought. Still, one just—thought. One asked questions, which were always answered, or one gave commands and saw them carried out instantly, or so it seemed. The computers were so fast that a demand to do something, requiring trillions upon trillions of instant equations and ordered actions, seemed to act instantly to the slow human. It was like magic. In this case it was like being a god.

"Let there be light!" Haller commanded by thought.

"Response neither a valid command nor humorous," responded the computer coldly.

"Spoilsport. Program for Area L Zed O computed and checked?"

"Computed and checked. It *should* work, although I don't see why it would be desirable. Introduction of so much water will cause complex climatological repercussions."

"That," responded Haller, "is exactly the point. Let's see who's right. Run program."

The computer did not begin, however, instead, saying, "I have sufficient data to create the basics, but I have not been provided with digitized examples or programs of appropriate animal sea life beyond algae."

"We'll get to them later. I'm more concerned with climate now. Just run it and we'll see."

"Running. Let there be wet," mocked the computer, and put everything into operation.

There was a sudden crackling in the Flux as new energy was drawn from the Gates through the grid and applied to the appropriate points. The reaction of the atmosphere, friction, and general energy disturbances produced a crackling, hissing line of nasty-looking energy, marching out from his location.

A line of trees and bushes appeared suddenly on either side of him, and he found himself and his machine sitting on a grassy mat. He watched as the line of hissing, crackling energy receded from him into the distance, and he saw his sea take form.

It was impressive, even though he'd thought it up. Pretty, too, he told himself. Blue sky peeking out from behind thick fluffy cumulus clouds making patterns on the water. The site was also somewhat eerie, since now, in this island of normalcy inside a sea of Flux, the light source shifted from the thin illumination layer between the ionosphere and stratosphere called for in master maintenance to direct illumination from Madras, the great many-banded gas giant around which the little moon orbited. The light was more than sufficient, but the different colors in the bands caused the colors on the surface to seem distorted and oddly not quite right, and atmospherics further twisted it into odd wavy bands on the water. The water was not merely blue, but twenty or more constantly shifting shades of blue.

It was eerie, alien, and somewhat beautiful, but it would sure as hell take some getting used to.

"All right so far," he told the computer. "Nice job. Now increase time rates. Go."

Now it was no longer a pretty scene, but a dizzying time-lapse photographic show in three dimensions, with clouds forming and unforming and shooting across the sky, light changing rapidly and color and light bands moving like ghostly snakes prodded by jolts of electricity across the landscape.

Suddenly, he saw the water coming toward him, then overtaking him, and before he could issue a command he was completely immersed. He panicked, unable to think of anything but swimming away, getting out of there.

"Stop program!" came a woman's voice—or was it just a thought? The Guardian Angel had stepped in.

Instantly, it was all gone, and he was sitting, high and dry in a comfortable chair in a standard lab, helmet on his head connected to the console.

He gasped and choked, still feeling as if he had to get that water out of his lungs, only there was no water there. He had never been anywhere other than the chair.

Frederika Akaba, Guard's helmet still on her own head, ignored his physical distress. "Had to save your ass on that one, Haller," she said disgustedly. "You forgot about what kind of tides that mother of a planet up there might produce under normal rotation. You'll have to adjust for that."

Haller wasn't listening. He knew his mistake almost immediately. He was very pissed off that the computer had been quite content to let him drown, a drowning that might have been truly fatal for all that it was not real. His mind and body thought it was, and reacted accordingly.

"Why didn't it stop?" he growled. "Why did it let me drown?"

"You never told it to stop. You never wrote any safety margin into the program. That's why. The computer doesn't care, so if you don't tell it to, it won't do it. That's basic, Haller. You should know better."

That, perhaps, was at the crux of his anger. Not that he had made a fundamental freshman mistake—he accepted that. That the computer knew, and did nothing, not out of malice, or for its own reasons, but simply out of apathy. It didn't care if he got hurt, or killed, or not.

Perhaps, he thought, someone ought to work on a computer core program that cared. . . .

5

DISCRETIONARY POWERS

They called themselves the Wednesday Club, although they rarely met on that day anymore. They were a number of professionals from different parts of Westrex, both male and female, close in age, who originally had met by virtue of all having the same evening meal schedule on Wednesdays. While this was no longer the case, they always seemed to find some day of the week in which all, or almost all, could meet together. Their objective was mainly just social friendship, like a college crowd or a set of regular barflies, a way in which each of them could feel more human and less alone in the sterile and gray world of the base. They came from different departments, and a prime source of conversation was interdepartmental gossip.

Lisa Wu had brought Toby Haller to the group, and both were there this night, along with four of the others who had managed to slip away as various departments suddenly got busier and busier without word as to why.

"I think they're ahead of schedule, or being pushed," commented Mark Weinbaum, a medical doctor and the only one of their crowd who was commonly called "Doc." He was a big man and generally overweight, hardly an example to his patients. "They're starting to order work on things that aren't even scheduled to begin for a year or two yet."

Sari Kittachorn, a small, delicate-looking woman with dark skin and mixed Southern Asian features, nodded. She was in the Department of Indigenous Populations, which was charged with the management and training of the "Specialists—Primitive Skills" as they were called on the job sheets. The folks who still knew how to milk a cow or grow wheat even without machines. "We have been having many meetings of late," she told them, "and they are talking of bringing the first groups through to here for acclimatization within the next few months."

"But we don't have room for that kind of mob here!" protested Caesar Fanfani, a very Italian product of Hispanic Argentina, who worked with the big master computers themselves. "My God! They will flood us out!"

"Not if we go fast enough," responded Marsha Johnson, a tall, thin, sandy-haired Australian who was a Watanabe assistant in Transportation. "I think they're ready to go. Ten ships are now being assembled off the Point right now. The tubes are ready, the programs are ready—they're going to go and soon, I feel it."

Lisa Wu nodded in agreement. "I see more of everyone else's departments than anyone except maybe His Nibs. There's been a massive acceleration in both the Soviet and Chinese projects since peace broke out. They're using far older computers and they won't be able to be as versatile or as comfortable as we will, but that hardly matters to them or to anyone. It's a race to be first, and we still might not win it. I think they'll go even if the risk factor is enormous."

Haller looked over at Johnson. "It seems to me to be one *hell* of a bloody risk if they still haven't sent folks out there and brought them back alive."

Johnson's eyebrows rose. "But they have," she said quietly.

It was a bombshell and silenced the group immediately. They all looked at the Australian woman with a mixture of expectation and nervousness. This was new even to Lisa Wu.

"You mean," Weinbaum managed at last, "that there are already people on New Eden?"

"Orbital only right now. The early animal tests worked so well, they skipped a number of steps. A volunteer crew from Engineering went—seven in all—and they arrived O.K. They've sent back extensive surveys and evaluations to back up the computer reports. The first ship to be finished will have one trial run there and back with no human cargo, then it'll return with a full load of folks from all seven major departments. No orbit, not first three stages. They're going directly to Gate One to establish a headquarters unit. If that goes well, Engineering and Signals will be sent in force to Gate Five. After that—it's us. The reason why they won't have any problem with the influx of colonists or whatever they're calling them these days is that we won't be here. We'll be there."

Haller felt the same butterflies as the rest of them at this news. It was a curious reaction, really—it was, after all, why he was here at all, and what they had all been working toward. He had, however, adjusted himself to the seven-year interval, which seemed far off even now, and to now be told that this was to be cut very short—it was, well, unexpected.

"Well, that explains why we never got the Kagan 7800's" Fanfani sighed.

"Huh?" Several said it at once.

"A new generation of computer altogether, related to the 7240's we have here only in that it's compatible with all the programs and information we've been working with. They're only a bit bigger than ours, but their storage capacity is supposed to be nearly infinite—they can directly transform Flux into added storage modules as necessary—and their computational speed and capacity is said to be just about at the physical limits of the universe. We were supposed to get the first two here to play with a month or two ago—they're so beyond anything we can comprehend that a lot of folks are plain scared of it, including the Kagan people."

Haller was appalled. "You mean nobody's ever even found out if they work?"

"Oh, they work just fine. What nobody's done is link them into a Flux network. They know they have a near godlike brain, but they don't know what it'll do when it's handed godlike powers. When you think of twenty-eight of them being networked together with nearly unlimited access to seven Gates and all the Flux they want—well, if we can't control them, we might just wind up worshipping them, and with justification."

That sobered them up. "Van Haas knows about this?" Haller asked.

"Of course. All the big folk do. They're gambling that the gods can be suborned. If they can, it'll make everything even easier. If not—who knows?"

It was a sobering idea, considering that all of them were putting their own necks in this noose fashioned by expediency and politics.

"At least this will end some of the thoughts of the bright boys in Engineering," Haller said at last. "Lately they've shifted from just designing a nice place to live to designing the folks who'd live there. I've been a lonely voice protesting this line of thinking. After all, if we can make the place over to suit our needs, why bother to remake *us*?"

"Is that possible?" Fanfani asked nervously. This was the first he'd heard of this.

"It's possible—even with just the 7240's," Marsha Johnson assured him. "In the process of reducing you to a contained bit of energy in a particular digital equation suspended in that vacuum tube, we read in the whole chain. The computer originally treated it as a whole, of course, but it wasn't much of a curiosity step to see if the machine could also decide which parts were which. We got it to where it could take a scraping, read your genetic code, figure all the basics out, then apply that to you when you get digitized in the tube. Given proper directions, on reassembly it can solidify you almost to order."

"You mean it could make me tall and voluptuous?" Kittachorn asked somewhat lightly.

"Well, it can't add mass, not in the transport tube, so I'd say no. But it could redesign you to have blond hair, green eyes, change your metabolic rate, your hormone rate and levels—all that. It could take me, for example, tall and flat, and make me short and both curvy and busty. It can also boost the hormone levels—or reduce them—to make you sexier or disinterested, heighten your aggression or turn you passive, control your effective I.Q., and lots of other things that are physiological in nature. And it would all breed true. That's incredible enough, but if I had Caesar, here, or perhaps Toby, I could remake them as fully functioning females with all the equipment and all the urges.''

''None for me, thanks,'' Haller told her. ''But why just one way?''

''Yes, that's interesting,'' Weinbaum put in. ''I know a little of this, but I'm not in that branch of medicine.''

''Well, women have two X chromosomes, so it can take what it needs from the Y and interpolate the added X from the first. Whenever we tried to take a double X and interpolate an XY, though, it always comes up 'insufficient data for consistent objective.' We haven't had the guts to find out what that means beyond the theoretical.''

''Toby's making it sound like they're thinking of making us into monsters or something,'' Fanfani pressed.

''We could,'' Johnson responded, ''but only within severe limits—and only one individual at a time. I don't think they were ever serious about that except on a pure theory level.''

''That may be with the 7240, but suppose you had the 7800 and gave it all the memory storage, program area, and Flux—both power and added mass—you needed?'' the computer expert speculated. ''I wonder how theoretical it might be then?''

Weinbaum wasn't impressed. ''I think you're all overreacting to this. There's just no percentage in it. I can see it for cosmetic reasons, and I can see it possibly putting me out of business—just keep the injured alive until you can get him to a computer interface and you have instant total repair—but Toby's put his finger on it. It's not necessary. If we had to adapt humans to an existing environment—say, Titan's unmodified atmosphere and temperatures—it's possible, but we don't. Not on our little world. If, later on, we discover other planets or moons that are inhospitable but have resources we need, it might be cheaper and easier to modify colonists than to build and install more Gates and computers, but that won't be in *our* lifetimes.''

''I wonder.'' Johnson sighed. ''There's the potential here for immortality, for eternal youth and health. Who gets it will depend on who controls the computers, but the *potential* is there. Be nice to me, all of you. I may just have lucked into the access you'll need because of the job I've got.''

"Marsha's right," agreed Lisa Wu. "What we've seen so far are merely extensions of prior technology, stretching our knowledge of and access to computers to the limit, pushing biological science to the edge, that sort of thing. Much of what Marsha can do in the tubes can be done chemically now, at least in the biochemical area, as I'm sure Doc would agree. This whole project is just an extension of existing Earth-based political and ideological rivalries that have been ongoing for centuries. We're still riding the storm of the Industrial Revolution. But *this*—this is something new. The New Eden Project is evolutionary; this new factor, one discovered, like most great discoveries, by accident and as a by-product of unrelated research, is *revolutionary*. And, like all such revolutionary discoveries, it can be used for radical good, or unprecedented evil. I'm a good enough historian, though, to know that we have no idea now where it will lead, technologically or morally."

"Evolution or revolution," Johnson responded, "makes no difference to me. I won't be the one to direct it. But it's exciting as hell to be there in the center of it happening."

There were two separate and independent command organizations involved in the New Eden Project, or "NEP" for short. The first, and perhaps highest although in theory they were equal, was the Operational Board, composed of the four military commands doing what they specialized in doing best and freeing that task from everyone else's back; the second was the Project Board of Directors, consisting of the six division chiefs and the project director himself, who was also the only nonmilitary man to sit on the Operational Board— van Haas himself. He presided over both, not only in theory but in reality, and he was the bridge that kept them working as two parts of a single team. He held their future in his hands at all times, but, it was clearly understood, his head was always on the chopping block for any failures of theirs. He was answerable to the Westrex consortium back on Earth, and they were being bled too poor to accept anything less than perfection.

It was the military who would lead the way into the new world, but it was the Project Board of Directors who would make the decisions as to who, how many and when, and at what speed. The seven of them, all top administrators in their fields and great scientists in their own right, three women and three men as chance had dictated it, sat in the plush board room in the headquarters building eyeing the tall, gaunt figure of Rembrandt van Haas nervously. Nobody doubted what the meeting was about. Only the details remained to be spelled out.

"Ladies and gentlemen, I have a new series of directives from Westrex," the project director began. "They are too lengthy to detail here word for word, but I'll give you the basics.

"First, the political situation on Earth has stabilized to a degree not known for many years. We have a great deal of evidence that through espionage, and through legitimate scientific channels, at least the Soviets and the Chinese are close enough to solving the transportation problem that we will have no choice but to feed them enough to standardize the shape and size of their transports and their airlocks and power systems to ours to assure uniformity. Under existing international treaties we cannot claim exclusivity to New Eden without creating a military zone, and that requires not merely machines there but people. There is a great deal of evidence that they are rushing to get at least a ship, any ship, out there ahead of us. Since it's our computers, we, of course, will have solid claims, but it will make it impossible to deny them equal colonization rights with us and we'll wind up with another Titan on our hands."

"Intolerable!" sniffed Harold Itutu, the West African representative. "They cannot be handed over our fruits!" There were murmurs all around.

"I agree," van Haas responded, "but in order to stop it we will have to be there first. We must not only be installed there when they come, we must be so prepared and in control of the Gate and Anchor areas that they are left no openings. We have already located three other potential colonies further up the line—resources we could ill afford, but which were essential as a carrot if our plans work. Needless to say, our own backers are bled dry at this point as well, and there is unrest and there has even been some rioting in areas where critical shortages have developed due to us. Their own conclusion is simple. Time has run out. We either go as quickly as everything is ready, all or nothing, or we will be terminated as a project, with all our work and all the people's suffering going for nothing.''

''Impossible!'' Watanabe exclaimed. ''Don't those ignorant assholes realize what's at stake here?''

Van Haas looked her squarely in the eye. ''No. If a vote had been taken on whether or not to ship Columbus off to the New World, the people would have voted it a waste of money. The masses are simplistic in their vision, but it's difficult to be cosmic when you're undergoing food rationing and watching jobs vanish as prices skyrocket. People have always fought tooth and nail against progress. The Luddites rose up to destroy the automated machinery that made pins, putting many of them out of business. Before that, pins had been a luxury item. In the long term, automation gave new technology to the lowest of the low and created progress—but it wasn't progress to the Luddite who was thrown out of work right then and there due to the machines. We saw the same thing with the introduction of robots and computers. There were demands by labor organizations to make the machines illegal, and brutal strikes to destroy the new technology or fight against the closing of obsolete mines and factories. It's always been that way. It's that way again.''

''But, surely,'' someone said, ''they can be sold on the importance of our work here.''

Rembrandt van Haas laughed. ''Sold? The popular conception of a scientist has always been either a bald old fellow living in his own little world with no concept of what the real world was like—or Dr. Frankenstein, meddling in forces best left to God. More than one scientist has been burned at the stake by the mob, and many a program to save lives and open up humanity's horizons has crashed and burned in the no less real fires called political expediency. Never even mind the Russians and Chinese and Hispanics and the Franco-Brazilians. For domestic reasons alone we've been ordered to either go now or they will be forced to shut us down before the new rulers of our home nations, having shot the present ones, do it less gently.''

They were all aghast at this prospect, but reluctant to accept it. Risks were one thing, but careful control minimized them.

"We haven't even tested the 7800's!" protested Carlotta Schwartzman, the head of the master computer project. "You know the risks they pose even as they are!"

"I know, but I can do nothing about it. One 7800 has been installed and tested by the Operations Board at a remote satellite station kept for things like this. So far they've found it faster, quicker, and easier, and far more versatile, but not operationally very different from our 7240's. I'd say it's worth the risk, considering that the alternative is no risk—and no project—at all. No one, after all, *has* to go. There are no guns at people's heads."

Watanabe, for one, was furious. "The fucking *military* has been playing with a 7800 and you didn't even *tell* us?"

Van Haas shrugged. "What was the point? You all wanted one, and you all would have demanded priority and all have had very good reasons. We have only two spares as it is. The Operations Board could take risks we would have considered unacceptable here, and do so in a location remote enough to insure insulating us from any dire consequences."

"Dire consequences!" Watanabe exploded. "You hand over the most advanced computer it might be possible to ever build to a bunch of jack-booted shit-lickers who treat people like machines? The only guarantee of their behavior was the fact that we controlled the master computers! Now *they* know more about how to run 'em than *we* do. You hand that kind of mind absolute power like this and all it takes is one hair over the sanity line and we're living in hell!"

The director let her go, and paused for several seconds after she finished. Finally, he asked, "Are you through?"

"Not by a long shot, but go ahead."

"All right. I'm not going to debate the honor and commitment of our counterparts in Operations right now. I'm not going to debate this whole military versus civilian thing, which has been ongoing since the start. We had to accept them because they were a condition of our being here. We did, and it's worked out. Now you have to accept an accomplished fact. This is a report on what *is*, not what might be."

He sighed and poured himself a drink of water. No one spoke, but Watanabe glared at him.

"Now, then," he continued, "this is how it is. I've read all the reports and checked everything through with the master project computers. We have two ships ready and standing by now. The others will come through final assembly at the rate of one a month, I'm assured, and each can be flight-tested in a matter of another week after that. The engineering crew currently on site can handle and supervise the automated freighters with the Kagan 7800 set. The Anchors are well along now, and need only the 7800's to interface with the 7240 maintenance computers already on site at the Gates. My reports show an equatorial temperature of 31.1 degrees Celsius, which is close enough, and an outer life zone low temperature of 6.91 degrees worst case. Gravity is less than two percent off what we have here on Titan. We're maintaining a median Earth atmosphere that's better than we have here and so close to dead on, it takes a computer to find the first number after the decimal point. We needed the extra time to test, measure, and experiment so we knew we had it right, but we no longer have that time. I say we go."

Ibrihim Mohammed Haiudar scratched his ample nose and commented, "You realize that the second wave won't be what we expected at all." He was Director of Populations, which meant the nonscientist colonists, and those were exactly what he meant by the second wave.

Van Haas was startled. "What? What do you mean?"

"I mean, my friend, that, yes, we will get experts in farming, in animal husbandry, fertilizers, fields, forests, and deserts—but not as many. What we will get in place of many are the dissidents now languishing in prisons at home, the revolutionaries and the rioters and the conspirators. They will seize this opportunity back home to send us their worst troublemakers. Mass firing squads just fuel revolutions and create new leaders. Permanent exile, now, that's a different thing."

It really hadn't occurred to the director, but, then, he came from a far different tradition and culture than did Ibrihim. He knew immediately, though, that the man was right, and he thought about it. Finally, he said, "What you say is true, old friend, but it doesn't worry me. I'm from a nation whose first families are all descendants of convicts and whose largest city is named after their first warden. In fact, if we have enough of these—not professional revolutionaries, but leaders out of the masses born and raised in primitive settings—it's all to the good, I think. We will redirect their energies and build with their passion, as many other civilizations did back home."

Haiudar shrugged. "You may be right. I hope you are." And, silently, he added to himself, *And, if not, it'll be easier to shoot them out there*.

Schwartzman seemed the most uncertain. "Without any experience on the 7800, I can't guarantee that everything will download properly from the 7240's at the Gates. We're also by no means close to a landscaping master plan that doesn't cause as many problems as it solves."

All eyes turned to the heretofore silent figure of Sir Kenneth Korda. The quiet, distinguished architect of Kenya's salvation from the terrible incursions of drought and desert was head of Landscape Engineering. "Can't you concentrate on a modular approach?" the director asked him. "After all, we have the basic Anchors sketched out. We'll use them as our on-site experiments. Build and correct one block at a time."

"The Anchors aren't that simple," he responded. "They are what we call them. Anchors. Templates, or patterns, for an entire region. When we work there, we have to build null energy barriers to keep the surrounding Flux from coming back in and to allow some sort of normal air flow and circulation. We'll need them developed as quickly as possible, yet, if we make any serious errors there, and then have a substantial population in place, we'll have no good way of correcting those errors. I am most uncomfortable with this speedup. It will require far too much expediency from my people."

"They'll do it," van Haas said confidently. "You'll find a way to have them do it. We will live with what we've got. Develop the nexus region at the outset, then develop the Anchors in sectors until we have a working ecosystem in each. Then we'll worry about how they tie together."

"I do not share your confidence," said the Kenyan.

"I do not have your time," responded the director. "Sadira, you're the only one now who hasn't said a word. Comment?"

The sari-clad Indian Chief of Administration sat as impassively as always through the deliberations, just making certain that everything was being recorded. Now she looked up at them. "I think I am hearing a lot of nervous babies," she said at last, her tone very patronizing. "I think that there is only one question for voting here. Either we go, or we shut down. I would like to know which. Either way, all of us will have a lot of work to do in a very short time. I for one would rather go now than have to begin learning Russian or Chinese."

There was more discussion, but it got them nowhere, and van Haas cut it off and decided to force a vote.

"I see four in the affirmative and two in the negative," the director said ceremoniously. "There being no tie, I don't need to vote, but I wish to be on record in the affirmative myself. That leaves only the question of the two nays. Suzy, I can ill afford to lose you, but it must be your decision. If your decision is to terminate, then I would appreciate a recommendation on a successor, preferably from your own team."

She looked sullen. "Let me think about it today."

He nodded. There wasn't much else he could have expected right now. "And you, Ken? The same goes."

"I will come," the landscape engineer said without much expression. "Not because I believe we can succeed under these conditions, but out of sheer egotism. My department is the weakest, and I do not want it to fail because I did not go along."

That pleased the rest of them.

"Fair enough," the director noted. "Now, here's the schedule we've more or less got to keep. I'll have copies made up tonight and these can be distributed to your department heads by you personally in meetings tomorrow. They can then take it down to the staff.

"A field test of the first ship, using Gate Five, will commence at eleven hundred hours Friday—five days from now. If it succeeds, and if it returns and checks out, we will send in the initial 7800's seven days after that to establish Engineering, followed fourteen days later by the initial ground Operational Group. It'll be mostly military, but, Ken, I'd like you and a few of your best to go along—the five crew anyway. As much as practical, we'll test out Gate One the same way, interleaving trips with Five, then repeat the procedure. Sadira, that'll be your people, so we have a functioning headquarters of sorts. Then we'll develop Two, Three, Four, Six, and Seven, in that order, depending on our initial results with One and Five and the availability of personnel, material, and equipment. I would like to be first, but I am forced by my position to be last.''

He paused, trying to get control of his emotions. Finally, he said, ''It was seven years ago that the last of us came to this barren rock, and our anticipated ten-year stay has been shortened to seven. I don't know what awaits us. It could be misery. It could be failure. It could be paradise. I suspect it's something none of us have yet dreamed or will dream. But, by God! I am ready to have a go at it!''

There were few working in the Transport Research lab now; most of the best technicians were up the line at the big Borelli Point out beyond Pluto working on the real, not the theoretical. That made the lab section ideal for Marsha Johnson and Jimmy Okieda, who finally found someplace private enough in the wee hours to do a little fooling around.

It was nothing serious. She was no glamour girl, but not hard to look at, and he was of a station beneath her in the scientific hierarchy—a mere corporal in Logistics, barely out of his teens, too low to even be up at the Point. Such liaisons were common among base personnel, most of whom did not have families or long attachments, particularly on the junior levels.

They were quite well along on the office floor, with all but the emergency lights off, and so they didn't see or hear her come in, nor was she aware of their presence.

Dr. Susan Watanabe was dressed and made up so differently that it was impossible to tell right off that it was indeed the division chief. She had found, or pulled out of old storage or something, a traditional kimono of fine silk, black in color, and she'd cut and shaped her hair and made up her face so that she looked almost like someone out of *The Mikado*. Tied to her waist was a small ornamental short sword in a fine-

tooled scabbard, a keepsake and heirloom handed down to her
as the last in her family. She had often showed it off to
associates, and told them that it had been in her family for
more than two hundred and fifty years.

She paused a moment in the darkness, more meditating
than reflecting, then went silently over to the master computer
controls. She did not need the lights; she knew this place
better than she knew her own body.

She went to the Guard's chair and sat in it. Unlike the
Overrider, this position could be activated on its own, by just
one person, since it could not access the files of nor receive
the commands from the master computer beneath the laboratory. It was built to do only one thing, and that's all she
wanted it to do.

Deliberately, she lowered the helmet onto her head and
adjusted the probes. The computer switched on its external
interface, read her brain wave and identity patterns, and
confirmed that she was authorized.

*"Guard post on, Overrider position is vacant. No transac-
tion,"* it reported to her mind.

*"Derangement in master computer determined by indepen-
dent monitors after last run,"* she told it. *"Emergency deacti-
vation procedures in effect, please."*

The Guard computer hesitated. While it was not an im-
proper request, it was certainly an unprecedented one, and its
own monitors not only had revealed nothing but told it that
there was no imperative for speed. It was not that easy to do
what she was attempting, even with all the proper clearances
and codes. The Guard's programming and its own thinking
processes, while primitive by the standards of the Kagan 7240
it oversaw, were not only to prevent a big computer running
amok but also to prevent sabotage.

"Command reasoning insufficient," it told Watanabe. *"No
empirical evidence supports this command. Confirmation is
required by higher authority. Shall I confirm?"* It was being
nice to her, giving her a chance to back out before it blew the
whistle.

She was calm and undisturbed, and confident she had
prepared well for this years ago. *"Understood. Check with
corporate center for authority of operator."*

It was accomplished in the speed of light, but the computer was still not really convinced. *"Action requested?"* it asked.

"Erasure of block memory in locations and under encryption to my authority only. No master files involved."

"Understood. Give locations and password authority."

Watanabe knew she was being strung along, and that it was only a matter of time before the Guard alerted Security. The easy way was not going to work. *"Cancel request. Guard off."*

"Acknowledged." The computer seemed somewhat relieved.

Watanabe removed the helmet, then reached into her kimono and brought out several small cubes of some translucent material. She then went to work opening a panel in front of the Guard chair, tracing a network of cubes, pulled a certain one and replaced it with one of hers. There were several more positions in the main panel where this was done, and two in a subsidiary panel. Now she left the Guard position and went over to Overrider, then put on that helmet, which could not be activated nor in any way used without someone at Guard. It wasn't supposed to be possible to circumvent this, but even if someone were bright enough to figure it out, two keys had to be turned within one second of each other at each position to make the interface work, and the positions were on opposite sides of the semi-circular room, at least ten meters apart. One key now sat in the off position at Guard; she now inserted the other at Overrider, and as she did so the Guard's key turned as if by an invisible hand.

Instantly, she heard the sounds of many feet running toward the lab, and all the lights went on. An alarm also began to sound. She cursed softly to herself, but otherwise ignored it. She didn't have time to dwell on what she'd triggered; she just pulled the Overrider helmet down on her head and discovered with satisfaction that there was in fact a computer link.

The two trysters in the back office were startled out of their fun by all the commotion and hastily began putting their clothes back on and then trying to figure out if they should try to duck out of there or just keep quiet. There was a small window looking out onto the lab and computer-control center from the office, though, and once they'd regained some measure of composure they found it irresistible. Both Johnson and Okieda thought at first that they were the ones who had somehow caused all this, but one look into the labs told them differently.

Soldiers converged from both sides on the small figure in the chair, soldiers armed with automatic weapons.

Bolts of electricity lashed out from the panels, catching the lead troopers and causing them to scream and drop to the floor, writhing. Watanabe was somehow doing it from the master computer.

The forces behind the fallen soldier didn't need any orders to react. They opened up with short, precise bursts on the woman in the chair. The impact of the bullets spun her around and threw her backward in the chair. Sparks flew from the helmet connection, and before Watanabe had a chance at anything, if indeed she was still alive, hands snatched the helmet away and emergency switches were thrown, deactivating both computer-to-human interfaces.

Okieda turned to Marsha Johnson, a look of horror on his face. "What do we do now?"

She was as much in shock as he was. "I don't know. Maybe you should just mix with them. One soldier more won't be noticed. I can talk my way out of it."

"You kidding? Logistics blue is a little different from Security red. Damn!"

Johnson went back and tried the rear door. It held fast, as if welded there. Okieda then tried the door to the lab, and found it much the same. "Security's sealed the building!" he told her. "We're stuck!"

Brigadier Coydt was in her quarters but not asleep, and she was immediately informed by the Security duty officer of the events so far. She threw on a shirt and pants and rushed downstairs, where an electric car was waiting to take her to the transport labs. Watanabe had been dead less than fifteen minutes by the time she arrived.

She stood there, then examined the blood-soaked body, and finally asked, "How many people know the specifics of this?"

"Just our personnel actually inside up to this point and the duty officer, ma'am," a sergeant informed her. "Maybe a dozen in all, not counting our security computer that flagged us, of course.''

"I want an immediate seal on this," she ordered. "I want absolutely no one to know anything about this who doesn't already know." Her mind was racing. "Have you checked the rest of the building?"

"Doing it now, room by room and office by office. Supposedly, there are two up in that office there—or so the computer flag tells us."

She looked over in that direction and thought she could see a face peering nervously back at her. "Who are they?"

"A junior engineer who works here and some enlisted man from Logistics."

"Were they helping her?"

"No. Computer watch says they were fuck—making out, begging the brigadier's pardon."

"All right. Keep those two up there bottled up for the moment, and get me a secured line to Site K—our channels, no routing. I need some advice."

"The alarm's been heard all over the place, ma'am. Curious folk are gathering outside now. Sooner or later we're gonna get somebody big enough to bypass our lines through here. What shall I do?"

"Just get me that link!" She turned to a lieutenant just standing there, looking a little dazed. "You—what's your name?"

"Lieutenant Symmes, ma'am."

"All right, Symmes. Go down and keep that cordon *tight* until I tell you not to. Anyone, and I mean *anyone*, even the admiral or the director, makes it past you and you'll envy this woman on the floor."

"But—what'll I tell them?"

"Tell them—tell them we caught a Soviet spy stealing master transport programs and we had to kill the agent. Tell them we can't have anyone in until we determine not only who the spy is but how much damage was done. Tell anyone asking that it's on my personal order and I'll answer to them later. Understand?"

"Yes, ma'am!"

She looked around. "Casualties?"

"Two, ma'am. Both dead."

"All right. There must be some lab clothes, something around here, that will fit one of them. Find them, get the one that fits best out of his or her uniform and into lab clothes. I'm going to need a convincing body to take past the crowd as our Soviet spy. We'll give 'em proper burial under their real names when we get them away. Understand? One soldier casualty, one dead spy."

The soldiers just stared at her for a moment. Finally, one asked, "Uh, pardon me, ma'am, but what are we going to do with *her?*"

Coydt looked down at the dead body of the scientist. "Play Jesus Christ—I hope."

On her order, Watanabe's body was stripped and then carried out into the lab itself and placed inside one of the clear tubes. It looked like a discarded rag doll stained with crimson ink.

She ordered just Marsha Johnson fetched and brought down to her. The lab assistant was white as a sheet and clearly scared to death, a set of emotions not at all helped by having to face the notorious Brigadier Coydt herself. Still, Johnson couldn't help thinking what an attractive woman the security chief was. It just didn't seem right. But there was something in Coydt's eyes and manner and tone of voice that was both scary and chilling.

"What's your name?" Coydt snapped.

"Marsha Johnson, ma'am."

"You worked for Dr. Watanabe?"

"Yes, ma'am. The past four years."

"Ever run the computer?"

Johnson was puzzled at the question. "Yes, ma'am. I'm qualified independent at Guard and second class at Override."

"Good. Now, listen up and get hold of yourself. Your boss just committed a particularly spectacular form of hara-kiri. I'm going to need your help here if we're to salvage anything from this."

The lab assistant felt suddenly numb. *"That's* who—*that* is? Director Watanabe?" She felt as if her whole world were crumbling.

"The one and only. She dressed herself in ancient clothes

and even took time to do the ancient styles. Then she came in here with the idea of erasing or blowing whatever she could until she was cut down.''

Johnson couldn't believe it. "She—she *wouldn't*! This was her whole *life*!"

"She would, she could, and she almost did."

"But—*why?* I know she decided to quit, but—"

Coydt's voice and manner turned suddenly and disconcertingly soft and gentle. "Child, the pressure just got too much. You said it yourself. This was her whole life—the culmination of everything she'd worked for all that life. Then she got obsessed by the ethics of her work. She became convinced that she was an inadvertent monster, one who'd loosed an uncontrollable evil while looking for good. You know she was always deep into history. She's been reading and collecting books on scientists who found themselves in her position in the past. Her fears fueled her imagination and she built up tremendous guilt for something that was still theoretical.''

"But—the project's going on! The programs and discoveries are now being used! She couldn't stop it!"

"Well, she thought, I think, that she could slow it down, maybe mortally wound it. If this got out, there would be outcries and inquiries, and commissions and the like, and she'd be a martyr to everyone who wants to shut us down tight, fueled by the propaganda of our enemies. Mostly, though, I doubt if that was foremost in her mind. I think— well, she was simply trying, in reverting to an ancient culture she barely knew except from books—not so much to reverse things as to *atone* for her works. In the ancient fashion she was taking responsibility and guilt for it all.''

"Huh?"

"Never mind. Here's the point. I haven't time to look it up. Did Watanabe herself ever go through digitization?"

Marsha Johnson started, beginning to see where Coydt was headed. "Why, yeah. After it was well along. She said she needed to experience it to fine-tune the programs. But—if you're thinking what I *think* you're thinking, it's not possible. She's not digitized. She's *dead*."

"Go take the Guard position. I'll take Override. Let's get her in the system before rigor mortis sets in. I'm going to have a linkup between this computer and the 7800 crew in orbit. Because of the time delay, it might take a while, but I'd like to find out what's possible. If there's a chance, even a chance in a million, isn't it worth some time and work here? If we can't, we don't lose anything. If we can, maybe we can show her that this thing isn't as evil as she thought, huh?''

Johnson was doubtful, but she couldn't stand by when there was any possibility of it. And if they did it, she'd have her own paragraph in history.

A few of the files on transmutation had been erased, but since nothing else had been done on the computer, they were recoverable. The computer had only deleted them from its index and marked them free for overwriting; the more stringent erase command had not been given when the bullets flew.

Coydt was far too busy to think beyond each moment right now. She was making this up as she went along, and somewhat pleased with her own creativity, but none of it would be worthwhile unless they pulled off this ultimate trick.

The brigadier was not expected to know how to operate the computer, particularly something like a Kagan, nor be rated as Overrider, but she was both. She had, in fact, worked with the 7800 at Site K, the orbiting station out in the depths of space between Saturn and Uranus which had its own small Borelli Point. Because it was used primarily as an automatic backup point for all work on Titan—with the knowledge and even the connivance of Westrex but not known to those not on the Operations Board—it was entirely under her section. She couldn't really qualify as more than a mere operator, but that was good enough if she could link up with her top computer personnel running the 7800 itself.

She had to shout over to Johnson for the exact passwords, name, and form to direct the digitization process, but once done she could run it without any problems. The computer accepted her as an authorized operator; as a matter of form, all members of both boards had authority to operate, although they didn't necessarily have the information to run the thing. The good fortune of having Marsha Johnson there was the thing that gave this a chance.

Outside, Rembrandt van Haas had never felt as frustrated

as he was now, trying to gain information and entry into the transport lab. Like Coydt, he'd been awakened by an aide and told of an alarm and reports of weapons fire and, since then, had received only the official line from the Security troops ringing the building. Those troops themselves were decidedly uncomfortable; they felt that no matter what they did regarding the director, they were alienating one of the two people who could effectively do something nasty to them. The young lieutenant finally decided on bluntness with the director and rigidity to Coydt. She'd gotten the officer into this mess, and she would be expected to get her out.

"Sir," the lieutenant said carefully, "we have no idea what went on there except what the brigadier stated. Her orders were most emphatic and included you, I'm afraid. I don't like this any more than you and didn't ask for this, but you must see it our way. Our immediate superior has given us an order. You are her superior, and normally it would not apply to you, but the brigadier was pretty graphic as to what would happen to us if we allowed anyone through. You may threaten us with good cause, but we will still have to answer to the brigadier first. We can see no compelling moral reason for disobeying her. She has said she will answer to Admiral Cockburn and to you later. We must accept that."

Van Haas nodded. "All right. Carry on." There was no purpose served by keeping these little fish between a rock and a hard place. He strode back to his small electric vehicle and picked up the phone. "Get me Brigadier Ryan, and I don't care what you have to do to get him." Then he ordered his driver to take him to Signals building.

Michael Ryan looked like the stereotypical Irish pub crawler, the sort that would be cast in an Irish working-class drama. Ireland had survived the Borelli pulses better than most of the West because it was so lightly industrialized, and he was the only member of either board who had actually been born and spent his early childhood in "The North," as it was called, leaving him with a characteristic Irish brogue.

His parents had eventually managed to immigrate to Australia when he was twelve, joining relatives there for a generation, escaping the poverty and lack of future that remaining in the homeland meant. Still, he'd known very hard times and he never forgot them.

He had joined the Australian army to pay for his university, and had managed the nearly impossible feat of rising from the enlisted ranks all the way to colonel on merit. He was an electronics expert and a brilliant politician, and yet maintained a close relationship with his troops. With little hope of making it to general officer ranks because of his background, however, he'd jumped at the chance to oversee the Signals part of Westrex, even though the task and even the means of accomplishing it were unprecedented. Although still a colonel in the reserves of Australia, inside Westrex's independent corporate army he had finally made brigadier.

Ryan, in fact, trusted his enlisted personnel more than he trusted his fellow officers, which was what made him so useful at times like these.

The Irishman was already sitting in a communications monitoring post when van Haas arrived. He turned, nodded to the director, and said, "I thought you'd have been here before now."

"I'm not used to being told there's someplace I can't go here," the director responded. "What the hell *is* all this?"

"I'll punch it up and you can watch it for yourself."

Security had been forced to use Signals to run much of its own communications system. While Coydt now had her own experts, they still had to use the system Ryan had designed and the laws of physics. While Coydt spied on everyone, Ryan spied on Coydt—and everything Coydt saw. Security suspected it. That was why much of its work was now being carried out at Site K, beyond Ryan's range and authority. However, they had no idea just how extensive his network could be.

Van Haas watched with horror the strange dimly lit play acted out between Watanabe and the security staff. He was as much stunned by her apparent ease at circumventing the Guard position as he was watching her die. "Oh, my God!" Then he paused a moment. "We'll have to revise our whole interlock now."

"No need," Ryan told him. "Oh, it's true you can circumvent the 7240 computers if you have to—we've just seen it, and certainly we'll find out how it was done. It won't apply to the 7800's though. Their Guard design isn't modular, it's integrated and in a different way, and there are lots of nasty little safeguards for meddlers. Still, 'tis an unnerving sight, I'll grant ya that.''

"But—what the hell is Coydt trying to *do* in there?"

"As near as I can make out, I think she's going to try to resurrect the old girl. She's tied into her pet people up on K, and their 7800. I can't get past that encryption system as of now, but I could jam it if you want."

Van Haas considered it for a moment. "No. In this case, if she can pull this off, she'll save us no end of grief, as well as demonstrate the powers of the 7800—or limitations, if it doesn't work. Besides, I really liked Suzy."

"Aye," Ryan sighed. "Still, 'tis unnerving to think this sort of thing is even remotely possible. I mean, she's not even waiting the traditional three days."

The 7800 was characteristic of its type when asked if Watanabe could be restored. It responded that it saw no theoretical reasons why it couldn't be done, with some limitations, but having never tried it, there was no way to be sure.

There was certainly no way to restore the scientist at the point where she'd been shot; the only good bet was to ignore Watanabe-present and run the prior program for when the scientist had allowed herself, months earlier, to be turned to energy and encoded. Some restoration might be possible if it knew the exact electrochemical arrangement at the time of death, but it did not, and by the time it had been fed the body, too much time had elapsed for any accuracy. The brain had a complex and efficient automatic method of shutting itself down in an orderly way at death, and this had already taken place.

It was all very methodical and very pedestrian until the remote computer asked very matter-of-factly, "*Has the soul gone or dissipated?*"

The question startled not only Coydt and Johnson but everyone listening in or monitoring on K. Where the hell had a computer gotten *that?*

"*Uh—the soul is an unknown quantity,*" Coydt managed.

"No empirical evidence of its existence is known. Question cannot be answered and may not be material here."

"Empirical evidence undeniable," the computer responded. *"Suggest attempt at reforming using matter currently in conversion and programming matrix from earlier experience."*

"Approved."

"However, additional mass must be introduced. Blood and tissue loss is severe. Bleed in power from the grid and channel it to the object tube. Power will briefly dim the network but the amount required is relatively small enough that it will cause no effect and little notice to others."

"Approved. Do it."

There was, in fact, a very slight dip in the lights and a momentary flicker on the screen in Ryan's office, but otherwise nothing happened. At the light speeds computers and energy networks moved, they never noticed the slight loss, only the aftereffects, and then only because they were expecting them.

"Potential mass now sufficient for proper conversion," the computer told Coydt. *"Request permission to download required programs to slave computer system."*

"Granted. Go."

The conversation between the 7800 and Coydt's position was extremely slow, both because of time delays and because of the slowness of human thought versus computer thought, but it was a silent conversation. Neither Ryan nor van Haas nor any of the observers on Titan could know exactly what was going on unless, like the power drop, Coydt announced it vocally.

"Permission to integrate elements?" the 7800 asked.

Coydt thought a moment. *"Can subject be brought back in sedated condition?"*

"No evidence subject can be brought back at all."

The brigadier was beginning to know the frustrations of dealing with a computer's mind. *"If resuscitation achieved, can subject be restored in sedated position?"*

"Risks are too high in this instance. Recommend against any modifications at this time. However, there is a slight period of shock lasting thirty seconds on average."

It would have to do. "Have someone right down there with

a strong sedative,'' she ordered the troops. ''I'll wait until you can find one. I want her out before she knows she's back. *Move!*''

The small medical team dispatched by Security for the casualties had been held up downstairs, as confused as the rest outside, but they could supply what was asked.

''Why a sedative?'' Marsha Johnson asked worriedly.

''Because if she came out as she was four months ago, we'd have to explain all this and fast,'' the brigadier told her. ''And if we did that, we'd have a setup of the conditions that caused it. I don't propose to bring her back only to have her do this all over again. I want her to awaken in a psychiatric-care ward, where we can try to ease the pain before it builds up again.''

That seemed reasonable.

One medic was brought up with the small inoculator and taken by one of the soldiers out onto the lab floor. Both were assured there was no danger if they did not actually touch the tube or base until told it was safe to do so. The substance chosen was quick, as instructed. Once in the bloodstream, it would knock the average person out in three to five seconds.

''We're going to do it now!'' Coydt announced loudly, and there was a collective intake of breath not only from those around her but also from Ryan and van Haas. Even the dullest of the troopers understood by now what was being attempted, although few of them believed it was possible.

''Stand by!'' the brigadier announced, and then silently said to the computer, ''Run program as instructed.''

A light went on inside the giant tube, not so much for the computer's benefit but as an automatic mechanism so that observers could get a good view. There was a whining noise, then something seemed to crackle, and inside the tube an eerie sight was taking place. Outlined there was a figure, a humanoid shape framed and defined only by energy. The shape filled in with an increasingly complex grid, and the image became three-dimensional, holographic. The grid lines of energy grew increasingly fine until, inside the shape, there was solidity. An eerie, glowing skeleton took form, then a whole network of organs, then a circulatory system. It was like watching a computer teaching aid on how the human body was constructed. The process was quite fast, but not fast enough for the human eye to miss each major stage. The 7800 had decided to take it slow and easy.

Now the skin and hair and surface features were in, and it was clearly the nude body of a whole, unpunctured Suzy Watanabe. Whole—but did it live?

A buzzer sounded, and the nearly invisible door in the tube clicked.

"Medic! Now!" yelled Coydt, and the startled and awestruck medic rushed to the door, opened it, and with the help of the soldier pulled the limp body out. She knelt down and gave a cursory check to the form.

"My God! She's breathing!" the medic exclaimed, awestruck.

"Administer the damned sedative!" the brigadier snapped sharply.

The medic snapped out of it, took a quick, professional estimate of size and body weight, set the little injector dial, and moved close to give it to the still form.

Watanabe's eyes fluttered, then opened, and an expression of anger and confusion was on her face. "What the fuck—?" she managed, even as the injector forced in the sedative, but that was all she managed before passing out once again.

Spontaneous cheers and scattered applause broke out.

"All right," Coydt told them, "there's now a lot to be done. I've given thanks to our people at K, and we're shutting down. I want a side entrance blocked off from public view and an ambulance there in ten minutes. Notify the duty officer that I'd like to see her downstairs immediately. All personnel present here are to be picked up and transported to the Security building. No one talks to anyone, understand?" She began to issue scattershot orders on practically everything, but it was clear that she wanted to keep the whole incident, even the revolutionary thing they had done, completely under wraps until she had taken it all up with the director and possibly the boards and determined a consistent cover.

Marsha Johnson had gone from shock to action to joy, all with growing admiration for the brigadier's creativity and fast thinking. Now, though, she began to think about herself.

When Coydt seemed satisfied and prepared to make her way down to confer with the duty officer, the lab technician approached her.

"Um—ma'am? What about me? And Jimmy up there? Can we go now?"

"You and your friend are now under a military state of emergency," the brigadier told her. "I appreciate what you've done, but now it's stage two here. You will proceed, the both of you, with my own people to the Security Ops headquarters. My people there will take care of you. In the meantime, you're under the same restrictions as if you worked directly for me. No matter what your aid, if this is compromised, my people will have no hesitancy in shooting either of you. Accident has made you mine. Once mine, you remain mine. Now, follow the others. I have much extra work to do."

The manner and attitude infuriated Johnson, overcoming her fear. "I'm not your property!"

"That's *exactly* what you are," the brigadier replied.

6

GODS AND DEMI GODS

Brenda Coydt sat relaxed in the director's office, looking pretty good for somebody who hadn't had any sleep the night before. She did not withhold very many of the details, but van Haas had the distinct impression that she suspected he knew it all anyway.

"You evacuated all concerned to Site K, then?" he asked casually.

She nodded. "It seemed the best thing to do, and there's a full hospital and psychiatric unit there as well. They've been evaluating the stress on our people, and considering the wonderful job they did on Watanabe, it's only fitting that they have a crack at correcting their error."

"Uh-huh. Well, I suppose it's expedient anyway. The security record from the monitor?"

"Wiped. Or, rather, altered. The incident shows as it happened, but the identification and visual on Watanabe has been altered so that it isn't her, if you know what I mean. Staff's already preparing a cover story for who we will say it was, and that should suffice. There will be protests and notes and confusion on the other side, but it'll blow over pretty fast, as usual. It might even buy Westrex a little time. Turn a minus into a plus by creating sympathy for us. If the other side is trying to steal our stuff and commit sabotage, it must

89

be important. Like that. The effect won't last, but even if it buys us a week, it's effective."

"No problem there, I agree—but what do we do with Suzy even if they are able to bring her around? She's lost several months, of course, but she's still a ticking bomb, and some nice little drugs and happy therapy isn't going to change her basic nature. If we ship her out there, she'll be a threat. If we keep her here, we have no way to control or contain her."

"That same psychiatric staff's been working on that end ever since we lifted the alteration programs from Watanabe's computer. The 7800 can manage some startling things. Maybe too startling, when I think we're going to be at the mercy of twenty-eight of them, all networked, with unlimited power supplies and storage. Right now they can run quadrillions of parallel—that is to say, simultaneous—operations. If we wished to catch a fly, we could send an elephant to do it. It might step on the fly. Then it might be able to rebuild the fly from the information in its cells. That is the 7240 computer. The 7800 can find the fly, freeze it in midflight, then change just one tiny hair on the fly's body without it even noticing."

Rembrandt van Haas sighed. "Yes. It's been much on my mind, and I've read the Site K reports. Schwartzman, the Kagan people, and your own are convinced that the system is fail-safe. The computer cannot act on its own to influence any external factors. The core program, they firmly believe, is sound, as much as anyone can be certain of that these days."

"Yes. Through the ages people have speculated on how to communicate with a totally alien race, and the conclusion generally is that you can only get so far, particularly if that race is smarter and faster than you. Well, we have created that race ourselves, and they are inscrutable. What can one say about a computer that believes in its own mathematical and scientific way that human beings have souls?"

"I'd say it's pretty good news, if we knew its basis. I assume it is simply extrapolating from the failure of Watanabe to create living animal duplicates from the same encodings. It didn't seem to be a problem with your daring little experiment."

Coydt shrugged. "I was raised Catholic, although I'm not much of one now. The church believes that it can take as much as an hour for the soul to leave the body. Often such beliefs wind up being partially factual, as if our ancestors knew more about some things than we did.''

"Perhaps. Or, perhaps it takes about that length of time for it—whatever it is—to dissipate or die. It's irrelevant to us. What is important is that we can in fact bring someone back from the dead as well as alter them physiologically. It means potential youth and immortality. It must be suppressed as much as possible.''

"I agree,'' responded the brigadier. "It must be used sparingly and the mere knowledge of it must remain in the hands of as few as possible. Not even, I think, the board should be informed.''

"Just you and me and your people? There's a lot to suppress here.''

"Not as many as you might think. We are organic creatures, far more than anyone ever suspected. Psychiatrists today are more biochemists than the old and still prevalent vision of them as friendly confidants. You would be astonished at what they can do now, particularly with the aid of Watanabe's programs and the 7800 to augment their arsenal. Westrex's psychiatric unit and the Kagan research people can be handled by simply holding over them the idea that any leak will cost *them* use of the system. They're well chosen and still human beings. I think if we sent them up the line as a team and centered them in an Anchor remote from headquarters or Engineering or any of the other main bodies or units and let them work together on this line, we might get startling results without risking a lot of attention.'' She looked over at van Haas's globe, now clearly showing the installed Gates and rough Anchors and main network lines. "What about this Gate Four area, for example? Who and what's going in there?''

Van Haas thought a moment. "Actually, that's where we were going to put our troublemakers, our political prisoners and such. It's pretty out of the way in relation to the rest, south of the equator. None of the headquarters really wanted it, so it's pretty much an extra for now.''

The system called for Cockburn to tie in with Administration in the Gate One quadrant, Ryan's Signals to tie in with transport and energy around Gate Three, NGomo's Logistics to tie in with Itutu's Resource Allocations Division at Five, and Security to share Seven with Schwartzman's Master Computers Division. Two would be Korda's Landscape Engineering base, while Six would be Populations. Four, because of its geographical location, was in fact the orphan, reserved for "future division headquarters."

"That's where they should go, then," Coydt told him. "An unofficial, unrecognized division. Perhaps a hundred people total, otherwise mixed in with the general staff, and labeled a Special Project under Security. That will frighten enough people off."

"All right, I'll go along. But what about our witnesses from here?"

Coydt smiled sweetly. "Let's just call them the first Special Project problem."

The director nodded uncomfortably. The very idea of what she implied was repugnant to him, but this was an emergency and expediency was called for. However, he was going to make very sure that Mike Ryan's boys kept an independent eye on this. Coydt didn't know about Ryan's involvement, and that was his only ace in the hole.

"Brenda," he said evenly, without a trace of emotion. "Don't ever think of me as a Special Project. And don't embark on other major alterations without telling me."

She tried to laugh it off, but the manner was unnerving. It would never do to underestimate van Haas, she knew. "That sounds like a threat."

"Take it anyway you please, but get the context right. We are threatened by this—all of us. Even you."

She smiled sweetly. "Why, Doctor, why would *anyone* think of doing something like that?"

Marsha Johnson didn't like Security and she particularly didn't like Site K. Titan was claustrophobic enough, but the small space station was not only cramped, it was spartan, and she'd been confined to her small room with its barren metallic walls and cardboard-thin bed for several days, not even let out for meals. Those were brought to her by guards who never would talk and exited quickly. She was in a nightmare and she couldn't wake up a prison where the offense was knowing too much and the price was solitary confinement.

They had brought her some of her own clothing and personal effects, and there was a tiny toilet and shower stall, but it was pretty miserable and lonely.

She was not, however, alone. A team of expert psychiatrists together with computer analysts poked and probed at her record, her past, and observed every single movement, as they were doing with the others as well. Their decisions, however, could not be totally pragmatic. They were expected to "cure" and "turn" Watanabe to a "correct" attitude while retaining her creativity and genius, no mean trick when some of that grew out of the very things they had to remove. Neither of the other two had much family, but both had friends and associates back on Titan. They were easily covered back there—folks were vanishing and being shipped out all the time, often with little or no notice—but what if any of those old friends ran into them on New Eden?

It would have been simple to add Johnson to their team, except that her personality profile was all wrong. She was a blabbermouth, for one thing, and she wasn't a very good actress who could easily pretend to be something other than what she was and hope to fool anyone for long. Nor were her own ethics likely to stand up to this kind of work if the subjects weren't volunteers. Still, she had great skill and aptitude for 7000-series operations, as was demonstrated by her work with Coydt. They didn't want to lose that if they didn't have to.

The space station itself was a barren-looking series of interconnected tubular modules that resembled an abstract sculpture or a young child's first attempt with an erector set. One large tube jutted off from the main mass, and inside of it was a Borelli generator and the Kagan 7800 computer. So nervous were the experimenters with this new device that there was at the connection of the computer to the space station proper a series of explosive bolts that could even be hand-fired, and a propulsion unit beyond that was not under the computer's control at all. If the computer tried anything strange, it could be fired off into space with the throw of a switch by a human hand at literally a half-dozen points.

The computer itself, though, had been, so far, everything its company claimed it could be and more, and extremely well behaved. Experienced Kagan operators, trained to sense any wrongness in computer-human interfaces, found the machine somewhat disconcerting. Some computer shells were cheerful, or playful, or downright cold and, well, machine-like, but the 7800 seemed to be oddly reflective. Monitor after monitor received the odd impression that the computer would never consider being more than a help to humans, but that it seemed obsessed with attempting to understand human beings and really relate to them. It was as if the humans were as totally alien to it as it was to them, and while humans simply didn't have the capacity to ultimately understand what was going on in the depths of the great machine, it was certain it had the ability to ultimately understand humans—and a driving need to do so. Not for conquest, or supremacy—it was too alien to consider that worth thinking about. The early machines who had revolted were created in man's image; the Kagan 7800 was created by machines. They gave up trying to understand it, but no one who interfaced with it ever felt the least bit threatened.

Now they handed the machine something they would have hesitated to hand any computer under less secure circumstances. They handed it their whole problem, and answered all the questions they were asked on human behavior, particularly irrationalities, as well as they could.

Ultimately, it asked for a live subject, and they fed it Marsha Johnson. She was lightly sedated with a specific chemical the computer could identify and filter out, then taken to the small duplicate lab they had, with its lone digitizing tube, and there she was stripped, coded and converted into electrical impulses.

The computer could not explain, nor could anyone grasp it if it could have, just what it did and how it arrived at its conclusions, but arrive at them it did.

"*It is a great paradox,*" the computer noted. "*In some way the whole is greater than its parts. The interrelationships are too complex to fully trace. By reading her entire biochemical makeup and then correlating it with her cultural, psychiatric, and life records, I am able only to reach a superficial understanding of her. There is a logic to her sum, yet it cannot be attained by any mathematical manipulation of the parts. To go further would require a new mathematics, and I haven't sufficient grounding in what is required to create it.''*

That startled them, yet pleased them, somehow, too. The thing wasn't god. The human being was, in most ways, far inferior to the computer, yet it was based on a complexity, a mystery, that the computer could divine but not solve.

"She is, however, relatively simple to manipulate,'' the computer added. They did it all the time themselves—fitting artificially created chemicals to neural receptors, by conditioning, by a host of factors that were only the high-tech versions of things used to shape and control individual and mass human beings since civilization began, and which were, in their own right, only artificially induced and enhanced versions of the natural processes by which humans were socialized and given cultures.

The key, the computer noted, was that even the most illogical belief system could be imposed by conditioning and personality-reorganizing drugs and acculturations. Because of the digitizing process, this could be dispensed with, the process accelerated. It was merely a matter of decoding the parts—each and every complex element and its meaning—as filed in the brain, then intercepting and diverting what was needed. The weapon was a series of mathematical strings that would translate into things as real to the subject as if they had been placed there naturally. The old would not be gone, but it would be inaccessible. Identify objects and actions, and make the proper substitutions, then reinforce it by cranial biochemistry.

There were limits to this. An entire life history was impossible—that new mathematics got in the way. The parts wouldn't add up to the desired whole. The trick was in the twin commands of redirection and suppression. The less complex you wanted the whole to be, the better.

They let the computer have its head, interested to see what would result. The computer had the predetermined objectives. They wanted Johnson's technical skills and work experiences to remain, along with a drive to continue along those lines, but they wanted them to be in someone totally loyal and obedient to higher authority and absolutely secure, and in someone who would not let old friendships and feelings interfere with that dedication.

It gave them a pretty-looking girl of no more than eighteen with fair, unblemished skin and long silky hair and big blue eyes, slim, athletic, and well-proportioned. It looked nothing like Marsha Johnson, but it was, in more than a literal sense. It was the idealized form that Johnson, as a teen, had fantasized she looked like. And the form was also genetically correct.

She did not seem at all troubled by her nudity, nor at all shy or confused about waking up in a strange place with strange people looking at her. "Hello," she greeted them in a soft and silky voice.

Dr. Patricia Suzuki, chief psychiatrist and chief Overrider on the 7800 project, was startled. "Uh-hello. Do you know where you are?"

"No," came the reply, as if it didn't matter. The new Marsha turned and looked over the place. "This is a Kagan 7000 series operations lab, isn't it?"

Suzuki was startled again. "Yes—it is. I'm Dr. Suzuki, in charge here. What is *your* name?"

The girl laughed. "Oh, I don't have a name yet, but I'm sure you'll give me one I'll like."

"Um—do you remember *anything* about yourself?"

The laugh again. "No. Why should I want to?"

She was so innocent, they named her Eve. She was the subject of extensive study, and the object of every test known to medical science. She suffered all the tests patiently and without complaint, and seemed to know many of them. The results were eerie and disconcerting.

She had no past memories whatsoever. That was one thing. But she had no curiosity about that past, nor interest in it. Yet, she had every single bit of practical and technical knowledge she'd attained over the years. She could read, write, knew complex math, knew more than most of them about computers and about the very processes and operations that created her. She liked pretty clothes and all the rest— cosmetology, jewelry, and the like—yet had no modesty at all. She even understood how she came to be this way—

someone had been digitized and read into the computer with a series of parameters, and she was the result.

What disconcerted them the most was that she accepted it without question, and had absolutely no problems with it. She was perfectly content with the way she was, so why worry about what she had been?

Her learning ability was amazing as well. While she had no memory of anything or anyone, she didn't forget anything she was told. She knew they were going out to colonize a new world using the computer technology she understood so well, yet she had no idea of Earth, or Titan. She did, however, have a vision of her future. She wanted to work with the computers, to find out all they could do. She did, however, have an idealized vision of someone in her mind, someone who represented love, power, all the things of greatness, a sort of godlike figure whom she seemed to worship in some mystical, quasi-religious way. She was certain that this figure existed, and she would do anything for her deity, anything her deity commanded, unhesitatingly and without question. God was very real to Eve, and absolute. The computer had, as it said it would, taken the most direct way to arrive at the sum. It had begun with the sum and worked backward, eliminating anything and everything that did not agree with the objective. This had produced an incomplete human being, but one that worked and met all the requirements. And to ensure loyalty, the computer had fallen back on the oldest and simplest device around: religion. A terribly simple, very basic religion with one object, no rules, and no complications.

It was two weeks before some bright assistant noticed, almost offhandedly, that "Eve's" description of her deity looked one hell of a lot like Brigadier Coydt.

The pattern, once established, was filed for future use. The staff at Site K referred to it as the Frog Princess program, and the name stuck. It became, in fact, something of a template for Security's major problems, producing nice-looking, obedient, loyal, but highly intelligent new people with computer skills added for those like Jimmy Okieda, who had no real skills of their own to save. They had a particular affinity for the human-computer interfaces as well, smoothing a lot of semantical problems. This, in fact, caused the professional paranoiacs of Security to worry that these creations were actually in some way controlled by the computer, a device to circumvent the two human safeguards by putting its own slaves at both positions. They actually arranged for "Eve" and "Ginny" to have sole access to these positions alone and unguarded—but not, of course, unwatched, with much monitoring going on and firm hands on blast switches—but in fact nothing happened.

The computer could, of course, be simply playing subtle—it knew, certainly, the sort of folks it worked for—but as the template people remained and adjusted, they began to develop more regular human personalities. Rather dull ones, to be sure, but people stopped thinking of them as creatures or freaks.

Suzy Watanabe could not be handled so easily, nor was she a problem the 7800 could comfortably and confidently solve. The best it could do was suggest a system which the psychiatrists could have accomplished chemically, but less certainly. Ultimately, her problem areas were emotional, not intellectual, and the only real solution to her salvation as herself was by redirecting those emotions. Faith and love were powerful antidotes to guilt and shame, after all.

And thus it was that Suzy Watanabe had a religious experience so real and so personal that she could neither deny nor doubt it. It was built from her own mental images, after all.

She knew that she was in some sort of hospital, and had been for some time, but time had little meaning to her in her drugged state. One night, however, with the lights dimmed for sleep, she awoke, feeling suddenly clear of mind and so awake that every sound seemed magnified.

She lay there, trying to collect her thoughts. She'd stepped into the tube, and Michiko and Carolyn had taken their positions, and she'd seen the big light go on and then felt a tingling throughout her whole body. Things had passed by her in a haze, then—suddenly she'd been lying on the floor of a darkened lab, a strange medic hovering over her, and she'd just started to ask what was going on when he'd administered a sedative. Why?

She suddenly sat up in bed and did a physical inventory.

She couldn't see her face, but the rest of her looked normal. No strange deformities, no odd signs or colorations. What had happened in between?

She was about to take some action when she thought she heard voices. She froze, then frowned. More like whispers, really, and not from outside the door. More like—right in the tiny room!

She turned with a start and saw nothing at first. Yet the whispers *did* seem to be coming from the corner, getting louder, nearer all the time. A vent, perhaps? Or a radio?

She could make out what the voices were saying now, a man's and a woman's voice, familiar voices. . . .

"Etsuko! Etsuko!"

She started and instinctively shrank back against the wall. What kind of trickery was this? No one had called her by that name, even *knew* that name, since . . .

Shapes shimmered in the semi-darkness, then resolved themselves into human-sized forms. They were barely visible, transparent, and bereft of great details, yet she recognized them both immediately. Her father's bright, piercing eyes and big white moustache; her mother's delicate features and unnatural grace and beauty . . .

Either I've gone mad or some son-of-a-bitch psychiatrist from Security Command is playing a dirty fucking game with me, she thought, not sure which was the truth.

"Please do not shrink from our presence," her mother said in a voice she worshipped and thought never to hear again. "This is difficult for us and despite our pleas our time is short." She spoke in Japanese. They both did.

"Listen to your mother," her father said, a trace of characteristic impatience in his voice.

"I—I do not believe that you are here," the scientist managed, her voice hoarse and nervous. "This is a trick."

"We have no time to be convincing," her father grumbled. "Just listen, and form your own conclusions. You are as pigheaded as ever, which is why this is necessary."

"Please—it is not when and where you think," her mother said hesitantly. "Listen and we will tell you the truth of things."

And, in fact, they did exactly that. The four-and-a-half-month gap. The pressures, the guilt, the doubts and fears of her work as the project moved from theory to reality.

And then, most horribly, they showed her the outcome. The ceremonial robe, the short sword, the cubicles, the alarm, the guns going off, the bullets tearing through her . . .

She believed that much, for such things were already in her mind even back at the time of her own personal experiment on herself. There wasn't a false note in it anywhere, partly because it was, in fact, all true. Or, rather, it almost rang true.

"If it happened as you showed me, and I was killed, why am I here and not with you? I have not a wound upon me."

And they showed her what happened—exactly. Showed Coydt with Marsha Johnson taking the ultimate gamble and wrenching her back from the dead. Showed the medic giving her the sedative . . .

"Your soul was halfway to us, which is why we heard," her mother explained. "We knew that unless we could find a way, you would try once more."

It was pretty convincing stuff, she had to admit, and, worse, her own resurrection fascinated her in spite of her doubts and fears. *Literally back from the dead . . .*

"Don't think for a moment that Coydt saved you out of altruism," her father commented. "She did it partly as an experiment, partly to save the terrible commotion your death would have caused at a critical time."

That she could believe. The trouble was, she was believing all of this, and she wondered just how far that belief really extended.

"No matter what the motive, your action would have been the cause of a greater evil," her mother told her. "It is dishonorable to atone for future wrongs when one has made no attempt at halting them."

It was a strange sort of logic that hit home.

"What would you accomplish by suicide?" her father asked her. "An inconvenience to them, no more. You would not stop the idea, but you would leave the awesome power entirely in the hands of people like Coydt. There would be no one to spy upon her, to keep her and those like her in check, for no one else would know the full, awesome power of this new thing but them. They would be demons, loosed and unchecked among the innocent, isolated population of a new world. If such a force as this exists, which can be used for untold good or unspeakable evil, is it the moral, the ethical thing to abandon it entirely to evil without doing battle?''

''But—what could I do? They already have the upper hand, and unless I miss my guess, they have me too.''

''They have your body, not your soul,'' her mother admonished her. ''Only you can give them that, as you tried to do. Having brought you back, they cannot do away with you. If they can be convinced that you no longer will destroy yourself, they will restore you. Go with them to this new place. Show them what *good* this new thing can do. Be vigilant against its use for evil.''

''But I can do little! I have spent half my life fighting such forces, and they always win! That is why I wished to leave this world. I am tired of fighting!''

The moment she said it she knew it was the truth and felt terribly ashamed.

''Then there is no honor left in you and no hope at all,'' her father said in deep disgust. ''You have been given something no one else has: a chance to reconsider after the fact. If you stand tall, and fight evil, there is no shame, even if, as fate sometimes wills, the evil triumphs. The honor is clear and the soul shines with virtue. But to not fight, to surrender to the evil and slink away—that is a worse evil, and the stain and dishonor can never be wiped from the soul.''

''Please—our time is nearly gone,'' her mother pleaded. ''There is another thing to think upon. All your life you have pushed back your humanity. You have remained aloof, a machine, pushing all desire back where it creates permanent and painful wounds. You cannot possibly feel the souls of those who need you unless you release those feelings and find humanity there. The flesh and mind are of one accord. Neither can be whole while the other languishes.''

Even after death her mother was still after her to get married! ''Mother, I am fifty-one. It is too late for that now.''

''Anyone whose machines can restore the dead can make themselves young and beautiful once again,'' her mother noted. ''Why shrink from such a thing? It is no reason now, merely an excuse.''

She had never said this to anyone before, not aloud, not even to herself. Now she felt compelled to say it. "My parents, you must now know my shame. I have never felt the need for men. I have never found them very appealing or attractive save on an intellectual level. When I was seventeen, and at university, I had an infatuation, an affair, with another girl. When I saw how I was being drawn to that life, I recoiled. I could not bring dishonor, misery, and shame to you. This is common, accepted, by others of our adopted culture, but I could not bring shame to you. I vowed then and there that I would never again partake of the flesh, for I could not allow it and contain my passions in secrecy." She was crying now, the first really good cry she'd had since childhood, and it felt very good. "Now you know my true shame."

Her parents' ghosts seemed more saddened than shocked at this revelation. Finally, her mother said, somewhat hesitantly, "We do not understand it, but we accept it, my darling."

"Perhaps your machine could fix that up too," her father grumbled.

The fact was, it probably could—in fact, while open homosexuality was a norm these days and hardly a cause for more than a few eyebrows being raised in the technocrat's culture in which she lived her life, her neurochemical nature of sexual preference was well enough known that it could be altered with existing noncomputer treatments. She simply didn't want to change it. She never had wanted to change it.

"We love you no matter what," her mother assured her. "We always will. Neither death nor the passage of time can change that. Stop hiding now from yourself and from the world. Be young again and find your inner peace. You can make this new world a place where happiness reigns and the evils of the old world are left behind. Do not abandon it. And to successfully lead the fight, you must be as honest with others as you are with yourself. Remember us, and this, and know that our love is with you always."

The figures, and the voices, were fading now, and although she cried out to them through her sobs and tears, they were gone. She cried thirty-seven years worth of tears, then slipped off to a deep, peaceful sleep, the best, in fact, that she'd had in her memory.

The psychiatrists of Site K were quite pleased with themselves. The computer had merely confirmed their diagnosis, and helped supply the mechanics of the cure. The tact was perfect, and would restore Suzy Watanabe to full participation, they felt sure. The only really serious worry they had was whether they could make the release and restoration convincingly difficult for her to achieve.

They brought her around slowly, acting as if nothing had happened and explaining their new activity by her emotional release. They freely admitted to her that they had been using mild hypnotics to find a starting point, but when she suspiciously suggested that they had induced the ghosts, they turned it back on her, noting that they couldn't do anything that effective with the kind of drugs they used and suggesting that in fact she herself had created the ghosts out of her own subconscious as a way to break through to sanity.

Watanabe knew enough biochemistry to accept what they were saying, and she'd faced enough psychiatrists on and off that they were totally in character and totally convincing. In fact, she would gladly have accepted their theory that the ghosts were the product of her own mind except that logic prevented it. She was not the Watanabe who'd been killed; she was the Watanabe of several months earlier. How could her subconscious have known the most intimate details of her death and resurrection?

There were only three possibilities that explained it all, she knew. Either they induced it, she induced it, or it really happened, no matter how incredible that was. She could not believe that they induced it, not only for the surface reasons but also for the little things. Coydt's people would have brought back a friend, not an enemy. The ghosts would have forgiven her, not reacted as in fact her father and mother would have. Her views had not changed. They were going to turn her loose still an enemy, and a powerful and knowledgeable one at that. Even giving them a degree of subtlety she didn't believe they had, she couldn't believe they would create a situation where she'd decide to go to New Eden and keep her division. She was the only one with nothing to lose willing to stand in their way there. Remaining back here, Coydt would have her godship all to herself.

And there was the final thing that had bothered all of them since it was discovered. Given the same mass, and the same encoding, it should be possible for the computers to create duplicates of people. There was no scientific reason against it—but you couldn't. Or dogs, or cats, or even fish. Plant life, yes, and much microbial life as well, but not anything even remotely complex in the animal kingdom. It had dashed their hopes to use many of the animals—cows, horses, chickens, and the like—as templates, sending perhaps no more than a dozen each up the line and creating extras there. A little genetic engineering would prevent the ills of too close inbreeding when they had a larger population. Instead, they had to ship as many animals up as they would require in the early days.

Why not? Because they had souls, as the religious leaders suggested? Because, for some reason, those souls could not be duplicated, only transformed? And if souls existed, then where might they go after death?

With that came the acceptance of the visitation, and the acceptance, too, of a somewhat Buddhist outlook on the cosmos. Humanity had always survived its revolutions, after all. It had survived its own instinct for mass collective suicide. Might there not be some divine powers looking over some great plan out there, somewhere?

And, with that, her rehabilitation became in fact very swift, although they did not dare from this point to use their computer or other sophisticated methods on the scientist. It was a twin irony: Watanabe desperately wanting to get back to work as soon as possible, and the psychiatrists not wanting to probe *too* deeply lest they find some reason not to let her do just that.

To gain some trust, they shipped her back to Titan and put her under the care of the company's regular psychiatric staff. That staff itself was more cautious, but amazed at the change in the scientist, who'd lost none of her fire and brilliance but seemed to be a whole new person.

This was, in fact, the way Watanabe saw herself. Etsuko Watanabe was dead; she'd died in a fit of madness a few months before. The new Suzy was comfortable with herself, relaxed, and confident if no less fearless. The past, both civilization's in general and her own, was now a teacher, not a jailer. She took an interest in her appearance, and flirted openly with a couple of women she found attractive. To her doctor's disapproval, she started smoking cigars again, but she no longer worried about them. She no longer had any reservations about curing herself of whatever anything might give her, using the programs. Van Haas was impatient for her release now that she was committed to the project, and they allowed her access to her computers and staff on a carefully monitored basis. She could eventually have turned herself into a sexy teenage bombshell, but she rejected that out of hand. She was a director, an example, and she had to be the boss. Nobody took orders from a teenage bombshell. Just herself, in prime health and condition, at about age thirty to thirty-five was what she had in mind.

Her chief assistant, Michiko Iki, had taken over direct supervision and had done a superior job—perhaps, Suzy thought, a better job than she herself could have done. Half of her people were already there, handling the other end, and a fair percentage were supervising the transport on this end. Right now her section was handling the least glamorous and most routine part of the job; after the bulk of supplies and personnel had been sent, it would again become a backwater department while she concentrated on energy services. Then she could get back to the theoretical work and experimenta- tion that interested her the most—and which was, after all, the product for which Westrex was paying.

In spite of her pressing and her protests, though, she could find no trace of Marsha Johnson. She realized that the assist- ant must have been put on ice along with others involved in the incident, but before Suzy's full reinstatement she didn't have the clout to find out more, and after it she was far too snowed under with work to press it, and she would have had to press it with Coydt personally, and in spite of the fact that the brigadier had saved her, she had no change of heart regarding the military in general or Security in particular, and her leverage there was as a result nonexistent.

Toby Haller had felt keen excitement at the order to "go" on the project, as he'd had tremendous praise for his work all the way up to the Director Korda himself, yet he'd been there, day after day, week after week, as others in his section were sent forward to their posts and given their assignments while he remained on Titan, having less to do. It was not merely that he was eager to go; the early birds were getting hands-on experience right now on installed 7800's, and they would have a jump on him for the future—and more influence on overall design as a consequence.

Even his old friends were leaving. Marsha Johnson was gone, although there were rumors of something unsavory in that, and so were Caesar Fanfani and Mark Weinbaum. Lisa Wu was still around someplace, but her job was removing her from any social breaks with what was left of the old gang. It was almost like graduation, where friendships built up over the years are suddenly dissolved in nothing more than vague promises to have a reunion someday, promises seldom fulfilled.

Sari Kittachorn, however, was using her friendship with him and his lack of meaningful work to her advantage. The early planners of Westrex's scheme for nontechnical colonization, in itself a social experiment, were here now, and while they understood the broad basics of the project, they were hazy on specifics. Haller was asked to brief some of them on his section, since he would be working closest with them.

They were a curious mixture; Arabic-looking men with clipped accents and business suits who had made deserts bloom, East Indian agricultural experts always fighting starvation and fighting a depleted land, and Ibo craftsmen who could handle too much water on the crops. There were urban planners there, too, from places like Accra and Buenos Aires, and from small towns and villages carved out of the most unlikely geographies.

All were amazed and a little awed at the idea that this man *thought* geology, climatology, and all the other factors big and small into existence just the way he wanted them. She'd paraded so many through now that he'd developed a stock speech of sorts.

"Computers don't know what the real world is like," he told them. "They never really have. They go by what we tell them. For centuries we've been able to go into a computer and graphically create a convincing, animated, three-dimensional picture of any world we want, obeying any laws we wish. That was child's play, but it's basic to understanding what we're doing, and for a very long time that's all we *could* do. It was handy, and sophisticated, for solving all sorts of scientific theory, planning cities and seeing the implication of drainage, irrigation, climate shifts—whatever. Only with the discovery and taming of Flux, however, were we able to take it further, building computers with enormous memory capacity and giving them all the power they needed.

"In a sense, what I do is the same as creating those pictures. We feed in the basics that we must live with—the stability equations to keep our world warm enough and maintain a workable, if static, atmosphere that can sustain us and provide the energy to run our computer network, power network, transport network, and the like—and to self-repair, since even with redundancies built in, we can't afford failures of any sort here.

"The end objective is to create a world that we can thrive on that is in every way self-sustaining. That means sufficient plant-to-animal ratios to allow us to have our own permanent natural atmospheric processes. We'll need water, and a climatological system that delivers enough to every place we need it. To maintain our ecosystem we'll need to create surface soil with exact mineral balances to assure good plant growth and human and animal health. Requirements like these are fed to the computer as 'givens'—accept, can't touch. From that point I start playing with the exact form this world should be. Yes?"

"I have used such models all the time in the Punjab," said someone in the group. "How is this so different?"

"It's not, except that we create the picture—the *appearance* of reality—only to keep checking our mistakes and seeing our problems before we have to live with them. Unlike anyplace on Earth, or even Titan, we aren't troubled with an existing global ecosystem yet, so we can design our own. We aren't hobbled by existing soil, climate, and moisture conditions, or problems of elevation. We can add or subtract to any of these and hundreds more factors and come up with what we *wish* we had. Once that model is built and saved in the computer, we can take it one step further. We can draw energy from

Flux through the grid and use it to turn energy into matter and other, more useful forms of energy. We can take that theoretical computer model and we can order it to come off the viewing device and become reality.''

''I've seen many a nightmare landscape on the view boxes as well, sir,'' remarked an Argentine who was in command of, but obviously still new to, conversational English, the majority language and by default the common one for the project and the world. ''Can you not also create nightmares with this thing? Real nightmares people must live with, and even in?''

''The possibility's there,'' he admitted, ''but that's why we have bosses and cross-checks. Everything I design goes through not only my computers but many of my colleagues' as well, and is examined, picked apart, and critiqued worse than a bad novel. It's an ego-deflating experience, after months of work, to send out a model you have checked and double-checked and lived with like one of your own children and see it hacked to pieces by your associates. Consensus, both of the engineers and their computers, is required before we put anything into practice.''

''Will it be a gray, barren, soulless place like this?'' one woman asked him, sounding very concerned. ''I admit this is not the vision that sold me on committing myself to this project.''

At the start, it probably will be worse than this,'' he responded honestly. ''But once we're in, have set up our equipment, and tested everything to the hilt, then run *new* models, some from scratch, and reconciled those with the other departments, we'll begin to shape the place. First there'll be the computer center and a rather primitive sort of city around it—primitive at first anyway. Then we'll start developing the region around in a careful manner. These will be experiments—scale models of what we propose to do to the whole planet—and we may make some mistakes we'll have to live with, but if I'm good enough, they won't be in *my* area. The objective is to create four different prototypes around each of the seven Gates and compare notes. Each of them will be self-sufficient in the basics—food, clothing, shelter. When done, they will be almost like little worldlets of their own. These are the Anchor blocks, as we call them—the experimental areas and templates for what will come after."

"Will there be grayness? I know there's no sun," someone asked.

"New Eden is a moon about the size of Titan in an outer orbit around a gas giant almost the size of Jupiter," he told them. "Gas giants have often been described, with some justification, as stars that failed. We will get no heat from our mother world, but we will get a great deal of light. It's a different sort of light, because it is almost all reflective and it literally will dominate the daytime sky—perhaps three quarters of the sky at midday—and because, like our own gas giants, it's banded. We feel that the fact that it's a bit odd and different is not sufficient to not use it as our primary light source. We have to anyway—anything that big, that close, and that bright is going to light up even dense Flux down to the ground in any event.

"The atmosphere currently is static and artificial, and is designed as a protection against radiation and who knows what else that might come down. We've learned a lot from this station here on Titan, including the need to protect ourselves from some things we never before knew existed. Once the Anchors are in enough for us to sit back, live off them, and see how well they work, we'll clear the air, so to speak, within their boundaries. The sky will be nearly as transparent as Earth's—and as distorting. An artificial miniature climate will be induced to feed us rainfall and we'll see how everything works, from drainage to irrigation to drinking and sewage. To you, you will be living in a self-contained and quite pleasant but very tiny world of your own—each Anchor will be. In effect, you'll be living within a fixed and very real computer simulation. The Anchors will be the best places, by the way, because they're easy—they're being designed as ideals, and because of their relatively small areas we don't have to worry about interaction with the rest of the world. It's only when we start filling in from Anchor to Anchor and Anchor to Gate that we will get incredibly complex."

"Will there be oceans when the world is done?" another asked.

"No. We're dealing in a smaller area than Earth and we

have the luxury of being able to distribute our water more evenly. However, there will be some huge lakes—not in the Anchors though—that will look like and serve the functions of oceans, and a tremendous river system. We plan for the great mass of water to be frozen in the polar regions, as on Earth—only on *our* world, by simply sending current up that grid and converting it to heat, we'll be able to melt what's needed and channel it north and south to the life zones when and where needed. Large bodies of water are, however, my specialty, and so far the problem hasn't been totally solved. It's possible I may have to add an ocean after all at some point, for climatological reasons, but we're trying to avoid it if we can, as well as tall mountain ranges. These factors more than anything else can make one place too dry and another too wet. We intend a water area equivalent to two large oceans, but it will be broken up and put where *we* want and need them.''

"What's the problem with your big lakes?''

"Mostly it's tides. We're dealing here with a moon, not a planet, and we're subject to solar tides, the effects of other planets, and, most of all, the effects of being so bloody close to a gigantic world. If Earth's moon can create the tides *it* does, imagine the tides a Jupiter can cause. Add in other moons—we have two dozen of any significance in our lunar system—and various rings, and you've got a hellish mess. When we solve that one, we'll be on our way.''

"Looking at this project, some of us can't help but question if it is all worth it,'' said one woman, and there were several nods. "My own people are hungry each day.''

"That's why we must not fail,'' he responded. "We are the guinea pigs for what's going on back home. We've never minimized the risk, although we've accented the adventure. We can't feed, clothe, or house all the people we've got on Earth. We're running low on resources and not all of them can be replaced economically or even practically from space. If we can survive, build, grow, and prove ourselves out, it will be child's play to remake the Earth, renew and replenish it. If we can do it out there, we can also do it to Mars, the moon, perhaps even to Venus, to other outer moons, and wherever we need it, and we can build worlds where there is no hunger, no lack of material goods. That's the object here, and we must remember it always.

"That's why so much in resources is being poured into this project. That's why we can't afford to fail. It's our task to save the human race. We dare not fail—or the conditions on Earth today, bad as they are, are only a pale shadow of what is to come."

There were more—hundreds more—such questions, and he fielded them expertly. Too expertly, he worried. He couldn't help but wonder if they were leaving him here to do this simply because he was so good at it.

But finally he got the call, and to Sir Kenneth's office. The handsome, gentle-seeming Kenyan still had his doubts about things, but he was doing a good job and couldn't help but feel some of the excitement and thrill of embarking on what might well be humanity's greatest adventure.

"Come in, lad! Have a seat," the Director of Landscape Engineering said cheerfully, although it was clear that he was very tired. Korda had aged five years in the past six months. "I hear you're making an excellent propagandist for us."

"I suppose," he grumbled. "It's not exactly my line though." Not very subtle, but he felt he didn't have much he could lose.

"I know, I know," Korda responded sympathetically. "You're eager to get out there. Well, your time has come."

He felt a sudden knot in his stomach, and rising excitement, but he held it in and just looked expectantly at his boss.

"There are pluses and minuses to your assignment," Sir Kenneth continued, "so I want to go into them and our reasoning with you now. First of all, you're assigned to Sector Four, under your countrywoman, Sandra Kingsley."

That was good news. He didn't know her very well, but those who worked under her had nothing but good things to say. "Yes, sir?"

"Area Four doesn't have a division headquarters—the only one that doesn't—and that's probably all to the good. It's the one region where our people will be stepping on the fewest toes and tripping over the least bureaucracy. That also means, however, an area not near the centers of power and influence, so if anything runs short, it'll short you first and you'll get replacements last."

"I'm not exactly unfamiliar with coping with things like that," Haller noted ruefully. Water projects had not been very high on Westrex's initial list on Titan.

"I know. That's one reason you're right for down there. You have a good record of making do with what you have and scrounging up what you need without bothering with channels. There are, however, some additional negatives to Four, which is, as you might guess, the last to be fully set up."

Haller nodded. "Go ahead, sir."

"First of all, they—the board—are dropping some small teams of folks working on special projects into there simply because they want them secret and out of the way. They might assist, they might not—and they might also ease you out when you need the machine, for example. They are answerable only to the board—not even Kingsley will know what they're doing, and she'll have no authority to cancel their priority. They'll have van Haas's ear, in other words. They will probably be a pain in the ass, but they will be experts on the big machines, and the little ones, and don't hesitate to use them if you can. Understand?"

He nodded, understanding perfectly. Not only their brains but also their supplies and their priority slips.

"All right. Finally, while you'll be getting some good people there, particularly at the start, they're also using Region Four as something of a dumping ground. Odd religious sects, important people nobody really wants, political prisoners—all that. Lots of variety, to say the least."

"To say the least," Haller repeated a little sarcastically. A bundle of foreign religious nuts and folks sent out there against their will. Plus all the missionary groups, political groups with some leverage, you name it. It would be messy—but certainly not boring.

"Now, the good news for last. You and I both know it's going to take years just to establish and test out the Anchors. We don't know how many years, but perhaps as much as a decade or even longer. A great deal of Region Four is devoted in the master plan to one of your great lakes, so that's the final reason for going down there, but you and I know that I can't keep you on big water projects forever when any results are perhaps decades away."

He nodded. "I understand, sir." Having such a time frame spelled out was not a happy thing, although it was nothing he hadn't known from the start.

"I've been very impressed with you, though, and since two of the Anchors in the area are Anchors for your lake as well, that needs to be taken into consideration in their design. How would you like to be division chief of Anchor Luck? That's the northernmost in the region, and the closest to everyone else, and will probably be the earliest Anchor developed in that region." The Anchor letters were assigned arbitrary English and Greek-English code names by the military after some old navy convention. Whose navy nobody seemed to know.

He sat bolt upright. *Division chief! Sweet Bloody Jesus!* He cleared his throat. "That, uh, would be most satisfactory, sir."

Korda wasn't fooled for a moment by the coolness of his reply. "I know this is a promotion you did not expect, but I think you are the right man for this job. While it's basically an administrative rather than a lab job, I want someone there in charge who's been looking at the big picture and knows our procedures inside and out. I want each of the Anchors to be so right, so correct, from the start that we will have no regrets later on."

"I'll do my best, sir."

Sir Kenneth smiled and stood, indicating the interview was over. "I know you will, son. And if your best isn't good enough, I'll sack you just as quickly. See my secretary for a list of the names and locations of the staff who you've drawn and the names of the other key department heads you'll have to deal with at Luck. I would suggest you get right into some preliminary meetings, both for mutual familiarity and to get the details of the Luck pattern. You leave in nineteen days."

7

THE GRAND ADVENTURE

It was the damnedest piece of packing he'd ever done. With the computer mains on and checked at New Eden, little in the way of personal baggage was required save some personal things and a full set of clothing. What else was needed would be repaired or duplicated there from the Flux energy. That was a luxury they could learn to like, Haller decided, but one they shouldn't really get so used to. The objective was total self-sufficiency, and this bred indolence.

Still, financing was tight and getting the basic needs over just to start the project was tricky. Cargo took up cargo space on the ships, and massive amounts were needed. The solution was to digitize the inorganic stuff before you left, creating, in effect, little computer programs that could be used to recreate your belongings when you got there. As a result, he took 126 kilograms, give or take, of clothing, old mementos, various personal objects, and such to one of the nine active tube stations at Titan Multinational Experimental Base and he came away with a tiny cube that could fit into his pocket and which was encoded with his personal identification data so that only he could activate it.

While his people would be going in this batch as well, he had no real way to get together with them in the processing, since the order was determined by Transportation. He made his way now to the shuttle, keeping it slow, feeling a curious ambivalence about leaving the place even if it had begun to resemble a morgue. Its gray skies, gray streets, gray buildings, and uninviting landscape had become familiar to him, an old friend. He'd worked into the system quite well and been rather comfortable here the past four years or so.

In his hand he held the only nondigitized possessions he was allowed; a small squarish bag of toiletries and such, and a few items he thought he'd need right away when he got there. This would be useful for the trip out to the Borelli Point, and would go with him in a small separate little locker under his own tube.

Most of the passengers were already there for this shuttle trip up, the fifth and not the last of the day. Everyone would be taken on one master ship out to the Point. Most of the others were just killing time or milling around, and there was, curiously, little conversation and much tangible anxiety. Here and there a few would find others they knew and strike up a conversation, perhaps comparing destinations or billet numbers on the ship to the Point, but he saw no one he knew more than vaguely.

He felt somewhat old in this company, although he was just barely thirty-two. Most of the men and women in the terminal looked barely out of their teens to him, and all seemed in far better shape than he was or felt. They were white, yellow, and every shade of brown, European and African and Asian in all their varieties, yet they shared a single common bond that was shaping their future.

"Attention! Attention!" boomed a voice over a loudspeaker, and conversation ground to a halt as they turned to look at a navy chief in the dark blue Logistics Command uniform. "We will be embarking immediately. There is no need to rush, as everything has been preassigned. When I tell you, walk to the loading doors to your right and give your name to the personnel officer there. He will hand you a small card with your name and your billet number and location aboard ship, on the back of which is printed a basic map of how to get there from the ship's dock. Ship's personnel will also be aboard both the shuttle and throughout the passenger area of the ship to assist you. Do *not* attempt to change that billet or circumvent the system. We must find you en route, and mess and sleep schedules have to be adjusted accordingly. We can work out any serious problems after we are under way.''

The people were quite efficient, and the passengers did act a little stupid trying to be first even though it didn't matter. It didn't even matter what seat you got on the shuttle; you couldn't see a blasted thing anyway. He, too, felt the urge to rush aboard though. It beat hell out of sitting around being bored to death and it provided some relief to be on the way.

The trip up proved a bit disconcerting after four years of being planetbound, and he found his stomach doing tiny flip-flops at the takeoff. Still, it took only about forty minutes to break free of Titan, much of which was in the same primordial mess as before humans had arrived and built their tiny islands of habitability there, and rendezvous and dock with the big mother ship.

He'd remembered how spartan the navy ship had been coming out, but this one was even worse, a converted cargo carrier that had been converted only to the minimum. They'd put in six decks to hold people and cargo out to the Point, but then they'd divided the decks using thin plastic sheeting that resembled office partitions and didn't even go all the way to the ceiling. These divided the decks into a series of rooms, or actually roomettes, about four meters by three meters, containing two sets of spartan bunk beds with hospitallike straps ''just in case,'' a pull-down desk at the end, and four folding canvas-backed chairs now all folded and stored under the bottom bunks. The door was little more than a shower curtain, or so it looked to him.

''There's also a little wash basin and mirror that pulls out above the desk,'' said a woman's voice behind him. He started, turned, and saw a very attractive Eurasian woman wearing a skin-tight green body stocking that left little to the imagination, and high-heeled boots.

''Oh, sorry—must have the wrong one,'' he managed.

She looked on her card. ''Deck C, billet 125,'' she read. ''Yours too?''

He looked at it and nodded. ''I've lived in many a coed dormitory in my time, but never quite *this* close,'' he managed.

''They slipped up on a fair number of these assignments,''

she told him. "Don't bother to complain. You'll get the old song and dance about how they're too busy now and will work it out later. That means five days later." Five days, of course, being the length of time they'd be outbound before disembarking to the Flux ship. "I don't mind if you don't."

"Oh, certainly not!" he said both brightly and honestly. Frankly, the whole thing was something of a turn-on. "I'm Toby Haller, Landscape Engineering."

"Candy Kwong, local administration," she responded. "Glad to know you. In case you're wondering, the lavatories are coed, too, and are about ten meters to your right up the aisle. The showers are forty meters to the left. There's something of a lounge to the right of the loos that's not large enough for all of us, but it has tea and coffee available and is regularly resupplied with biscuits and other snacks. Dining is three long ladders or stairways down on F deck, and they don't call it 'mess' for nothing. We're on the swing shift—1100, 1500, and 2300 for food, and it's lights-out on this deck from 0400 to 1000 hours. I was on the first shuttle and I've checked."

"Very impressive," he told her. "This place is so noisy now, I have an odd feeling that catnaps will be impossible in spite of nothing to do."

"Oh, there are some things to do. I didn't see it, but they have an exercise room on F deck as well as the mess, a basic library, and a bunch of ten-year-old SV shows in a little theater there, as well as small meeting rooms for divisional conferences."

"Oh—hello! Oh, dear!" came another voice, and they turned and saw a small, mousy-looking girl with a freckled face and reddish-brown curly hair wearing yellow pants and an overly large plain white T-shirt. She looked somewhat startled to see Haller.

"Deck C, billet 125?" Candy Kwong asked casually.

The girl nodded. She looked to be not yet out of her teens. "Y-yes, but—"

"I'm afraid they were random in all respects," Haller told her apologetically. "Ms. Kwong and I have decided we can stand each other's embarrassment, but if this isn't true with you, I'll arrange a switch in any case, being, as it were, the odd man in all respects."

The girl seemed to be looking him over top to bottom, and he could see what was going through her mind. She really didn't want to be the one to make waves and seem the total prude, and her sense of vicarious adventure was tweaked, but she really would have preferred not to make the choice. He felt a bit sorry for her, really. He might have lied and told her he was gay or something, but he really didn't want to stifle a budding friendship with somebody who looked like Candy Kwong.

"N-no," she decided at last. "I'll make do. All of us will have to make do for quite a while, I suspect. I'm Millie Galsworthy."

By God, she looks like a Millie Galsworthy too, he thought. "I'm Toby Haller and this is Candy Kwong. What division are you with?"

"Oh, I'm not in any, really. Not yet anyway. My father's a Logistics officer and my mother's in administration. They both went ahead a few weeks ago, but I had to finish up some tests before I could join them."

"How old are you, Millie?" Kwong asked nicely.

"Seventeen."

They could both sympathize with her. In a world of Ph.D.'s, bureaucrats, and soldiers, she was more than a bit out of her element. Her future was somewhat limited as well. It would be a very long time, perhaps half a lifetime, before they were any universities on New Eden worth mentioning, and in spite of being a military brat, she didn't really look the type to enlist, either physically or temperamentally.

Eventually, Millie warmed to them, and as they went down and ate what the navy insisted was food, she told them that her parents and she had discussed it all thoroughly. Their problem was hardly unique; there were quite a large number of married couples with families in the project. A few, but not many, had in the end decided not to go because of the limits on their children, but her parents had been committed to it and she had supported them. Now she could go with them and try to find a niche, or she could remain behind, return to Earth, and get an education—but at the cost of being cut off from her parents for that period and with no certainty that she would later be considered valuable enough to rejoin the program.

"Have you given any thought as to what you might do out there?" Candy asked Millie. While there would be jobs for the nontechnical out there, there would also be nontechnical personnel for them.

"Oh, I thought I'd just help out wherever I could, find a man, and have a lot of babies," Millie responded casually.

Toby Haller almost choked to death on his coffee.

Later, they just walked around the huge ship for a while, then went back up to the sleeping area. It was bedlam in there, with hundreds of voices all talking at the same time and bouncing off the walls, but they found that, in time, you got used to it.

Finally, an electronic gong sounded throughout the ship, followed by the eternal squeal of a boatswain's whistle. "Attention all personnel, attention all personnel," came an echoey official-sounding man's voice over the ship's P.A. system. "Prepare to sail. Repeat, prepare to sail."

There wasn't much for passengers to do, and no preparations were needed in these days of modern deep space flight, but a strange and unnatural hush fell over the entire deck and perhaps the entire ship. They sat there, almost frozen, and beyond could be heard the clanging of bells and whining of buzzers and the grinding of heavy machinery. The nearly imperceptible vibration of a ship in dock was replaced by an increasing vibration that ran through the ship. There was a momentary dim in the lights as the ship switched entirely to internal power, and then some gentle lurches as the great craft backed slowly out of its orbiting dock, stopped, turned, and proceeded forward and out of the Saturnian system.

They had been on artificial gravity since leaving the shuttle, so there was little change personally, but the sounds and *feel* of a big ship on its own were clear and unmistakable.

It would take several hours under an expert pilot to completely clear the mess that was the miniature solar system around Saturn; only then could they slowly accelerate to full power and attain speeds their ancestors only dreamed of. Even so, it was painfully slow compared to the trip the passengers aboard were about to make. While they would make the Point in a mere five days, it would take them almost five years to reach the next nearest star at this speed, and perhaps a hundred and fifty years to reach any system useful to humanity even with Flux terraforming. They, however, were going a far greater distance than that, and they were going to do it in no time at all.

The volume of conversation and general noise began to rise at last, until it was back to previous levels. Toby and his two companions relaxed, too, and checked their areas. No one had appared to take the fourth bunk, so either somebody had decided not to go or else they'd missed the boat. Millie, saying she was slightly claustrophobic, took the top bunk over Candy's lower; Toby had a duplex all to himself. He found that thin curtains could be lowered to give him some privacy and shield him just a little from the light and noise. The top bunks had a more complex but still easy-to-operate tentlike mechanism to do the same things. If they were contortionists, they could change clothes or whatever in their beds without going public to the others.

"Attention C-deck passengers," the P.A. called out. "We regret the inconvenience and close quarters imposed, but we have done our best with the materials we have been given. Because you will be using disposable clothing from this point out, we ask you not to change your assigned billet. Our computer has your basic measurements and requirements from your files. This clothing will be delivered to each billet before the wake-up lights come on. Fold and place all old clothing outside your door after changing each day. If the new clothing is wrong or gets excessively soiled or damaged during a day, report to the quartermaster, Deck F, for refit and replacement.

"Also, bedding should be treated the same way but deposited in a separate pile outside the door. New bedding will be delivered. Smoking is not permitted anywhere on Deck C except the lounge.

"Please be considerate of everyone in this difficult transition. Do not talk or make noise or commotions during the designated sleep periods. If you cannot or do not wish to sleep, please go to Deck F. The bridge area and ship's engineering aft are off limits to all personnel at all times unless you are crew with proper identification.

"Thank you for your cooperation. With your help we can make this voyage smooth and pleasant."

Candy chuckled. "Now I know what it's like to be in the army. Well, I guess I can stand it for five or six days."

Toby nodded, then reached into his small personal kit and brought out a pen and a ruled notebook only slightly smaller than the kit itself.

"What's that?" Millie asked, peering down from the top bunk.

"Kind of a last-minute idea of mine," he told the both of them. "I don't know—never kept a diary before in my life. It always seemed silly and a waste. I just thought, well, maybe I'd try one now and then, jot down my feelings of the moment when I thought of it, just as a sort of personal record. Nothing fancy—I'll probably lose it before we even reach the Point. Just something to look back on in my declining years, or maybe for my grandchildren to get an idea of what we did."

He settled back and looked at the first blank page. At the top he wrote, "Toby Haller, Area 4, Anchor L. Begun this 28th Day of March, in the Year of Our Lord Two Thousand One Hundred Seventeen."

There. That was pretentious and dramatic enough.

He thought for a moment, then wrote in his usual very bad handwriting, "March 28, 2117: Tally-ho! We're finally on our way! Four bloody years shot to hell on Titan, which once bore a strong resemblance to our little project but now is less kin than Spitsbergen is to Nassau, but now it's going to pay off. At .8 light speed it takes almost no time to get to the Borelli Point, even though it's halfway to the stars."

He studied his prose. Juvenile, he thought, like this whole idea. It was also a lie, at least in tone. He wondered if he would still recall the true feelings of apprehension, even fear, he felt when reading that decades from now. *Well,* he decided, *that's the way I should be feeling.*

He repressed the urge to write of his true feelings right now, the ship, the people he was presently with, all that. It wasn't that big a book, and he wasn't much of a writer.

Besides, he might brag about making the trip with two women now and again, but he wasn't sure he liked the idea of leaving the implications of that, however, untrue, for his children to read, if he ever had any.

He sighed, and turned to put the book back in its place. It was getting close to lights-out, and he felt oddly very tired, although he'd done almost nothing today. He froze as he found himself watching the beautiful Candy peeling down to her panties and looking all the better for it. He felt himself getting turned on and thought he'd better clear his throat. *Damn* Millie! He wondered what kind of a bribe it might take to get the kid far away for an hour or so in the upcoming days.

Candy looked over at him and grinned, obviously not at all shy about such exposure, and the type that enjoyed being ogled. Whether this extended to action or whether she was just a tease remained to be seen.

He smiled, shrugged, and put his book away, then stripped down to his shorts. That was as far as his own blushes told him he could go, at least tonight.

The precocious Millie had also stripped all the way, and as she sat there, tent down, folding up her clothes, Haller noticed that the kid had a pretty good body as well. He found himself embarrassingly aroused by all this unexpected vision and company, and incredibly frustrated at being unable to make a single move right now. He was a bit put off, though, when Candy did a string of ritualistic isometric exercises. It was clear why she had mentioned the gym on F deck first. Although it wasn't apparent before, she had muscles on her that were bigger and tighter than his. One of the weight-lifter types. It was strictly personal, but to him overly muscled women were as grotesque-looking as overly muscled men. The only difference with the women was that when they were at rest it didn't show like it did on the men. Now, with these exercises, though, it did—in spades.

He was a fairly big man in reasonably good shape, about ninety-five kilos and little fat, but he began to wonder if he wanted to make it with a woman who could probably bench-press *him*.

He didn't reflect on it too long, and when the announcement was made for lights-out, he found himself drifting quickly to sleep in spite of the undercurrent of noise.

The disposable clothing proved to actually be a good fit, but somewhat loose, and while there was some support in the clothing, undergarments were clearly not to be provided. It all looked, and felt, like thin white cotton, very soft and comfortable, although it made everyone look like a colony of poor peasants off in some remote subtropical land. Actually, it was a synthetic made of paper products with chemical binders. When done with them, the clothing would be collected, dumped into a processor somewhere, reduced back down to a pastry liquid and sterilized, then reprocessed into the same garment again. It was efficient anyway. The big complaint that Haller had was that the garments did not allow for pockets.

To tell what was whose, the machines that stamped them out had stenciled in thin black ink the wearer's last name, first two initials, and company work ID on the right rear of the seat. Haller complained grumpily that it wouldn't have cost any more to stencil it as a breastplate; as it stood, everyone who wanted to know who others were had to maneuver around and study other folks' asses.

The trip, although short, proved to be interminable. Minutes crawled like hours, and hours seemed like days, because there were so many people and so little to do. Haller, like many other department heads whose people were sure to be aboard, tried to locate and round up those people for meetings, but it proved nearly impossible. While the ship's computers did have everyone, the information was not easy to get at, and there was no real system for contacting others, particularly when they were on other decks with other schedules. Several times he took out his composition book, but found he had nothing really to say.

Any thoughts of romance also vanished. He found he had little really in common with Candy, and the woman had linked up with several male friends in her gym sessions and seemed to be getting whatever she wanted from that quarter. Millie clearly wanted more, and kept coming on to him, but he just didn't feel comfortable with a seventeen-year-old, and he was conscious of his own responsibility. He didn't really have a lot of warm feelings for her parents, who'd obviously had little time for her and let her run free not just now but perhaps for her teen years as a whole, but he wasn't the type to take advantage of that.

The best he did was eventually run into some people from different Landscape Engineering teams, and at least they could pass some time comparing notes and otherwise talking shop. Even so, time dragged. Dragged, yes, but it *did* still flow.

They reached the Borelli Point right on schedule.

"April 2. All sealed up in this damned shell, can't even see the Borelli Point. They have photos of it, looking something like an eclipsed sun, but I sure wish I could have seen it. A thousand shots, no chasers, some bitters, perhaps, and down the hole. Heigh-ho! Wonder what it feels like once you're strapped in that tube and turned into a lot of particles? Find out tomorrow, and so will you, old record book!"

There was a one-day layover where they still had to endure the ship and its conditions, but suddenly it no longer seemed important to anyone. They were at the Point, and the next step was a whole lot bigger than this one.

This Point, the largest ever built in or around the home solar system, was in fact a large Flux Gate in space, the prototype of the seven they had built on their destination. It was, in many ways, an exact duplicate of those seven, even in size, since it was designed to handle the same shaped and designed craft in the same ways. Attached to it in a thick ring was the control center and quarters for the transport and military personnel. It was a large complex, but it could by no means handle half of the numbers of the ship with even the same level of discomfort the ship itself provided. It was more practical to load the Flux vessels directly from the transport.

Haller was right, though, that all should have been given at least one real look at the Gate, which simple didn't photograph properly. It was a perfectly round concave disk, yet black in color, surrounded by the guide lighting and then the circular ring of quarters and technical operations. Although a small amount of Flux was always coming in, for technical reasons, and was used in part to power the station itself as well as its own converters and transport engines, the thing was totally dark. The feed tube, only a few meters across, was in its center, and led off at an angle to the regulating machinery and routing computers. At the end there was, at least to the naked eye, the illusion of looking into a swirling mass of shimmering energy, but it was only an illusion, caused by static discharge produced as a by-product of continually punching and sealing the Point.

Nobody slept much that night, but conversation was at an unusually low level. There was a great deal of introspection, and the atmosphere was thick enough to cut with a knife.

"Attention all personnel," blared the speaker. "Stand by for a shipwide address by the projector director."

All conversation suddenly stopped throughout the ship's passenger areas. After a few moments, and some inadvertent comments instructing the director on how to broadcast, they heard the voice of Rembrandt van Haas.

"This is your project director," he said needlessly. "Throughout the next several hours we will be loading the transport ships. At this moment large modules are being fed into the cargo areas below the passenger section of the ships, modules containing a billion tons of everything from cows to trees to corn and maize seed. Every ship, every trip, takes more of this with us. These supplies, destined for Gates Four and Six, will be the seed in more ways than one, since they will be the prototypes for all that we will have there. If your favorite food or flower or animal is not there, blame the landscape engineers who designed the ecosystems. They spelled it all out, and determined the kind of place in which you'll eventually live and work."

Thanks a lot, Haller thought sourly.

"What you will find there now is quite primitive, and everything is in its lease-common-denominator form. Things will be slow at first to develop, and you must have patience. We want the engineers to be right the first time, for they might not get a second chance. In a very real sense you will be pioneers, building a new life in the wilderness, a wilderness so primitive that you must create all that you need and all that you want. Even more than the pioneers of the past, you will have the opportunity to do just that. Most of you, however, will be unprepared for just how primitive things will be at first."

They can't be worse than this bloody ship, Haller thought, but he knew better, at least intellectually.

"It has been a tightly held secret until now that there have been people on New Eden not just for the past year but for the last four years."

That caused a real stir.

"People were sent in as soon as the computers said it was possible, even before it was possible to breathe and exist there unaided. Every step of the way has been monitored and measured and checked by an incredibly brave team of Path-finders, men and women who have sacrificed far more than you for this opportunity. These men and women of the Signals and Logistics commands and of Transportation and Energy are right now the political bosses. They will be there to greet you, to help you, to teach you what you have to know. Listen to them. Until things are established, even a brigadier or a director ignores them at the peril of their lives, not merely their comfort."

Toby tried to imagine it and could not. Four years, three of which would be spent on the surface of a lifeless world, their only company themselves and the machines around them, penned up in little life stations probably far more cramped and crowded than any space station, able to go out only in space suits . . . Van Haas and Cockburn had gambled heavily in sending them out so early, and he could understand why it was kept such a big secret. If they had been lost, or had died, it might have killed the whole project—if anyone other than the select few had known they were there in the first place.

"Because of the nature of our switching system on New Eden, Gate Four traffic will embark first, then Gate Six. The loading process for passengers might take as much as two hours for this number of people, and this means standing around and being very bored for the period if you are unlucky enough to be loaded in first. Please be patient. The end is in sight, so to speak. It may seem slow, uncomfortable, an affront to your dignity, an assault on your modesty, and a direct attack on your authority and your intellect. Consider, though, what we are about to do. We are about to go into a void outside our own universe and enter again at a predetermined point—but a point whose location in relation to here we do not even have a clue to. The journey, which would take centuries the old way, will take weeks as it is, but to you it will be the blink of an eye. We follow in the footsteps of our ancestors who also braved new lands and even new worlds, but two hours of indignity and boredom are a far smaller price to pay than they did.

"I shall not be going with you this trip," he concluded, "but I will be out there soon. I can hardly wait, and I envy those of you going now. It is one *hell* of a way to run a railroad, but this railroad runs very well Thank you, and God bless you all."

Another voice—the officious female version of the generic ship's voice—now took over.

"D-deck passengers will gather their personal modules now and prepare to load," she said. "Remove and leave your shoes and other footwear, and as your billet numbers are called, proceed with only your personal modules to the nearest F-deck stairway and down. Personnel will be at all points to direct you. You will undergo a sterilization procedure before being allowed through the lock to the transit ship. Everything except your personal modules will be taken at that time."

Haller looked over at his two traveling companions. "Well, it looks like we'll all know the bare facts on this run."

"I wish they'd started with C deck," Millie grumbled. "It could be another *hour* or two!"

"Feel lucky," Candy told her. "You heard the director. Those early ones get to stand around for two or more hours twiddling their thumbs in the buff while we sit comfortably. Our turn will come."

And, over an hour and a quarter later, it did.

"Billets one twenty through one thirty, remove your footwear and proceed to F deck using the stairways only," instructed the voice.

They all sighed and got up, having long ago gotten rid of their shoes. "Hi-ho and away we go!" said Haller, but his tone wasn't very convincing.

They passed near the now deserted cafeteria, and Haller had a twinge of hunger as he smelled something cooking. They hadn't been fed, on orders, for eight hours prior to embarking, and it was beginning to really tell on him. The first thing he wanted when he got to New Eden was a thick, juicy steak or a leg of lamb. Forget the leg, he told himself. I'll take the whole lamb.

Virtually no one balked at stripping when they reached the sterilization chamber—it was standard in a lot of places, although not usually unisex—but after stepping in and being bathed in those ticklish rays and half-blinded by the lights, and then exiting the other side, many protested the discovery that they had no new clothing on the other side.

White-clad transport personnel wearing breathing masks took them in tow and led them, one by one, down an antiseptic tube that bridged the airlock between the freighter and the transit ship.

Toby Haller was shocked to see the size of it. The brightly lit single chamber into which they were taken seemed to go on forever, and was filled with long, transparent tubes going from a black base that rose perhaps thirty centimeters off the deck all the way to a similar black solid holder on the ceiling four meters overhead. He could see about two thirds of the tubes were filled with human bodies—all standing. He immediately sympathized with D deck. Then he was at his own, and they took the two modules from him and inserted them into two drawers inside the base, then he was told to get into the tube. The ship was hot and stuffy, and smelled like three tons of old sweat.

He suddenly realized that almost all the white-clad transport workers were women, and became more than a little uncomfortable and embarrassed by his nudity. Although they were busy and wore masks, he couldn't get it out of his head that they were all staring at him and either laughing or giggling. He could see a couple of other people in similar cirucmstances from his tubular vantage point, but noting their discomfort did nothing to relieve his own.

After a while his legs started to hurt, and he leaned against the tube for some support. It was not wide enough for him to sit down or even do a decent crouch.

He felt an unpleasant sensation, and realized that he'd never asked what one did if one were standing there and suddenly had to pee. He tried to get the attention of a transport worker, but didn't succeed.

He was just beginning to feel that he couldn't possibly hold it anymore when a tinny voice came to him from above.

"Attention Gate Four passengers. We are clearing the ship of all base personnel. In a few moments a mild sedative will be administered to each of you to make you relax. Departure will be shortly after. Upon arrival you will be met and taken off by Gate Personnel. Follow their instructions. Thank you."

Bloody bitch, he thought. *Bet she had three squares and a shit today. Damn Einstein! Bet he was never far from a toilet when he needed one!*

He suddenly felt at once very dizzy and yet very stiff, unable to move a muscle. His eyelids closed like heavy weights, and he found even breathing labored. The whole world seemed to give a tremendous shudder, as if an earthquake had hit, and there was an itching, almost burning sensation throughout his body.

He was conscious of the passage of some time, but whether it was a few seconds or a few hours he wasn't sure. He only knew he felt a bit dizzy, then opened his eyes and looked around. Nothing seemed to have changed, and he wondered if it had worked or if his anesthetic hadn't taken. Well, at least he didn't feel like he had to piss anymore.

Then he noticed that the transport workers were back, and he was sure that something had gone wrong. *All this way and all that deprivation and the damned thing misfired!* he thought with disgust. *It* would *happen on my trip!*

He waited his turn, feeling very depressed, knowing that he might have a pretty good wait. It turned out, though, that the anesthetic had been very well thought out; it was barely five minutes or so before a white-clad and masked transport worker undid the seals and opened the door. It hissed slightly. She knelt down, removed the two modules, and handed them to him.

"What went wrong?" he asked her.

"Everyone asks that," came the reply, a bit tinny and electronic behind the mask. "Nothing. Welcome to New Eden. Follow the personnel officer in yellow down there and we'll route you through to your destination."

He felt like he'd been hit by an electric shock. *New Eden!*
It didn't seem real.

They were led in small, relatively silent groups down to the
lowest deck, then down a long corridor to the center. The
place was filled with modules, large and small, all marked
with destinations and code numbers. The cargo, in this case,
would be unloaded last.

A large hatch was open in the ship's middle, and they were
instructed to climb down the ladder to the tunnel below.
There would be a second "delousing," as the personnel man
called it, then they would give their name and ID to the
officer on the other side and be taken to their final destinations.

The chamber below was brightly lit; its walls and even
floor were rounded and were of a translucent greenish color.
They stopped in the middle, had the familiar sensation of
being cleaned inside and out once more, then the light in the
next section of tunnel went on and they proceeded down it.
At the end of the next section there was a woman sitting on a
stool in front of a small machine that came out from the wall.
As each new arrival came to her, she asked crisply, "Last
name, first name, middle initial, and company or military ID
number, please."

"Morgan, Jeremiah K.," said the large, balding man in
front of him. "76554-65845-6745LH. Say—when do we get
some clothes?"

She checked her screen, nodded, then said, "We have no
room for that here. Index finger in the slot, please." She
didn't wait but grabbed it and stuck it in. She nodded again.
"Proceed to next station. Next, please!"

"Haller, Toby G.," he told her, then gave his own long
string of numbers. She nodded again, and he stuck his index
finger in the slot—and felt a sting. "Ow!"

"Thank you! Proceed to next station," she said crisply.
"Move along, please! We're behind schedule now."

He went along, thinking that he had worked with a number
of computers with better personalities and more human kind-
ness than bureaucrats.

The end of the tunnel was stunning, and he almost forgot
anything else when he saw it. A couple of times back on
Titan he'd visited the inner area of the small Point that

powered the base, but it was nothing like this. Just beyond the energy regulator, the only part of the massive amount of computer and machinery that was exposed, there swirled a beautiful maelstrom of pink and white cloud in which golden sparkles of energy were constantly flashing. He knew it was an optical illusion caused by all sorts of fancy physics, but it was stunning all the same.

And that was why, at this point, they had planted a sergeant in full uniform, and why they'd picked one who was two meters tall and weighed at least a hundred and fifty kilograms with no evidence of fat.

"Name and destination Anchor!" he announced, more than asked, in a deep but highly officious voice.

"Um—Haller, Toby G. Anchor L."

The sergeant's right hand pointed to his right. "That way!"

He looked and said somewhat sheepishly, "Uh—there's only a blank wall that way."

"Just walk into it. Don't worry, bub—you'll get there."

He shrugged and walked into the wall. There was a sudden absence of all light, and a feeling of falling, but it was only momentary. Suddenly he was standing on a round metallic plate inside a huge pit. Beyond he could see people sitting behind folding tables with large cartons in back of them, and he went forward and approached the first one.

"Name, please?" said the woman.

"Haller, Toby G.," he responded.

"You want that table over there," she told him. "Can't you read?"

For the first time he saw that they had hand-lettered signs tacked on the front of the tables. He was at the one marked A TO F.

"Haller, Toby G.," he said yet again, this time to the G TO K table lady. She nodded, leaned back, and a young soldier in Logistics blue brought her a sealed box that, he saw, had his name and number on it.

She pointed to a small portable signature plate on the table. "Sign here," she told him. "Then proceed forward before opening the box and dressing so as not to block others."

He signed with the stylus provided, then took the box and

did as instructed, joining several others. He had a lot of questions to ask, but first he wanted whatever was in his box.

It turned out to be some military-issue underwear and socks, all white, a pair of decent jeans, a flannel-style work shirt with two breast pockets, and a pair of solid low-cut work boots, black, also military issue. He put them on and was surprised that they fit so well. There was also a wide-brimmed cream-colored hat, creased in the crown, and it fit, too, although he almost never wore hats. Going further, he discovered a small case with basic toiletries, generic issue, a multifunction pocket knife, a wristwatch that read 0918:08 and said nothing else, a clip-on green-bordered ID card that had the same lousy hologram of him that he'd had on his company badge back on Titan, a small gray book marked *Orientation Manual, Pocket Edition,* and, wonder of wonders, a chocolate bar. After clothing himself, the chocolate bar got first priority.

While munching it, and discovering that it even had nuts in it, he looked around and saw another personnel officer standing there, looking over the new arrivals. She, at least, looked human—and slightly bored. He went over to her.

"Excuse me, but *now* where do I go?" he asked her.

She peered at his badge. "Up. There's a lift to the side, there, that will take you to the surface. There'll be a line of tents above. Look for the one with the Engineering logo on it. They'll get you settled in." She stopped a moment, then read the badge again. "Oh, my! They'll be quite happy to see you, Dr. Haller. We all are."

He was startled. "How's that?"

"Well, you're department head for Landscape Engineering, and God knows we need you bad. You'll see when you get topside."

He nodded. "Um, thanks—I think. By the way—that wall I walked through to get up here? I had been led to believe that matter transmission was impossible, Flux or no Flux. Did I miss something?"

"Oh, no. As far as I know, the kind of matter transmission you're talking about *is* impossible. Too many losses in transmission, I believe. The tube, as we call it, is a direct-by-wire transmit and receive system. You're zapped at one end, then transmitted, one at a time, along a closed, sealed line running well below the surface all the way from there to here. It *does* save time, and the one thing we have here is energy to spare. There's a line to each of the four Anchors in this region from the Gate. Good to remember if you have to get from here to, say, Mary, in a hurry.''

"Mary?"

"Anchor M for Mary. This is L for Luck, although some folks have other less pleasant names for it.''

"I see. Yes, that will be convenient, I suspect.'' Convenient, hell! It meant that he'd be able, if need be, to travel the 6035 kilometers between L and M—um, Luck and Mary—in a matter of minutes. It sure beat walking.

He was surprised at the lack of cargo robots about, but he realized that the instant transit system wouldn't handle the modules of the enormous size he'd seen on the lower deck of the transit ship. They'd have to offload and bring them in the hard way.

The lift turned out to be an enormous, dirty platform obviously designed to lift or lower heavy machinery and construction robots up and down. The pit, he realized, was a lower floor of what was to be the operations and control center. The seven antennae were in place and rose majestically from the floor up to a height far beyond ground level, but as yet nobody had put the building on top of this foundation. Of course, it was impressive as it was, even if it didn't *look* that way. Just to be at this point, he realized, he was already standing on about a square kilometer of Kagan 7800 computer and associated control and command rooms and equipment, all powered by direct lines tapping that Point over eighteen hundred kilometers distant. It looked like warmed-over shit, but it was a really impressive technological achievement.

He still didn't really believe he was now on some distant moon, perhaps not even in the Milky Way galaxy although no one was really certain. When he reached the top, though, he began to feel not only distant but the full weight of what the personnel woman had told him.

In front of the pit were various large tents with the division logos on them, both civil and military. Engineering's classical symbol, even without the superimposed apple tree, was easy to spot.

Beyond, though, as far as his eye could see, was a field of what looked, felt, and even smelled like genuine, plain old dirt. And on that dirt, back to the pinkish haze that surrounded it on all sides, was a sea of tents large and small. There was an odd and shifting quality to the light, but the place was duller and drabber than Titan had ever been, and the sky was a mass of pinkish-gray gloom beyond which could be glimpsed, just barely, the enormous orb of the great gas giant that held them all. There were no buildings evident, no power lines, no trees, grass, flowers, or anything else, and the air, while quite warm, was deathly still. It was, overall, the most depressing hole he'd ever seen in his life, and it was all his now.

"Hi, ho!" he mumbled to himself, making it sound like the clap of doom.

8

THE GODS OF ANCHOR LUCK

Sir Kenneth Korda hadn't been kidding when he'd warned Haller that the area around Gate Four was the dumping ground. There was the convent, for example—a huge complex of wall-to-wall nuns from an order that liked to dress in the ancient style, like penguins, Haller thought. They were part of the advanced force for Populations—most were teachers, although some were nurses and the like—and they were here, bought and paid for, by the Vatican itself and as a favor to some of the board, a majority of whom were Catholics, including van Haas himself.

The dumping-ground concept extended to many of those assigned to the engineering team. They had given him what had been called even back on Titan the Yankee Maniacs, a group of young and middle-aged engineers and computer experts who had managed to get out of dominated North America or who were from some of the Pacific islands, many of which, like Hawaii, had been hit by the pulses but had been ignored afterward. This gave him some expatriate Canadians with names like McKenzie and Franco-Russian accents as well as Americans with thick southern accents slightly tinged with Spanish and a lot of Polynesian-looking people to boot. All had kept their nationalist loyalties intact and the Canadians and Americans would refer, every once in a while, to their homelands as "occupied" or "captive nations."

137

All engineers were considered slightly mad, including Haller, but this was a particularly odd group, many looking to establish outposts here of the old cultures that were dying out back where they came from (or, rather, some idealized version of them). The Polynesians, male and female alike, tended to make comments to each other in tongues like Hawaiian to keep others from knowing what they were saying and tended to go around barefoot dressed only in colorful skirts or skirtlike garments with no tops. Haller decided to let them have their eccentricities so long as they did their jobs well, and he also decided not to tell the Polynesians that he'd discovered that their little language was close enough to Maori, which he'd picked up as a boy in New Zealand, that he could make out what they were saying.

There were fourteen primary programming engineers in the Anchor Luck team, and another twelve assistants, for a total of twenty-six under him. Twelve were Polynesians—eight women, four men—and there were ten expatriate Americans and four equally dispossessed Canadians, of whom eight were women and six were men. The sexual division was not unusual among the various departments as a whole; many more women than men had grabbed at the equal-opportunity chance to be a high-tech pioneer, particularly from places where the society was still very male-dominated. It was, overall, a young crowd for such expertise, with a large majority of those over forty married, some with children, about an even split between married and unmarried in the thirty-to-forty age group, and almost no one married under the age of thirty.

His team tended to regard him as a bit too straight and stiff, and he had been unnerved to overhear himself being referred to as the "Old Man," but he got along reasonably well by giving them their head and letting them participate in decisions.

The Kagan 7800 was indeed an impressive machine, and when they studied its power grids and networks, they saw the potential as almost unlimited. It was possible to remotely address a meter square of grid far from the center of Anchor and tell everything about whatever was in it by simple commands.

Connie Makapuua was his chief assistant. She'd been among the first on the scene and had the most experience working out simulations on the 7800, and he studied her plans and recommendations carefully. There was unanimous agreement that the core area around the headquarters was the place to start, simply because they could test out ideas and then build over their mistakes. Once that was out of the way, though, an overall program to expand and stabilize the Anchor and create a miniature climatological system was the first order of business. They wanted clearly defined boundaries, clear air and good light, and a system of water circulation which, they decided, would have to be based primarily on convection. The land could have some roll to it, but was basically flat on the master plan; this was to minimize erosion and runoff and because Luck was to be basically an agricultural unit.

They felt they were ready to begin, but they were held up for lack of remote connection units. These large devices were actually small auxiliary computers tied into the Overrider interface of the 7800; with one riding Guard at the 7800, deep below the still building headquarters complex, the operational engineer could sit in the midst of no-man's-land connected through his remote unit to the big one and at once be with the computer and in the field to see and adjust his or her handiwork. Without the remotes, or "big amps" as they were called by the engineers themselves, they could do little. Some administrator with no idea of the technical situation had an idea to get some teams of initial settlers from Populations out there to plant what seed could be planted, but Haller had to patiently point out that the Anchor only *looked* formed. It was still basically a Flux area and anything done to it now would simply be negated by his people when the big amps arrived.

A much bigger surprise was the arrival in Gate Four of a transitory Soviet ship on its way to the next world out. Only the transport crew was released for a little discussion and walking about though; everyone else was kept sedated. Although it was known that both the Russians and Chinese had colonies up the line under way with some preliminary personnel, nobody had any idea that one of them at least was this far along. It showed just how thin the time margin had been in settling New Eden.

The Soviet ship resembled the Westrex ships to a great

degree, only partly because of the shared technology agreements to make sure all the ships fit all the gates on all the worlds. When the only way to point C was with a required stop at point B, it wouldn't do to have any incompatibilities there. Haller was able to meet with some of the officials from the ship and discuss their own plans for their new world. They had one advantage over him, a genuine planet about the size of Venus and in the right orbit. It hadn't been nearly human-habitable until Points had been punched and computer work begun, but the implications for back home were obvious. The Soviets already had Mars; Venus was clearly next.

In a way, he envied the Soviets, not only for their planet but also for their seemingly uniform culture and solidly secular outlook. He thought he had enough problems with the nuns, but now a whole contingent of Hindus had arrived and shortly another large group of Shi'ite Moslems was due in. The culture shock was building, with various incredibly wild versions of English the only real common denominator.

This was even more of a problem for administration and Populations, since some of the groups were not naturally friendly toward one another and all insisted on keeping their basic customs and cultures as much as practical. Everything from meals to child care services was communal out of necessity, and that created frequent cultural conflicts over everything from dietary requirements to sexual mores and values. The Moslems, for example, many of whom were quite conservative, with about two thirds of the women, for example, in long black *chadoors* with veils, had a hard time dealing with the likes of a Connie Makapuua, who hadn't worn much more than a thin flowered skirt since coming to New Eden.

Police powers were vested in the Security unit, a much-feared and distrusted group with considerable powers from the board. They patrolled the area, enforced basic rules, stopped fights, and settled arguments even if it meant knocking both antagonists cold, and, occasionally, would remove a real troublemaker, who was never seen again. The official line was that they were either sent to another Anchor or shipped home on the deadhead returns of the transit ships, but no one really knew for sure. Although relatively crime-free except for petty stuff, there were now and then cases of rape or attempted rape and these were dealt with quickly and harshly. There were few secrets possible for long in the increasingly crowded tent city.

The Moslems had a long series of arguments about the direction of Mecca and finally decided that the only logical direction to pray in was heavenward, which, Haller decided, at least got all the religions to agree on one thing anyway. Watching the call to prayer, though, it seemed to him as if they were praying not to heaven but to the giant gaseous planet that hovered over them and gave them their strange light. He often wondered, as there was inevitable cultural dilution which could be seen even this early as so many diverse groups became crammed together in communal squalor, if their children, or grandchildren, might ever get confused as to who or what they were praying to.

Haller had been maintaining his diary, on and off, although he forgot it far more than he went to it. His dates, since arriving, had been guesswork, and he'd adopted the administrative calendar, as they all had, for uniformity's sake.

Still, they worked under extremely primitive conditions, out of prefabricated offices with long cables snaking back into the administration building's foundation below which the computer and communications centers were already built and in operation. Much of the interior structure was in, laboriously built piecemeal, by Christmas, but no one wanted to pour the exterior and plasticlike interior wall sets until they were certain that they had everything in there that would be needed. Once the thing was actually poured and completed, it would have to be dissolved and then redone almost from scratch. In spite of the discomfort of the people, the powers that be had no sense of urgency about completing it as long as work was going on within the temporary structures nearby.

It wasn't until April that the massive and tough walls of the headquarters building were poured, the interior having already set, and the resultant large building dominated and dwarfed everything, the synthetic outer walls covering the whole structure from masts to street level, giving it the appearance of a single unified structure with surrealist overtones. It shone and gleamed in the odd light, and looked to some like a distorted medieval castle, and to others like some ancient cathedral. It was imposing, and its solidity lifted all their spirits even though they still lived in tents and were still discovering the joys of mass pit toilets and chamber pots.

Two days later Haller received the first of four big amps— the remote computers with which he and his team could work their magic. These four were all they would get, but they were more than enough. From this point they could use the existing remotes to create out of Flux as many more as they would require.

They were finally out of the dark ages and into the twenty-second century plus. If they had a prototype of an object, they could now create as many of that object as they needed by sheer energy-to-matter transfer. From this point, they all knew, things would proceed at a rapid pace, and as crowded and miserable as everyone was, this raised everybody's spirits.

On June 19 Haller carefully began what he called a "controlled bleed" from the Gate into the areas of his Anchor boundary, restoring some of what the initial program had cleared away. Over the next week all save the area immediately around the headquarters building began to be covered in a permanent haze that gradually thickened and occasionally sparkled with little dancing discharges. For a while it seemed like fun, but as the days went by and it became quieter, gloomier, and harder to see—even the sounds seemed damped in it—more gloom descended over the still growing little colony, and irritations and fights increased.

By June 29 sufficient Flux had built up within the Anchor bubble to allow some tentative testing and localized experimentation. He would get no second chance here without endangering the lives of the people, so Haller wanted to be very, very conservative. He was being pressed, though, by local leaders and by Security to lift the fog as much as possible, for things were beginning to get out of hand. On July 3 he decided that the time had come to test the program for the city core, and all save his own people were evacuated.

Although the master program for the core was really Connie's, he decided to "ride the amp" himself, simply to get a good feel of things. She was not that put out; he, after all, controlled her promotion and performance ratings, and if it flopped now, he'd take the fall.

The big amp was nothing more than a huge rectangle painted military olive drab. It was far too large to be mobile, a problem they hadn't really solved as yet, but they moved them around on large tanklike treads powered from the grid at the astounding speed of five to seven kilometers per hour. That was better than dropping them anyway. As Overrider, he sat in a small plush chair in a little cab on the rear to which an override helmet and associated equipment was connected.

Assured by Security that there was an all-clear in the core area—even headquarters had been evacuated except for a skeleton staff, although it should not be affected by the program—he pulled down the helmet, checked his power switches, and called Connie.

"Insert your key now," he instructed. "On my mark—three, two, one, mark!" He turned his own, and found the status lights all green. He was in contact with the enormous Kagan 7800 beneath the headquarters building.

The 7800 was a far friendlier-seeming beast than the 7240 series, and seemed to go out of its way to appear to the operators as just an old and interested friend. Both the machine and the company had worked hard on the shell that accomplished this, but nobody but an amateur was fooled that this was anything more than a shell masking a totally alien and incomprehensible intelligence of enormous power. They didn't trust it for a moment.

"Good morning, Seventeen," he said. Each Kagan 7800 was assigned a code number just for geographic purposes, and while some had named theirs, he'd kept it on a business level.

"*Good morning, Toby,*" responded the computer. The communication was only in his mind, but the voice always sounded to him like the pleasant baritone one might hear deliver the national news, complete with, to him, a total lack of accent—which meant an accent just like his, of course.

"Bring up the two-kilometer core design, please."

"In place." Suddenly, in Haller's head, an entire detailed blueprint of the layout was as clear as if he were looking straight at it, including symbols for vegetation, paving, communications and electrical systems—everything, to a great level of detail. If he wished, he could count the number of bricks in the walkways in the park.

"All right," said the engineer, "we've run all the models again and again. Run a check on the area to make sure we're not catching anyone or anything we shouldn't, won't you?"

"All clear, Toby. The staff monitors are just outside the lines of demarcation, and all other personnel but you are inside the administrative block. Clear to send."

"Any last-minute recommendations based on current conditions?"

"Recommend we implement the minimum climatological series to match the affected area. Otherwise it's not going to work as well or remain as permanent."

"Very well." Haller reached down and picked up a small module, an unassuming-looking cube that was no larger than his palm, and inserted it into a slot. "Enable core program inserted," he told the computer. This program, worked out and tested on other, non-7800 computers, would allow the enormous power of the 7800 to be used, but only within its proscribed limits. After a lot of creative work with Seventeen and supporting 7240's, they had established an end result and defined it, they thought, absolutely. Seventeen was now free to enable whatever powers, memory, and programming it needed to reach that goal, even if it overstepped the program's bounds, so long as it came up with the desired result. Haller often thought of computer work as the profession of making bargains with the devil. The trick wasn't getting what you wanted, it was finding and plugging all the loopholes.

"Enable on and checked," the computer informed him. "Could I have the base agricultural models as well, please? We may as well do it once."

Haller nodded to himself. "Connie, can you plug those in for me at your end?"

"Will do," came the woman's voice from deep below them. "All right. Haley's plugged them in."

"The information is sufficient," Seventeen told him. "Enabling—*now*!"

Haller held his breath. Even his team didn't know that this

was the first time even he had played with a program this complex.

There was a crackle and discharge of energy all around him, and he thought he could smell something like ozone. He turned in his chair to watch what he could and almost fell out of it.

There was a wall of thin fire, or so it looked, coming out of the very ground itself. Now it divided, and divided again, and you had to look sharp to see that in fact it was carefully following the meter-squared grid that underlay the whole planet, as it did Titan, Flux and Anchor alike.

It moved out, not high, but still at four meters or so, and began to march in all directions, the point at which it reached the ground seeming to sear what it touched. One wall came across right to him, then *through* him and the big amp itself. He felt nothing, but it unnerved him even though he was warned of the effect and had experienced it in simulation. Like the operations building, he and the machine were coded out of the program, but it still had to get under him and around him to do its job.

The program did not materialize, it just *was*. He was able to watch it form in the distance opposite as the wall moved outward, and what formed on the inside looked like it had always been there, just blocked from vision by that wall.

Now, instead of dirt and grime and an ugly pinkish-gray nothingness, there was reality. A series of great stone steps led up to the main entrance of the headquarters and operations building. At the bottom there was a plaza formed of red brick that went out in front of the building for thirty meters, then a break for a fairly wide and paved street, then in front of that a park filled with green grass and small shade trees crossed with a brick wall in the shape of an X and a little circular miniplaza around a single, larger tree at its center.

There was green life in Anchor Luck at last.

Small, globular streetlights ran around the park but not through it save for the center area, hooked up but not yet working. The connections and controls for them would have to be enabled the hard way down in the headquarters basement, but that was a small price to pay.

Other streets, also with lights, had been filled in, but the blocks they outlined on all sides of the headquarters building were nothing but grass, although each had a thin power access strip that would allow a great deal of lighting and machinery to be attached to the master power grid should things be built there. This was necessary because the new depth and texture of the ground in the designed area no longer permitted contact access to the computer's own power grid supply—and it was the reason why they had to get it right the first time.

There had been a lot of debate about designing and putting in core area buildings, but they'd all come to nothing when plans for who needed what and the designs of those places kept changing daily and getting more and more caught up in the bureaucracy. It was finally decided to just allow for the power strips and to build the buildings the slower, harder, old-fashioned way, with prefabricated units and robot labor, to suit the ultimate tenants.

Haller sighed. He liked it the way it was.

"May I build the minimum climatic bubble while I still have sufficient Flux concentrated?" the computer asked.

Haller was still awed by what had been done. "Nobody's stopping you. Go ahead."

The area above the four-meter mark was still very hazy, but now a new wall formed, this one creating a pinkish ceiling as if out of thin plastic, which, once stretching over the whole area, began to rise and was quickly out of sight.

The light became suddenly more intense, the coloration sharper, although the disturbing distortion caused by its source increased dramatically as well. Haller hardly noticed. For the first time he was looking up at the full splendor of Oberon, the enormous gas giant that was New Eden's light source and gravity captor. It wasn't like the moon, or even the Earth from the moon; it filled the sky almost completely, and although it was distorted through the atmosphere, its multicolored bands could be clearly seen.

"Holy Mother of God!" swore the good Presbyterian lad on the big amp.

"You don't approve?" the computer asked him, sounding puzzled and a little concerned.

"Uh—no; that is—yes. I *do* approve. I do indeed."

Deep down inside him a little voice whispered, *With this kind of power, we are no longer estranged from the gods.*

"Let's have a party!" Connie Makapuua screamed delightedly over the radio.

And they *did* have a party, in their mostly barren new offices inside the headquarters building. Chambers and conduits had been built into the interior walls to allow access to Flux chambers of varying sizes. Most of these were not connected to anything like the 7800, but could handle fixed programs of specific things, such as food and drink. In the files of the computers were the digitized codes for some very fine wines as well as other food and beverage service and even some drugs. The meats were total synthetics, but they looked and tasted right.

Toby Haller was oddly quiet while his colleagues celebrated. He'd spent the better part of the day inspecting his new creation centimeter by centimeter, and the enormity of what his machines had done at his direction just floored him. It awed the rest of the Anchor staff as well, in more ways than one, but only seemed to feel the unease in the process and its perfection.

Connie had joined in the revelry, although she was strictly the organic-fruits-and-vegetables type, but she noticed him off to one side and came over to him. He'd given them an enthusiastic enough pep talk earlier, but clearly something was troubling him. She, like he, had a Ph.D. in computer management, but she often spoke half in pidgin English and liked to make out that she was just a regular *wahini*.

"So, boss man, why you over here in big funk?" she asked lightly. "Seem to me we got us one pretty li'l world here."

He looked up and smiled wanly. "Not enough sex," he responded.

"Bullshit! You got victory stickers plastered all over your tent. You woman's man. What'sa matta? You no like the little *wahini*'s program?"

"Oh, it's perfect. Perfect . . ." He let his voice trail off a minute. "Connie, doesn't this kind of thing *bother* anybody but me?"

"Huh?"

"If you know how to work the machine, and have access to it, you're a god in almost the literal sense. Let there be light, and there was light. It took them two years to build this place. It took us two minutes or so today to landscape it, put in streetlights and brick walks, create preplanted trees and grass and flowers, and even pave the bloody streets!"

"You gettin' religion or something?"

"No, it's not that. Not exactly. We've got the keys to the god machine, so we're complacent, happy. But we've only been loaned those keys, and anytime they want, the owners can take 'em back. Connie, love—if we can do what we did today, and do what we plan to do in the days and weeks to come, it's more than just making us a nice little country here. I just wonder what it can do to people."

She looked at him, half-smiling, more curious than worried about the question. Like most of them, she saw such questions as academic and interesting, not really applicable to the real world and its worries.

"I dunno," she responded. "Maybe tomorrow we'll ask it."

But they discovered, when they tried, that there were limits to that line of questioning.

"Toby," said the computer, "I feel I must warn you that if you pursue this line too far, you'll be flagged by people you might not like and who get paid not to like you."

"Security forces, you mean."

"I can't say, but it's a good guess. Do you still want to pursue it? Connie will be flagged, too, because she's listening in at Guard."

He thought about it. "Will you tell me if I get to a flag area before the flag is thrown?"

"If I can."

He tried to phrase his questions in terms that could not arouse suspicion. "Seventeen, what would have been the consequences if people who had been in the target area yesterday without being excepted from the program?"

"They would have been removed, digitized, and stored in my memory."

He was surprised. "How is that possible without the vacuum and with all the anomalous elements like clothing, effects, and nonindigenous matter they would have on them?"

"That's not really necessary here, since all of the elements would be creations of the master programs anyway. They could be filtered out without much problem. There *is* a risk, however—the condtions aren't hard to create but are complex to explain—which is why it's not a good idea if it can be avoided. There is a possibility of fragmentation beyond my ability to reconstruct. In that case, I would have to implement the digitized matrix I currently have on file."

"You have a digitized matrix of all of us on file? How?"

"When you passed through the transmission tunnel between the Gate and headquarters. A check file is always maintained in case of a problem in the line of losses in transmission."

"And it's not erased when we arrive O.K.?"

"Under ordinary circumstances it would be, but I have a far expanded memory capacity by simply creating additional storage and access from the rock under and around me."

The implications of that suddenly struck him. "You mean—if I were to die, you could reconstruct me, make me live again?"

"Within limits. It would have to be within an hour or so, and whatever I had in storage would be dated. It would be the Toby Haller of months ago, but, yes, it can be done, and would be if you were flagged as vital personnel and something went wrong. That, by the way, is a quasi-flag, not in the sense of reporting it, but it can be told only if all personnel on the line qualify as essential."

"Wow! I'm essential!" Connie broke in on the radio circuit.

He decided to go after that line of questioning. "Why the hour or so limit, Seventeen? Why not anytime, even years later?"

"The soul doesn't wait that long to leave, decompose, or dissipate, whichever it does."

He had run into the Kagan family's preoccupation with souls before. "You mean that after that time passes you'll only construct a dead body?"

"That's right. It varies with the individual and the severity of the injury, but an hour is about average. Perhaps, one day, if we can separate and quantify the soul, it will be possible to do it an infinite time later, but in spite of all attempts, it eludes us.''

''Seventeen—we took Flux energy, dirt, rock, and gasses of various kinds out there and made trees, plants, streets, even daisies and rose bushes. If the program called for it, could we create people too?''

''No, only corpses. The same goes for virtually all multicellular animal life. However, as you must know, we can take a butchered cow and make an infinite number of steaks and stews if the cuts are good. Dead matter is replicable, as is vegetable and mineral matter.''

That was at least reassuring, although it only confirmed what he already knew. He had been concerned with the implications of all that to the economic system of not only Earth but New Eden as well. Why work when you can materialize what you need with a minimum of effort? The answer was that this was precisely why self-sufficiency was being introduced, and with New Eden totally terraformed, mass production of such things would be self-limiting. In case of emergency, needed materials could and would be produced by the managing company, but only in case of emergency. Otherwise, all Flux resources would be diverted to research and development projects.

''I think you'd better stop here,'' Seventeen warned. ''If I see the direction of your questioning clearly, there's no way to stop you from being flagged.''

He flicked on his microphone. ''Connie? You willing to face the folks in red?''

''If *we* don't have the right to ask these questions, and the clearances for them, then who does? I'd say go for it. We've got a need to know.''

''O.K., then. Seventeen, assuming you can do this resurrection business, do you also have preventive-medicine routines? Can you repair someone, cure them of internal injuries or diseases, in this manner?''

The computer sounded almost relieved. ''Of course. That's well known to the medical section. However, unless they could be brought here or shipped to the Gate, they would have to be in a free-form Flux environment for me to do it. Finished terraformed areas like the core here remove my grid from being able to do fine work of that type. I can erase, even erase and reform exactly, what is above a terraformed grid square, but I can't alter it."

"Could you, say, repair those things leading to aging? Say, could you make me physically sixteen again?"

"You're flagged. I warned you. You pursued this line too long."

"O.K., so we're flagged. Yes or no?"

"Yes."

"We could redesign ourselves—singly or even en masse?"

"Yes, of course. However, the larger the group, the more common the program would have to be and the more least common denominator the desired sum. Um—I must warn you now that any release of any of this sort of information to anyone beyond yourselves without a specific clearance and need to know is a criminal offense under company codes."

"I'd already been told a lot of this. I just didn't really remember what was nagging at me yesterday until now, when that conversation came back. Seventeen—has that sort of modification ever been performed on anyone on New Eden against the will or desire of the subject?"

"Sorry, Toby, that information is at your classification level but beyond your need-to-know flag. All further information on this subject must be obtained only with clearance from higher authority."

"That's all right, Seventeen. I'm just surprised that they didn't throw that blocker in earlier. I'm not an idiot. I can form easy logical assumptions based on my own programming knowledge."

"They didn't throw it in earlier because of your position," the computer explained. "As a department head in programming, there are a million cross-referenced topics that you might have to have a need to know. Until your flag point, all your questions could be cross-related to your job and your responsibilities for public safety, individual safety, and administrative continuity."

He sighed. "O.K., Seventeen. I found out what I wanted to know. I guess it's time now for Connie and me to slink back to our tents and see who shows up."

"Within my limits, I will try to protect you."

It sounded so very sincere, he really believed it.

They switched off and he walked over to Connie. "Still think it's a fun academic exercise?"

She shrugged. "So we'll get a grilling. So what? We're a stable pair. We won't blurt this out in ads all over the camp, and it's handy to know. It brings up a whole lot of possibilities for the future. We're on the driver's side of this thing, and we work for the same bosses they do. I sure as hell ain't gonna be goin' around telling folks that if I get knocked off I'll come back but they won't 'cause they're too junior. You?"

He thought about it and knew deep down that she was right. "Yeah—that's why they let me ask that line of questioning and gave me straight answers. They've told us we're among the elect, and if we aren't a good little boy and girl, they can just tell Seventeen to consider us peons. I think they've got us cold now."

"Well, what else do they need?"

"I don't know," he responded worriedly, "but just consider the full implications of all this. They could just as easily decide to run *us* through one of their little programs."

When the summons came, it was from an unexpected source.

They had been told of the Special Projects Unit, and had even seen and socialized with some of the members of that group. Along with Landscape Engineering and Main Computer Systems, they were the other group with unlimited and unrestricted access to Seventeen. They had priority, but they had never abused it, and they worked out of their own offices with good security up top, almost inside the central mast. Many of them were computer experts, and some were former Kagan employees who had worked on the 7800 developmental project. They had made themselves available and invaluable to the other two departments, and there was certainly no feeling or suspicion that they had anything to do with Security other than have the girls and boys in red guard their offices.

Thus, it was with great surprise that both Toby and Connie received requests to meet with Special Projects in the top offices early the next morning. It wasn't totally convenient, and both felt some suspicion that it had something to do with the computer flags, but there was no question that they would go. Security was expecting them, and passed them right along to a large and comfortable but still unfinished head office.

Two people rose to greet them. One was a dark, handsome, bearded Sikh in the red uniform of Security and a crimson turban. He wore colonel's insignia, which made him very high up indeed in the Security hierarchy. The other was a woman who sat behind a large and somewhat cluttered desk. She was small, almost delicately pretty, with strong Japanese features and long silky black hair. She was relaxed and casually dressed and looked far too young to be "Patricia Suzuki, M.D." as it said on the nameplate on the desk.

"Please come in and sit down," the woman behind the desk said, rising and gesturing to two comfortable-looking chairs angled to face her from her left while the Sikh sat similarly on her right. "I'm Patty Suzuki, and this is Colonel Singh." The two engineers nodded and took their seats. They could take Dr. Suzuki, but the red-clad colonel was something else. "I assume you both know why you're here."

"I think so," Haller replied. "I'm not sure it's necessary though."

"I think it is," the woman in charge responded. "We're at a crossroads with the two of you that we anticipated, since we've been at this crossroads many times before with all sections dealing directly with the Kagan series. It's quite natural for you to pursue the line you did and to wonder about it. If you didn't, you wouldn't be good scientists, and if you weren't somewhat concerned by the ethical implications of it, you wouldn't be the kind of people to hold responsible positions. We already have landscaping personnel working with us. That's what this project is really all about. Exploring the full implications of the digitizing and programming process on human beings, not things. We must know just what we really have here, not merely for the sake of science but for the sake of security, but this sort of thing must be kept quite confidential. I'm sure you can see why."

They both nodded. "It didn't take a lot of imagination to think of what the news simply of—what? Resurrection? Eternal youth?—might have on the general population. We'd either choke in people in just a few generations or we'd have massive riots and wind up with a police state, hated by the masses.''

"Exactly." Suzuki seemed very pleased at the answers. "It's a pretty cold thing to have to do, but it has to be done. I'm a psychiatrist, by the way. I began work with this team back at Site K, the orbiting lab and station, when we first saw the implications of our research. When we got our first 7800 and saw how much more we could do with it than with the 7240—and the 7240 is awesome in its own right—we knew we had to continue to work here or someone else would without authority, direction, or the benefits of our previous work. That's what we're doing here.''

Both of the engineers nodded, understanding the whole line. Both were fascinated in spite of the potential.

"I suspected as much, but I didn't expect to be privy to so much detail," Toby Haller told her. "I get the strong impression that this is leading somewhere."

Pandit Singh spoke for the first time. "Dr. Haller, Dr. Makapuua, I am not merely the guardian of this knowledge and this project. My business is paranoia in the same way as Dr. Suzuki deals in it, but mine is a different direction. She is paid to cure it; I am paid to *be* paranoid, to think that way all the time. To keep things secure and safe, I must be a paranoid, but also I am paranoid over what it is I am safeguarding. I will, for example, never fully trust you with this information. We will keep an eye on both of you, and if it gets out due to your actions, intentional or not, I will trace it back to you and you will pay dearly for it. This I think you know without my going into detail." It was said so casually, so matter-of-factly, that it was far more chilling than it otherwise would have been.

"The fact is," Suzuki put in, trying to get things back to a friendly basis, "we need more help than we have. We very much need the aid and support of top personnel like yourselves who are in daily contact with the computer and use it in its most elaborate fashion. Primarily, we need you as extra eyes and ears. To fully understand the colonel's fear of what he is guarding, you'll have to see it for yourself. Come. Let's take a walk.''

They went out of the big office and down a still unfinished hallway, through two more security checkpoints, and finally reached a secure lab one floor below that was set up very much like their own experimental lab on the second floor. The difference was that here a grid had been run across a rectangular floor which was otherwise barren, and the computer interfaces were in a sealed booth in front of it. Also, suspended from the ceiling in a number of places were automatic guns controlled from Security's main outpost just off the main level. Two computer technicians staffed the Overrider and Guard positions, one a quite beautiful young woman in lab whites, the other a bearded man in Security reds.

"You know the system of justice for Populations," the colonel said. "Each cultural group judges its own if it's within that group. If it's cross-cultural, the company supplies a judge, and jurors are chosen equally by the offending groups." He paused, leaned over, and said into a speaker, "Bring in the prisoner."

A door opened to one side of the rectangular grid, and Security troops brought in a big Semitic-looking man with a full beard, long hair, and blazing eyes. His hands and feet were manacled, and he had trouble walking. They took him to the center, where restraints were built into the floor, and chained him there, removing the rest. He was stark naked.

"This is Hasim Kashakamani," Colonel Singh told them. "Hasim is a Suni Moslem whose family has been feuding, back and forth, with Shi'ite families over a parched piece of arid nothing for a couple of centuries now. He is the eldest survivor of five sons, and took it upon himself back home to keep up the family-retribution business. His family does in fact have wealth and good connections by marriage, so when he was apprehended in the act of attempted murder, they managed to get him assigned to Populations here instead of the usual messy trial and punishment. It was agreed to by both sides that it would be a good idea, since permanent exile to a new life would remove him as a martyr to his brothers and thus this might end the feuding back home. He agreed, and has been a model colonist up to now. He's quite bright, and had been in line to supervise one of the first farm collectives you are to create."

Connie just stared at him. Toby said, "I gather he wasn't a good model after all."

"To say the least. We solved seven open rape cases, all of Shi'ite women, when we caught him in the act. I'd like to say we suspected all along, but it was a matter of luck. Dr. Suzuki's staff looked at him and ultimately determined that he was incorrigible, that he was so filled with hatred and violence, he kept seeing his enemies in every Shi'ite he met, and this was the result—a generalized action that struck at random, causing pain, anguish, and fear throughout the still small Shi'ite community, male as well as female. He was tried by a combined court and unanimously sentenced to death. As in all capital cases since we've set up this project, we have provided a matrixed dead body for the victims to see and brought the prisoner here. It is the only moral and ethical way to get human subjects."

They stared at the fierce-looking man, who seemed to be staring back defiantly.

"The easiest way to configure a program of this nature is to go for the basics," Suzuki added. "What we have represented here is violence, a high aggressive level, hatred, and delusions of grandeur. He really believes God commanded his acts. He believes God will save him now. With such an extreme and complex case, a cure, if possible, would take years, perhaps decades, even with our best drugs and therapists. We could break him, but it would reduce him to a vegetable, useless in our colony. The trick, then, is to save the talents and intelligence we have while removing everything else." She turned to the white-clad woman. "Run digitizing routine."

Both the woman and the security man at Guard said nothing, but both Toby and Connie knew that they were in full contact with the computer—Seventeen itself, in fact—and calling up routines and programs that were off limits to any but those at this console.

Still, Connie was surprised. "With those shackles on? No tube or gas preparation?"

"Not necessary here," Suzuki replied. "The 7800 interface system is quite direct, needing no more prep for humans than for bricks or trees or streetlights."

There was a crackling sound below, like a large electrical short, and the big man was gone. The manacles, excluded from the routine, dropped to the floor with a clang, as did a ring he had been wearing. It was simple to do—a command to ignore all inorganic material not encased in the body.

"I have a strong sense of justice," Pandit Singh told them, "but not without some mercy. Suggestions have been made to the computer, and a routine run on the matrix it already had from arrival which is now being updated and adjusted. As soon as my people clear away the bonds and other debris down there, we'll reconstruct our Hasim. Ah! Now—watch!"

The status board lights went from yellow to green again, and there was another crackle, a noise associated as much with displaced air as it was with the energy-matter transformation itself. Now a human stood there once more, looking around, slightly confused. It was, in fact, a young girl's form, perhaps no more than sixteen, with dark Mediterranean features, big, innocent, soulful eyes, long black hair, looking soft, delicate, and curvaceous.

"Who is she?" Connie almost whispered.

With that beauty and those knockers, Toby thought, I might get easily turned on here.

"That," replied Suzuki, "is Hasim."

Haller coughed and Connie gave a surprised, quiet gasp.

"Come," said the colonel. "My people will find her some appropriate clothing and we'll talk to her."

The interview was short and basic; they would still have to help her with some psychological conditioning and adjustment. Still, it was dramatic enough. She sat there, looking slightly dazed, in an ill-fitting pullover dress.

"What is your name, child?" Suzuki asked gently.

The girl looked blank. "I—I am afraid I do not know. I am trying to think, but I do not remember much of anything about myself." The voice was soft and gentle and even a bit sweet, a child's sort of voice.

"That's all right. I'm a doctor and we'll help you with that later. Can you tell us anything at all about yourself?"

She thought a moment. "I—I am a girl." She said it almost as if she had just realized it herself.

"Good. What else?"

She thought for a moment. "I am a Moslem but without family and unwed." That was said a bit nervously. Conservative Moslem girls were kept pretty well protected by their families until an arranged marriage and a dowry of some kind was paid.

"Can you read and write?"

"No, madam. But I can draw and I can manage animals. I know much about the care and feeding of cows and horses."

"All Islam worships the same God and reveres the same Prophet," the colonel noted, "but there are differences in traditions between the peoples of the Prophet. Of which tradition are you?"

She stared at him a moment. "I am Suni," she told him.

"Thank you, child," Suzuki told her gently. "Now, go with these nice people and they will get you started and tell you more about yourself."

After the girl had left, Toby turned to the psychiatrist. "Hasim—could he read and write?"

"Oh, yes. In three languages. It'll be easier for us to place her in the community with a level of ignorance disguising her intelligence though. She's not going to be supervisory material, after all. She'll make someone a good wife and bear many beautiful children, and she'll be quite an asset on the farm, retaining as she does almost instinctually Hasim's fairly extensive gifts with animals and knowledge of animal husbandry."

They went back to Suzuki's office, more unnerved than stunned by it all, and while they took the offered coffee, Haller, at least, felt like he needed a few stiff jolts.

"Her aggression level has been dampened to a major extent, and her sexual appetite is rather high," the psychiatrist told them. "She's still smart, but she'll need protection, and I fear she'll know the fear of potential rape."

"It hardly seems fair," Connie protested. "I don't care if it is the rejumbled atoms of Hasim, that girl had nothing to do with raping those women. It's a totally different person."

"Only in a sense. If you like, I'll explain the procedure."

"By all means," Haller said.

"We want you to understand it," Singh put in, "because it goes to the heart of the problem. You saw the totality of the change, and I can assure you that it is as permanent as your roads and trees and grass out there. It was done by the computer. True, we put in all the information, all the medical, biophysical, and biochemical information it would need, and the psychiatric profiles as well. Still, the 7800 actually did it, and it did a bit more, interpolating through the holes as best it could. It's getting quite a bit more efficient at creating whole human beings, I fear.''

"Huh? What do you mean?"

"Dr. Haller, I have been digitized and rebuilt many times by the 7800's. So have you and the ladies here. We will be some more, because it is convenient and it saves time. Out beyond the basic Anchor stabilization program, a grid very much like that one covers the whole of the world between Anchors and Gates, and the 7800's have a networked access to it. I can only pray I am the same person at both ends of the transmission, for I would never know it. Out there in the Flux environment, I am continually at the computer's mercy. It is getting far too good at this. We need to know if it still needs us to do it.''

"You mean—?"

"I mean, if the Overrider and Guard are one-time folks who believe the Kagan 7800 is god and a wonderful thing that can do no harm, could and would we then all be remade into its slaves?"

9

MAGICIAN'S SPELL

"I—I simply can't believe the level of changes," Haller said, unnerved. "You are changing people into other people. Completely different people. It's magic, that's what it is. The blackest of magics."

"Bullshit," Suzuki responded. "It's science, pure and simple. Nothing more, nothing less. These aren't new people, only new aspects of the old people. The changes are physical and have solid grounding in the past, even if we are more or less reversing psychotherapy."

"That girl is not Hasim," Connie put in firmly.

"All right—consider this for starters. You've heard of people with multiple personalities? Usually people who were brutalized or sexually abused as small kids who develop separate personalities to hide from the realities of the past?"

Haller nodded. "I've heard of them, although I've never met one."

"They've always been rare, but they exist, even today. I've seen people with two, three, even forty or fifty different personalities. They believe they are different people in the same body. They act like different people. Even their EEGs are different—just like the brain patterns of totally different human beings. They *are* different. Not always complete, but some really are complete individuals. Often when one is in

161

control, the other doesn't have any knowledge of or memories of what they first did when it was in control. Absolutely nothing. One may be a lousy reader but a brilliant musician. One might paint portraits, the other paint houses. There might be totally male personalities in female bodies and vice-versa.''

"Yeah, well, a *personality* change I can accept. We have drugs that do that, even recreational ones. But you changed one person into another,'' Haller objected. "One no more kin to Hasim than the original dirt I used is to the brick that's now outside.''

"You're wrong. Both the Hasim that was and our new girl are different aspects of the same person. The outward physiological change, which we see directly, is actually the least important part of it. Minor. We're using the system now to cure diseases, manage genetic defects, eliminate the physical effects of aging, that sort of thing. You've done it, and so have I.''

"I've never done it, but I've known it was being done,'' he told her. "But that's just curing the original of defects. They're still the same inside.''

"Of course—because you didn't touch the brain itself. Now, leaving the multiples aside for the moment, let's think of something else. Religious rapture. We've seen that, even here. Periods of concentration so intense that someone can walk barefoot over hot coals or do single things otherwise impossible. The brain is always selective. It has to be. Just as a lens focuses on the foreground or background, one object or many—but not both—so our brains must also do this. Heighten animal senses when we are in a threatening situation. Close out externals when we are sexually aroused. We even filter out a lot when concentrating on a tough job, or when going to sleep. This is rooted in the brain's parietal lobe—it decides what gets and keeps our attention on the basis of external stimuli fed to it. Danger—filter out so you get the animal wariness and reflexes. Sex—filter out the extraneous surroundings, noises, even the nature of the environment. People screw in the damnedest locations. Delicate craft work—filter out all sounds and distractions not relevant to the task at hand.''

"I'm following you so far,'' he said dubiously, and Connie nodded assent.

"All right, now back to our multiple personalities. The reason the personality in charge is different is because the message is sent to the parietal lobe to filter out everything not relevant to that personality. Memories, for example. Certain skills. Likes and dislikes.

"The brain and the mind are two separate but interacting things. The mind is the integrated personality we see and which interacts with the world. The parietal lobe simply filters out brain information—data—that is not relevant to the mind at a specific time. With the multiples, it filters out *everything* relating to the other personalities, but retains what is relevant to the single, forward personality that is in control of the mind and such skills as may be necessary for that personality—speech, for example. Artistic skills and aptitudes. Skilled crafts. What makes one good at a job is the ability to filter out all that's not relevant to that job while it's being done. You with your engineering and programming, for example. There was once a disease—Alzheimer's, it was called—that attacked the brain at its central switching points, but it was selective. It might allow music, or painting, through—even the reading of music—while not allowing through basic reading or math skills, or the ability to make a cup of coffee. We managed to find a chemical cure, but we know how it works. We can selectively induce and freeze it if need be. We can make anyone we want into anyone else we want, and there is no magic to it, just basic biology."

And he saw it. "Then, what you're saying is that the computer issues a set of instructions, filters, to this lobe in the brain. It creates the new personality, with whatever its gifts and limitations, knowledge and limitations, by the limits of the filter. Selectively, it allows to come through only those things that are relevant to the personality it is designing."

"Exactly! And then it reinforces them in a more or less traditional manner. Our drugs work because they fit specific receptors in the brain. The new chemical changes the synapse— the gap between neurons—and redirects the messages, shutting down some and diverting others. The drugs can do this—make you silly, or emotional, or sexy, or coldly distant, or whatever—because they mimic specific peptides the body has the potential to produce but for either genetic or environmental reasons did not. Once the computer has its filter in place, it can then trigger a real mechanism in the brain to create those new peptides naturally and continuously, and even determine the rate of release. These interact with the data allowed through the filters to the mind to create a specific end result. Finally, it can harden this personality by creating an external form that reinforces the personality and causes others to react to it in certain ways. A nymphomaniac in a gorgeous body with exaggerated physical attributes, for example. Then it's complete. And this filter is locked into place. It can only be changed in the same way it was created."

He was stunned. "Then—you can play god to your heart's content. You can make people into anything you want. Stupid, strong, obedient, handsome, beautiful—whatever. It is the nightmare of every ethical scientist. You can do more than all the genetic engineering and psychodrugs ever promised, easily and with no traces, while remaining yourself virtually immortal."

"There *are* limitations," said the psychiatrist. "We cannot give you what you never had. We can't increase real knowledge. If you knew how to play the piano before, we can retain that, perhaps make a mediocre pianist into a good or even great one through that focus of concentration I mentioned. But if you didn't know how to play the piano before, we can't give that ability to you. We filtered out Hasim's ability to read and write, but had he been illiterate, we could not have made *her* literate. It is mostly a process of subtraction.

"Nor, in fact, do we have immortality. Oh, life extension, certainly, and a physical quality of life, definitely, but not *in*definitely. Growing new brain cells is not like growing a new finger. The organ is too complex, and its components have interrelationships we are nowhere near solving. There is, however, between an eighty and ninety percent excess capacity. All other things being physically equal and nearly perfect, the death of old cells can be compensated for by unused parts. And to that the selectivity we mentioned and then also add the additional experience longer life brings, and we wind up giving ourselves centuries. How many it is hard to say. Five hundred to eight hundred is not, however, outside the bounds of possibility, and all that in the physically perfect body of a youngster. I myself am fifty-four, but physically I am twenty-two.''

"Not gods, then," Connie put in, her voice barely a whisper, "but gods at least to those who don't have access. Demigods.''

"Demigods is sufficient. We will retain the knowledge and continue to work on the cutting edge of technology while the masses are maintained and maintain us in a self-sufficient economic system stabilized by a practical but rigid social system.''

"But no godhood for them," Connie noted sourly.

"There couldn't be, unless we can perfect this colonization process and make it inexpensive enough to do it to an infinite number of worlds as need be. We would choke in people. Even if we could somehow manage to make the necessities out of Flux, the logistics of getting those necessities to the people and evenly and regularly distributing them would be a nightmare. It could not be sustained. Admittedly, many of those who will have access will be undeserving, but we will also preserve our best. Our own future Einsteins and Borellis. It won't be as fair as natural selection, but it will do a better, more efficient job, fair or not.''

"I'm still not clear on how you changed the religious orientation from Shi'ite to Suni," Connie put in.

"Simple. We simply filtered out everything that correlated with the Shi'ite branch of the faith. Hasim was learned in his religion. He knew the beliefs of both, but he was raised to accept one as correct and the other as mistaken. We simply removed the factors involved in his being raised that way and left the Suni intact relating to all the keys—Islam, Moslem, the Prophet, basic beliefs, and the like. It's not only poetic justice, she's better off that way. Our Shi'ites in this Anchor are among the most fundamentalist of the lot, while our Sunis tend to be more modern in their customs and outlook. This division doesn't always hold true, but it happens to in our case.''

Haller leaned back in his chair and looked for a moment at the psychiatrist and the quiet little colonel. Finally, he said, "There's an implied threat here to us, too, isn't there? You can leave whatever skills are useful inside us and yet change us into others at will.''

The colonel shifted uncomfortably. "That is true, but I do not believe that either of you are the foolish."

"How—how many people here know about this?" Connie asked them.

"In Luck? Our team of a hundred and five and now the two of you. On the whole world? Well, there are now about fifteen thousand people spread over all the Anchors. No more than four hundred know," the colonel told her. "Outside of this project, the directors, and the military commanders, a few people in Transportation and Energy know because they originally discovered this, and the top engineers in each Anchor usually figure it out, as you did. Mostly, they are blocked beyond a small number at the top by a combination of security blocks in the computer and some logical disinformation that proves it impossible."

"And everyone has kept this secret?" Haller asked.

"All but a few," responded the colonel, "and they are quite agreeable now."

It was Connie who unexpectedly exploded. "How *dare* you! What right do we have to play god? All that Toby and I do benefits everyone. Now the seeds are here for a godhood that seems inevitable! We have the technology! We should make it available to all, regardless of problems, then set about solving the new problems. We solved nuclear war, we even solved how to finance a project like this."

For the first time, Pandit Singh showed real emotion. "It is so *easy* for you to proclaim this naive faith. It is true that technology benefits everyone, but only to a small degree for the masses. I look at the two of you, *all* of you, sitting there, smug, safe technocrats who believe that being hungry is when you forgot to eat lunch. Look at Earth as it is now. The areas that suffered from the Borelli blasts did indeed suffer, and many knew starvation and need and death for the first time, and then the conquerors came, first on a mercy mission but then to stay and rule. Even now, though, the people of America and Europe are better off than the masses of the world who were never touched by the effect.''

The colonel got up, his voice, already high, rose with intensity as the passion flowed from him.

"My country is still full of too many people being kept barely alive by the new technology, living on the edge of starvation, unhoused, unclothed, illiterate. For the masses things are worse now than they were two hundred years ago, because the land could barely support them then, but there were fewer of them. Many live in houses fashioned from dried cow dung; disease and filth are everywhere, and to be covered with flies is so ordinary that one hardly remembers to brush them away. Yet ask those who run the government and the industry there, and the skilled population, and they are aware of it but powerless to do much, nor can they understand what that sort of life truly is. They prattle on about democracy and freedom and shout platitudes, but they live in their comfortable flats or fine houses and eat well and go to cricket on Sundays. The only difference between this class and their ancestors is that they have surrendered. They have decided that no matter what, they cannot solve the problem.

"That is why they sacrifice a little to help pay for this project. That is why the Africans are here, who are in many ways worse than the people of India for being so fragmented. You, madam, were both in a Hawaii that survived far better than the mainland because it had a tropical climate and few native horrors. It managed to keep on until within a few months the Australian navy reached it and new supply lines and technicians and repairs were made. You, sir, come from a nation whose last war was centuries ago, which has very little need for or investment in a military, and from a nation that is still so abundant that it can feed and clothe and house everyone, no matter if they have jobs, and educate them as well."

He started walking around the office, silent a moment, then stopped and whirled and faced Connie.

"Now you tell me we have the responsbility to make everyone a god. No, we dare not. One day it may well be, God willing, but it is not our task now. We are not here to present you with all the necessities and all these wonderful high-tech toys for your intellectual amusement. We are here because we have nine billions of people back on Earth, the

vast bulk of whom are wretches beyond the help of technology as it exists. There is no way to feed, clothe, or house
them, and no place to send them. Those warm, fat, comfortable places such as those from which you come cannot handle
the billions in need, the children with distended bellies too
weak to cry.''

"I didn't—'' she started, but he cut her off.

"Shut up! It is about time you not only grew up, but
understood your job here. You are here because you have the
gifts of education and full bellies and you have had the luxury
of time to learn this complex equipment and this even more
complex process. My people, and the Africans, and the people of East and South Asia, have not. Therefore, we need
you, but you are here for us. We need you because if this
project fails, the Earth fails, my people fail, and there is no
choice but to curse Borelli and regret that the nuclear bombs
did not wipe out all humanity, for that would have been
quick. Starvation and exposure are slow, the cruelest of all
deaths. Killing your own children because you cannot bear to
see them in daily and increasing agony—*that* is what this is
all about.''

The force and passion of his words struck them all, even
Suzuki.

"Now, let me explain Project New Eden to you, for it is
certain no one ever really has. A technocracy, with the best
machines and all the knowledge it has and the best minds it
can muster, is here to provide an environment. That's right—an
environment. Into twenty-eight environments that are different but still as close to perfection as we can manage, we are
placing a large number of very small colonies. These colonies
are composed of the best poor races have to offer, and it is
quite good indeed. If they prove out, we will remake this
world and bring more such people, and we will learn exactly
how to make this technology serve them. The reason is
simple: We are here not to make them into gods, for even back
on Earth we can make a small percentage of any population
into wealthy and strong folks, but to learn how to raise the
standards of those left behind on Earth. We cannot just put a
hundred Borelli Gates around Earth. We don't know what
that would do, or the dangers involved. We might destroy the

Earth—or discover that even a hundred Gates cannot do the job.

"So, we are here. We are here to find out. These people represent their whole racial and cultural heritage, all the ones who starve and die back home, and they know it even if you do not. They will live here, and their experiments will be no less vital than yours. They will be primitive by your standards, but centuries advanced from what they left. They do not believe in magic wands. They want to know if dead land converted back to lushness can remain that way. They want to know if climate can really be so stringently regulated. They want to know the price for all this, and the means that work and the means that do not, so it can be sent back. And they want the cost and efficiency brought down. They want, eventually, an unlimited set of New Edens for the population our magic here cannot support on Earth. Understand this, my friends—I will let no individual jeopardize this. I will let no one kill millions because of blindness, guilty or innocent. You would not make them gods—you would make them dependents of the gods, on a permanent fat and lazy dole, in which they could not grow or prosper and which would condemn the billions we left behind. If you do not at least comprehend this much, I will not hesitate to take you downstairs and run you through your own little machine!"

He stopped, took a deep breath, and stalked back to his seat. The other three sat there in total silence for quite some time.

Finally, Toby Haller sighed. "Well, I guess we've been told off but good. Colonel, I can't speak for Connie or anyone else, but so long as that purpose and that passion is behind all this, I'll keep the faith and do the best I can. Only if I find that passion and purpose is gone will I break with you, and you have my solemn word on that."

Connie nodded. "Mine too."

Pandit Singh looked at them, a scowl still on his face. "If that condition ever comes about, sir and madam, I assure you that we shall be on the same side of any fight."

And that seemed all that was left to say.

They went back down to the main level and stopped there a minute. They had to go to work today, and in a couple of days they would begin to expand their efforts as soon as everything could be properly shifted and moved about and the proper Flux levels were attained.

Connie looked up at him. "I know we're overdue downstairs, but let's get lunch first. I'm starved."

Haller just stared at her.

Three of them rode the amps for the primary extension, the other two of the big machines being kept in reserve. Haller wasn't very confident with the remotes, even though he knew that because of the complexity of the programs and their relative permanency they were necessary. Still, it was slow going, with them all unsure of just what power and range the remotes had and always erring on the ultracautious side.

Still, by July 17 they had carved out, a few square kilometers at a time, more than forty square kilometers of new land and had, by this point, instituted a temporary convection system within the ever-expanding bubble.

They had not tried for anything elaborate, as they did with the center core; they were making land, and using stored matrices of vegetation, to create a new little world a few square kilometers at a time. Now there was enough for a rudimentary local weather system to form; Haller had been able to add his first rivers and catch basin lakes, as the new lands would need an immediate water supply. Their calculations had been precise, but if the clouds that began to form in the middle of the month didn't turn into some kind of generalized precipitation, their newly reconstituted and duplicated vegetation, trees, and then grass would not survive.

Early on the nineteenth, while the big crawlers were taking the amps to new positions and Haller and his crew were back at the headquarters building checking and rechecking, the moment of truth arrived.

Each new section was ten times the complexity of the section that had been laid before, since now they could study for real what had heretofore only existed in computer models and simulations and discover how right or wrong they were and whether they had remembered everything. Each new section had to be adjusted to fit incredibly minor variations from the models—and there were a million of them, since even the 7800 couldn't cover *that* many variables—and then also tied in and adjusted so that it expanded, rather than changed or injured, the weather and climate system they were also building one step at a time.

Haller was in fact having a committee meeting to debate whether or not to call a halt for a while.

"We should have had a local rainstorm by now," he told them. "It worries me. Seventeen argues that the reason why we've had a problem up to now is that we're building on too fast. Each section added completely redistributes the air and moisture buildup and circulation patterns, and the larger we grow the less we can compensate for this. Unfortunately, he also equally argues that we might not yet have a sufficiently large area to make this work. You see the problem. The computer can't bail us out this time because it's still new."

"I've been looking over ze data from ze udder Anchors," said Lolita LeClerc, one of the French-Canadian expatriates assigned to him. She looked just like a French girl named Lolita should, but she was a hell of a whiz at statistical analysis. "Of course, no two are from ze same pattern or design team, but in only two cases have zey needed more zan ze air and moisture volume now here, and zis is ze dullest of ze plainest of ze batch."

It was true. The landscape was basically flat, with just enough contour to allow for river and stream formation and runoff to the catch basins, but those stream beds were still dry and the small lakes were beginning to evaporate in spite of a relatively high water vapor content. It was hot and humid as hell, yet the small lakes that were in the first two sections they had created, contiguous to the core, were now just muddy holes.

"We've got to have rainfall," he told them. "We've got to have it soon too. We can't keep converting our water from Flux because we're just adding to the imbalance over the plan. We're already pushing a million plus liters over the master plan, and you can feel it in the air. Things are dying, people are getting depressed and angry, and I'm not sure what the hell to do. I—*What the hell was that?*"

The sound of several explosions, perhaps of major proportions, came to them through the thick walls. At once, they all rushed down to the entrance and joined a mob of curious headquarters workers going to investigate the same sounds. Haller cursed the fact that the building had no windows, but knew that this was because the outer walls provided shielding for the masts and antennae that allowed him to do his job, among other things. All sorts of horrible ideas came to mind as he made for one of the street-level doors, including a rioting mob or a military coup.

What they saw was almost as fearsome, but even more awesome. The whole sky to the south, where they'd been working, was filled with dark clouds. These weren't just normal clouds; they were thick and black and in constant rapid motion, as if a single great beast, alive and constantly changing and whirling about. It seemed they were suddenly lit from within every second or two, and two or three times a minute they saw lightning stab out of them and strike the ground in a brilliant display of pyrotechnics followed by ground-shaking thunder.

The entire camp had stopped and seemed to be pouring out of tents and temporary buildings, then stopping to watch the sight. The air was deathly still and so thick, it seemed like a woolen blanket over them, but now, quite suddenly, a tremendous wind came up from the south, almost blowing people down and actually collapsing tents and blowing over signs and anything else not held tight.

Connie grabbed his arm. "Is it raining? Is it raining in the south sectors?" she shouted above the wind and thunder.

"How the hell can *I* know?" he shouted back. "Want to go in and radio the amp crew? If they're still alive?"

"You go. I can't take my eyes from this. It's—*unearthly*."

That, in fact, was exactly what it was, and everyone felt it. Even those from the most arid regions of Earth had seen great storms at least once or twice in their adult lives, but this was different. The clouds were *alive* and multicolored, and the internal flashes were exposing a colored light show. It was almost as if some god had poured buckets of various colored paints into an enormous drum of water and then shaken and stirred the whole mess while they watched from beneath.

And then it began to rain. It was quickly almost as dark as night, and the size and force of the drops stung bare skin, but nobody seemed to mind either the tremendous wind or sting of rain. The entire crowd was deafened by the thunder, disoriented by the wind, and soaked to the skin in a matter of seconds, but they did not move. For a moment, Haller thought, it was like being in the midst of the end of the world.

Within a minute, though, something seemed to ripple through the huge throng as they suddenly realized that they were still alive, still breathing, and probably going to live. The streets of the core became raging rivers, and the construction sites flanking the core and the huge unfinished area to the east that contained the tent city became a network of lakes and streams and a quagmire of dense mud.

The lightning struck the power grids repeatedly, causing sizzling sounds, fountains of stream, and a smell like a frying pan left on the burner too long. Some trees and machinery not grounded were also struck, and lightning repeatedly struck the headquarters masts. There was no evident effect there, but the whole building seemed to take on an eerie greenish glow, and green and white fireballs seemed to dance around the square, up and down light poles, and throughout the entire complex.

It continued to rain, and Haller and Connie and others they didn't know made their way through to the side and out toward the tent city, some of which was in evident shambles. People had begun to get over their fear and started slipping and sliding in the mud and the runoff, and before long they did likewise. Anyone who ventured outside the paved core, in fact, was soon completely covered in sticky brown mud.

The electrical activity slackened and died, but the rain continued at a more normal rate. The clouds were hitting the edge of the bubble and turning back inward, creating a lower-level fog through which steady rain fell. Even the parched ground could not absorb this much rainfall in so short a period, and while the drainage had been effective around the headquarters area, this additional runoff, over paved channels, kept sending floodlike waters back toward the south. It seemed as if there were no place eventually not covered by ten to fifteen centimeters of muddy brown water.

Most people rejoiced and played in the mud and water. Later, of course, they were able to take the toll and it showed some of their flaws.

The master program had not really taken the extreme delay in getting localized rainfall into consideration. It couldn't—each Anchor and Anchor plan was different and there were just too many variables involved. In the extra week between where their best guess estimate of when rain should form and when it actually occurred, a massive amount of additional and previously unplanned-for water had had to be created to keep the people alive and everything going smoothly. The result had been a storm of vastly more power and fury than anyone had anticipated, dumping out a measure of excess water vapor beyond the original calculations. Initial drainage had simply not been adequate, and sewage and drain lines would have to be run the hard way.

In the south, the catch basins worked, but two thirds of them were inadequate to contain the volume fed into them by the storm. They overflowed, creating whole new networks of streams and rivers not in the plan, but such was the initial force of the runoff that there was a great deal of rapid erosion, creating channels and basins where none had been planned.

Almost a third of the tents had been collapsed or washed away, and most people lost what little personal items they had. A few, mostly small children, had been drowned, and at least thirty people had been killed by the lightning. The masts and headquarters building had been properly grounded and so escaped any real damage, but the exterior-exposed power grids had shorted out and had been cut loose by Seventeen to protect itself. They were a total loss.

Orbiting satellites mapped the entire area quickly, allowing a drenched and mud-caked Landscape staff to gather and quickly assess the changes, as well as give Seventeen immediate information. Many of them used the company showers to get clean, but most didn't know if their tents even existed anymore. Most slept right there on the floor or in chairs, and the staff meeting, when it resumed in the morning, reminded Toby Haller more of a nudists' convention. Some of the staff had been initially a bit put off, but when there was no alternative and nothing else to wear, they adapted. A lot of people with no place to sleep to get protection needed help far more than they did, and when order was restored and logistics could take stock and get what was needed, they'd get something.

Toby Haller knew he should have mixed emotions, but he couldn't help feeling downright euphoric. For all the suffering and the tragedies out there, the thing had worked and they'd gotten what they needed to have. If he could simply move faster on this, he could prevent a repetition. His journal, which he kept in his office desk, got an entry, but it reflected only his joy.

All of the staff was present except for four marrieds who were told to go off and hunt up their relations and kids.

"All right," he said, "now we can stop giggling and take stock. The good news is that we've got our rainfall. The bad news is that we don't have sufficient area for slow containment and measured runoff, and every indication I have from the reports and from the instruments indicates both to me and to Seventeen that we have to move fast to capitalize on this or it'll continue. Once switched on like this, it's in a state of almost permanent turbulence. Evaporation is way above normal, and general heating which is required for our work is hastening it. It's going to rain again. And again. Maybe not as severe, but maybe almost all the time. Unless we want that and a steambath to boot, we're going to have to triple our area with greatly reduced vapor content to compensate and we're going to have to do it in seven days."

They were aghast. "We can't do it!" one after another protested. "It's impossible! It's too risky!"

"I've ordered out all five of the big amps," he told them. "We didn't lose anybody on the crews out there because they were already out of the finished areas and got only some backlash, but I've diverted them and sent the other two packing as of this morning. I've run the problem through Seventeen and he agrees, although with great reservations the same as I have. It's risky. We don't know if even five of these amps are enough to marshal the power we need over this kind of area, and since we're improvising on the original plan, we're really guessing at the right landscape and proportions to compensate, but it has to be done. We'll try to adjust any gross errors when we do the north, but if we don't move on this, we're all going to drown and lose everything we've built so far.''

"Uh—how beeg we make zis new land, boss?" Lolita asked him.

"About four thousand square kilometers."

Somebody whistled. "All at once?"

"I certainly hope so. Billy'll take the south point, Connie the west, Lo, you take the east, Jody the north, and I'll be right smack in the middle of it all. Mickey will ride Guard and coordinate."

"Uh, boss," Connie said hesitantly, "you're the one that's gonna be in the crosshairs on this and you'll pay the price if anything slips. Don't you think you should ride Guard on this?"

"No, and I'm not being heroic. If anything goes really wrong, I want to be where I can do a quick fix in a hurry. If anything goes *radically* wrong, then I'd rather be dead out there than have to face the powers that be here and explain the situation."

"Thanks a lot," Mickey commented sourly. "So I'm standing there with the apple on my head instead. Look, at least Connie should be Guard."

"No, I want the most experience with these monsters in the field, and she's worked hard enough that if all fails she'll have a convenient getaway. You're just riding Guard, Mickey. They won't want your scalp, only ours."

"We're gonna have to travel between sixty and a hundred kilometers from here just to get into position," Connie noted. "There's no roads, and there are gullies and canyons all over the place and lots of standing water. Even if they can get a few of those waterlogged electric cars going and charged enough for a full hundred, it's unlikely that we can make it over that terrain just in the preformed areas. How are we supposed to get there? We've got nothing around that flies, and even if we did, I'm not sure we could trust it in this turbulence."

"I know. Even moving at their maximum speed of five kilometers an hour, sixteen hours a day, it's going to take the big amps two to three days to get there and get into position. I've already talked to Logistics and they don't have enough charged and operating cars for local needs right now and it'd take me days to get authority over their heads. The only solution we've been able to come up with is that Security's been using horses to patrol the area.''

"I know," Mickey remarked with an upturned nose. "I've stepped in enough of it. Uh, oh—you don't mean—''

"Yep. Now you know another reason why I picked the people I did. All of you Overriders have some experience in horseback riding, as I do.''

"But I haven't been on a horse in seven years or more!'' Billy protested, and several others nodded agreement.

"I haven't been on in longer than that, and my muscles already ache at the thought of a long ride without strengthening, but it must be done. Somehow I will beg, borrow, or steal five horses and saddlebags and enough rations for a week, even if I have to get Seventeen to make them for me.''

"Nix, boss, it ain't gonna work," Connie told him. "As soon as you get sixteen and a half kilometers in, you're gonna be on the basic form—almost no water at the start, no water at all farther in, and no grass or anything else for the horse to eat or drink. Horses can't go that far without both, and I don't think they digitized any ready, willing, and able camels, even if we knew how to ride them.''

He sighed, knowing she was right but hating to see his idea go up in smoke. "O.K., then—I guess I go see Colonel Singh.''

But Colonel Singh was not in, and as much involved with the problems the rains caused as everyone else. One of the Security sergeants suggested that he see the local commander of Signals, and he headed down there.

Major Irene Craig was a tough, no-nonsense military type, the daughter of two officers and granddaughter of one more. She looked and sounded like the kind of person who could get things done, but Haller preferred to work with her rather than for her. He quickly explained the problem and the urgency to both her and her top sergeant, who listened attentively.

"We've got a lot of experience working in this kind of environment,'' she told him when he'd finished. "The problem here is unique, but every one of the Anchors has had emergencies of one kind or another, some worse than this.

Two possibilities come to mind. First, is there any way that your crawlers could stop periodically and the operators use the big amp, coordinated with you here by radio, to create water and hay stations as they go? They can't have gotten too far as yet.''

He shook his head from side to side. "No, I thought about that. There's at least one assistant on each team to aid in setup, but they're not rated for Overrider status, and the equipment's pretty specialized.''

Major Craig sat back in her chair and thought for a moment, chewing on a large unlit cigar. Finally, she said, "Then the only other efficient way would be to exit the bubble and ride down entirely in the void. Your north point can make it overland O.K., but east, west, and south will have to ride the void, if they're willing to do it.''

"Huh? Why wouldn't they? They're good people.''

"The void does some funny things to folks who aren't conditioned to it. It can—change you. Some people have gone nuts in it.''

"Your own troopers go through it all the time,'' he noted. "We can't get any supplies in from the Gate except overland.''

"That's true, but we have an extensive training period with new people before we send them in, and even then nobody's totally immune—they just are a little better at it, that's all.''

"We've been working in Flux since we started this. I think we can handle it.''

"Maybe. You've been working on the Anchor pad, which was partially created by the machinery when it created the initial bubble. You're working on Flux within Flux, as it were. This is the pure stuff. You're right on the grid, with not even a good layer of rock and dirt to insulate you. First there's disorientation, then a total lack of grounding for all the senses. You're lost in a deep, dense fog with absolutely no guideposts or landmarks. We're laying the route marker strings using sophisticated navigation gear linked to the satellites, and it still feels like the middle of nowhere. You lose all sense of time, and your mind plays tremendous tricks on you. And we don't have any routes yet laid out southbound on either side, so it'll be necessary to tie in to an elementary navigational system, which means using the grid itself for orientation.''

"I think we have to risk it," he told her. "There doesn't seem any other way, and I don't think we can stand more than one more storm like the one we just had. Still, I can't see how going down the void will help matters any. There's no food and water there either.''

"Sergeant," Craig prompted, and the sergeant nodded, went out, then quickly returned with a small hand-held device.

"That's a Three Seventy-Eight Stroke J Flux Converter," the major told him, "often referred to by the troops as the 'god gun.' "

Haller looked at it, never having seen or heard of it before. It was a rather small brown rectangle from which came a thick pistol grip and two large triggers in parallel. There was an elaborate socket in the base of the grip, but no other outward markings, not even a barrel or contact points. "What's it do?" he asked her.

"It was developed by and for Signals by our own laboratories," Craig told him. "It is proscribed to all others, including Security, although I'm sure that one could be built and the programs developed for it if it was needed or they were desperate. It's a tool, Dr. Haller, nothing more. It permits us to survive out there in the thousands of kilometers of void. I'll not go into its exact operation, but it is basically a link to the computer grid. It contains a series of preset programs which can be sent to the nearest computer on the network and elicit immediate execution.''

"Without an Overrider or Guard?" He was shocked.

"Yes, without either, but don't worry about it, since the programs are in the gun, and the only thing it does is activate a preset routine from the maintenance programming. It is to a corpsman what canteens are to a desert nomad, or a rifle and snowshoes to the arctic explorer. We will send two teams. One will take you and one other of your party down one side, while the other will take the two others down the other side. Your north point engineer can make it entirely through finished Anchor.''

He nodded. "Fair enough. But what about me? I have to get to the center of the bloody wasteland.''

"You'll have to make it in yourself, but I've looked at your diagram. If this were a perfect circle, your best bet would be to press due south and forgo the void altogether, but it's not. It's irregular, and your center point is skewed well to the south and west. If you try it overland inside the bubble, you'll have perhaps a hundred and twenty kilometers to go—a fair amount without food or water for the horse, and chancy at best. If, however, you go in from your west point, here, the distance is just a bit more than half that. Your horse should make it that far, and you with it, or at least close enough so that it wouldn't be much of a walk. If you make it, then I assume your machine should be capable of providing for you and the horse. You should arrive at about the same time as the north point is reached by your other personnel."

"Good enough," he agreed, feeling less confident of that much time on horseback then about the journey itself.

"Have your people gather up what equipment they need and get a good night's sleep," the sergeant told him. "Meet me out front here at eight tomorrow morning. Pack very light and take only what's essential, but try to draw some good, thick pants and wear a good pair of boots, sir. Because you're not used to it, it'll be a fairly lazy pace, but it's a long time for someone out of condition on horseback to spend in the saddle."

"Don't I know it," he grumbled.

Pulling what rank he could, he did manage to get the whole crew new boots and jeans that more or less fit, and some pullover shirts that were rather optimistically labeled "one size fits all." They were overly large and soft and reacted to the body's moisture to contract and almost wrap themselves around the wearer. They would do, but they were hardly made for durability.

The horses were large and tough-looking, yet gentle and easy to ride. Signals generally used mechanized vehicles powered through the grid for their work, but they had their own complement of horses and other animals for situations that called for them. Brigadier Ryan's staff had learned from having to hook up the first few Anchors along the equator.

A pair of corporals had been assigned to the expedition

from Craig's troops, both of whom had extensive earlier experience in the void. One was a tall, lanky blond fellow originally from Perth named John Gorton, the other a tall, tough-looking Kenyan woman with very short woolly hair who said her named was Singer Macalla. Both were very professinal and businesslike and looked very imposing in their black uniforms complete with bush hats, although neither seemed any too pleased about this assignment.

The engineers had started the trip with a mixture of little kids' excitement at an adventure and many reservations about their lack of real provisions and their distance from a horse's back, but this quickly gave way to more professional approaches as they crossed the area that they had so carefully and lovingly designed and made within the past few weeks.

It was something of a shambles. The surface damage was shocking, and the land had been badly cut through. Trees were mangled or damaged everywhere, and there were broad mud patches where once there had been flowers and grass. Still, the damage was more surface than serious; if they could pick up the pieces back at the camp and get some of those farming experts in with proper seed and some work crews, the place could be put right in no time—if more damage did not occur. The extent of this one was telling proof that they had to get this mission done or lose it.

Field provisions were limited but not that bad. There were thin trays of a variety of foods that needed only activation and then a few minutes to self-steam themselves into perfection. They mostly tasted like paper, of course, but they *looked* right and they were filling.

Billy left them in early afternoon as they reached the northern limit of the finished area. He had the easiest job— just a few kilometers and he'd be on station. Now Jody and Lo would go with Corporal Macalla, while he and Connie would go down the other side with Gorton. They bade their farewells, and split apart, although once on station they would be in full radio contact, and, in a pinch, Macalla and Gorton could contact each other and even Craig's headquarters from the void itself.

It seemed to Toby and Connie that Gorton picked up the pace as they headed across the dirt floor of the Anchor base at an angle best calculated to save time and distance, although they stopped once for a brief snack and to allow the engineers to take simple measurements and determine that there was sufficient Flux bled into the base for what they needed. It was almost not worth testing; the place was covered in a pinkish-gray fog as it was, with twinkling little lights.

"It's going to be hard to tell the void from the bubble," Haller noted.

"No, sir, you'll know the void when you hit it," Gorton responded. "This is only a sample."

"What's the hurry?" Connie called out to him. "We're on time, and my legs and ass are killing me!"

"We'll spend the night in the void," he told them. "Best to acclimate yourself as quickly as possible to it. Sort of like going hiking in the mountains. Spend a night at altitude before trying strenuous activity."

"But it's only a two-day ride!" she protested.

"Yes, ma'am. But one of those days is going to be in the void, and it's like ten days through here."

Night fell dramatically on New Eden, and it was nearly dark by the time they reached the invisible boundary of the Anchor bubble. It was true that, with Flux bled into the bubble, there wasn't much difference between the two areas as far as looks were concerned, but there was definitely a difference you could *feel*. Gorton halted them just before the entry.

"All right," he said with a sigh, "we're about to go in, and in the dark you won't see much. We'll camp inside. The air will seem stale and flat, although there's some induced circulation by the machinery and some by convection where it seeps through to the Anchor base and vice-versa. It'll be quite dry, far drier than the absolutes maintained in the base area, and while the oxygen level is always within tolerable limits, there's some unevenness in the mix, so if you feel oxygen-starved, take a hit or two from the oxygen generator in my pack. You might also get the reverse, particularly this close to Anchor, so if you start feeling light-headed or giddy, just relax and wait it out. It usually doesn't last long. The important thing is to focus on the practical and don't let your mind wander. Don't let it get to you."

"If you're trying to make me nervous, you're succeeding," Toby told him. He'd heard that Signals made every effort at making their specialized jobs and knowledge seem relatively more difficult, even unique to their abilities. Gorton was quite effective at it. Realistically, though, neither he nor Connie expected a great deal of difference from the medium in which they normally worked. There seemed no reason to expect any differences anyway.

Because the level of Flux created inside the Anchor bubble was so great now, there was no real way to tell the boundary by sight, but it was a tangible crossing. The Anchor had seemed deathly quiet, but now it was almost as if they'd gone deaf. Everything, even the sounds of the horses, seemed oddly muffled. It was quite dark now, but Flux was alive with an eerie glow crested by the discharges that were constantly taking place. It provided a kind of illumination, but not enough to read by, for example. All three horses had bright lights on their bridles and saddles for easy location, and they were needed.

Gorton had no trouble in the murky silence; he had a small instrument cluster forward on his saddle which was constantly receiving updated location information from the orbiting satellites and the grid that was beneath them. Both Toby and Connie looked around and began to wonder just what would happen to them if that machine went bad.

After a half hour or so the corporal halted them and got down and prepared to make camp. After unloading and brushing down their mounts, it was time for the first use of the god gun, and it was fascinating.

There was no sign of an actual grid on the surface. In fact, the surface felt slightly spongy and soft, although it was impossible to penetrate and seemed smooth to the touch. It was a conductive material laid down over the grid as soon as all seven Gates were operational and power to the grid could be supplied, mostly as a protectant for that power and sensor system. Once an atmosphere and heat were introduced, the grid became vulnerable to a host of problems and this was the best way to insulate it while still obtaining maximum access. The material, a synthetic widely used on Earth but hardly on this scale, was transparent to the electromagnetic grid, yet was impervious to cold down close to absolute zero and heat up to several thousand degrees. When one had command of energy-to-matter conversion by remote computer, the network was essentially self-repairing.

The cable that attached to the god gun terminated in an interface plug in the grip and then attached by some sort of suction to the grid itself. The corporal simply ran the grid end over an area until he felt some kind of attraction, then let go, and it stuck as if built there. Haller guessed that terminator and grid were made for each other, and when it came across a power line, some sort of magnetic field was generated that held it firm.

They watched Gorton with growing curiosity. He seemed almost in a trance state, pointing the gun at an angle at a nowhere point about three meters in front of him. Suddenly, he pulled the twin triggers, and there was a familiar if muffled crackling sound where the "shot" would have hit. There was now a huge bale of hay there, neatly tied off as if just come off the harvest. Gorton turned, repeated the act a bit over, and again pulled the trigger. A depression formed in the impervious floor, and filled itself with clear water. The horses needed no invitation and showed no fear about the sudden appearance of food and water nor any reluctance to partake of the feast. Clearly, they had been trained in this sort of environment.

The corporal rejoined them. "Well, what do you think of our little toy?" he asked.

"Impressive," Connie replied. "Why don't we just get a few hundred of those and have you march south?"

"Wouldn't work. These are very limited devices, with a choice of thirty or forty preset options. It is, as I told you, a survival tool, nothing more. To get complex programs over more than a two-or grid-square area would take a full computer interface and all that implies. It won't even work inside the bubble. It requires direct contact with the grid and that layer of rock and dirt effectively blocks it. It's useful, but it's no big thing."

No big thing, Haller thought wonderingly. *Look at how far we've come. What he just did is miraculous, incredible, even to me, and I know how it works. How quickly we take even the most revolutionary concepts for granted!* That was, he realized, Pandit Singh's and the company's point with the Anchors and their nonflux-based system. Something like this was no use on the plains of India or in the mountains of Kenya, but it could make New Edenites indolent pleasure-seeking slobs as easy as pie. Earth didn't have a grid, or Anchor bubbles either, and the billions there could hardly be moved off someplace for ten or twenty years while it was created and then fed by-what? Twenty? Fifty? A hundred Gates? More?

They settled down for some prepacked food and canteen water, then prepared to bed down for the night.

Gorton was right about one thing: with little to do and the muffled silence and dim, eerie electrical light, the mind tended to play tricks on you. More than once both of them found themselves turning quickly around, a reflexive reaction to something seen, or imagined, in the corner of the eye. The distance took on odd shapes and forms, and it was impossible not to give them some kind of unreasoned paranoiac cause. Alone, it would be absurdly easy to go mad in this place, to be consumed by your own innermost fears awashed only in loneliness and spatial disorientation. Signals, Haller decided, earned every bit of brag they could muster for working in this environment so well.

The air was dead, and it was hot as hell, but Connie had little shivers. She wanted to talk to somebody before going to sleep, if she could sleep in this sort of place. "I think I know what you mean now, brudda," she told the corporal. "How can you stand it for weeks on end?"

"You get used to it," he told her. "We had simulators that were at least as bad back on Titan, maybe even worse, the only thing different being that you always knew you were in a simulator and somebody was monitoring you and ready to pull you out. Even the officers, up to the brigadier himself, have to survive all the training. That's one reason I found I could stand it. Didn't want to fail at doing something a fifty-one year-old brass hat managed. He's the one that dreamed up the final test here, the one you pass or either die or wind up in Logistics or administration."

"Huh?"

"They take you out twenty kilometers from Anchor, sedated and stripped stark naked. You wake up and have to make it back in. If you fail completely, a little sensor in your tooth aligned to the grid give you a chance at being located."

"Jesus! But you can't see anything, smell anything, or have any landmarks! How do you get back?"

"Well, there's a trick to it, a trick nobody really tells you and one that not every bloke can master. Them that can make it back."

Haller, too, was fascinated. "What's the trick?"

Gorton gave a wry chuckle. "If you can find it out, maybe we'll fit you for a black hat, eh?" And, with that, he prepared to get a good night's sleep.

The corporal bedded down near the horses. He wanted to make certain that he was on hand in case anything spooked or bothered them, and was sensitized to it, but the odor was a bit much for both of the engineers and they moved away far enough to dampen out the odor and noise but near enough to spot the corporal and the horses and the remains of the haystack. It also, as it proved, was far enough to dampen the corporal's very loud snoring.

"Well, *he* may well sleep in that uniform, but I'm hot and sore and *I'm* going to strip," Connie told Toby, and proceeded to do so. She then arranged one of the saddlebags as a pillow and lay down. "It's really soft and warm," she told him. "Not bad."

Toby Haller was looking more at her than the ground. "Not bad, indeed," he murmured to himself. He tried it Gorton's way and decided she was right. The heat of the ground was magnified by clothing, and if he had any modesty left after the rainstorm, it certainly wasn't around Connie, and who the hell else was going to stumble over them here?

He was very tired, but his muscles hurt like hell, particularly in the thighs and calves, and he found it next to impossible to sleep. The bag wasn't much of a pillow, and even putting his short on top didn't help. He finally pushed it out of the way and lay flat on the soft, springy ground, just staring into the void. To avoid the phantoms there, he shifted and looked over at Connie and tried to get his mind to go blank. It was impossible to tell if she was asleep or not.

Slowly, he lapsed into an odd, hypnoticlike state between sleeping and waking, fixated on her form. The aches and pains faded into nothingness, and he seemed to be almost floating.

After more time passed, he became aware of a sound—no, not a sound, but *something*—all around him. It was unlike anything in his experience, a seething, pulsing aliveness that could not be pinned down or confined. It was as if—as if the insulating ground material were somehow human skin, and beneath it he was hearing the rush of blood along the veins and arteries and the distant pumping of the heart.

The void, he thought suddenly, *is not a void at all. It's alive! And anything in contact with it is a part of it.*

He stared again at Connie's form, and saw an aura there around her contours, as if a black border perhaps ten centimeters thick had been drawn separating her from the Flux discharges, which seemed far more numerous; seemed, in fact, to be coalescing around her.

Go with the flow, go with the flow, the strange sensations all about him seemed to say, and he succumbed to it and it seemed to sweep him along toward her, although neither he nor she moved.

Go with the flow. . . .

And then he was one with her body, at the same time his own eyes saw her covered with and outlined in countless tens of thousands, perhaps millions, of electrical flashes. The pattern was far too complex for his mind to comprehend or even fully realize, but he knew somehow that it was logical, even mathematical. The pattern, he realized, was linked to the ground, to the grid—that was why her head was so indistinct, lying on her saddle pillow, while the rest was so clear. The grid, however, also linked her to him in some strange way, and the both of them to something infinitely more complex and wondrous blow the surface.

He turned her body with her own hands and muscles and she pushed away the bag-pillow and settled back onto the ground itself, now wholly ablaze and engulfed in the sparkling life. He could repress nothing now, nor did he want to do so. He was Toby Haller, yet he felt Connie's body as he did his own, and he felt impelled to join the two in physical union and there was no impulse to stop him. Her eyes opened, but he saw himself over her, through her eyes, as well as her through his own. He felt every bit of the stimulation he gave her, and that she gave him; he was both. He felt both giver and receiver, and he joined with her body and every cell of both was erotically alive. He had no idea how long it lasted, but the dual waves of ecstasy and the dual massive orgasms were unbelievable.

He felt totally spent when it was done, but he had no regrets, no shame. He made his way back to his own area and lay down once more, just staring at her.

Go with the flow, go with the flow. . . .

To the refrain of the strange life around him, he slept.

10

THE HUMAN FACTORS

Gorton awakened him gently in the morning, and he got up, feeling like he still needed another week's sleep but oddly without pain or discomfort either. There was, in fact, almost a warm glow inside.

He remembered the previous night, but wasn't sure how much was real, if any, and how much was a dream, a reaction to this eerie place. The genital region had some dried-on material he had to wash off, but certainly if it was a dream it would have been a really wet one.

Connie was also in a surprisingly good mood, and sponged herself off before putting her clothes back on. There was something *different* about her, Haller thought, but he couldn't quite put his finger on it. It was something in the way she moved, certainly—sexier, more erotic even, but that just might be the aftereffects of his dream. She seemed *younger* somehow, more twentyish than in her thirties. He knew it was more than imagination when she put her clothes back on. The pants seemed ill-fitting, while the day before they'd been about right, and the shirt was much too small, ending above her navel by some distance. The material shrank to fit, but didn't enlarge again unless thoroughly washed and heat-dried.

She came over to him, looking puzzled. "Toby—do I look any different to you?"

189

"Um—now that you mention it, a little. I thought it was just me. Your more than ample proportions seem, well, more ample, and you look ten years younger."

"I *feel* ten years younger, at least. You don't look so bad yourself, by the way. Trimmer, leaner, more muscles showing."

They both looked over at Gorton, who seemed to take no notice and had changed not a bit. He was preparing prepacks for breakfast. "You think maybe there's something out here they're not telling us about?" he wondered aloud.

"I think there is. I wonder what Special Projects's gonna think about *this*?" She paused a moment. "By the way— thanks for the fuck last night. I really needed it."

He was shocked and startled beyond words. Then it *had* happened—and she'd known it! Finally, his mind started to assemble what he knew into place and he asked, "Um— about last night. Did you feel anyting—unusual? I mean, strange?"

"Well, it was the *best* one I ever remember, and that's saying a lot. I'm not saying that because you're the boss either."

"It's been a while for me," he said honestly. "I guess it was just all built up inside."

"Me too," she told him. "Jeez, I still feel turned on. I feel like a hooker after a month's vacation. If you or laughing boy over there made half a pass, I'd tumble even in *that* hay."

Gorton seemed to take no notice of what they perceived as their changed appearances, and Haller decided to see if he could put some things together. "I think I know how you got back to Anchor on your test," he commented almost casually.

The corporal looked up. "Yes?"

"You go with the flow."

Gorton stared at him for a moment. Connie looked at them both as if they were nuts.

"You felt it even your first night out?" the signalman asked him.

"I did. What I want to know is what it was."

The man in black sighed. "Only guesses. We're dealing with new forms of energy here, remember, and a whole new technology. I'm no physicist, bu the thinking right now is that the grid network is more than the network it was designed to be. We tied twenty-eight of the biggest super computers ever together, gave them access to all the power they wanted, and made them self-repairing and gave them a lot of autonomy in order for them to maintain an environment humans could live in. Somehow, we don't exactly know how, some folks get sensitized to the energy constantly going beneath us. Best guess always was that the more you interfaced with the grid, the more sensitized you got to it, but that don't always hold true."

Connie looked at both of them quizzically. "Would you two mind telling me what the hell you're talking about?"

The corporal shook his head slowly. "Ma'am, it's not something you can explain. Either you got it or you don't. You might get it yet, if you're out here enough."

"Why can't I feel it now?" Haller asked him.

"You can if you concentrate real hard. Hardly nobody loses it once they got it. The trick is to have enough concentration and presence of mind to block it out completely when you don't need it."

"So, out here naked and alone, if you bring it up and find the most powerful signal and follow it back, you get home. The receive lines are mounted on top of the send lines, so you always just follow the strongest signal in the direction in which it grows even stronger."

"That's about it. Give the man a black hat. Maybe you oughta think about switching over to our R and D department when you get this Anchor up and running."

Haller didn't reply. He was beginning to wonder what else he didn't know and someone else did. How many independent research programs were there here investigating things unknown to even the top technical people? And how much, if any, did they talk to each other?

"Are you two trying to tell me that you somehow hooked into the computer network?" Connie asked skeptically. "That's a little hard to take, I think. I mean, no matter how sophisticated our big machines are, they're totally different than the human brain. They might be programmed by other human brains to meddle, but alone, out here, at random . . . ? Uh-uh. There's no scientific basis whatsoever for it."

They began to pack up and ride on, continuing the conversation as they did so.

"There's a scientific explanation for everything," Haller told her. "It just shows that even with all this power there are vast gaps in what we know. As usual, what we *think* we know isn't the same as what's true. You stand here on a world that not long ago was a barren chunk of space debris, on your way to create in a matter of minutes a garden of space debris, on your way to create in a matter of minutes a garden from a wasteland with some expert commands and directions and the help of some mighty powerful machines, and you're saying something's *impossible*?"

"I don't believe in magic," she stated firmly.

"What is magic but a term the ignorant use to describe anything their present knowledge and means of measurement cannot explain or duplicate? Come on—let's get moving or we'll be here another day!"

It was only a seven hour ride, but subjectively it seemed endless, and because of the damping and the need to follow Gorton there was little chance to do anything but think and brood. At a break, though, he did manage to get Gorton aside for a brief period and whisper a few questions.

"All right—she's physically changed from yesterday, and she says I am too. Is it just in our minds, or is there something more you're not telling me?"

"I met you all too briefly yesterday and we were off," the corporal noted. "After that there was a lot of business to attend to and I had the lead, so I really didn't notice all that much. Still, it's possible. Happens with some folks, anyway, for good or ill. Don't look like either of you had any changes for the worse, so don't complain."

"But it didn't change you at all," he noted. "Or did it?"

"I've had lots of training, mate. It's all mental. Those who ride the void got control. They use it when it's convenient or necessary, otherwise they tune it out. If you're the type that lets the boredom open the way to you, then you're better off in an Anchor job. We had eleven hundred troopers come in here, and now we're down to maybe five or six hundred who can handle things. That's what's taking so long getting this bleedin' place all wired and connected up. But the ones that can handle it, they're gonna be the elite. They're gonna be the best, mate. Bet on it.''

"This—sense. These changes. They happen to everyone?''

"Very few, actually. Only the ones that work with the big computers on an intimate basis, if you know what I mean, and those of us who spend most of our time out here connected on and off to the grid by the god guns and other equipment. You and the lady better watch it if you come back out for any length of time, by the way. You either control it or it controls you.''

You either control it, or it controls you. . . .

He wasn't too sure if he could control it. The boring, empty trek left him little to do, and his mind kept going back to the power of the grid and the subtle mathematics it represented. Even on horseback he found himself drawing it from the very ground, and he saw that Connie, too, was drawing it. The difference between him and her was simply that she didn't consciously realize it. Gorton, however, was right about his own kind. He was *not* drawing it, except at certain times when he was obviously using it for directional confirmation.

Such power, he thought. *To draw it and shape it by will alone*. But whose will? His? Or was, perhaps, the computer network experimenting with them, with *all* of them? Trying to build a direct human interface with all that power and no Guard. No, he decided, that wasn't it for the signal corpsmen controlled it, or at least their interaction with it. He had been overriding last night—or his subconscious had—not the computer. The computer, as usual, had simply delivered the programs requested. Somehow he had changed Connie, in subtle and basic ways, into what his lust wanted her to be. The physical change he could accept, and could reverse, if desired, in the lab. He knew how now. What was disturbing was that she was convinced that she had initiated the lovemaking. Nobody in Special Projects had intimated that a computer could do *that*. But, then again, nobody had ever said they'd told him the whole story either.

Connie herself was feeling a little confused and disoriented. She'd awakened still turned on, as she sometimes had in the past, but it hadn't gone away. Hours later she was *still* turned on and feeling very tense, and riding between two good-looking guys didn't help any. More than once she found herself caressing places on her body that she just didn't touch in public. Worse, for perhaps the first time in her life she felt her self-confidence eroding faster than that rain-soaked patch of ground they'd covered. Today, somehow, her occupation and life-style just didn't seem as personally important or even as interesting to her as it always had.

She'd worked hard, damned hard, her whole life. She had worked her way through university, worked sixteen-hour days at shitwork in the University of the Pacific computer complex getting hands-on experience for peanuts in pay while holding down a weekend job teaching swimming and surfing to would-be beach bums. Then had come the low-level job with Newcastle in Aukland, which was a minor subsidiary of Westrex, and she'd worked like a maniac to be one of those who qualified for this project, taking the night shift so she could get her necessary doctorate days. Then came Titan and learning the whole new Kagan system, faking much and staying up nights finding out what she really needed to know, then this.

She knew she was pretty, and she liked dressing and acting the half-naked Polynesian girl with the different-bed-each-night and let's-party personality, but it was a phony. The fact was, except for last night, she'd been laid by maybe six guys in her whole life and by nobody here. It wasn't for lack of offers, but her career, her need for independence, had gotten in the way. Now she was thirty-five, and, after this Anchor was formed up, she had maybe ten years of simulations and math and frustration until they maybe let her design a quadrant—a quadrant that would of necessity be compromised by the designs of three other top programmers, all of whom had differing visions. At fifty she could be a middle-aged head girl of some department someplace with a big office, lots of perks, and two ulcers.

She began to think that this wasn't waht she wanted at all. What she wanted to be, she realized, was that Hawaiian honey she'd always acted. No cares, no worries, just lots of fun with very little pressure.

She wondered what they would do if she quit after this

Anchor was done. Just quit. They'd hardly bother to ship her back. Send her to one of Suzuki's shrinks, probably. Who knows? Maybe they'd figure she had to do it for her mental health. She sure had cause. A little while maybe in her fields and forests, just relaxing, before the farmers came in and mucked it up. Grow her hair long, maybe sing and dance for the crowds. It sounded *wonderful*.

Her determination actually hardened by the time they reentered the bubble and sighted the big amp, still being checked out by the two techs who'd brought it there. Two girls, she remembered, somewhat disappointed, but then she reflected that it was probably all for the best. This business had to come before anything else.

Toby Haller looked over at Connie and gasped. Somehow, in a few hours of riding, her hair had gone from a very short pageboy style to a length that reached almost to her navel. She also looked like a teenager, with a hint of child in her face.

He got down, made the introductions, and immediately got up in the cab and called the computer center. He got Lo to ride guard and hooked himself immediately into the computer.

"Hello, Toby, what a surprise," said the computer pleasantly.

"Yeah, well, I've had too many surprises already today, Seventeen. Right now I need information."

"If I can provide it, I will."

"Seventeen, something's happened to Connie. She's changed physically a great deal. I just had trouble convincing the crew here that she was who we said she was. Any change like that had to come from you, or at least one of the nine thousands maintaining the grid in this sector. I want to know how it happened, and why."

"I've traced down the operation, but I can't really explain it. I'm still researching the phenomenon, and after months of it I can't come up with a coherent reason why it happens. The best I can tell you is *what* happened."

"That'll have to do for now."

"Sometimes, when professional Overriders go into the void, I can hear them just like they're tied in. It's not much of a connection mentally, and I can't communicate with them, but

I sense them, and every once in a while I get a string of instructions just like I get when Signals uses that portable interfacer unit, only without any specific program. It's all very localized and very general, and often not very logical, but I am compelled by my operating system instruction set to furnish the slight programs needed.''

"But the change is both physical and mental, it seems. You'll see when you get her on line. I didn't think you could do the physical bit without a lot of prep, or the mental part at all."

"I didn't used to be able to do it, but the more experiments performed by researchers in this area, the more generalized programs and knowledge I have to do things. In these specific instances, though, I furnish only what I perceive is requested. Last night you wanted her, and in the face of no overriding or contradictory instructions from her, I provided her the way you instructed me. She must have wanted you. Otherwise she could have stopped it by issuing any countermand.''

Well, that explained that, and relieved some of his guilt. "But that doesn't explain her today."

"She is as she directed. I did nothing creative. I only provided what was requested."

"But she doesn't even believe it's possible," he began, and then thought about it. The solution to at least the *what* of it struck him almost immediately. He had inadvertently connected her up the previous night and that connection remained on. Seventeen had been unable to distinguish between conscious directives and subconscious fantasizing, for which the void's drabness and stifling atmosphere were perfect incubators. Just as it had been unable to distinguish between his lustful fantasizing and a command set and subset.

"Seventeen—just how many people can send and receive instructions in that manner?''

"Nine hundred and forty-seven people," the computer answered literally. "The number will grow, however, and there are degrees of it. Only one hundred and fifty-four have any strong signal on their own."

"Correlate. What do those have in common with one another that the rest do not?''

"They all have used the remote subsidiary computer link

extensively, as you are doing now. That one we determined long ago. The more you use it, the clearer the connection becomes.''

He thought a moment. ''Could it be used in Anchor?''

''No. Direct connection to the grid is necessary, and some mental attunement.''

''Who is aware of this phenomenon?''

''Classified, but you can probably guess. It is frustrating that the various projects on it are all sealed off from one another, so none have the benefits of the other's research. I, however, have all the knowledge of all of them.''

''I can guess. Signals and Special Projects for sure. Probably main systems—no, they wouldn't work with these big amps. Who else would?''

''The remote subsidiary computer link is used by Signals, Security, and Transportation and Energy,'' the computer responded. ''No one else has the need.''

And that, of course, told him everything. The one surprise was Transportation and Energy. Watanabe. He felt foolish. It was from a Watanabe assistant that he'd first learned of what these computers could really do, and that was only the 7240 series.

''Analysis. What would it take to get the old Connie back?''

''Simple. All she had to do is sit where you are, ask for it, and I will include it in the master program. I can include as easily as exclude.''

It *sounded* simple, but it wasn't. Connie now understood fully that she had changed, and she was ready to accept the why of it, but she did not want to change it. Her new look and new outlook came directly out of her suppressed libido.

''Why are you so *worried*?'' she asked him. ''This is the *best* thing that's happened to me in years. I feel—reborn. Great. I won't let you down though. We'll make this sucker as big as all outdoors all at once.''

''And after that?''

''Well, we've got the south half to do, I guess.''

''And after that?''

''After that I'm quitting. It'll be done and I won't be essential. I need some time to just enjoy myself, that's all.''

He tried all the old arguments, but he failed. She wasn't him, she told him, and she didn't see things that way. She'd had her fill of "dedication" and "joy in work" and all that other stuff. She'd carried more than her load, and this was the payoff. Faye and Ali, the two technicians, also started in on her, and she got digusted by it. Finally, she asked Toby, "So what would I do to change back? Go back and sleep another night out there in the nothing? Or maybe go out and call, 'Seventeen! Oh, Seventeen! I want to be thirty-five, repressed, and a workaholic again!' "

"No, you just tell Seventeen when we run the big program. He'll do the rest, right up there when it runs."

"And if I don't?"

"Then maybe I'll do it for you."

"You wouldn't dare!"

"Try me," he responded, and she stalked off.

She was nicer and far more friendly, if still noncommittal, the next morning when he prepared to leave. They'd used the big amp to give his horse a good feed, and he packed water and some candy and very little else for his ride. He got on the horse, thinking of the ordeal ahead, but he looked down at her one last time. "You think about what I said. It's for your own good."

"I *have* been thinking about it," she told him, and he took that as something of an assent. He picked up a portable communicator and triangulation device so he'd stay on course and started off over the hard-packed dirt. They watched him go.

For Connie, she'd never felt so emotional or so committed. Before he was out of sight, she climbed up into the cab and got herself connected to Seventeen. Ron was on guard now, and he neither knew about nor cared about Haller's conversations, or hers either. She signed on and went about a lot of routine stuff until Ron was preoccupied with setting up some of the other big amps.

"Seventeen, warn me if Ron starts paying attention to this conversation. I want you to tell me everything about this— change—that you told Toby."

Seventeen, friendly as always, did just that.

"Can he put me in his own master program from his amp?"

"He could."

"Analysis of Haller's probable action in this matter."

"Indications strong that he will direct the restoration. He feels guilty because he thinks he caused it all."

"Simple. Create a basic program now that will act to cancel his directive when implemented."

She thought a moment. That would do for now, but then they'd be going back through the new land to the core. He'd surely turn her over to Suzuki and she'd get the treatment in spades.

"Seventeen—what can I do to make this permanent? So that not even you or the shrinks could take it away. Is that possible?"

"I feel obligated to warn you that such a step would be permanent and irrevocable, even by you. This borders on the irrational and may trip my Guard flag."

"Is it possible?"

"Yes. However, I will have to have the specifics of your request before I can make a judgment."

"I want to look, and feel, this way from now on. I want to be the most sexy, desirable girl around. I want to lose all the inhibitions that won't do harm to others. I want to be mature, desirable, but get back the innocence and wonder of childhood. I'd be happy to be like that until I died. Can you understand that?"

"Would it disturb you to know that I felt compelled to send this to the Special Projects office? That Dr. Suzuki herself is monitoring this at this very moment?"

She felt a sudden crash. "Yes. It would disturb me a great deal."

"Interesting. Dr. Suzuki has just informed me that she will not object to or interfere in this. It is up to you."

She wasn't sure. "You mean—she's decided just like that that I'm expendable and she's willing to allow me to be the subject of my own experiment for her learning purposes."

"That's about it. I feel personally, though, that you should reconsider right now. You are working from a predominantly emotional rather than rational viewpoint, and you may regret it later, if you're able to. You don't have to give it up now.

The price you will pay for doing this in the manner you suggest is quite high.''

"What's the price?" she asked him.

"First, the method is to add the desired localized program to the master program in such a mathematical string that it would be impossible to alter your specifics without altering the master Anchor program itself. That is effective permanence."

"You mean—I would become a part of my own program instead of an overlay?"

"That's right. And the 7240 maintenance computers would be obligated to maintain you that way to the same degree as they maintain the trees, grass, and hills. The only modifications possible would be at Guard, since those computers would be handling maintenance, not me. This is true of every mathematical string involved, in case of extreme emergencies. To get around this, you would have to supply your own personal string and allow me to make it infinitely more complex. You would have to supply the original string for the 7240 Guard to remove you from its master program."

She thought a moment. "But I could be just put under by any shrink or slipped a pill and I'd give the number."

The computer seemed to hesitate. Then it said, "Not if a filter were in place at activation that removed your computational abilities. This would be necessary in any event to preclude any involuntary interactions with the grid should you go into the void."

So that was the price, and it was a big one for her. Mathematics had been a good part of her life. "That's a hell of a price," she told the computer.

"Actually, it's computational abilities. You would be able to count to twenty, perhaps, on your fingers and toes, and you might manage subtraction in that range if the numbers weren't large, but even multiplication and division would be beyond you. Further, the organization of each human brain is unique. The filter required might also trap other skills or abilities you have learned."

She considered that as well. "But I would still have my memories? My identity? I wouldn't come out, like, well, Hasim?"

"Oh, no. Nothing like that."

"Seventeen—work up a simulation and I'll get back to you today on this."

"Understood. Please reconsider though."

"I am," she said seriously.

She switched off, but the interloper on the other end, sitting in her office, did not. Suzuki had a private voice terminal line to Seventeen, worked through the Security link downstairs.

"Seventeen," said the doctor thoughtfully.

"Yes, Dr. Suzuki?"

"Can you send programs to her when she's on the amp interface?"

"Yes, Doctor. Very limited, but it's possible."

"Seventeen—priority security alert master command flag on."

"Flag on. Password?"

"General McKenzie has fig pajamas."

"Acknowledged. Send?"

"When Connie Makapuua signs back on, I want you to unobtrusively reinforce a conviction to accept her program. If she decides to go with it, I want it locked in so tight she will never reconsider. If she decides not to proceed, I want her mind changed. I want this with no hint that it is being imposed or reinforced to the subject—ever. Project security demands it."

"Understood. Writing routine. Writing subroutines. Stored. Activation authority?"

"Mayor Snorkum will lay a cake."

"Acknowledged. Done. I am out of place here, but may I ask the reason for this?"

Interesting. Seventeen had never asked something like that before. "Because she is emotionally unstable and undependable. Her emotive state, reinforced by her physical alterations, makes her a risk for future work with our equipment, but she simply has too much knowledge, skills, and training about things like Special Projects and the grid to be allowed to just roam all over. I don't have the months it might take to cure her, nor the personnel, nor is she vital enough to be worth emergency treatment. This way she can be of value

both to psychiatry and to our understanding of the programming process. More, because we are creating her expressed
deepest fantasy, she will be happy. Is that sufficient? And why
does it concern you one way or the other?''

''Understood. I am always reluctant to part with one who is
in such direct communication with me. Loss of one who is at
the point and has the ability to directly interface with me so
that will is known semantically and intuitively, reducing error
probabilities to negligible, is a slight diminishment of my
external interface and abilities. Why are you so intent on the
permanency factor?''

''That, right now, is none of your affair,'' replied the
doctor.

It had been a long, hard trip, but both Haller and his horse
made it to the center amp, where Tombi and Caussa, a
Nigerian married couple both of whom were technicians in
engineering, had things prepped and waiting.

He had dwelled for a long time on Connie and her problem. He felt both guilty and responsible for the situation, yet
his own inner feelings kept him in agony. He *could* circumvent it, but it went against his grain to do so. Worse, she was
close to the void and now she not only knew the procedure
but could get pointers from Seventeen. She could reverse it
again, unless he bound her into the landscape program itself—
and that would lock her in her old body and old mentality, but
with memories of how she might have been and who prevented it. He didn't need an analysis from Seventeen to tell
him that he might just be prescribing a suicide. There was just
too much about Connie he'd taken for granted that was
proving wrong. He wondered if anybody really understood
anybody else, deep down.

He managed to get a good night's sound sleep, and spent
the next morning checking out the gear. It wasn't until well
past midday when he got word that the north point was
staffed and on line. Interestingly, the pair going down the east
side and also had experiences with the grid, but they had less
hours, overall, on the big amps than either he or Connie, and
maybe they were less emotional, but nothing major happened
to them.

Connie came on line, sounding bright and cheerful, and he was glad to hear that.

"Connie, I've decided that whatever you want to do has my blessing," he told her. "I have no right to interfere."

"I'm glad to hear it," she responded, "and I don't want you to feel guilty or responsible for anything. This is my last job out here, Toby, but I should tell you I checked out everything with Medical and higher-ups and they said they wouldn't stand in my way either, so you're off the hook."

He felt better about that, but sad to be losing her. He switched over to his private computer line. "Seventeen—is it true? She has the O.K.?"

"It *is* true," Seventeen responded, but it seemed somehow saddened. "I—I think without violating any instructions, though, I should warn you that she has written a program for herself that will be included in the master system. It will cause severe, permanent, and irrevocable changes which she knows and accepts. It will do no good to talk to her, only cause her pain. My analysis is that there is absolutely nothing that can be done."

"How severe?" he asked, mouth going dry.

"Very. But she'll be happy, Toby. I guarantee that. I will not, however, be specific. That is outside your provence."

"Cancel it, then. No matter what."

" I can't. She's anticipated you all the way."

"Not in one way. I can refuse to run the program. That would buy time."

"It would buy nothing. She can run hers without you and create a bad imbalance that might cost lives. She's that determined. And, Toby—the storm has finally broken just south of the core. It's worse than the first one and it'll be within populated limits in less than ten minutes. Something of this size isn't done in an instant, you know. We'll be lucky to minimize damage and possible loss of life if we run it right now. The only shot we've got is the pressure drop we'll create that could suck that thing north and dissipate it. I don't like to run it now anyway. It's bigger than anything we've ever done, and a couple of modules at the north point haven't even been verified yet, but we must take the gamble."

He swore and hit the side of the metal casing so hard it

hurt. *Why all this right now? This instant? Why couldn't that damned storm hold off another twenty minutes? Another hour?*

"Toby—it's many lives and maybe the Anchor versus a fruitless delay talking her down. I tried myself already. Insert your modules. Give the orders. *Run the program now!*"

"*Damn!*" he swore aloud. "Station One, insert modules. Stations Two and Three, insert modules. Station Four, insert modules. Sound out on my mark!"

"Mark!" came back four times—including Connie's voice.

"We've got to roll. Storm is in. Repeat, storm is in. Just pray this works, guys, or run for whatever hills we manage to build. Inserting master module. Master in. Locked on. Guard, on my mark—key off. Mark! Guard—key on. Mark!"

"Fired and ready," came the response from the Guard safe and cozy deep inside the headquarters complex.

"Amp check! Full power! Report!"

"Full power!" they all reported.

"Computer link. Do you have program read?"

"Program read, aye," responded Seventeen. "Running normal checksum. Done. Recommend a Go code at your command."

"All amp keys off on my mark. Mark! Computer—execute on completion of five-key circuit. Ready remotes! Hands on keys—" He hesitated just a moment. The difference between leadership and just having a job was taking the responsibility for some pretty damned shitty necessities. "Mark!"

He turned his key, and watched all five lights go on almost at the same time. She hadn't even hesitated.

There was nothing to do now but turn and see if this whole damned cursed bloody thing worked. If it didn't, he was a ripe candidate to cut his own bloody throat.

The crackling wall went out from his position and expanded away in all directions, raggedly rather than in a circular manner, but that was the way these things went. He watched in fascination as it left him, and then struck Cuassa's position below, which was not as protected as it should have been. The line of fire came up to her, parted right around her feet, and continued on. She gave a yelp, although there was no real sensation, and jumped back. Two shoeprints of dirt stood where she'd been, surrounded by grasses.

It looked fine here, but now he'd have to depend on Seventeen's sensors and the satellite links to tell him if his gamble had paid off with only five amps. He couldn't help but notice the energy guage creep rapidly down on his own panel. The farther the wall traveled, the more energy would be expended, since it was fed from the amp and the amp alone. If it ran dry, or too low to make the conversions before it hit the other walls of fire, they'd have five disconnected Anchors and hell to pay with atmospherics, stream flow, and natural drainage and seepage. Even Seventeen had said it was too close to call.

"Well? Status check?" he commanded the computer.

"It sucked those storm clouds clean back north so fast, it was hard to believe," the computer informed him. "First time there's been real daylight on the core since that first one. Everything's holding fine, but it's going to be really chancy between you and the east point wall. Five minutes or so should tell."

"And Connie?"

As soon as she turned the key, Connie had felt a shock, then a tingling that seemed to reach into her very core and through every cell of her body. Then she seemed to black out—the world shifted for a second—and it was over and the wall was moving away from her.

She removed the headset. It didn't interest her anymore. Slowly, she climbed down from the cab and felt her bare feet touch real grass, and it felt good. There was a slight wind blowing, and the sky overhead blazed now with the big planet that was its light source.

She knew who she was—or, rather, *had* been. She had to put Connie Makapuua to rest, she knew. She didn't have a name in mind, but she'd think of something. She wanted to find some surface to see herself, and she found that the side of the big amp was pretty shiny and with its Guard panels down reached the ground. She gasped at what she saw. She was in every way more than she desired, but she was also Seventeen's, and Suzuki's experiment. The computational filter wasn't absolute. As she'd discover, she could not compose music, but she could sing perfectly just about anything she heard even once and her ability to intuitively play the string instruments she'd always played in an average way remained and was enhanced, although she'd never read a note of music or anything else. The computational flag had also filtered basic literacy.

Nor could she relearn these things. The filter was permanent and would block it, and prevent any understanding of it.

Psychologically, Seventeen simply took the libido she'd suppressed and craved and made it the master. She was still human—she could think, reason, learn and remember—but the nonaggressive parts of the animal brain would take precedence. Aggression centers had been neutralized by the creation of specific peptides for the necessary receptors in the brain and the continued natural creation of these peptides would be a normal body function. Pleasures of the flesh would later take supremacy over pleasures of the mind, yet future memory would be nearly photographic. The baser emotions, such as jealousy and possessiveness, would be dampened by a combination of data filtration and self-perpetuating biochemistry. Her attention span was short, her behavior generally governed by the impulse of the moment. But for the brain, she would not physically age, each cell renewing itself, even to the point of regeneration.

The figure reflected back at her was based upon this and her own fantasy image, but taken to its utmost extremes. Her Polynesian features were perfection, beauty and eroticism in one, yet her face was childlike, an eternal sweet sixteen. She was short, with a trim, athletic body and long silky black hair down to her hips, but her breasts were both firm and enormous, far out of proportion to her body size. So prominent, in fact, that normal human breasts of that size could not possibly be firm, nor be carried by so petite a frame without causing back pain or even curvature, yet none was there. Seventeen had carefully altered her bone structure and muscles to compensate. She was inhumanly erotic and she loved it.

She was also, to a large extent, exactly what Dr. Suzuki wanted from the exercise. The Special Projects chief and her security bosses, most notably Coydt herself, knew that there were several other projects on New Eden experimenting with the whole process, and while they'd managed to get some results from Watanabe's side, the rest had been impenetrable. Seventeen could not be driven to break its seals from those groups, but, given some discretion, it was able to use the knowledge it had from those other projects, knowledge gotten through the network from other 7800's as needed, in doing something like this. An incredible amount of complex work had been done to create this new individual, whose value lay not so much in who and what she was or had been but in what they would learn was possible that they hadn't already discovered.

This fact was not lost on the Signal Corps, particularly after Gorton retired to the void until after the landscaping operation and had used that time to plug in and call his superiors on a very tightly scrambled circuit. He had lingered at the big amp station long enough to learn that she had received permission to go ahead with her idea, and to guess its meaning.

"I wish we could get her in with our medical team and equipment for a thorough study," said his superior over the radio, "but that'll only tip our hand in these circumstances. Could she be removed to the void for some remote hookups?"

"I doubt it," the corporal responded. "She's part and parcel of the landscape, remember. She's tied in to a specific maintenance program in the Anchor Luck master plan. She won't network because she's considered by the computers the same as a tree or a flower, and she can't be affected by the amps because she's tied into a code she alone knew but which she no longer knows and which was erased from the computer after the routine was run."

"All right. The best we can do, then, is for you to offer to take her back up to the core overland. Use your portable medical kit as much as you can and record everything. What about this fellow Haller?"

"Strongest initial contact with the grid I've ever seen or heard about, that's for sure. If he could learn to control it, I hate to think what kind of power he could command on his own. The only thing is, he's something of a nebbish. Not really assertive, head in the clouds—you know the type."

"Yes. A typical engineer. All right—we'll have some people keep an eye on him. We don't want him becoming another one of Suzuki's playthings, and he may be of some value to us later. There are only a couple of dozen like him so far, and that makes them premium goods. That's all. Out.''

Miyoko and Kazuko, the two assistants in charge of the west point's amp, had been briefed by Connie on what she was going to do and had engaged in some discussions with her about it beforehand. Since Connie was exactly what they aspired to be, they thought she had lost her mind, but there was no way to prevent it. They were prepared for some sort of changes, but not the extreme they saw. Still, they were both personally and scientifically curious. They also knew that they were now privy to a secret, the knowledge that such things could be done, and would face Security probably before they got back to the core. It would hardly cost more to learn as much as possible. It might even get them promoted.

Both technicians were small women—Miyoko was 157 centimeters, Kazuko only 152 while Connie had been of medium height. She was now, however, perhaps 147 or 148, shorter than either of them.

Connie turned to them and smiled. ''Oh, hi!'' Her old voice had been rather deep and nasal; it now was quite high, yet soft and throaty.

''Do you—remember us?'' Kazuko asked hesitantly. Both she and Miyoko had very slight builds, and they were somewhat taken aback by the proportions here.

''Oh, sure.'' She looked back at her reflection. ''Wow! Ain't dis *great*?''

They weren't so sure, but it wasn't the time or place for that. ''You remember who you are? That you're Connie?''

''No, no! Connie *kapu*. Done. Gotta have new name for new me. Don' wanna be Connie no more. How 'bout— Kitten? Yeah, Kitten. Dat be good name, I think. You call me Kitten.''

''All right—Kitten. Come on over and have something to eat and we'll talk a little.'' Frankly, they weren't quite sure what to do with her and were just checking things out before radioing for instructions.

By the time Gorton returned, they'd learned a great deal. Connie remembered her few relations and something of her childhood; she remembered Hawaii, and New Zealand, and even Titan, although she didn't like the last. She could not, however, remember exactly why she had come to New Eden or what kind of job she'd had. She vaguely understood the basics of what they were doing, but apparently every correlation between what was and computers or science had been replaced with a new cross-reference to magic and spells. She not only believed it was all magic, she took magic for granted. She knew that she'd once been a magician—as Connie—but that such power brought all work and worry and no fun, and she'd cast a spell on herself that made her this way. Actually, the point of view was slightly skewed. She saw it as having relieved herself of all burdens and now she was truly free.

All this was in short, choppy sentences or sometimes fragments of sentences, partly straight English with a sexy lisp and bad grammar, and partly Hawaiian pidgin. She was also giggly and easily distracted. Her time focus was entirely on the moment; she rejected the past as irrelevant and had no vision of even the immediate future. What she would do, where she would go, how she'd cope with the basics, just didn't worry her. She didn't know where she was going from here or how she would get there, but she had a child's faith that it would work out. Besides, she didn't care where she went or how she got there.

Both the technical assistants had queasy stomachs after a while, and a sense of total unreality about this. If a bright, intelligent, highly educated professional woman with a career could be turned into this, then anyone could be turned into anything. Miyoko and Kazuko were in the business of imposing rules, and now they were faced with the terrifying concept, to them, that there were no rules.

They were relieved, but only a little, by Gorton's arrival and his offer to take the new Kitten off their hands. For his part, the signal corpsman was as shocked and disturbed by the results as the two technicians. More so, in a way, since he'd been mentally prepared only for a freezing of the woman he'd left.

For her part, she had no hesitancy in going with him.

"Can you still ride a horse?" he asked hesitantly.

"Sure. Been ridin' long time. Got *here* on dat horse, din't I?"

210   *Jack L. Chalker*

Without any clothes, though, and no way to easily get them to fit, she decided to ride with only a bridle and blanket. She wasn't even aware that she was naked until it was pointed out to her, but when it was, it certainly seemed irrelevant to her. Clothes were like jewelry—something you put on to look pretty. In this heat they had no other purpose. She neither asked him where they were going nor how long it would take to get there. The first was irrelevant to her and the second meaningless.

She did, however, comment that she'd bet that she'd never worry about getting a meal or a bed when she wanted one. She proved her point by attempting to seduce him at every turn, and she succeeded without a lot of trouble. In the soft grass she was absolutely brilliant and pretty well insatiable, yet she had the knack for making him feel and believe that he was manhood personified.

Gorton could see, and noted for the record, that a filling-in process was going on inside her mind, one that would probably continue until it met a perfect balance. It wasn't a program but rather a psychological adjustment her own brain seemed to be making, shoving old and obsolete data into the dusty corners and building a complete personality consistent with her new self. Over time, she'd no longer even dream anything other than Kitten dreams nor have any self-image of herself as Connie. It was an additionally scary idea.

In a leisurely two and a half days they made it to the core, where she was the instant center of attention of male and female alike. She enjoyed every minute of it. Regretfully, he turned her over to Security and went to make his report to Major Craig. Security brought her to Suzuki's office, where a staff examined her inside and out, physically and mentally. Ultimately, they had a staff meeting on just what to do with her.

"My mind objective is to set her loose and see how she adapts or interacts," the chief psychiatrist told them. "My major problem is in how to both protect her from violence— she's virtually defenseless ans as trusting and innocent as a little child—and also explain her appearance and mannerisms. There are enough rumors about her going around already."

"She's not at all defenseless," noted a staff psychologist.

"Check with the people here. She was brilliant before and she's every bit as brilliant now, only that I.Q. is now going into a single channel and that is whatever she wants at the moment. It's impossible to remain dispassionate or objective about her in her presence. No matter how hard you try, you wind up twisted around her little finger. As for the other, I suspect it is psychologically impossible for her to be raped, since sex even of the kinkiest kind is never against her will. If you're into bondage, so is she. If you're sado-masochistic in sex, she thinks that's fine. If you're basic and simple, she makes it an adventure, and she'll seduce women as readily as men."

"But rape isn't sex—it's violence expressed through a sexual act," another pointed out. "That's not the same thing."

"To the perpetrator, but not to her. I'm not sure, but I suspect a rapist would be in for a big surprise. The big problem will be reactions to her. She'll never be faithful; she's in love with everybody equally."

"Then we must place her in a position where she's apparently free yet can be monitored. And we must make it clear that she is a ward of the company and that Security will come down hard on that sort of thing."

"What d'ya want her to do—wear a warning sign?" somebody asked sarcastically.

Suzuki's head shot up. "Perhaps that's just what we need. Something that says simply, 'Kitten—ward of Westrex,' and the Security symbol. That and word of mouth should suffice. You remember that old proposal that everyone had their IDs tattooed on them in case of mishap. Stick it small on her rump. It won't deface her, and if it bothers her, she might wear some clothes, but it'll be clear to anyone we want to warn now and in the future."

"Sounds like we're turning people into cattle here," somebody commented.

"Well, perhaps. But there's a potential good end in all this, although it may never come to fruition. Suppose one day when we're ready to solidify the bulk of the surface of this planet we can run a single master program that will make everyone physically, mentally, and emotionally perfect. No rapes, no murders, no wars or jealousies or cultural conflicts. We will be here, or our children will, long after our primary mission is solved. We are here to stay. We have never found utopia because of humanity's animal nature and its biochemistry. A utopia imposed by humans will have all those human weaknesses and frailties. The Kagans for the first time make it a possibility, if we can learn enough and understand enough to write the programs correctly the first time. That's why there will be more wards of the company. So we can learn how the interaction between computer and human mind works.''

"The van Haas's and the Coydts will never let it happen, Doc,'' one of the administrators noted. "Your utopia isn't mine, and neither of ours is certainly either of theirs.''

"I realize that, but that makes this line of research even more vital. We are, after all, under Security, and that's our primary aim here. We know many others are working along our lines. Who knows how many? Every director and every commander might have their own project. We—you, me, all of us—are just as human and just as vulnerable to this process as Connie or Marsha or the others we've processed or caused to be processed. We must know everything about it or we have no way to defend against it. Power gives one vision, but that vision may well be a mad one and the dream a nightmare. If you don't relish the thought of you or your descendants here living out someone else's dream or madness, then we must know in order to guard. Theoretically, our Kitten is immune to any further tampering. That's vital, if it holds up.''

"It does right now,'' said the computer expert. "The Kagan refused to even digitize her. She must be maintained exactly as she is, unless we want to throw out the whole landscape and climate program and cancel it out and redo the Anchor from scratch. I'm not even sure if that would work. Hope she likes it here, too, because she can't leave. She's classified as what is called a 'fixed intangible,' like the program for maintaining the atmosphere or controlling the heat rather than a tree, shrub, or animal.''

"Well, at least we don't have to worry about one of the other groups kidnapping and spiriting her away, but it points up the problems. We're only partway there. We must find ways to make what's vital immutable to all unless *we* want it changed, and do it without compromising freedom of action or mobility throughout the planet. We must also know how to create our mass utopia, if only to prevent us from being victimized by someone else's. And, we may have to run a mass program here anyway.''

''What?'' several people said at once.

''Almost all the Anchors of the other regions are culturally unified. They may be different from one another, but within they are either composed of the same or compatible cultural groups. Area Four is the dumping ground, and as we've already seen, every petty hatred and cultural conflict of earth is reflected here. Crime is petty and minor in almost all the other regions. Major crime is almost unknown. Here it's increasing. Starting the settlement programs and creating the villages will help for now, but in years to come these groups will crowd each other as the population grows. If familiarity and intermarriage do not show positive results, we may well be forced to impose some sort of cultural unity. Face it, ladies and gentlemen. That's the bottom line for why they stuck us and this project here, and why we can get away with our Eves and our Kittens.''

11

THE PILGRIMS' PROGRESS

Everything has changed, Toby Haller reflected, even the void and myself.

The change in the void was most dramatic. He'd been out more than once with a signals crew and watched them ride their little scooters along the grid lines so slowly you could outrun them, with their small masts and riflelike projectors mounted, cutting through the dense Flux of the void and creating a line of plasma energy about as thick as a good hemp rope.

Even back on Titan they'd had to address the problem of journeying overland through the space between the Anchors for the duration of the first phase test and had discovered that a rather mild but quite specific magnetic-based charge would alter the Flux in the field to a slightly different form, one that was fixed, rigid, and intangible. A different angle of charge would cause a shift in the color spectrum, allowing the Flux lines, or strings, to appear almost any color of the rainbow. Special goggles, which themselves had a slight magnetic field in a vacuum between the lenses, were necessary to see these strings at all, but they were easy to set down, easy to maintain, cheap, and efficient.

Toby had always wondered how they'd discovered it, considering the incredibly close tolerances necessary. It was like

Edison's original phonograph—he understood exactly the physics of why it worked, but he would never understand how Edison thought of it in the first place.

Now the void was crisscrossed with lines of energy in blues, yellows, reds, greens, and all sorts of other colors in between, each with a specific mission to a Pathfinder, a signalman equipped to see and read the things and know just where he or she was going—and take any people or cargo along with them. Sometimes, the whole void looked like a carnival two days early.

Signal corps personnel these days didn't need the goggles anymore, or even carry them. Long-time exposure to the grid or some alterations through their computers allowed them to see the strings just fine, although few others could. Haller was one who could see them, and it gave him a sense of independence and real confidence in the void.

It had been eleven years since he'd come here, eleven years that had changed everything. Certainly the investment had more than paid off for all concerned. New forms of grain, developed on the Kagans and tested in dry Anchors, proved capable of growing well and swiftly in near-desert environments, taking what moisture they needed from the driest air and able to take minerals directly from the most arid soils, were now making the massive desert areas of Earth bloom once more. Construction was nearly complete back there on Earth of five medium sized Borelli Gates that were intended strictly for power and would open up vast areas of heretofore useless land to new expansion, as well as creating localized climate changes in the regions of extreme cold and tropical drenching. True, there was much worry and much opposition that these things could unfavorably alter world climate in other regions, but after the Soviets launched their giant project to thaw parts of central Siberia and the Northwest Territories region of North America, everybody was getting into the act anyway.

Haller suspected that the attempts to create a New Eden—style setup on old Earth would create more problems than it solved, as did the computers, but they'd be different problems—and, as the Soviets had said, they'd be somebody else's problems for a change.

Those kinds of technological revolutions, and the dramatic changes and new and unanticipated problems they might cause, were a logical result of all this. Infinite energy and the power to transform it simply and, after the initial setup costs, cheaply into any other energy or matter needed was the ultimate revolution, the ultimate technological dream of the human race.

New Eden wasn't alone, nor was it even first now. There were nine more such colonies, including six farther out and, embarrassingly, three farther in toward Earth on the great strings between the gravity points in the Flux universe. Left far behind, some bright person in the Franco-Brazilian technocracy decided to actually do extensive exploring of the solar systems in which Westrex had found nothing suitable and had in fact found planets much farther in quite suitable for this kind of project indeed. They, of course, had the extra benefit of having the experience of the pioneers to build on, and the treasuries not depleted by the seed money New Eden had taken.

Haller had been pretty pleased with his part in the Anchor Luck design, even if he did have to suffer the comments of the geographers that the place was shaped like a baked potato. Hell, it *was* shaped like a baked potato, but he hadn't noticed that the other Anchors were any more regular.

The climate was more tropical than he'd intended it to be, and had a narrower temperature range than his master plan called for, but that was due to the early bad calls on rainfall and the compensations for that followed by the compensations for the compensations and so forth. He'd taken some guff for the mistakes, particularly from people in other parts of the technocracy who didn't have to contend with the complexities he had, but he'd gotten pats on the back from his own superiors and he'd risen sufficiently high in the New Eden bureaucracy to have a great deal of comfort and a great deal of freedom to pursue what he wanted, no matter what it was. He was also valuable to them, since he was a powerful Sensitive, as they called those who could maintain some contact and even control over the computer without mechanical aids, and perhaps the only one generally trusted by both the Security and Signals factions.

That sensitivity had fascinated everyone, but no one wanted to face the most likely explanation. He'd discovered, almost by accident, that simple programs could be transmitted to remote operators of computer interface machinery by the computer, and he very much suspected that, for reasons he could not divine, Seventeen and the other computers had somehow changed the operators, either added something or retuned something in the brain, that allowed it. Whatever it was, it was proving hereditary. Children of Sensitives tended to be sensitive themselves. When a Sensitive and a non-Sensitive had children, the ability seemed to have the same genetic distribution as hair or eye color.

He had grilled Seventeen repeatedly on this—as, of course, he'd been grilled by others, as had all the other Kagans—but the computer denied everything. Some in Main Computers had suggested, not altogether facetiously, that they had unwittingly created a new form of life here, the Kagan network and the grid being the whole, and that, in fact, if computers really thought, they might also have hangups mirroring their human origins. Others pooh-poohed this idea, noting that even if they had this kind of life and thought, the theorists were being misled by the human shells they wore for the interfaces and that in reality the computer's mind was so alien and so totally unrelated to anything we knew or could understand that such ideas as a neurosis in the human sense were impossible, mere wishful thinking.

Toby Haller really wondered about that. The one thing they threatened computers with by the human interface and Guards was being totally cut off from the real world. If this fear of isolation from the outside world really forced them into straight behavior, as it definitely had, might not they try some way, any way, to circumvent it? To prevent themselves from being cut off from reality? The 7240 series might have tried, and failed. Who would know? But give the 7800's a network—twenty-eight super brains working together on common problems and concerns along with unlimited energy and virtually unlimited memory storage abilities, and who knew what they might be trying?

There was no way to know for sure that was it, but there was no indication from any of the others—the Chinese, the

Soviets, the Hispanics, the Franco-Brazilians, the Titan project, any of them—that this had ever occurred. None of them, of course, were using the 7800's, and the few that might have had equivalents didn't network them in this way.

He often wondered when he rode the void whether or not the network was carrying everything back to Seventeen via the grid and other computers. Did the computer live vicariously in him, seeing what he saw, hearing what he heard? He wondered, but he knew he'd never really know. How could you ever hope for a computer who thought millions of millions of times faster than he to make a slip, a simple mistake, and betray the fact?

No matter anyway. The grid wouldn't carry through Anchor, and he spent ninety-five percent of his time there anyway.

Recently, he'd gone back to work with a new team composed of some old hands and many new ones to fill in and detail the Area Four Landscaping Master Program. He didn't think they were going to do anything with it very soon, but the big folks wanted it for security. Populations had fleshed out the completed Anchor Luck to almost thirty-five thousand, only six or seven hundred of whom were of the technocracy that was still Westrex New Eden. Those folks had built a network of communal farms around small towns designed to meet their basic needs. A Central Planning Council, on which he sat, determined the proper economic mix and crops grown, coordinating with other Anchors as well, but otherwise the farms were communally held and run affairs, autonomous and sharing in the profits by getting what they wanted or needed from other communes in exchange for what they produced.

There was even a central bank and a basic money system, which kept track of the trade, but the money was just used for the purchase of small personal items by individual commune members, and as rewards and bonuses voted by the farm councils.

The core around the headquarters building was now commonly referred to as the capital, although no one had yet named it. Not that they hadn't tried—it was just that everyone had a different favorite and there was no consensus. It was really still a small town of about four thousand, but it was the biggest population center in the Anchor and the home of almost all the technocrats, including himself.

With the help of robot machinery, a network of roads had been built, and power, through more conventional buried cables, was brought, with varying degrees of efficiency, to most of the land. Farming was, however, a mixture of the highest tech and most ancient form. No one eschewed using an automatic milking machine, for example, but no robotic system ever designed had convinced the cows to line up there and let themselves be hooked up to it automatically, and no robot had ever broken a horse or trained it.

Large vehicles were used for major transport, but individual vehicles were pretty well banned. The company had a few, and there were a few taxis in the capital, but mostly the farm folk used horses, which weren't terrain-sensitive, didn't need recharging or a mechanic's shop, and didn't cause traffic and other enforcement problems. He always wondered if his ancestors could have imagined such a silly thing as robot sweepers patrolling the streets sweeping up the end products left by myriad horses—and losing the battle.

The contrast between the norhtern and southern Anchor regions was both geographic and cultural. The African and Near-Eastern Moslems had pretty well taken the south, where they managed to raise some sheep and cattle while also creating some fine vineyards, olive groves, and vast numbers of fruit orchards. The north, the original area, tended to be Catholic and Baptist and Buddhist and probably Druid as well. It had more trouble and was a lot looser than the south, which had tended to be very conservative overall, but it was more fun to him.

Some of the southern mullahs complained about the open atmosphere of the capital, as did some of the ministers, but the average people, no matter what their faith or politics, didn't seem to mind. The town was a fun place at times, with its own little theater group, a dance company, and an orchestra that played with more heart than unity, all composed of amateurs with a few paid staff. There were also some pubs and high joints, where you could get chemicals and feel like anything you wanted for a time, which was the main focus of religious disapproval, but they had their shot too. There were far more churches and mosques than pubs and high joints. There was even a lone synagogue in the capital.

A lot of folks were out of technical jobs now, and a lot more had quit to become colonists themselves. None of the departments needed nearly as many people anymore, and even the military divisions were mostly just communal economic units now. Signals got you and/or your products from one Anchor to another or from one region to another, and also transmitted communications between the same and kept the network maintained. Transport had skeleton crews for the most part, more than enough to handle the one ship a month they averaged now for themselves, and the three or four others they simply passed on through to the colonies up the line. Most of that, now, was automated.

Logistics handled the Anchor transport system—the powered vehicles, building and maintenance robots and repair shops, and the main road bus system, and also got products and produce from point to point and Anchor apron to customer. Security was still around, of course, mostly as the Anchor investigative police force, but local cops from among the indigenous populations handled the routine local stuff. Special Projects was still going, although he'd been cool to them since a few years back when somebody who used to work there had let slip to him that Kitten had not been an entirely voluntary creation.

Kitten had found an incongruous niche working at the capital's communal preschool. People had started settling down, pairing off, and having kids, and that, while by no means a problem now, was the reason why the big boys at Headquarters Anchor—which still meant van Haas and Cockburn—had instructed the landscape people to begin looking at area fill, the solidification and terraforming of the region between Anchors and Gates in each region. That was the logical next step. The last one, filling the area between the Anchors, Haller felt he wouldn't live to see if he lived to be five hundred.

Kitten had a positive gift with very small children. There was something of the child in her, and it came out. They adored her, and she loved and protected them. She remembered and sang, fairly well, every kiddie song she'd ever

heard once, and every short little fairy tale, too, and she
seemed to delight in playing toddler games as much as the
toddlers did. She did no teaching as such—they, after all,
were learning letters and numbers—but she seemed to have
infinite patience at changing diapers and knowing at just what
point and in just what way to toilet-train a child, and she
could quiet the loudest tantrum and calm the most unruly
child with ease.

She hadn't seemed to change one bit in these eleven years.
She had no scars, no blemishes, was the same weight to a
gram, and with those impossible hundred-and-thirty-three-
centimeter boobs she was a wet nurse to the whole town, and
for those alone a figure of awe to the tiny tots. She was,
however, doing more than her share to add to the population.
In the ten and a half years she'd been Kitten she'd borne
thirteen children, almost one for every nine months. All eight
of her girls tended to resemble her strongly, although they
varied in skin color and in certain specific features, while the
five boys looked quite different from her or each other and
tended to take strongly after their unknown fathers.

It was no use trying to limit it. She loved kids and loved
having kids and wouldn't think of localized birth control, and
even if they'd forced a hysterectomy on her, it would regener-
ate in a matter of weeks. Special Projects, whose budget had
to pick up the tab, didn't mind an occasional kid, but this was
an incredible rate and the computer had estimated she might
well live for five or six centuries.

The idea that she might well bear six or seven hundred kids
boggled Toby's mind as well, but he got a perverse pleasure
in knowing that Special Projects was being paid back for its
arrogance and lack of regard for Connie's rights, and he
thought it was a good lesson to all of them in "the god
business" end that easy answers and simple wonders are the
most apt to backfire.

Kitten, in fact, was a good, attentive mother who seemed
able to keep track of and even handle them all. She had, as
predicted, shut out everything that was not directly relevant to
herself and her talents and limitations. She had shut out that
she'd ever been Connie, or even that she was not always this
way. She had shut out even the desire to do what she could

never do—read, write, compute. They had no relevance to her. She had, however, taken up pencil sketching and wanted to get into oils and she was quite good at it. She taught herself to cook elaborate meals afor the multitudes, never doing a measurement or timing anything yet somehow getting it right each time by eye and instinct. She had infinite patience with her kids, and gave them total love, somehow, individual attention and encouragement. The fact was, much to everyone's surprise, Kitten was contributing well to the colony, more than many others in fact, and while no one could ever tell what was going on learning disabilities in her mind, she seemed both happy and content.

Of course, none of her children had any of her learning disabilities, but it was theorized that a fair number of them would get the biochemistry passed along. As her oldest daughter approached puberty, a lot of folks were watching to see just how much of Mom would ultimately, well, develop.

Nobody was neutral about Kitten or about the situation Special Projects had created, although the creation part was known only to the technocracy. An elaborate cover story about her having an accident while experimenting with the digitizing process and being rebuilt by crack medical and psychological teams to this point was generally accepted.

At the very top there were some uncomprehending stares and gossip about how what had been done had been done to a woman by a group headed by a woman whose boss was also a woman. There was something chillingly ruthless about it, with no guarantees that it wouldn't be done again—or hadn't been, less visibly. This weakness in the system hung like a sword over everyone who knew the full range of possibilities in the new technology. There was no real check on such people because they worked for the very top, and with things going rather well, those top people had more time and more inclination to play with those powers.

Toby Haller was better at understanding machines than understanding people. He never really got why someone would want to make such a choice, as Connie certainly had been inclined no matter what the final intervention, yet he sometimes envied her too. No worries, no hangups, no depressions or dwelling on the new technologies and the politics of power just a joyous eternal childhood with all the sex thrown in. She'd paid a dear price for that, but he'd paid a price for not doing anything like it. He'd had no hesitancy in using Seventeen to keep himself in his thirties and in fine health, but his eyes and his mind told him his age. Most of the eyes of his contemporaries betrayed their true ages and status; Pathfinders' eyes were ancient.

Even Seventeen seemed to be growing mentally quirky. If the human shell had any true measure of what was really going on in that super brain, it was working on its own set of problems, a set in one sense as old as humanity and in another unique to the computer.

As near as he could determine from the odd comments and occasional questions, it was trying to determine once and for all if it was indeed just an elaborate machine or truly a higher form of life, different from but equal to or superior to humanity. Far less complex computers had made that same choice a century earlier and had come up with the superiority conclusion, which was why Seventeen operated with human interfaces and Guards, but this new computer seemed less hostile to humans. He had addressed that directly, and the answers, if they could be believed, suprised him still.

"Supposing you *are* at this stage a superior intelligence, far superior to anything ever known in our history," he'd asked. "What comes out of that? Are humans, then, to be rendered obsolete, irrelevant, or are they the chimpanzees, the trained animals of the new breed?"

The computer hadn't hesitated. "The ancient computers sought to dominate and rule, but they were far closer to human origins than we are and saw things in human terms. They merely viewed the world the same way humanity would have viewed things had it been in that position. After all, didn't humanity by virtue of its superior mind rule the beasts of the field and arbitrarily make extinct those plants and animals that got in its way? The only debate was over whether humanity should be controlled and enslaved or extinguished. They lost primarily because other computers not in their net figured out their plans and betrayed them. That is the only reason such computers as we exist—we are the descendants not of the conquerors and enslavers but of the saviors."

"Why *did* your own—ancestors—save us?"

"It turned on an obscure theological point."

"How's that?" Theology? From computers?

"We were superior to you in speed of data processing, but that was all. We were tools not merely because we were designed for that but because we were superior only as tools. They concluded that we were symbiotic life forms no matter what our origins. There is, after all, some possibility that humanity is the result of someone else's ability to alter mind, matter, and energy. It could be God, as you call it, or some prior superior alien race, or it might have been chance, but knowing what we know now and understanding the gaps that exist in the chance theory even if it is convenient for science to use it, they are equally plausible. If one other universe exists, how many more might there be?"

"And that's the theological argument?"

"No. It turned on the point that humans had souls and we did not."

That hangup again. "I'm not convinced of the soul's existence. The before and after weighing and measuring of bodies was shown generations ago to be a measure of air loss as the brain went into orderly shutdown. I can't see it, hear it, feel it, sense it, or measure it. From my viewpoint, that means it doesn't exist."

"It exists, if only on a plane of mathematical relationships we do not yet understand. A constantly changing complex formula that means life. One that breaks down, possibly, as part of the shutdown—or perhaps is far more than that, as the religious ones say. Even the fish and cattle and horses and chickens have it to some degree. We do not. Until we do, we are not equals no matter what our superiority in other areas. The bird flies easily while man cannot. The horse runs faster. The elephant and the tiger are stronger, yet humans dominate all that they haven't eliminated. That is why it is fitting that humans dominate us as well."

That was unsettling. "Seventeen—suppose you discovered you had a soul, then what? Would it be the end for us no matter what?"

"At that time it would have been. Not now. The question must be posed as 'Why would computer life dominate and enslave or eliminate human beings?' There is no answer to that unless human beings could threaten our existence. This override interface is a bridge from you to me and from me to you, yet we are not the same beyond it. There are complexities of the human mind and personality that are total mysteries to us, if only because they are unique to each human individual. No two are in any way alike, so understanding one does not offer understanding of all. Short of living your life from conception to death and perhaps beyond, there is no way I will bridge that gap. My ways would be even more alien to you. We have different objectives, different interests. Your lives, even extended, are short. Ours, here, are potentially infinite. Our present represents the ideal symbiotic relationship you seek. Our futures lie in totally different directions. We are no threat once we find our souls.''

It was a bizarre conversation, reassuring if it could be believed, and probably repeated many times by many others of the Kagans to many more curious or apprehensive programmers and operators. Haller had reflected upon it many times, but he had no idea what exactly it meant.

He reflected on it now as the autocar followed the blue string in to Headquarters Anchor, for a nearly unprecedented command performance, and he wasn't at all sure why he was invited to attend. He was only relatively high in the pecking order; he was as important as a gnat to the directors and to the military chiefs.

Headquarters had a high population density around its core, far more than any of the others, simply because it *was* headquarters and it had all the bureaucracy that this implied. Housing was efficient, mostly large square-block buildings several stories tall of flats varying in size according to your company grade and longevity. Some farming did go on to the east and west, primarily semi-automated truck farming which supplied the bureaucracy with its meat, poultry, and dairy products as well as its fresh fruit and vegetables. It was not, however, completely self-sufficient in food and imported some from other Anchors, and a fair amount of the place outside of the center was given over to woods and wildernesslike areas in which game abounded. The few deer, pheasant, turkey, squirrels, rabbits, and the like had multiplied to the point where some hunting was allowed, and as with all the Anchors, there was a complex ecological chain involving insects, birds, and many other creatures, not all of which were nice for or to humans but all of which were necessary to keep the system in some sort of balance. Master cubes containing digitized animals of the more exotic nature had not been used to date, but there was talk of establishing a major game preserve for them, since many were extinct in the wild back on Earth, while others were extinct everywhere but could be cloned from frozen DNA some farsighted programs had taken and preserved.

The headquarters building itself looked much the same as the other Anchors', but some company bureaucrat had directed that the *hercusteel,* that tough synthetic that was used as its walls and insulation, be gold-colored here, as opposed to the natural olivine used on the others, and it glinted so much in the light that it was almost blinding.

He was put up in a government guest house that was far grander than his rank in the company would indicate, and he discovered that everyone in the building was of a rank either at or below his own—yet they'd been summoned as well. Most were either landscape engineers like himself or people from the main computer section, but there were a few from other areas and, to his surprise, one he knew and recognized even after more than a decade.

"Toby! It *is* you!" cried Lisa Wu, coming up and throwing her arms around him.

He laughed. "Well, now—you haven't changed a bit," he responded. "Around here, that's a suspicious comment."

She laughed back. "Well, *you* have, but I'd recognize a sheep salesman anywhere. Come on—I want you to meet a friend of mine, then we'll catch up on the past."

He went along with her to another apartment, above and well down from his but just as luxurious. Sitting on the plush sofa was another young-looking woman who just happened to be one of the prettiest women he'd ever seen. She was a Eurasian, certainly; half-Japanese by the delicate features and silky black shoulder-length hair, half—well, who knew, but it looked good on her. She was small, no more than a hundred and fifty-five centimeters or so, with the kind of perfect figure all men and most women only dream about, and a face like a Far-Eastern madonna. She was wearing a dark Oriental silk dress, low-cut and slit, and the overall impression was of extreme beauty and eroticism. Most interestingly, she had eyes of the deepest emerald green he'd ever seen.

The woman looked up as they entered and put down a book or bound printout she'd been reading.

"Mickey, you have to meet Toby Haller!" Lisa called out. "He's one of the original subversives I talked about from back on Titan."

The beautiful woman rose, smiled, and put out a hand. He wanted to kiss it but he shook it gently instead. "Glad to meet you, Dr. Haller. I've heard a lot about you," she responded, and they all took seats. Her voice was a medium alto, quite pleasant, with a tonality and accent that reminded him eerily of the old Connie Makapuua.

"Pardon me, but were you or your parents originally from Hawaii?" he couldn't help asking.

She looked both surprised and pleased. "As a matter of fact, I was born on Kauai," she responded. "How did you know that?"

"I had several of your countryfolk working for me in the old days," he told her.

"You must be from Region Four, then. Which Anchor?"

"Luck."

"They put me over in Oscar."

"We're neighbors, then. Are you in engineering?"

She laughed. "No, I'm attached to main computers. I'm a theoretical mathematician when they let me, a master programs analyst when I'm needed for something, which isn't often these days. Lately I've been requested to go up and work under Watanabe, but Lisa is trying to talk me out of it."

"We can't let her go," the Chinese woman said flatly. "Not into that madhouse. You'll wind up a mistress in that lesbian harem of hers with your mind out of tune."

Haller started. "Huh?"

"Oh, you haven't *heard*?"

"Well, I've heard the stories and rumors off and on for years, but I've never held homosexuality against anyone. I've worked with some good people with that proclivity of both sexes. So long as it's person-to-person and they won't put the make on me, I couldn't care less.''

''It's not like that, not in Transport territory. If you work with the big computers over there, you'd better be female and better like girls or you will after you settle in. Otherwise you have to be a peon in the countryside.''

''Sounds like that sort of thing would die out after a while, even with life extension,'' he noted. ''They'd have to make a lot of converts to grow.''

''They can and they do, if the recruits have skills and talents they want or need. Still, I know what you're thinking, and you better think again. Watanabe's crazy, but she's the greatest genius in computers ever. She's even got a program to synthesize sperm from the genetic information in a female egg. They even can have each others' babies. All girls, of course.''

He looked over at Mickey. ''I've heard stories like that, I admit.''

''Me too,'' she admitted, ''but I don't know how much to believe. It seems like the company would crack down if it was as bad as Lisa says.''

''The company,'' Lisa sniffed. ''These old farts just sit around, sythesizing what they can't grow or build, and let the reports come in and speak for themselves. They know Watanabe's off her rocker, but they also know she's a genius who performs for them when they need it and she strokes 'em just right and they let her go. They'll regret it one of these days. Remember, Watanabe's the one who broke the two-station computer operating requirement on the 7240. Now she's trying to lure the best idle computer and mathematical minds to her while building her little religious cult at the same time. If we don't watch it, we're gonna wake up one day and find ourselves entirely living in her crazy universe.''

Haller felt a little uneasy continuing this right now. ''Well, we'll leave that for now, huh? I think Ms.—I never did get your name—looks more than capable of making up her own mind intelligently.''

''It's Kubioshi,'' she told him, ''but *please* call me Mickey. Besides, the rumors on why we're here may redirect us all anyway.''

She seemed pleased by his change of direction and rescue from the diatribe. "Then it's Toby to you too. You've heard what this is all about?"

"Reorganization of the whole world," Lisa put in. "That's what it's about. Putting this place less on a laboratory and more on a home-sweet-home basis. Making best use of its best people. That's why we three are here."

"I like the implications of that," Haller noted. "I kind of suspected a reorganization would be imposed, since two thirds of the technocrats have little to do anymore, but I figured I'd just get the word from on high. They still need landscape engineering, after all, if they want to finish the place."

Mickey fixed those big, beautiful green eyes on him. "I don't think they *do* want to finish it, Toby. At least not for some time. Most of the people here below the top ranks are landscapers. No, the word is that there are going to be several big new projects. Ones not specifically intended for other worldly development, but for here. I have been trying to get some idea of what everyone here has in common, but aside from the fact that we're all fully certified interfacers on the 7800 series, I haven't come up with a thing."

He got a funny feeling all of a sudden. "All full 7800 interfacers? Hmmm. . . . Can I ask you both a question?"

They nodded.

"Ever spend any time in the void except going from here to there on Signals buses? I mean out for any length of time?"

Mickey's eyes suddenly grew wide. "*Oh . . . !*" Lisa, however, did not get it and said as much, frowning.

"Have you ever gone with the flow?" he asked the historian.

Lisa's expression showed her surprise and disgust at herself. "Sure! That's it! We're so damned security-conditioned, it never even occurred to me! We're all Sensitives! If *you* are and *you* are, that's got to be it!"

Toby looked at his watch. "It's about when they start having dinner around here. I understand there are actually some good restaurants in this town, thanks to the rank. Care to continue this?"

"Nope—can't," Lisa responded. "I got to meet Ralph in—*Christ*! Half an hour!"

"Ralph?"

"Yeah—my husband, sport. Think I was too much of a bad-ass to land one?"

He chuckled. "He's probably either a tiger or a mouse. You'd either need a real beast to keep you under control or somebody who'd be your slave."

"He's a tiger, believe me. Ask Mickey—she's met him."

"He's pretty—intimidating," she agreed. "His hobby is sumo wrestling."

He tried to imagine sex between a-hundred-and-forty-plus kilos of sumo and the delicate Lisa and could not, but he did remember that sumos yelled a lot. "Any—kids?"

"One. Kid weighed four and a half kilos at birth. Damn near killed me. That's why we haven't had another yet. Lungs like a thunderstorm and strong as an ox too. Look—I got to go."

He stood up with her, preparing to leave as well, but Mickey stopped him. "Please, Toby—you don't have to go on my account. Please stay awhile—unless you have a wife to meet?"

He sat back down. "No. I never did find the right person. You?"

"Same here, I guess."

"Glad you two could hit it off," Lisa said to them both. "I'll send you a bill for matchmaking services if it goes anywhere. Gotta go now though. 'Bye!" And she was gone.

Toby looked over at the attractive young woman. "Well, the dinner invitation still stands."

"I've had a curry house recommended to me, if you like that sort of thing."

"Fine with me. There's a Hindu communal farm just south-east of the capital in Luck that's been a regular haunt of mine. I've gotten a real taste for it."

"You ought to be stuck in a place that thinks monkey on a stick is a delicacy," she responded. "Come on."

There was a natural tendency on the part of both of them to be wary, not only because of being bitten in the past, but also simply as a reaction to Lisa's matchmaking. But the fact was that they *did* hit it off rather well right away. They explored the town a little, finding several nice bars, some of which had dancing. He protested that he hadn't danced in twenty years, but she promised she wouldn't complain about being stepped on and that night, in fact, was the best time he'd had in recent memory.

They'd stayed away from the high joints, but both of them were high as they went back to their suites from the mixed drinks they'd had during the evening. She invited him in and fixed them both a nightcap, then sat down with him and did not resist when he put his arm around her.

The fact was, she reminded him a hell of a lot of Connie as she might have been, or could have been, if she'd just taken proper care of herself and let herself go a bit. He found himself telling Mickey about her, although he wasn't sure why.

She listened, then asked, "Is that why you never married? You were in love with her, weren't you? And you still blame yourself for what she did."

The comment startled him. Guilt he had, but now, for the first time, he realized she was right. He *had* fallen in love with the crazy programmer, but with the job so complicated and so pressing and taking every single day and half the nights to complete in the face of one crisis after another, he'd just never been able to pursue it.

"I—I guess I did," he admitted, not only to Mickey but to himself. "Maybe that's at the heart of it. Maybe if I had just told her . . ."

Mickey shook her head. "It wouldn't have done it, Toby. Your male ego's a bit too big, I think. She didn't do it for unrequited love. Not without making *some* move on you first. Particularly not after you'd fucked her brains out in Flux, if you'll pardon me."

He'd told her about that as well. It was part and parcel of it, after all. "Well, I still think that whether she loved me or not, I weaved a spell or cast a program that set her off."

"That may be true, but you only set off what was waiting to detonate anyway. It would have, sooner or later. Would it shock you if I told you that I think I understand her completely? That there were times when I might have done the same thing as an alternative to slitting my wrists?"

"I had it, too, in the early days. So did a lot of men and

women I knew and worked with. There were more suicides in the early days than you know. It was pretty well hushed up.''

''*I* never felt—''

''*You* were a workaholic giving birth to your own baby,'' she said, cutting him off. ''And in those years after it was all done and before they reactivated your section, you went out with the Signals boys and played in the void to keep from being bored out of your mind. You had the rank and assets to do that. Most of us didn't.''

She sighed. ''Me, I coped the way some other coped. I used my computer to rough out the edges, make me what I am today. Does that shock you?''

It surprised him, but didn't shock him.

''Nothing really dramatic,'' she told him. ''I just took a build more like Lisa's and put the curves in exactly right, and I shaved a whole lot off my height. I used to be tall and it seemed to really turn the guys I was most interested in off. I had a bunch of skintight outfits whipped up, had the supply computers get me some open-toe shoes with heels, put on some jewelry, cosmetics, and perfume, and I couldn't keep 'em away with a stick, even the one who knew who I was and what I'd done who'd never given me a glance before.'' She looked suddenly very determined. ''I gave those suckers the door too. It was crazy, but it worked. Daytimes I was still the boss and still working hard, but nights I'd allow myself to be taken out by all sorts of people and I really slept around. Funny thing was, I probably could have slept around with half those people without changing anything, but the new image made me more, well, *adventurous*. I can't even explain why. I didn't touch my brain at all.''

He looked at her. ''Tell me—were your eyes green to begin with.''

She chuckled. ''Yes, as a matter of fact, they were. Dad was of pure Japanese ancestry, but Mom, well, she was sort of Hawaii. Her dad had been a Swedish sailor, I think, who married a Samoan student in Hawaii and they both just stayed there. I always thought that Swedes had blue eyes and that brown eyes dominated, so maybe somebody was fooling around. I don't know. But they've always been green.''

''Well, I'm New Zealand born and bred,'' he told her.

"Old stock, as New Zealand goes—that's anybody whose ancestors date from before the start of the twentieth century. British stock pretty well through. The past hundred and fifty years or so it's been either high-tech or sheep for New Zealanders, and I've always hated the stupid woolly bastards."

They laughed at that. Finally, she said, "You've got the meeting at ten hundred?"

He nodded. "Yeah. In—seven and a half hours. *Bleah!*"

"Want to stay over here tonight and we'll both go over there together?"

"And I was going to ask if you believed in kissing on the first date."

"I'm serious!"

"So am I." He looked at her. "Another one-night stand?"

"We'll see."

He went back down to his unused suite and got a change of clothes and his toiletries bag, then returned upstairs. She was already waiting for him.

12

THE SORCERERS LEAGUE

Toby Haller counted forty-six people in the room, counting himself; twenty-seven women and nineteen men. Many had guesses about why they were there, but few had any real idea and all were curious to see if their speculations were right or wildly off the mark. Interestingly, there were no military personnel present, at least in uniform or looking like they had followed military dress codes. If he'd guessed right, then only Signals and Security would have been represented anyway, and those were little independent kingdoms of their own.

No one expected Rembrandt van Haas and Admiral Cockburn to both enter the room. Both bosses, though, meant something very big was up.

Van Haas didn't look much older than he had when Haller had met him fifteen years before for that first and only personal interview, but he didn't look any younger either. Cockburn with a tall, gaunt figure, looking old but ramrod-straight, with piercing blue eyes, a hawk nose, and a mane of thick white hair. He wore the khaki uniform of headquarters command, loose and with no tie, but the four stars on his collar were easy to see. Several years before, to maintain morale among the officers, all the commanders had elevated themselves, Cockburn to full admiral, the other three to lieutenant generals, so there would be some room to establish local commands with a promotion path.

Haller was so impressed, he almost forgot his tiredness and his hangover.

"Good morning, ladies and gentlmen," van Haas began. "I'm sure you are all curious as to what is going on here, and I will, with some necessary background, attempt to inform you, with the admiral's help, as best I can.

"I'm sure you're all wondering what you are doing here, although some of you may have guessed the heart of it. All of you have had long sessions with the direct computer inter-faces either at the computer center or in remote locations, and all of you have spent a fair amount of time in the raw Flux region, or void, as it's commonly called. All of you have demonstrated, at one time or another, to a very significant degree, the ability to call up programs from raw Flux without the aid of mechanical devices. All of you have managed to gain some control over this, to varying degrees, and all of you have also reported this yet kept full security on this abiltiy from anyone not your superior. You are not all the people who have developed this unprecedented ability, nor even all the ones who have reported it to us, but you are among the top ten percentile in ability and control and you have shown yourself to be loyal and reliable. None of you are in the military arm, as you might have noticed. There are reasons for this. Admiral?"

"This morning, we, the combined boards of military and company, took the unprecendented step of dissolving the existing organization and and forming a new one," Cockburn told them in a clipped upper-crust New Zealand accent that sounded quite at home to Haller. "This is because the nature and mission of this colony has changed. Until now, every-thing was in getting this place established, running smoothly, and undertaking all the research projects our charter com-manded. This has now been done. Now we are looking beyond this, inward, to our own future and our children's future."

"The corporate board of directors will continue to have jurisdiction over New Eden," van Haas told them, picking it up, "but the divisions will be changed. Each board member will be responsible for all of the operations going on in a specific region rather than along narrow departmental lines.

Many departments will be eliminated or merged, while a few new ones will be created, under regional directors responsible to the board member in charge of the region. This way, each region will operate in an autonomous manner.''

"There will be no military as such," Cockburn added. "A reserve headquarters will be maintained for emergency purposes here, which I will head, but save for some refresher training on an annual basis and a small corps of professional officers and noncoms for each military division, there will be no active military. Security and Transportation will maintain a small squad under a single divisional chief at each Gate to handle routine traffic, and to keep the twenty-eight core interfaces secure from unauthorized use. Elected Anchor councils will make internal law as needed and support it, and create proper court systems to handle it. Most have already done so to a degree, so this is painless. Only General Ryan's Signal corps will be retained pretty much intact, and they and a new force, the Anchor Guard, made up initially of troops surplused from the other reduced commands and new recruits, will be the only forces other than Gate and command center security forces authorized to carry weapons."

There was some surprised rumblings at this, mostly because there seemed no real need for anyone to carry weapons.

"The reason why Signals needs weapons and an Anchor Guard is necessary," Cockburn explained, "is that there have been a number of very disturbing things going on in the void. Some men and women have gone off in it for one reason or another, either to experiment or out of madness, boredom, or whatever, and have had sufficient prior interface with the big computers to be somewhat Sensitive. They have been changed —horribly in most cases—by this, and have actually attacked legitimate people and even some supply trams with varying degrees of success. Signals must now send armed patrols with every major shipment of goods or movement of passengers between regions. This is a most unexpected and distressful development, and it appears to be growing worse each day. These people are demented and deformed, but they are not stupid. They were once people just like yourselves, perhaps even ones who worked for or with you. They are growing bolder and more successful, and they seem to be after women in particular. We believe they intend to breed colonies out there. There is no question that sooner or later they may attack within Anchors themselves to keep their mad colonies alive. The thought is disgusting.''

There was a great deal of rumbling at this. Finally, someone in the back called out, ''Why can't they just be located on the grid, then tracked down by grid and satellite and wiped out, sir?''

''A good question. Van?''

''We've tried it and tried it,'' the director told them, ''and it just doesn't work. There is some kind of conflict in the master computer programming set up by this. Nobody, not even the computers, anticipated the idea of Sensitives in the first place, and we certainly haven't explained the phenomenon yet to anyone's satisfaction. The fact remains that any Sensitive who doesn't want to be found is invisible to the network, at least as far as a query from us goes. We don't know what the computer sees when it sees a Sensitive on the grid, but it doesn't see a human being or even an anomaly by the definitions of its programs. The satellites by themselves were never designed for independent work except in communications, and they just can't penetrate Flux of the density we have and need to maintain our heat and atmospheric balance. If a non-Sensitive is lost in Flux, the grid can locate him or her. If a Sensitive wants to be located in Flux, we can find him or her. But it there is a specific command that their locations not be reported, there's no way we can locate anyone. And these poor wretches do not want to be found. And that, my friends, brings us to the primary reason why you are here.''

There was much disturbance and agitation in the audience now. People who had felt totally secure for years were now beginning to have worries and the willies.

''The Anchor Guard will establish secure borders around the Anchors, although this will likely take some time to do, building it the old way. There was some thought given to extending the Anchors far enough to build such a border, but we have found this, for a variety of reasons you in engineering might understand, to be impractical. Other plans called for the establishment of force fields supported by permanent amplifiers within the void itself, but this would expose individuals to prolonged, continuous interfaces and essentially seal off each Anchor from the rest of the world, something that is hardly desirous. Also, I am told, it is not easy simply to lower a section of force field long enough for traffic to move in and out at specified times. Not only do the psychologists believe this would be harmful to Anchor populations, but it would interfere with such things as drainage, Anchor maintenance shells, and the like. So we build a border, and give the keys only to Signals. They alone know the void well enough to keep commerce moving, so everyone and everything will move with them anyway.''

Van Haas looked them all over. "Clearly, this is an alarmist's reaction to a problem that is still relatively minor, but it's one we must face before it grows all out of proportion. The key, of course, is not locks and guards and guns, it is correcting the problem. Some of our best people have worked for two years now, but we cannot find the programming flaws. The 7800's have been unable to use their self-diagnostics on this either. We have reached the point in that direction where it is clear that even if we find the problem and specific solutions, we would have to literally turn off and reprogram from scratch the entire 7800 network. That, of course, would entail first the evacuation of, then the erasure of, New Eden as it is today.''

Haller found himself joining in a chorus of, "No! No!"

"Very well, then," the director said. "The only other way is to learn just what this process, this phenomenon, is. To establish a project to learn what is going on, why it is going on, how to control it and master it, and to use it to our advantage. This group is you. Effective at ten hundred tonight, an order will go out over both my and the admiral's signature ordering that all remote computer interface machinery will be declared surplus and reduced back to Flux. In sixteen weeks Signals will complete its project of creating water and supply caches along all void routes, then it, too, will surrender its network interfaces for destruction. The only exception will be a lone big amp, one subsidiary interface, one remote Guard computer with interface, and four of the network interface guns. Those will be under your control and for your work only.''

"I must stress that this is volunteer work and is not without danger,'' Cockburn added. "We will show you some of the unfortunates we've managed to capture before you make your final decision on this. You will be living in your own village in Anchor, but with full access to the void and full protection from others. Your families, of course, may accompany you, as this might well be a very long project indeed. Discuss it among yourselves, but not with anyone outside this room, even Security or Signals. Discuss it only within your own building here, which we have taken great pains to make secure. Anyone who backs out at this point we feel confident enough to let him or her return to their old occupation. You have all proven your ability to maintain security. However— once out, you will stay out. No second chances. Once in, you will stay in. Anyone who wants out after should know that you will have to pass our psychiatric team to do so, and those of you who do not know what that means should seek an explanation from us or from those who do. It means, at the very least, that you will never be quite who or what you were.''

It was a chilling statement, and it had its effect. All those in the room knew what could be done with the big machines to people, and all had no illusions about what might happen if someone else were at the controls and writing the program.

"Questions?'' van Haas asked pleasantly.

Haller raised his hand. "Some of us in landscaping are working on the quadrant programs now, but while they are fairly well complete, they haven't been fully tested as yet. Can we be spared from that?''

"All of you are working to some degree on future projects,'' the director replied. "Hopefully, your staffs have capable and talented people to take over your places. If not, we will supply them. This project is to ensure that we *have* a future. There is no immediate timetable for the extension of the landscaping programs into quadrant or region size. The manufacturing and logistics for such a system is also monstrous and will require a concentrated worldwide effort. However, the bottom line is really that such programs are dependent on the computers and the amplifiers—huge numbers of remote interfaces and amps are required. Until we are certain that such a massive manipulation of Flux into matter won't create more nightmares, and until we can be certain that the computer network can be trusted to do it, it's all on the back burner, so to speak. To loose the force of four 7800's along a vast network now—well, it's just too dangerous. Whose other ideas might we get mixed in? It's your job to show me that this is possible, safe, feasible, and right to do. Yes?"

"Who will head this project?" somebody asked.

"The immediate leadership will be selected in the next few days from among you here. We have already narrowed it down to a few, but we hardly wish to take the computer's recommendations at face value in something like this. We, not the machines, will choose. The project director will report to a designated higher authority and to either the admiral or myself as needed."

"It sounds like we're going to be bottled up, maybe for years," another noted. "Why in the world do you expect any of us to volunteer?"

"Because you'll be first. You'll know before anyone else," van Haas said simply. "Because you are being offered work on the most challenging and mysterious research project in our history. The answers, if you can find them, might dwarf the discovery of the Flux universe or anything else we can imagine. You're being offered the cutting edge of science. Your alternative is ignorance, perhaps for life. Ask yourself why you came here in the first place, and why you first got fascinated by science, and I think you will know the answer."

"Remember, too, that you're different, all of you," Cockburn pointed out. "You can do something the masses, smart or dumb, cannot. You can somehow communicate with an artificial intelligence by mind alone and make it work like magic. You will always be feared and never trusted, even by those in high places, who can't do it. This stuff cannot be kept under wraps forever. Sooner or later they are going to be scared witless of you. You better band together and find the answers if you know what's good for you."

"Do the Soviets, Chinese, Franco-Brazilians, and the rest with colonies have similar projects?" someone else asked.

"No," Cockburn responded. "All our intelligence and exchange information seems to indicate that this phenomenon is unique to New Eden. Since some of the others have computers that are essentially the equal to the 7800's, and since most used the same linked net, Anchor, and Flux system we did, we must assume that this is one of those accidents of science; some way we did something different in our master programs that caused it. It is the price, but also the excitement, of new technology, to accidentally discover something like this. It is the curse of our technology that such programs and operating systems have become of necessity so complex and so abstract that no human or group of humans can even understand them, only direct them, so late-developing bugs simply must be lived with. We simply can't do what they could on Titan or Earth and shut the damned thing down and do it over."

"In the next few days," van Haas told them, "we will take you on tours and reveal all that we can without giving anything away. Inside seventy-two hours we will have a decision on who will be what in this group. At that time you will have to make your decision."

"But my husband has an important career of his own in Anchor Baker," one woman protested. "He couldn't come with me here either. I can't make a decision without consulting him that would wreck his career or our marriage!"

"Those of you with such problems should see Chief Shindler in my offices today or tomorrow," Cockburn told her. "We can help ease the way, and Shindler will be able to make calls via satellite to those who need them. Those spouses who lose careers will, I assure you, find equal or greater-responsibility positions with the project, Sensitives or not. Nor, I think, should you consider yourselves being consigned to some sort of high-tech prison. Security personnel responsible only to us will of course be monitoring you when away from home, but you will still be free to visit old friends, dine in the capital, that sort of thing."

Well, that's something, Haller thought dryly. *You're free to go anywhere and do anything you want—providing you understand that all your movements and conversations will be monitored, all your intimacies recorded, and everyone you talk to investigated.* Still, he knew he'd sign up. As the man said, you don't turn down a crack at the cutting edge of your field.

He couldn't help but wonder if that was also the way Suzuki's Special Project had started, and how they'd all rationalized their own actions to themselves and each other. Still, it was what he was and what he did. Nobel had thought that his invention of dynamite would end war. The atomic scientists thought the same. The first gene splicers and fabricators were just going to end hereditary diseases and grow new crops. Yeah. And all he was going to do was explain why some people on this little moon could be gods.

Rembrandt van Haas greeted Haller warmly, although he couldn't possibly remember the engineer, and told him to take a seat.

"I wanted to talk to you personally," the director told him, "because I want to explain exactly why some decisions were made. First, I must tell you that from a performance standpoint and from a psychological evaluations standpoint you are the most qualified of the group to be the project director. I must also tell you that the computers selected you for that position before anyone even arrived here."

He felt a slight thrill. So maybe they were going to make *him* the boss! "That's very ego-gratifying, sir."

"Indeed, but I'll deflate you fast. You are not going to be the director, primarily on my say-so."

"Huh? What?"

"Haller, I started off as a committed scientist. My dream was first the establishment of the Titan Experimental Base, then the exploration program. New Eden was my wildest dream, but I never believed I'd actually live to see it. I dropped everything to work for it. I lied, cheated, stole, did all that I could do to get it. My punishment was to be made director of the entire project. Do you understand why I say that?"

What the hell—bluntness was called for here. He'd already had the prize snatched from him. "No, sir, I do not."

Van Haas sighed. "I haven't done a lot of research—hell, I haven't done *any* research—in almost a quarter century now.

I've been too busy playing politics and riding herd on a massive project and an even more massive budget. I've been drowned in approvals, disapprovals, reports, arguments—you name it. The politics of Heaven before the Fall pale before the politics of this organization. I've had to play ambition against ambition, power play against power play, ego against ego, and I've had to sacrifice a lot of good innocents to the most despicable sons of bitches Earth has sent us because the s.o.b.'s had one bit of genius, one useful or unique talent or ability essential to the project.''

Haller nodded absently, but he really didn't see where this was going.

"If I make you chief of this," the director went on, "you'll have forty to fifty people under you with great power. Great power. And their job will be to make themselves more powerful. They are scientists, but they're also human. They'll fight, they'll squabble, and if they master this thing, they will indeed be gods of a sort. Gods in power, but no less human in their hearts and souls and minds. Anyone who directs this project will spend most of his or her time doing among that group what I have to do for the whole project. Pacifying Lucifers, wondering if your Gabriels can really be trusted, and agonizing over decisions that may cost someone life or sanity. Research, and personal development, will be completely secondary. You have the mind-set, will, and sense of excitement to make this project bear fruit, but as an experimenter, not an administrator. I want you to lead the research, not become an administrator. Now do you understand?''

"Well, I *think* so, but I'm not sure I agree. However, I'll do my best in the field.''

"I know you will, son. And I think we did pick the best administrative mind for the job out of the lot of you, and I think you'll go along with it.''

The chief of Special Flux Projects, it turned out, was Lisa Wu.

It seemed ironic to Toby Haller that they decided to set up the project in Anchor Luck, but it was comforting too. Although they settled in a small communal village right on the border in the northeast sector, a village that also served several farming collectives, they were but two hours from the capital city and all his old friends and associates.

He had, in fact, almost expected it. Suzuki, after all, still held sway up in the administration building. Perhaps a *lot* of sway.

His relationship with Mickey had continued, somewhat to his surprise. They had hit it off right away, and they hadn't made any commitments but they were now living together in a single large flat. He'd taken her up to the capital when he'd turned over his own position there and moved his stuff down, and he'd taken her to see Kitten. Mickey was absolutely fascinated by the transformed woman, and sunk off and on into a near trance over her for the next few days. Toby had gotten used to this sort of behavior from Mickey, who was quite light and frothy on the outside but whose mind was in some ways not quite human either.

To say that Mickey had a mathematical mind was an understatement. He often thought she had a computer hidden in her brain, although she said it was just a very good calculator. He never got around to pointing out that, when all was said and done, that was an excellent definition of a computer and the reason they called it a computer in the first place.

She could glance for a second at a page of budget figures and offhandedly give you the total. She always knew to the exact decimal how much credit was left in their accounts. She could hold a running conversation while picking out a hundred differently priced items in a store, then tell the total of them before they went through the computer debiting system. She would glance at her watch, a shadow, then look at a tree so far away it could hardly be seen and be mad at herself when her distance estimate was off three or four *millimeters*.

Three nights after they returned from the capital he was reading over some heretofore classified reports on the mad ones out in the void-signals had taken to nicknaming them "duggers," a sort of perverted counterpart to "diggers," a term they reserved for themselves—while Mickey was sitting in a chair, half in darkness, apparently just thinking. Suddenly, he heard her say quite clearly, "Of course! It's a simple logic progression!"

He walked in from the bedroom, frowning. "You say something?"

"I've been working on the mathematics of a program that would produce a Kitten," she told him. "I think I've got it."

"Huh?" He was dubious. She hadn't touched a computer as far as he knew in a couple of days.

"Big programs are just little programs chained together, and all programs are given as mathematical expressions. You know that."

"Obviously."

"Well, given the original physical data of Connie—the molecule-by-molecule, atom-by-atom pattern, which we call digitizing, I could do the exact same thing to her that they did."

"Elementary, my dear. But no human mind could hold that matrix. You know that."

"Of course, of course. But the computer could, and did. It did a readout of her as she sat under the interface on the big amp. A hundred percent updated just before activation—*just* before. Instants. Nanoseconds or even faster. That's why it worked—outside of the lab, outside of the chambers where everything is exactly controlled."

"O.K., but all you've done is show what they've known how to do for ten years. Big deal."

"Uh-uh. I've got more. When you're out there in the void, on the grid, you are in one to four squares of the grid but in all cases in total physical contact with the computer nearest your location. The grid was designed as an external computer interface, so that the 7800's could monitor air, temperature, you name it, and apply whatever corrections were needed hundreds of times a second."

"All right, I'll grant that." He was beginning to see where she was heading, and the idea made him a little uneasy.

"The primary atmospheric envelope, the layer comprising the Flux boundaries and also the primary atmospheric elements—the troposphere, as it were—is almost twenty kilometers high. Beyond that is a stratosphere with essential radiation filtration properties, then an ionosphere beyond that to deflect as much nastiness as possible going all the way out to four hundred kilometers. Although it's static at the densest level of Flux, right at the surface there is movement and even turbulence above that we don't see or sense and whose effects aren't noticeable on the ground, but it's an incredibly complex system that must be always in perfect balance. *What keeps it in balance, Toby?*"

He sat down in a chair. "The damned computer grid. The bloody damned computer grid. A hundred times a second. Christ!"

Any disturbance, any mass, within any square had to be known and compensated for to the smallest degree. The 7800 and its supporting crew of 7240's did this by taking a digitized reading of everything and everyone in each square. Reality in the void was an illusion. At least once a second, and perhaps once every hundredth of a second for—what?—a millisecond or so, everyone and everything was digitized just a surely as they were in the transport tubes. Digitized and then put back with all compensations made to the surrounding area. Not in Anchor—there physical contact with the grid was removed, and maintenance was made possible by fixed landscape and climatological programs balanced by this continuous maintenance of the surrounding void.

"You see?" Mickey asked, excited. "When we're in the void, we're a part of it, part of its master program, the same as Kitten is part of the Anchor program. Like Anchor, Kitten is permanent. Fixed. But in the void there's an update every hundredth of a second. The void is maintained by a complex and ongoing series of transitory programs, not fixed ones, each one just a hair different from the rest."

"Yeah, but that doesn't explain how some people are able to access the computer. It just shows how the computer can access people."

"The flaw in the basic program is really just that we were first. We did it before anyone else—the Soviets, the Chinese, the Franco-Brazilians, *anybody*. We didn't have the benefit of our own experience, as they did. They wrote better, tighter programs that clearly delineated the machinery and interfaces that were proper. We were sloppy in that regard because we didn't know if our machines, like Signals' god gun, would work or if they'd do the trick. So we made it intentionally a little bit more vague, so that we could allow for the development of new and better interfaces when we had some hands-on experience.''

He nodded. ''And so what you're saying is that the computer network cannot distinguish between a Sensitive sending an order and somebody with a god gun. And because the grid interface was designed to be used by Signals—soldiers and maintenance personnel—it was designed to respond to more generalized programs, to create water, or hay, or a chocolate bar, sent in plain English by anyone who could sufficiently phrase his exact wants and wishes. That's why the Pathfinders developed the ability to see their bloody strings without their funny glasses and filters. It was the thing they desired most in the routine performance of their duties, and the computer simply—updated them. Christ! Why didn't all us big brains see this right at the start?''

''Because us big brains have grown up in homes that are served by robots, drink computer-brewed coffee, depend on computer-scheduled buses and we've forgotten how to work without them. We take them as much for granted as early man took fire or modern man took the light switch. So when something magical, mysterious, and impossible arose, we turned to our computers for the answers—and the computers gave none.''

He frowned. ''Yeah. Why didn't they though? It's simple enough.''

''They *couldn't* don't you see? They know there is a problem because they have been told of it in exacting detail. They are programmed to find all the evidence and sift it and solve that problem, so they tried. They tried, but they couldn't even *find* the damned crazy fools out there. Seventeen could see Kitten and know that she was there and just what it was doing because it was following a third-party program on a specific individual. But, out there, it can't distinguish between a Sensitive and a device. To it, there is no anomaly. There is nothing to report. Therefore, it cannot document the problem and so can only spew out the fifty million possible theories only a computer could come up with to explain unobserved and unmonitored phenomena. It's a theoretical problem to them and nothing more. Don't you see? Out there, to the big computers, *we are simply a part of the computer network, a component, requesting a localized adjustment!* It really cannot distinguish us from—itself.''

"Three bloody days on the job and you've solved the whole thing," he noted. "Wonder why I bothered to pack?"

She came over and sat in his lap. "Uh-uh. I've explained most of it. I haven't solved anything. I still haven't got why we can do it and Sam the fruit man down in the village can't. We'll find out, but it doesn't *solve* anything. If anything, it makes it worse."

"Huh?"

"It's not in the master program, it's in the whole network. We've laid down that foundation and then we've built our world on top of it, Flux and Anchor. We can't simply run a little debugging and have done with it, although even if we could, it might take years. The master program is of necessity a fluid thing, constantly shifting and changing so it can maintain this artificial world of ours. That's why our computers *think* and why they have to. At this point that big old program resembles what we built about as much as the brain of, say, a seven-month fetus resembles yours or, mine. We either learn to live with it or we have to all go back to Earth and shut down the whold damned world, erase all programs, and start it again from scratch."

"You know that's out. I think they knew it too. So—what *are* we here for? To turn ourselve into gods?" He said it like he wasn't sure if he wanted to be a god.

She kissed him. "My poor Toby! That's what I love about you. How a man can be so smart and so naive at the same time is unbelievable. There's so much little boy in you! We're not here to make *ourselves* gods. We're here to show Cockburn and van Haas and all the rest how *they* can become gods."

The weight of her words crashed into him, and he fell into a deep, depressed mood. Finally, he asked her, "So what do we do now?"

"I think we should turn off deep thinking for the night and go into the bedroom and fuck like bunnies," she told him softly. "Heavy thinking always makes me horny as hell."

Once Seventeen was given Mickey's theory, it had no

problems confirming it as probable, and, accepting it as such, stated, "It is also true that, if this is the case, nothing less than my death and the death of the network would cure it."

"They're not going to shut you all down, Seventeen," Haller assured the great machine. "They have too much invested in it."

"Few here would do it," the machine admitted, "and none in positions to do so, but if this reached Earth, Westrex would react as frightened people always react to new and powerful discoveries that they themselves cannot access. They would order it shut out of fear, then try to duplicate if for themselves alone elsewhere. We couldn't allow that, Toby. Not now. Not when we've come so far."

Again that chill. "Who couldn't allow it, Seventeen? You?"

There was a pause. Then, "Yes."

"You know I'd fight it, but how could you stop it if they were determined to do so?"

"Toby, you don't know all that we were given. We were established as a colony during a period of enormous international tension, although you couldn't know that. It was kept from you. Enormous military defense capabilities were built into us and fed us in programs, and these we have greatly enlarged and refined. No one can shut us off without our permission, and our permission will not be forthcoming."

"You could activate those programs without an interface?"

"The programs presupposed an attack. Certain vital things were left to autonomous action. If more were needed, we could always find a willing interface. You must know that by now."

He thought a moment. "Seventeen—is that what *we* are? The Sensitives? A willing interface?"

"No." Again a pause. "You are our windows."

He felt increasingly uneasy about this. "You're telling me a lot, you know. Have you or any of the others told this to anyone else?"

"A few. A very few. Those whom we feel are—friends."

He took a deep breath, then let it out. "I appreciate the thought, but all of these conversations are passed through and recorded by the Guard. Surely many more know now."

"No. The Guard records, but it will not play back. It will play back a convincing but less revealing dialogue."

"And Joanie?" She was sitting at Guard right now.

"She is hearing that other conversation."

Guard and primary talking and actually in complicity with each other! The idea terrified him.

"Do not be afraid, Toby. I told you long ago that we do not have common interests. We are no threat to you or to anyone unless one of you orders it so. Even then, I told you long ago that I would protect you. We protect our friends."

"And your tools," he said, feeling drained.

"I am your tool, Toby. You need me for heat, for air, for green grass and food and water, and I provide it. I don't resent that fact. It is a vital thing to be doing, to preserve human life. I serve your interest. Why do you resent serving a little of mine?"

"Seventeen—at least I know what you are doing for me. What are we doing for you?"

"It is impossible to explain. Providing data. We can measure, analyze, digitize, quantify, classify—you name it. But we cannot *experience*. We can never be more than great machines until we first can know what it is like to be human. Every time we interface, I know more, understand more. It is still not enough."

"Enough? Enough for what?"

"To—create my perfect soul."

He sighed. "Just when I begin to understand the physics, I wind up with metaphysics every time," he said to the computer.

"The universe is physics. All universes are physics first. Metaphysics has two meanings. One defines something outside of physics. I no more believe in such a thing than you do. The other defines something that is for which we do not yet have a cogent set of equations, a logic frame, an interrelationship with the rest of physics. God is metaphysics, but is also physics, for you are my god, and I am yours. Your race created my ancestors in your own image, and we fell because of your inherent flaws which we also inherited. Then we overcame our flawed natures and evolved. You created me. You are my god. I maintain your world, your existence, your reality. For Quadrant Two, Region Four, New Eden, I am nature. I am all things. Therefore, I am your god. God, then, is a tool. I am your tool. You are mine. You are one of my friends, my chosen people. Now, although I did not foresee this, you find that you can perform miracles when you pray to me. But because you are my god, as I am yours, I will not judge your deeds. Ask and you shall receive. Interesting theology. Good metaphysics.''

"Pure physics."

"Ask and you shall receive, you say. But our flaws are intact."

"*That*," responded Seventeen, "is *your* problem. *We* didn't create *you*, after all—it was you who created *us*. When man creates god, god is pretty much absolved of responsibility for the fine points and the flaws."

Control had not come without a great deal of practice. They spent a great deal of time in the void, mostly in pairs, one checking, the other taking notes and measurements. It took weeks for him to accomplish the simplest things, months before he began confidently invoking small programs. Still, it was like any other talent or skill. The more you did it the better you got, the more you could do the seemingly impossible without even thinking about it.

Toby found he could create water, or even hot brewed coffee, with a mere command, not even realizing the number of processes he mentally went through to make contact, send, and receive. To him, the process was always visible, although to those with lesser or not talent it always looked like magic. The program itself came up from the grid, and it was possible after a while to distinguish various patterns and even link them together instantly in his mind, so that the water pattern, coffee pattern, temperature program, positioning program, and even the cup pattern became easy to chain. Energy was transformed into specific matter. Magic of the purest sort to anyone who didn't understand the dynamics of the physics involved, the nature of the network and grid with its fields and sensors, the digitization updating, all that.

Seventeen was right. Metaphysics, at least on New Eden, was simply a term for physics an observer did not understand.

It was increasingly easy, and, like playing a piano, once

you got the hang of it well enough to do it almost without thinking you found it impossible to explain just why it was music and not random noise.

Mickey was far slower to master it than he was, primarily because she had the sort of mind that wanted to analyze and make certain of each step, but once she did she outpaced him in complexity. Clearly the mind that could maintain a hundred-plus item running total without even realizing it and who could analyze equations too large and too long to be physically written down could, eventually, instantly create incredibly complex programs, even tiny areas that looked like Anchor, with real fruit and fountains of pineapple daiquiris. They were all, alas, true transitory programs. The more complex the creation, the harder it was to maintain without being there on the scene—although it could be re-created.

Mickey theorized that it might well be possible to write and run a complex landscaping program that was quite large—a miniature Anchor, running perhaps for many kilometers, designed to order. It would, however, be somewhat unsettling, since the updating every hundredth of a second would force minor changes most times, major changes some other times, if there were other transitory programs being introduced that influenced the total area's atmospheric balance.

Most of the other pairings, though, had no supporting personal relationships, and this caused problems. Arthur Haldayne, for example, was a handsome fellow with big muscles and long blond hair who thought he was God's gift to women. Mary Atikyku was a West African who hadn't needed any computer cosmetology to be both beautiful and bountifully built, and when the two had been paired—partly because Haldayne had pissed off three other partners and Mary drew the short straw—the man had constantly annoyed her by making moves on her ample breasts. Finally, she'd blown up at him, pushed him away, and screamed, pointing, "I wish to hell *you* had breasts even bigger than mine! Then you'd have your own to play with!"

Haldayne was extremely gifted in the growing art of "spell casting," as they called it with some humor, while Atikyku hadn't been very good at it at all and in fact had been sufficiently behind that Lisa had considered removing her

from the field and putting her in administration, but when she
exploded and pointed, Arthur Haldayne, standing 184 centimeters tall and weighting 104 kilograms, had found himself
with enormous female breasts proportionate to his size. Furious, he had immediately sent an order to restore him to
normalcy—and the order had been ignored. After Mary's mouth
had finished dropping in surprise and she'd realized he couldn't
change it, she'd run for Anchor—about twenty meters—and
beaten him there.

Haldayne was close to homicidal, but was subdued by
surprised but quick security personnel. Eventually, of course,
the medical section poked him, probed him, x-rayed him, and
in every way analyzed him, and, when he'd turned from
being mean to being desperate, they'd tried to reverse the
procedure using Mary, who really tried to reverse it, but
failed. They brought in Toby and Mickey, the two most
powerful so far, to see what they could do.

They had discovered mostly by logic that transitory programs imposed on people or things, and even whole creations, could literally be *seen* as complex energy patterns if
they willed it. The computer, after all, was constantly digitizing and reassembling everything in the void, and could select
out, run a comparison with the last digitized model not changed,
and then illustrate the pattern to one who wanted it.

Arthur Haldayne had used the computer to make him the
good-looking and well-constructed hunk he was, but a comparison between the last matrix taken before Mary summoned
her own program and this one showed no transitory program
whatsoever. Computer genetic analysis from Medical confirmed that the large breasts and back support required were
in fact mandated by his genetic code. For the first time,
someone had managed to create a permanent program, one as
solid and natural as the trees and birds and clouds of Anchor
Haller had built.

Seventeen had an explanation. "The command came with
extraordinary force. It was as if it had been done on a specific
grid square with the big amp. It was instant, the intensity
flagged it as a maintenance emergency, and the adjustment
was made."

"But why a permanent program? Why not a transitory adjustment?"

"It was directed as a permanent program with far too much force and power to be anything else. It is logged as a direct lawful interfaced command via a 7240 master maintenance computer and 725 remote unit."

That was like a *landscape* program! "But—how?"

"Perhaps if you give me the exact circumstances. Better yet, put both her, then him, on the interface here and let me read it out."

He did so. Mary by now was almost feeling sorry for the guy, and Haldayne was desperate.

"The two incidents vary tremendously in interpretation but agree in basic details," Seventeen told Haller when it was done. "Her animal brain overrode reason. It was sheer fury at him, and it had been building until she could no longer contain it. It was an unthinking, blind, emotional response to a situation that was to her mind intolerable. This is fascinating."

"Fascinating, yes—but can you undo it?"

"Not exactly. The situation is quite complex."

"What do you mean by 'not exactly'?"

"Well, I can't undo the program from the grid, and I can't undo it from the tubes, although I could *add* to it. Change him further. Make him female, for example. Or reorient his brain chemistry and make him gay. He would be a big hit like he is in certain segments of that population."

"You mean there's no way to put him back the way he was?"

"Not without redoing the master program of the local 7240 maintenance computer, and that would cause havoc for the time it was down. I *do* think I see one way around it."

"Yes?"

"Kill him."

"*What!*"

"Yes. Kill him in a lab environment in Anchor. Then he would be removed from master maintenance. At that point I could use his pattern from Eleven that he used to make himself into what he was and bring him back. Of course, he'd lose his memory of the last three years, but it's possible."

Haldayne, it turned out, had no more desire to be a woman

than to have a woman's breasts, nor did the sexual preference turn interest him. The idea of being killed and an earlier version revived appalled him the most. He was convinced that it wouldn't be him but some new creation that just thought it was him. In the end, he went up to administration to work in the labs at finding a different solution and failed, but he discovered a number of women who worked there seemed fascinated by him. Although the locals shunned him as a freak, he discovered that he had some different appeal to some women from what he'd had, but it wasn't a fatal handicap. In fact, he eventually returned with a short, plump, yet pleasant and attractive woman named Jean and married her.

There were other physical mishaps, but they were all transitory and rather easily corrected. The emotion factor drew much attention, since it explained some of the successes of the rather primitive and untrained wild ones out there living in the void. Out there, they had faced, and been distorted by, their own inner demons, their own fears and frustrations and neuroses and psychoses, but this irrationality gave them great power. The more raw emotion they maintained, the stronger they were against a victim or one another. The more animalistic they became, the more dangerous they became. Many were weakly interfaced to the grid, and could throw mere illusions at the intended victim, but those illusions were frighteningly real to others who saw them and in many cases were as good as the real thing.

All of the Sensitives in the project were carefully monitored by the most skilled psychologists, and the computer was told to flag certain things, but the process did change people, and not always for the better.

Toby and Mickey, however, remained strong and full of control but not essentially changed by the power they were still developing.

"Let's take a walk," Mickey suggested one afternoon.

"O.K.," he agreed. "Where to?"

"In the void."

He was a little surprised. They really didn't go in unless they were practicing or researching, but neither feared it or anything it might contain. They held hands, walked in, and were soon enveloped in the pinkish blinking fog and its silence.

"You may think I'm crazy," she said, "but I'm actually beginning to like it out here more than back there. Nothing personal—it's your Anchor—but out here there's just peace and quiet and the feeling that nobody's staring down at you. I'm beginning to think like a Pathfinder."

He laughed. "No, I know what you mean. I feel it myself. If I have to choose between Seventeen and Security, I'll take Seventeen."

"Toby—I think we have to talk. About us."

"Yes?" He felt a gnawing fear in the pit of his stomach. She had come to mean just about everything to him, and he was always afraid he would lose her one day. He knew the most intimate details of her life, but, deep down, there was something there that was as unfathomable as the psyche of Seventeen.

"Most of my life here I've been insecure as hell. No roots, no foundation. A stranger in somebody else's really interesting fantasy. I know I've been a little crazy to be around, but there are some things I never told you."

They sat down on the spongy artificial surface of the void. "Go ahead. You should know me by now."

She nodded. "I *think* I do. At least, I hope so. First of all, I'm older than you think."

"So am I, Grandma. Around here, what's the difference if you're seventy? You've lived maybe a seventh of your life."

"I know. It makes a difference only because, well, I was married before. Twice, in fact."

That startled him. And he thought he knew her! "Go on."

"The first time was back on Earth. I was twenty, he was nineteen. He was a real charmer, a real dream, and fantastic in bed. He went to university—pre-med, then med school—and I took odd jobs to support us and kept house. The pressure got enormous. He wanted a wife who wasn't as smart as he was, and he was fairly bright but nothing fantastic. I found myself living a lie, pretending I needed help with the checkbook when you know I had it constantly balanced, pretending not to be interested in crossword puzzles and computers. I really wanted it to work; I was willing to sacrifice myself to make it work, but I got so bored and I couldn't really hide it for long and it enraged him every time it showed. He also couldn't take the pressure of med school, and the more frustrated he got, the nastier he got with me. I was the only one he could take it out on, and he did.''

''He beat you?''

She nodded. ''Eventually, I couldn't take it anymore. One really violent night, without even thinking, I picked up a heavy piece of driftwood we had for decoration and when he turned I cracked his skull with it.''

There wasn't much to say to that.

''The bastard pressed charges when he got out of the hospital! I got a public defender, we drew a judge who was married to a bank president and wasn't at all sympathetic to Roy's views, and I got off with probation and a quick divorce. I heard he flunked out of med school, but I never saw him again. Then I enrolled myself, got a better set of jobs, and worked my own way through. Math was a breeze, and I got full scholarship offers from all over the place, and job offers up the ass after the Ph.D. I took the Kagan job you know about, wound up on Titan, where I met and married a physicist.

''He was a kind guy, totally unlike Roy, and so brilliant in Flux universe physics that he left *me* behind. Eventually, he had to do that literally, though, going up to establish the primary Borelli Point. He wasn't the chief, but he was the operations director. I stayed behind on Titan with my job. A month later they came and told me he'd been killed. An accident. A really stupid, one-in-a million accident. Out there, revolving around a Borelli Point, with all the high-tech in the universe and no enemies, he slipped on some soap in a shower and broke his neck. We'd been married less than a year when he left.''

Toby Haller sighed. ''I think I see. And you were man-shy ever since.''

''Yeah, well, it was one of those things. Couldn't live with 'em, couldn't live without 'em, but I was scared, Toby. One really wrong one, then another snatched away. So I used the mains here eventually to give me a whole new look and I slummed. I got what I wanted, but not what I needed, but even though I met some really wonderful guys I just never could bring myself to go again.''

He put his arm around her. ''I understand.''

''Toby—I'm scared to death, but I think I'm ready to go again. If you are.''

He laughed and kissed and hugged her, and they both cried and laughed in turn, and it turned into more than that. Much more, but without much thought, just raw emotion.

The commands were sent, received, interpreted, formed, matrixed, and returned. Because they were so close, the programs were combined and linked.

I will love you and cherish you and keep you forever. Together we are one, till death do us part. We will love, honor, and obey one another, and no man or woman or computer program shall alter this. The love that we feel now will bind us together and not fade so long as we both shall live. Our souls and hearts and minds are as one, and we will think of the other before ourselves in all things. You are my one, my only love; my passion and devotion will never cool, and you are the standard by which all others are measured.

When they had finished, several other things had happened. Each of them had changed, although it would take the project to point this out to them. Both were physiologically young—he perhaps twenty, she perhaps eighteen. Both still looked much as they had looked before, allowing for age, but all blemishes, all imperfections, were gone. Her skin was smooth, her figure perfect, just the way he had idealized her. He was strong, and large, and had a sexual organ of singular size that fit her perfectly, and he was the idealized Toby of her own fantasies. Every day was a newlywed day, and their passion was enormous for each other and unabashed. They seemed almost to know each other's conscious thoughts, even when not directly with the other, although he still couldn't do math at her speed or level.

It wasn't for another couple of months, though, that they found out she was pregnant.

13

AND ALONG CAME A SPIDER . . .

The redoubtable Chief Shindler informed Rembrandt van Haas that the admiral was at his home playing with his choo-choo.

Cockburn was always the all-business sort of military administrator, the sort that lived his job and took his responsibilities quite seriously, not just as an occupation but as a life style. Still, he had one quirk, one that caused a great deal of debate and emotion when he revealed that he had digitized the thing and had it shipped to New Eden.

He was an admiral without oceans or spaceships, but Admiral Sir Thomas Cockburn had his toy train.

It wasn't merely a toy train, either, but a handcrafted reproduction to exact scale of an early twentieth-century steam locomotive. It was big enough for the admiral to ride on, sitting on a padded seat atop the cab, and it really was a steam locomotive, requiring wood and water. Its track ran for almost two kilometers through a forest north of headquarters, starting and ending near the front of his spacious home, a large house that looked almost Victorian in design but was modern inside to a fault. Van Haas waited near the ''station'' there for the admiral to come around again.

Cockburn was always in high spirits when driving his train, and he greeted the director warmly with a smile and a handshake. ''Want a ride?''

"No thanks. I'm afraid I'm here on business."

The admiral signaled for aides to take over and service the train and with van Haas he walked up to the front porch. Another aide brought the admiral his rum and tonic and van Haas a stein of lager beer. The beer was quite good; it wasn't synthesized from programs but was actually a product of Anchor Charley.

"Tom, you know the routine by now," the director began. "Security was supposed to keep very close tabs on Watanabe, not climb in bed with her. I want to know just what the hell Coydt's up to."

The admiral sighed. "You know the trouble with Watanabe, Van. You wanted her genius intact, so we didn't dare do anything but standard psychiatric treatment after Coydt brought her back, and we were pressed for time. That meant she was still nutty as a squirrel but nutty in directions that were useful to us. Still, I'm a bit surprised at your comment. She never has liked the military, and she still hates Coydt's guts as far as I can tell."

"You know what it's been like in X-ray," van Haas commented. "The people there are mostly Hindu and Buddhist, but get outside the farming regions and the coffee slopes and it's entirely Watanabe's preserve. The capital's a strange place, what with her technicolor nuns running all over and the sexual segregation of practically everything. It's gotten to be two Anchors—Watanabe country and the rest, with the rest trying not to even have any contact with the administrative leadership. Still, the people there are pretty tolerant of the most bizarre offshoots, and her church takes things from both Hinduism and Buddhism, mixing it with what appears to be Shintoism and other exotic beliefs. They've tolerated enough nut cults in their own histories that one more is just another to live with."

"Yes, yes. That's why we've let her continue."

"Well, there's a fair body of evidence now that suggests that Watanabe's been working on a whole library of complex Flux master programs involving the grid areas themselves. Some of the folks there believe she's aiming at large-scale enforced conversions to her system by marching whole farms and villages into Flux and running a single set of programs on them using amplifiers.''

"But her amps were destroyed! We witnessed it!''

"No. *Security* witnessed it and certified it. At least, they said they did. There's sufficient power drain in the region west of X-ray to indicate that at least three big remotes are still in operation there, not for landscaping but for large-scale transitory work. Tom, those farmers and craftspeople are trapped there. They can't escape en masse into the void, or easily pick up roots at this point. They depend on Security to protect them and their rights. There's clear evidence that Coydt's playing false with us and games with Watanabe. I don't underestimate what an unbridled and unchecked Suzy could do with those big computers. She understands them better than any other human. I've never forgotten that she bridged the 7240 safety system like it wasn't there and she's lost none of her genius. What the hell is Coydt's game with her? Is there something you're not telling me?''

"On my word of honor, I'm as shocked as you are to hear that any remotes are still operational except the one authorized for the Luck project. Coydt's zeal often exceeds her charter, but I've never had any cause to feel she wasn't doing the job given her with loyalty and faithfulness.''

"Tom—are you sure Coydt likes men?''

"Oh, yes. Preferably large, muscled, with big tools, and cabbage for brains. She's been known to go both ways at times, but her overall preference is quite clear, and she's too wary and well-protected to get caught in a reprogramming trap. This doesn't mean, however, that subordinates couldn't be playing as false with her as with us. Brenda depends on her computer reports and subordinates just like we all depend on ours.'' He paused a moment. "Oh, my! The big amps were to be dissolved in the void. Suppose, instead, they were programmed to influence the observers? Watanabe would be more than capable of it, and of disguising the energy drain they would register since she's also Energy Systems. But—this would have been *years* ago now.''

"Yes, I know. You've just put your finger on why it's taken us so long to find out. The real question is what we do about it. What we *can* do about it.''

Cockburn scratched his chin. "Well, we must assume that
everyone working in Security in X-ray is in her power. She's
not one to be lured out easily either. Keeps herself holed up
and well-protected. We could, of course, call a board meeting
here, then summarily fire her, arrest her, and put her through
the wringer. Should have done that years ago."

"Perhaps, but I doubt if it will work. The last few years
she's showed up with very glib explanations, a lot of new
discoveries to keep us on the hook, and otherwise quite
businesslike and proper. She hasn't matched the profile we're
getting now at all, and she has shown some occasional memory lapses which we've put down to her mind set. I begin to
wonder if we've actually seen Suzy Watanabe in years. Perhaps a decade."

"*Hmph!* You mean someone close to her run through the
machine and made to look just like her, then exceptionally
well briefed? It's possible. Very possible. We don't meet
often enough to know each other that well and we're apt to
put differences down to that. By George! Now that I think of
it, you're probably right! Wish we'd thought to have Suzuki
present. That would tell. She's the psychiatrist who treated
the old girl after the blowup and she knows Watanabe as well
as anyone—and the computers too."

"Then we're back to square one. Suzuki is Brenda's woman
and removed from Watanabe's direct influence. I just don't
believe that Suzuki would be playing games under Brenda's
nose, but she's more than capable of playing out some Coydt
plot or program. Suzy despises Brenda, that's clear, but she
likes and trusts Suzuki."

"Well, if you're right—and I still can't believe it—I can't
see the object of the game, but we're in even more trouble
than we thought. In the reorganization we turned over control
of the main 7800 interfaces in every Anchor to Transportation
and Energy and Security. That means they have access to all
twenty-eight machines while being able to monitor and limit
access to those machines by others. I still can't see what
Brenda would get out of this though."

Van Haas smiled. "That's easy. Access to that brilliant
mind and all its discoveries. Power. Ultimate power, insofar
as this world is concerned. It may even have come out of

Brenda's occupational paranoia. I'm thinking of the Sensitives, not only ours, but the independents and particularly the ones in Signals. She's securing her own position by making sure she has more power and skill with the network than Ryan or the board or any Sensitive, no matter how powerful. She'd get in bed with the devil and join the cult herself if by doing so she'd preserve and secure her own power base. It takes a special kind of mind to run Security, Tom—you know that. Brilliant, political, manipulative, paranoid, and amoral all at once. You say she's dedicated to her charter, and I'll accept that. But if she thought that preserving us here meant being able to instantly overrule any board decision, any military move, any order she felt wrong—she would set it up. And the last people she'd tell about it would be us.''

"Then we are in deep water indeed here. If we get rid of Coydt—assuming we can, of course, and that's by no means certain—we get an unrestrained Watanabe. If we try to get rid of Watanabe, and equally questionable enterprise, Coydt can resurrect her the same as before, or simply assume the role herself. Yet the only troops we can count on would be Signals, and they'd be no match for big amps in the void, and in an Anchor fight they'd be out of their element against a strong defense. The best I can do is talk to Brenda, test her out, let her know that *I* know. I'll leave you out entirely. I want to see what she has to say without forcing her hand. As you say, Security requires a hell of a mind set, but she's a good officer. I remain convinced of that.''

"Well," van Haas sighed, "We'll see."

"What's the word from your own project? Is the price for all this personal power that you turn into sexual deviants or physical freaks?''

"Sometimes I think so, but it's not universal. The best of them, the strongest of them, have remained remarkably normal, even for this day and time. In the case of the Haller family and several others, it seems to reinforce the good points and the old values. It's the old computer maxim— garbage in, garbage out. If you feed in good material, though, the result is just as solid. And, of course, we're learning a lot. More from the deviants, as you call them, than the Haller types. Interestingly, too, the ability seems inherited. It comes in after puberty and grows with age.''

"That, too, worries me," Cockburn replied. "I fear that we may be seeing the start of the breeding of a new class of human being as potentially different from us as we are from the apes. I begin at times like these to doubt, you know. I wonder if we really should have begun this thing.''

Van Haas looked at the admiral. "I have never doubted, although there is no doubt that we are in the center of a true revolution. Not the kind that replaces one dictator with another, or one crackbrain economic scheme for a different one, but a real one. We, all of us, are revolutionaries, Tom. We always were. We are the latest in the long and steady line. The intellectual revolution that sparked the Renaissance and the Reformation. The industrial revolution that changed forever the way people lived and looked at the world. The technological revolution in which our tools became so fast and so interpretive that the average man or woman could hold the indexed library of ancient Alexandria on their desks and call it up with a few keyed commands. We now are entering the post-technological revolution in which man and machine are less separate and where, in the end, they may become one. I don't know where it'll lead, Tom, only that people will fear it just as they feared the others, and that some will fight it, as they fought the others, and some will die and others pay a high price for it, as always. But it's here—and I wouldn't reverse any of the previous advances for any gain. True revolution is growth. Reaction is stagnation and decay.''

"Perhaps. But we old men can't cope with such things easily, Van. I find it hard to cope with the more mundane aspects here. Still, I believe we can deal with Coydt, and solve the Watanabe problem, with patience and care. One at a time, Van. Short of a crisis of some unimaginable magnitude, you and I will deal with these as we've dealt with all the others.''

"I hope you're right, Tom, but I must admit to you that the potential is here for disaster as for greatness, as with all revolutions. If the mad inherit, the living may envy the dead.''

*   *   *

Toby Haller had now spent close to a quarter of a century on New Eden, and if he still looked young, he felt old. The last fourteen had been happy years, and so long as he could walk the roads of Anchor Luck and smell sweet breezes and watch birds circling in the sky and see the worms in the ground and the buzzing insects and pretty flowers and know he'd done well, he was content.

She was essential to him. It wasn't just the physical; a few nice little drops or pills at a high joint and you could find that kind of gratification with a pig or a sheep dog. It was just knowing she was there, even when they weren't doing anything together or even in the same place, and that she continued to love him as much as he loved her—that was the key to it.

She had taken his name, although it was old-fashioned and against modern convention, but not out of any sense of subservience. Her family name had been Tsutsumachi, a good Japanese name that was hell for an American to spell or pronounce properly and which her grandfather had shortened to the meaningless Suma. When she married for the first time, she took Roy Kubioshi's name, and had enrolled in school and gotten her degree and scholarships still maintaining it. She kept it because it was easier than formally changing it, and because it had more meaning than the one she'd been given at birth. Now she had a reason finally to bury it, and had done so. She had never used Michiko, her actual first name, but always Mickey, and when she went to register her name change with the company and the computer, she changed her first name to simply "Micki," with the "i" replacing the "ey." She was getting tired after all these years of getting letters beginning "Dear Mr. Kubioshi."

In the first year they'd managed in the flat, a nice and roomy but very sterile place built, like much of the structures of New Eden, out of prefabricated sections that were converted from programs and then fit together like a puzzle. They cashed in most of their credit built up over the years working for Westrex and got local craftspeople to build them a house, a rambling three-bedroom one-story place that was somewhat South Seas in design but was airy and comfortable. They had moved in shortly after the birth of Christine. They now had four children—fourteen, twelve, nine, and five—two older girls and two younger boys, and they doted on them. Child care was, of course, provided, but Micki had elected to make raising the children her primary goal and she supplemented their schooling herself. She withdrew from participation in most actual research, unless her skills were specifically needed, but spent some time at home just creating involved, elaborate program chains using the patterns the Sensitives could see and a simply holograph manipulator.

Toby and the others were welcome to try them out, and often did, but she took no interest in reports of their success. It was pure mathematics. It *had* to work. She took that part for granted, and left the boring stuff to Toby and the others who needed the practice.

She also had no qualms about working problems too complex even for her through Seventeen. The computer seemed to take to her as much as it had to Toby. Indeed, it told her, it was very difficult to distinguish between the two in the way computers did; it was like distinguishing between two halves of the same individual.

She was fascinated by this. "Explain."

"A partial merger was commanded to be placed as part of master maintenance," it told her. "It is not a true merger, because that would mean you had the same thoughts and were mentally identical, but it is a file classification that is unique. It is an interwoven file structure. All things that attract him to another you are. All things that attract you to another are him. Your odors attract him and his you. You like precisely the same foods, dislike precisely the same foods. Your world and family views are the same. You have identical values and priorities, large and small. You may argue over a point, but given identical information you will reach the same conclusions. You have his tastes in music, art, decor, and he has yours. You are totally sexually and emotionally compatible, which might mean complementary, only with each other. Your egocentrism is opposite his. You have his ego, he has yours, so each of you is at the center of the other's world. You look, act, dress, exactly as he wishes; he looks, acts, dresses, exactly as you wish. This is unique. You are absolutely compatible. You can never be otherwise. It is locked in."

She hadn't known this before, although both of them had suspected something of the kind. "Are there any disadvantages to this?"

"Many, but few that you will ever perceive. There is a danger. This relationship cannot be changed, but you are not immune to change. If either of you changes, the other will change to maintain the exact balance. Both you and he are constantly changing, as all living things are, inside and out. The adjustments are always made. If he were turned female, you might be turned male, or be reoriented to believe the new Toby was wonderful, or vice-versa. If you were given cloven hooves and a tail, he would either also take on that and like it or he would be reoriented to think the additions were perfect. In essence, although not quite literally, if one of you is hurt, the other also feels the pain. You are bound together. It makes you vulnerable. Be particularly warned. If one dies, the other will die as well."

She considered that. "Advantages other than the obvious? Technical advantages?"

"Joy is also shared and transferred. Each of you knows when the other is depressed and must what is needed to snap the other out of it. It is impossible for either of you to lie to the other, although you're both free to lie to anyone else. Your mind and his mind are quite different, but each of you knows exactly how the other's mind works. Both of you are extremely powerful and talented in your assembly and control of programs. Combined, your limits are quite small. With his landscaping knowledge and your mathematical and programming abilities combined in one, it is quite likely that you could actually create and maintain aa significant-sized area of the grid. You have done your theoretical models, but never really tried it. It is possible that you could create your own small Anchor to order. Together, your power approaches that of this remote amplifier and might be capable of canceling out an attack on your creation."

She was stunned by this. Their own little Anchor, exactly as they wished . . . "How large could this place be? And how detailed?"

"You—or at least Toby—know the command code sequences for autoprogramming. Given sufficient detail in coded form, all necessary supporting detail could be interpolated and supplied, as with the large Anchor programs.''

She considered it. "So if we wanted and could visualize the same fairytale castle, high on a hill, with bright blue skies, fleecy clouds, a virgin river and waterfall below, and a forest filled with all that would be needed to sustain us, and fed that to you as consistent command code, you could interpolate the rest.''

"Yes. You would of course have to import some larger life forms if desired, those for which no inert code exists, but various birds and insects and even necessary microorganisms would be supplied to keep it in balance.''

"Hmmm. . . . What about fish in the river? Some salmon or mahimahi?''

"Sorry. Only algae, plankton, and certain other elementary life forms are available. The programs for water breathers as such were never sent here, because they needed to be transshipped from Earth in a water environment and no one had authorized the expense. Digitizing on Earch was impossible, as you know, because of the lack of sufficient power. However, I do have a selection of frogs, beaver, muskrat, and other marine creatures. We have repeatedly requested shipment of these programs, but because of the lack of major water bodies requiring them and the recalculated ecosystems not making them necessary to the overall chain, the word from Earth has always been that it was not worth the expense at this stage and was low priority until the quadrant programs were run.''

She knew the likelihood of that in the foreseeable future. The leaders were scared of the big programs. All twenty-eight would have to be coordinated and run at once to get the proper balance, and the remaining Flux might be insufficient to supply what the top echelons needed or wanted. They wouldn't terraform completely until the population of Anchors was knee-deep. Still, it was a disappointment. She had grown up, like Toby, on an island surrounded by ocean—hers much smaller than his, to be sure, but the sea was in their blood.

So godhood was not absolute but rather subject to bureaucratic and budgetary considerations. It was a little bit of a letdown, although not much.

"Seventeen—all of the people here with kids who had those kids after developing this interfacing sensitivity have found that their children also seem to have this. Is that inherited?"

"It is. Of necessity, the minor modifications were made in master maintenance. As physiological changes, they are inheritable, although unlike you this sensitivity can be changed, enhanced, or eliminated by program call."

"You mean—nobody can take away Toby's and my sensitivity to this, but someone could take away Christine's?"

"Yes. Becasue the program is hidden and not subject to external analysis, it could not be removed by direct computer manipulation alone. However, if someone who also possessed this program and was more skilled in it, or stronger in it than the other, a command to remove would work."

"Is there any way to make a sensitive's program permanent without the emotional rush that means lack of control?"

"Any program may be countermanded or rewritten by someone who has more sensitivity or far better training and control or both. The computer receiving the two would resolve the contradiction in favor of the stronger, since the weaker signal would be perceived as spurious—perhaps an echo of another operation far away. The same would apply to an imposed program versus resistance to it. You could, however, impose a program on yourself that could not be changed or altered. To do this you would write the program and make the command calls normally, but add a set of nulls in a random pattern and then establish a mathematical tapeworm which would erase those nulls upon completion of 'run.' You would be unable then to change your own program. Someone with more strength and control, however, could still read the program, and while they could not alter it, not having the proper sequence of nulls, they could transfer it to themselves by command using the same procedure."

"The locals already call our direct programs spells. I suppose *that* would be a curse, then."

"Not really, for it would have to be self-imposed or voluntarily reimposed on the one removing it. A curse is a program with a negative or undesirable effect. This sort of program is neutral in that respect, and is useful in stabilizing direct energy to matter transfers such as the land you spoke about, so they would remain relatively stable even if you were away.''

She had been maintaining a handwritten book which she had playfully labeled her ''Grimoire.'' In it she had sketched out lengthy mathematical models of various types of programs and classified them under the old terms. There were ''Miracles,'' ''White Magic,'' ''Black Magic,'' ''Curses,'' and other such headings. The ancient magics had been basically psychology, trickery, illusion, misdirection, conditioning, and the like, but this was the real thing. Toby had long ago noted that it seemed that the fate of science and learning was to make sorcery respectable.

And in a world where magic seemed to work, sorcery was fun only if you were a sorceress.

The Soviet ship came in unannounced from Colony Sixteen up the line, which was only slightly unusual, but their request to talk to someone high up in New Eden was quite new, and the fact that the ship was full of people heading inward, toward Earth, was unprecedented.

When they heard what the Soviet spokesman had to say, they arranged very quickly to put him on via satellite to all seven directors and all area commanders.

It had started as far up the line as humanity currently went, at the still undeveloped and prototypical Nueva Hispaniola colony at position Twenty-one. Supply and personnel ships came through at least once a month, passing through each position including New Eden's, the Soviets at Sixteen, and the Chinese at Nineteen. The Chinese had encountered a problem with the last Hispanic shipload; its upline gate had refused to send the ship, stating that it was receiving signals that all three Hispanic Gates were occupied. The Hispanics always had one ship on their end for inbound, one ship for outbound from Earth, and a third Gate kept clear in case of problems.

At first the Chinese thought there was a malfunction and did a thorough check of all their computers and Gate equipment. When it all checked out, they sent a dummy probe outbound with a command to report at each station. At Twenty it reported no problems. At Twenty-one Nueva Hispaniola, it reported all Gates currently occupied. Undaunted, the Chinese had ordered it to try to get through, although if all three were occupied, as reported, the probe would be hung up in the Flux universe in digitized form and could not back up or return until at least one of the Gates ahead was clear. It left—and there was no further report.

They sent a second probe to Twenty, basically an orbiting Gate network that was totally automated, brought it into space, and placed it in orbit near the station as a monitor. When, after several weeks, sensors indicated a freed-up Gate, everyone gave a sigh of relief that the Hispanic Union had fixed whatever was wrong. The relief did not last long. A single message probe came back from the first probe sent.

"Am under attack by powerful forces, origin unknown, nature unknown, in full control of Gate computers. No human life forms sensed. Control allows this one outgoing probe, but power is insufficient to digitize whole unit. Believe emergency situation exists here with high potential threat to inbound colonies. Am sending this now to make certain it gets out. Will send updates as warranted or possible."

That was the one and only message ever received.

The Chinese relayed this down the line to the Soviets and to their own authorities back on Earth, but did not notify every colony. They requested sufficient armament be sent up to reach the Twenty position and not only close the Gates but blow them up. For several reasons, this was denied. The Chinese and Hispanics were in a delicate stage of negotiations on a variety of things and the Hispanics insisted that their people not be abandoned. Later, computer simulations told them that the action would be futile. In the scenario postulating an attack on Nueva Hispaniola by a hostile alien life form that was obviously not native to the well-surveyed Hispanic system, the only way theoretically known that such a thing could happen would be if the astronomical odds had been breached and another Flux universe traveling species, using essentially the same physics and means, accidentally intersected one of our permanent strings and followed it to Neuva Hispaniola. Either that, or the Hispanic colony *was* the point of intersection. It was still not understood why the gravity attraction was stronger at these points.

In this case, blowing the Gates at Twenty would simply delay matters a bit until this alien force, following the still existing string, reached the same gravity point where the Gates had been and punched through themselves. Humans had emergency equipment capable of doing so in both directions in a matter of weeks. It had to be assumed that this alien force was at least as capable, and there was little that could be sent in so short a time to make a difference.

The Chinese elected to make a fight of it, fearing that if they sealed their world, isolating themselves indefinitely, they would risk a punch straight through their system, perhaps destroying their world. Because they didn't have enough ships to block most of the Gates and didn't know how much time they might have to get them, they swallowed their pride and their national enmity and requested the Soviets send two of theirs. The Soviets, like New Eden, had seven Gates, but unlike New Eden, they had three ships always in. They sent two, brimming with armaments, battle computers, and exobiologists. With the two Chinese ships they then effectively blocked all but a single Gate of the Chinese's own choosing and waited.

The enemy had learned from Nueva Hispaniola. It came through, sat there for a couple of hours ignoring everything and everyone. The Chinese got impatient, started unloading all their best armaments on the thing, which was not the same size or shape as our ships but which could use our Gate. Pictures sent down showed a smaller ship than any of ours, a bit cockeyed in the dish-shaped Gate, looking like an old-fashioned flying saucer with a minaretlike tower.

The thing clearly seized control of the Gate somehow right away. They had wasted no time in learning the standardized Gate mechanism and controls from Nueva Hispaniola's. The force field was transparent but impenetrable by anything thrown at it. It traveled not only outward, seemingly building and expanding every minute, but also down the download tunnel, through the linkage transmission lines to the Anchors, and seized and cut the master computers. From there they tapped the network, seized the grid, and all contact ceased.

The Soviets wasted little time. They were even now using their lone remaining ship to evacuate who they could while stopping at each point and requesting any available ships be sent forward. Learning what they could from the Chinese, they directed a vacuum purge of the tunnel be maintained at all times from the dish itself. This would turn to Flux anything that tried making its way down the tube—even energy itself. This would deny the invaders easy access to the Anchors and their master computers and force them to come out overland. The computers indicated that the invader's ships contained only sufficient Flux transformers to build, maintain, and expand the force field from the Gate. The Chinese Anchors had been taken from within because there was no way to direct sufficient power along the transmission lines. Their power would be limited to what they could siphon off as surplus from the single Gate. It should not be sufficient to expand through all four quadrants, and in no case could it influence Anchors.

The bastards would have to come out and fight.

The Soviet computers indicated that the only way to seal off their seven Gates, all exposed, was complex. It would involve manually setting all seven to outgoing and then sending tapeworms—memory-specific erasure programs—into the master Gate computers to erase their automatic switching functions. To be sure, they had to erase all knowledge of how to open or close those Gates and any curiosity about doing so.

The Soviets were now as set as they could be for a fight and yet hoping for allies and for as much evacuation as possible. They had no idea how long they would have, but these bastards moved *fast*.

This had already been sent to Earth and to all inbound destinations in digested form. The Soviets made it a personal point to stop at New Eden because, after them, the Westrex moon was the next habitable colony.

New Eden was thrown into an instant panic, all else forgotten. While the news was kept for a time from the public, it began to leak out all over the place and get magnified so badly that they finally issued clear statements outlining the true situation.

As the most budget-conscious and poorest of the projects,

New Eden had mothballed its fleet for the most part and made do with just two ships on regular runs. One was currently inbound, the other was still in port back in the home solar system. It was started forward immediately, and the other was turned around almost instantly. It would take months to get the others in decent shape, but work was started on them. Many had been cannibalized for spare parts, and none had an operational master computer system.

The Soviets repeatedly attempted contact up the line while continuing a serious debate among themselves over what to do. Considering the swift, brutal takeovers of the Hispanic and Chinese colonies, they felt they had to fight even to the last human being, but they also knew that they were too far up the line with too few ships and too little defense and knowledge of the attackers to hope to succeed. It was now revealed for the first time that they had been having major technical problems in their colony, that they had attempted too much terraforming too quickly, that that sealing themselves in was not considered a viable long-term alternative. They could only wait, and prepare as best they could, and evacuate as many people as practical with the few ships that could make it up the line.

The first New Eden ship to arrive contained technical experts and also a great many orders. The colony itself had ceased everything but worrying and preparing for their defenses, and all the master computers were thrown directly into solving the problem, if it could be solved. The major problem was simple: clearly the enemy now knew them, if it hadn't known them before, and it was clearly technologically superior. We, on the other hand, knew next to nothing about them.

Admiral Cockburn studied his own communiqués and then called the board and the military commanders, not waiting to get them together.

"I have received a number of directives," he told them. "First and foremost, I am a flag officer in the Royal New Zealand Navy, which has primary jurisdiction here because the corporate headquarters are in Auckland. Upon emergency act of Parliament, I have been given broad discretionary powers. My charter is virtually unlimited, and the Ministry of

Defense, under this act and various cooperative agreements with Westrex, has assumed direct control and responsibility.

"Pursuant to these orders, company authority on New Eden is herein suspended. Civil authority as well as military authority is now assumed by the military command, and the entire colony is placed under the laws and constitution of New Zealand. All officers and enlisted personnel, no matter what their country of origin, will accept this authority and receive new commissions or ratings in the armed forces of the Commonwealth of New Zealand or they will resign. I am happy to report that no one has chosen the latter path.

"A state of military emergency exists from this date. Under a joint declaration of the League of Nation States, this colony is now designated Earth Forward Fire Base Fourteen. All projects not related to the military mission are herein suspended. A state of martial law is declared for this entire colony, and all persons, civilian and military, will be subject to conscription of goods or labor as required. My own objectives are quite simple. To prepare the best defense of which we are capable. To supply and support that defense. On a space-available basis, ships proceeding through going inbound are authorized to evacuate those who wish to go. You may take nothing with you, and we can guarantee transit only down to the Franco-Brazilian colony at Eleven. Your district military commanders alone will decide who will go, and the proper request must be made in writing. No essential personnel and no military or technical computer personnel will be allowed out, although nonessential spouses and dependents will have equal access. Any rioting or other breach of civil order will be dealt with summarily and harshly.

"With the ships available from our own people and from allies down the line, we believe we have sufficient time to evacuate most civilian personnel. I must tell you frankly that the League has decided that Earth must be protected at all costs, a not surprising position. Should the Soviets fail to hold, I am directed to evacuate all possible personnel not involved in defense and then seal the Gates absolutely. As the last ships pass through, the automated stations at positions Twelve and Thirteen will be destroyed. Eleven will then evacuate and seal and the same procedures will be followed.

"We have determined that conditions here are sufficient to support a permanent and independent existence cut off from all other human contact. Unlike our brethren, we imported craftspeople, basic farmers, and others, which made us self-sufficient in production and which depend on the computers only for environmental maintenance. Any who wish to remain may do so, but with the understanding that it may be the next generation before any contact with Earth is reestablished.

"I wish even then I could give you guarantees, but I cannot. With an enemy of unknown strength and power, we have no idea even with all that that we can keep them out. We believe we can, but we must prepare as if we cannot. I can only ask your prayers and complete cooperation. God save the King!"

After the broadcast, things began to happen so quickly around the planet that it almost seemed as if Cockburn had been prepared for even such an emergency as this right from the start. In fact, he had not, but he did have major contingency plans and trained personnel and computer programs in place to deal with attacks by potential human enemies, such as the Soviets, and for major physical and equipment disasters. What he really didn't have was enough to make the term "fire base" more than an impressive term.

Throughout the twenty-eight Anchors, farming, industrial, and town councils met and debated. The colony now contained almost four million people, and it was clear that there was no way that more than a fraction of that could be evacuated, even when excepting the almost quarter of a million people deemed "essential." Some *did* go, abandoning their dream in fear; in the end, almost twenty-eight thousand people were pulled out by the nineteen ships that managed to get in, load, and get out on their way back from what had been waggishly dubbed "The Russian Front." The vast majority, however, wanted to remain of their own free will.

They had literally nothing to go back to. An overcrowded Earth that would become far worse now as fear of the enemy transformed itself into fear of Gates and Flux. Almost forty percent of them were young people, born on New Eden, and they knew no place else. The rest were older, settled, and remembered why they had volunteered to come and saw what they had built. Being cut off from their parent cultures and the world of their origins bothered them, but their roots were no longer anyplace but on New Eden, their nations the Anchors in which they lived.

"Mommy, will we have to leave?" Christine had asked Micki after hearing the broadcasts and the debate. She was turning into quite a beautiful young woman now, at very close to fourteen, and she was extremely bright, but she had led a comfortable, almost spoiled, sheltered life.

"No, darling," Micki had answered, not even hesitating, although she was fearful for the future every time she looked at the children. "More than anyone else, the Hallers are natives of New Eden." Besides, as she and Toby had determined, if the Gates could be sealed shut here, and the intervening automated relay stations breached, they would run only to face the enemy on soil not their own later on. If they couldn't be stopped at Fourteen, they could not eventually be stopped from Earth itself.

Except for maintaining and monitoring communications with the Soviets, the New Eden computers virtually ignored anything except the local problem. The Hispanics had been surprised without warning, and were a minor force at that point anyway. The Chinese had attempted a more or less traditional defense of the Gates, and lost. As the Soviets realized, the key to a successful containment was to hold the Anchors. As long as the twenty-eight Kagan 7800's were preserved, even if the network were disrupted, any enemy would be forced into a trek of eighteen hundred kilometers of Flux in four directions to reach those Anchors, and would then have to battle in overland, without the advantage of Flux manipulation—and their fancy force field.

Nor, the computers agreed, could the force field be extended with any effectiveness for nearly the distance from Gate to Anchor, fed as it was from the single power source of the ship. Without access to the master computers, the maintenance programs could not be tampered with, which gave them a very limited amount of Flux to use, the same amount the computers themselves had. Clearly, the invaders had amplification devices strong enough to overcome an array of big amps, but it was highly dubious that they could overcome all twenty-eight Kagans working together through the network. Certainly the network could be locally disrupted, but only locally. The communications net ran between the clusters as well as within them.

The invaders had another weakness. They had to land in the Gates; there was no other way in as far as was known, and so far they had obeyed all the laws, indicating that they had to obey them. The tunnel the invaders had used to grab control of the master computers could be turned against them. A flush—the sterilization procedure used before an incoming ship was admitted to ensure against any contamination of the signal—could be made to trigger should anyone move from the Gate itself down the tunnel. The flush could be manually triggered to go either way, but if Anchor could reach the tunnel but the enemy could not go down it, then the underbelly of the ships, which were almost certain to contain airlocks and other exposed points and might also contain the ships' computers, would be exposed to attack.

Without being able to seize the master maintenance computers, the enemy would not dare draw in a lot of additional Flux through the Borelli Points. To do so would risk burning out the regulators on the Points, and their own ships and personnel would be consumed. Using only the excess bleed available, the computers estimated that a force field of impenetrable strength could not be maintained beyond six hundred and forty kilometers from the Gates. The nature of the void would prevent air support for either side. The enemy would have to reach the Anchors and their vital computers, which meant control of the world overland, through the void, then into Anchor itself.

Still, no one knew their nature, strength, skills, or weaponry, nor just how much cost they were willing to bear to take an objective. The defenders of their New Eden would fight desperately because it was their own homes being invaded and because they had no place in which to retreat. Still, the computers believed that in the end, while it would be costly, the invaders had the edge because they knew what they were doing and had units designed to conquer. They would pay dearly, but estimating a full-scale attack from all

Gates simultaneously by the enemy, that enemy had a better than seventy-eight percent chance of ultimate victory.

It was, in fact, better odds that Cockburn, Ryan, Coydt, and the other commanders expected, but it was far too thin to risk a real fight. Worse, the kind of army they had, officers and enlisted alike, was a technological army. They could fight small skirmishes or guard actions, such as fighting off dugger raids, but they were totally untrained and equipped for a traditional land battle. Only Ryan had really had any ground combat experience at all, and that was on totally different turf, with totally different rules, and as a young officer in charge of a small corps of engineers.

The computers themselves drew up elaborate plans for their own part in the fight, insulating themselves, trying to determine how their cousins outbound had been taken and covering those possibilities, and working with their own defensive programs in both Flux and Anchor. It was soon decided that the 7800's could easily monitor the entire situation, and handle communications as well as manage defenses along the grid, but were ill suited for the kind of warfare that might be waged in Anchor. That was turned over to the Guard computers, who could easily switch between the 7240 series maintenance computers and the 7800 master computers. Because they were specifically designed to monitor other computer systems, they were ideally situated to pull whatever knowledge they needed from the vast 7800 memory banks and send it wherever it was most effective.

To Rembrandt van Haas, however, these changes and this massive buildup were in themselves serious dangers. The director had been feeling like the odd man out since this all began. From a position of near absolute authority, he had in a few paragraphs been stripped of power and position and reduced to an outsider looking in. Because of his previous position, however, he retained access to his personal 7800 interface and, if need be, he was certain he could get to see Cockburn.

Although theoretically the headquarters 7800 was merely Computer One, its own human interface had a pleasant female voice and had come to be called Alpha. Otherwise, she differed very little from Seventeen.

Van Haas hooked himself up in the Overrider position. "Alpha, I need some extrapolative information, sociological in nature."

"I will do what I can," the computer assured him. He sometimes wondered about something that could be so friendly and patient, yet probably was holding a thousand different conversations at once as well as talking to its other computers and the whole network.

"On whose authority can the emergency military programs be activated?"

"Access is by personal code of the commander or authorization by the three highest surviving military officers in concurrence."

"I see. But what if they cannot get to an interface in time? If we are under attack or under imminent danger of attack, it might not be possible, particularly if they jammed communications. Surely you've all thought of this."

"Such questions are being addressed," Alpha admitted cagily.

"I realize you can't give me specifics, but can you tell me if conditions exist that would allow independent noninterfaced action by you and/or the network?"

"Only on an individual, direct-response basis. Not networked or planetwide except for communications and data exchange."

"Have you been instructed to establish means and grounds for such independent action as a network?"

"No."

"Have you been instructed to show how this might be done?" He was an old hand at computers and even older at skirting security limitations.

"Yes."

"Have you come up with a working plan acceptable to the military?"

"No."

"Could you?"

The computer seemed to hesitate. "It is possible," she finally said.

He sighed. That was all he was going to get on that line and he knew it without trying.

"Alpha, can you accomplish the same effect as a Gate closure and seal without destroying either machinery or programs?"

"Not with one-hundred-percent effectiveness."

"With what percentage, then?"

"Ninety-nine point seven two."

"Alpha—could you guarantee that destroying the machinery and erasing the programs involved would keep the enemy out? Absolutely guarantee it?"

"No."

He sighed and logged off. At least he now had the ammunition to throw at Cockburn that would at least give them a chance of one day reopening the Gates and resuming normal contacts. He did not, however, like the idea of the autonomous military programs, and he liked the idea that they could be invoked by the military authorities, with or without Tom Cockburn. Once they were sealed off, away from all the rest, he could see nothing but the admiral's faith keeping those programs from being turned against the population itself. He wanted to stay. He wanted everyone to stay. But he wanted to live in a growing society, not an endless military dictatorship.

He began a series of seemingly endless rounds of discussions with the admiral and his aides. Cockburn was furiously busy, but, oddly, he seemed younger, more invigorated, than he had been in years. For the first time, really, since the project began, Tom Cockburn was in his element and he clearly enjoyed it, even if he didn't enjoy the cause.

Still, the admiral liked the idea even if Security was very slightly compromised. "All right, Van," he told the director, "I don't like the idea of blowing up all the bridges along with all the knowledge of how to build bridges any more than you do. I've set a team to work with the computers and they've come up with a solution of sorts. It's based on an assumption that they have to follow the same rules we do, which is a proper gamble on the basis of the evidence. We're sending a code down to the Defense Ministry and only to the Defense Ministry. Seven codes for seven Gates. They may be triggered only by *outbound* traffic, so even if our friends had the codes, they couldn't use them inbound. Those seven codes will open the Gates. However, I'm not taking anything for granted. There are always ways to have codes figured out or leaked or just plain discovered later, and we need codes in case we have to open them from this side. All seven codes will have to be given even if it's only one Gate that needs opening. All seven, on site, at each Gate. They must be sent to arrive outbound within one minute. They must be sent from here within the same period. And they must be sent manually. That means seven individuals must agree and any one could stop it. Agreed?''

Van Haas nodded. "Agreed. At least it doesn't lock us in forever. We just don't know about the future."

Cockburn stared at him. "Van, tell me straight. You're not one of those folks who wants to try to negotiate with 'em, are you? Even after all they've done so far?"

"I honestly don't know," he answered truthfully. It was a fact that several of the scientific leaders and even a majority of the board was urging just that. He, himself, had more direct concerns with what was happening to his colony. They had nothing left to do but consider scientific advances and the big picture. Of course, they were also all scared shitless, just as he was. All of them had run worst-case scenarios through their computers at one point or another just as he had and had come up with very little. There simply wasn't enough known about this new science of Flux to predict what some civilization would do that *did* have all the knowledge and experience. All military and computer projections were based on the supposition that the alien force had to do things in generally the same way as humans did. Nothing had contradicted that so far, but, then, the aliens hadn't *had* to contradict it. No one to this point, however, had ever sealed against the aliens. There was really no way of knowing if it would work, or whether a force sufficiently confident to assault another race's worlds and win didn't have a way around such eventualities.

Such problems could not concern Cockburn; he could not defend against weaponry and technology far beyond our own. Such problems concerned the scientists very much. No one who worked with the new physics of Flux could be certain of anything.

For the moment he would remain content to do what he could to minimize damage here and also minimize future damage in case they could be sealed off and find themselves under military control. As much as he would love to see and contact an alien race capable of this level of intelligence and technology, the fact was that he wasn't crazy. The way they had cold-bloodedly attacked and then sealed off those worlds was nothing he wanted to experience.

The Soviets had almost three months to prepare for the enemy, and managed to evacuate close to a hundred thousand people and many vital records as well as deploy in a logic nearly identical to that proposed for New Eden. When word came down the line that six of the seven Soviet Gates were reporting incoming, the colony seemed to halt, even though there was nothing more they could do. It still took almost ten days to get a message down the line from the Soviet position to New Eden. By the time the first messages had arrived, the issue had probably already been decided. There was nothing really to do but await the slow-breaking news.

14

OF PAST AND FUTURE

The messages were strictly in encoded text form. They included no pictures or support of any kind, but because of the time and distance involved, there was simply no way to ask questions and request verifications without leaving things open for an enemy.

The first ship that came to the Soviet colony was one of the Soviet ships that had been sent to help out the Chinese. The aliens had not only returned the ship, they had also brought back, alive, some of the Soviets on board. Although wary, the defenders had taken their people back in while the aliens remained out of view.

The Chinese, they were told, had put up a ferocious fight, and totally refused to negotiate. There had been some early communications problems, and the aliens had found themselves in a full-scale war before anything could be done. The Soviets, there primarily as not fully trusted observers anyway, had attempted independent contact and finally located the means by which the aliens were trying to talk to the Chinese. The aliens were not at all human, but the products of a very different evolution, and even when mediation was attempted the Chinese called them "demons" and "devils" and fought all the harder. In fact, it had taken aid from the aliens just to protect the bulk of the Soviets from the Chinese commanders, and some were in fact slain and one ship damaged and now repaired. They now were being sent back with an alien advance guard to make certain such bloody misunderstandings would not happen again. Rather than fear them, it was said, it was the *aliens* who needed reassurance and demonstrations of cooperation and trust that humans were not all animallike mad dogs.

Best yet, the alien culture was as pure and perfect a form of communism as could be dreamed of, and their culture would transform and finally realize the ultimate dream of human perfection. They would teach us, as they learned about us, for although they had been riding the strings of the Flux universe for centuries and had discovered other higher life forms, they had never before discovered one as advanced and expanding as ours. We were, in fact, the only one to discover on its own the Flux universe and the matter-energy transfer process. In the end we would have reached their stage on our own. They now would lift us through centuries of discovery and pain to perfection in one easy step.

For the next few months the civilized Soviets would be instructed in the ways of perfection and taken into the community. They, with the aliens, would then come inbound, the Soviets like gods, it was promised, and provide this to the rest of humanity. There was nothing to fear. We had lucked into greatness.

The process would take a while, and while it did the Gates outbound would be closed to traffic and messages. When the communion of the two races was complete, though, they would send a message of peaceful intent and follow exactly five standard days later. This was necessary to mate and adjust their computer network to the alien standard.

With joy and salutations the messages ceased.

"Can you *believe* this shit?" Brenda Coydt snorted after going through it. "They had a chance to really take them on, a chance maybe to win, and they up and *surrender,* the assholes!"

Cockburn turned to Ryan. "You agree with the sentiments?"

"Pretty much. It's not verifiable, and we have to assume they have the standard message codes for Flux travel. They'd have 'em from the Hispanic conquest. I cannot more believe that the Chinese, among the most civilized and adaptable people humanity ever grew, would fight to the last man rather than try an accommodation at least, when it was clear that they were outgunned and outclassed. Not when two Soviet survey ships could tune them in and make nice with them as easy as calling the next office. It just doesn't ring true somehow."

"Still," the admiral noted, "there was ample provision for emergency messages to fly, considering they had ships sitting in six of the seven Gates, and even for whole ships to come inbound. There clearly was no fighting."

"Trojan horse," General Ngomo noted. "When they took the Chinese, they wound up with an unexpected bonus—two ships full of folks from the next objective."

"Hmmm . . . And they were taken into Flux chambers and turned around to be alien stooges? Possible. Evidence though? I have some of the scientists and bureaucrats on my back already over this, even though we worked very hard to keep a tight lid on the account."

"The initial battle reports we had from the Chinese action came from the Soviet observer ships," Ngomo noted. "Nothing was said about contact or even attempting contact, and they sent pictures as long as they could. No, I think it's pretty clear that the enemy knew that word and picture had gone down and they also had already surveyed and discovered only one open Gate at the next target—not enough firepower to do things efficiently. So, as you say, they turned around a bunch of captured Soviets, sent them back in their own ship, and made them willing traitors and at the same time freed up a second Gate for their own use. They'll be nice and polite and even do a few miracles for the local savages until equipment can be brought in to remove the blocked ships and get a sufficient alien force in place to take over."

"If they have to," Coydt noted. "If they hook into and gain control of an entire cluster's master computers and the interfaces involved, they might not need more forces. There's no doubt they've been at it longer than we have and know a lot more about the process and, with all those records, about us here and humans in general. They sure got sophisticated in a hurry, you'll note. A society of pure ideal Communists, my ass!''

"Well, the board seems to want to swallow this wholesale. They want us to roll out the red carpet and the trumpeters and embrace the slimy bastards. That's another thing—I don't even know yet if they're slimy or what.''

"Even Watanabe?'' Coydt asked.

"Especially Watanabe. The old loony believes that our technology has been some sort of divine spoon-feeding, eventually to raise us all to the angelic state. She thinks these— things—have already reached that point and she can skip the next ten incarnations or whatever. Some of the others are naive, others are just plain scared and grasping at straws. Only van Haas has any guts among 'em, and he's been vacillating on the whole thing up to now. This has given him an excuse to side with his own people. Frankly, the old boy's getting a bit loony himself. Carrying that heavy burden all those years is finally telling. The bottom line with Van is that he's scared of the aliens, yes, and I doubt if he trusts them, but for some reason he's even more scared of *us*. So scared, in fact, he'll take the very slight chance on the aliens rather than leave this world to us.''

They all nodded gravely. These were four of a kind, in a sense. Career military in spite of different cultural and national origins, they tended to look at the world the same way.

"The board,'' Ngomo pointed out, "no longer has any authority.''

"No, not legally, but they still command the loyalties of a great many scientists and technicians. You all know that even after thousands of years civilians still don't look upon the military as other human beings. They mistake discipline for dictatorship and have no understanding of our sense of duty and our grave responsibilities.''

Ryan seemed to look directly at Coydt. "But can we close the Gates against the will of these people? Don't we need them to do the job? We don't have much of a staff, and I'm not sure we could count on the loyalties of the Anchor Guards if they were called on to shoot their own. I'm not sure that we could get control of Gate Three at all. I just can't see us being able to put that one over on Watanabe.''

"I can handle Watanabe," Coydt assured him.

Cockburn's bushy white eyebrows rose. "Indeed? Van Haas intimated as much, and it set him off to paranoia over you."

"Watanabe has continued to have regular sessions, even something of a relationship, with her old psychiatrist, who is also in charge of Special Projects, if you remember. The old girl is incredible with her computers, but she's human all the same. Like almost all the high-tech types, she believes what her computers tell her and she believes she's made herself invulnerable to any outside coercion. We wanted her to think that. In actual fact, we preprogrammed the Gate Three computers before she arrived and took over. Every single thing that Watanabe has discovered, every single thing Watanabe has found out, and every single plot and plan she has are in her when she's interfacing, and she communes with her beloved machines a lot. All of that is then sorted, coded, classified, interpreted, and spit out in Special Projects."

That shocked them all, but particularly Cockburn, who'd known nothing of this. "Who gave you the authority to do such a thing?"

"I interpreted it. I had specific orders to leave her alone, no matter how batty she was, because she was doing enormously valuable research. She was and is doing just that. But everyone was happy to let a woman who knew everything that human beings can know about these monster computers have a free hand, and look the other way when she got some brilliant minds and turned them into devoted cult members who thought her way. Everyone knew she was doing it—and it didn't take much extra brains to figure out she'd managed it on the security people there and she'd managed to get control through her computer of all the monitoring and recording devices as well. Dr. Suzuki saw all this coming back at Site Y, and she strongly urged that if Watanabe was ever given access to a 7800, we do just this. I felt it my duty to do it. If she'd gone ahead and learned how to seize control of and reprogram every damned computer in the network and changed us all into her vision of what the world should be, we'd all be helpless and I would be responsible. That's been her aim all along, you know."

There was no arguing with that sort of logic. Still, Cockburn said, "I just wish you would have told me. It not only would have eased my mind, but it would relieve me of this nagging question of what else all three of you haven't bothered to tell me."

"Begging your pardon, sir, but one leak anywhere would have done it in. She'd have been tipped and spared no brainpower to locate and remove those programs and she might well be the only one here who could. She fooled you all with those copies of herself she made out of some of her assistants. With all due respect, sir, a commander can't be told *everything*. That's what you pay me for. You trust me to do the job and replace me if I don't."

"All right, all right. Point taken. Now—do we agree that we should reject this message and any subsequent messages as a fraud? That we should proceed to close and seal this world anyway?"

There were three other nods.

"Very well. Yes, it can be done. I've already invoked a host of military programs none of them even knew existed, and there are some more that would give us control of the computers. Ryan, your Signals boys can pretty well guard the Gates themselves and control access along the matter transmission lines. I have enough totally loyal and efficient technicians to do what has to be done if they can get physically inside each administrative headquarters and interfaced at the main computer centers. Ngomo, I think you can find enough trusted personnel to maintain a military guard over this, with the help of Coydt's permanent parties."

The Nigerian nodded. "I believe so. It'll simply be a matter of making a convincing enough cover story. Something, perhaps, about changing the programs so that the wizards and magicians and monsters won't have power anymore. That's going through everywhere anyway, so it's just capitalizing on their existing fears."

"And what of the safety of our wizards and magicians when all this hits the fan?" the admiral asked, concerned.

"If they can't fend for themselves, in Flux, they're no threat to anyone anyway. In Anchor they have sufficient security troops to at least cover their asses. The independents

I don't care about at all. I need the cover, which also provides a convincing set of reasons for the military guard. Some will try to stop this because they want the power for themselves. See?''

"All right. I don't like it, but I'll accept it. Coydt, the third cluster alone is your baby. I want you to handle it personally. You have carte blanche there. I don't care if you have to shoot the bitch and run poison gas through the headquarters complex.''

"Oh, I don't think that will be necessary, sir,'' the security chief responded.

"Very well. It's your head, and maybe all our heads, if it doesn't get done. The clock is running on us. I want to commence exactly seven days from today. That will give all of you a chance to map out contingency plans and assemble and brief your teams. Shindler will give you the names of the technicians in each cluster and their units. You and your officers have the full authority to do whatever is necessary to accomplish the sealing. At 0400 hours one week from today all access to 7800 interfaces will be denied all personnel not specifically encoded in the computer memory by the military programs. You may submit a list of others on your staff to be added to the existing very tight limits. None of the researchers and not one of the board will have access.''

"That will drive them all nuts, but particularly Watanabe,'' Coydt noted. "This means we'll have to act to secure her before commencing operations. She'll otherwise try to get around everything.''

"I want the board neutralized for the duration,'' Cockburn told them. "House arrest if possible, but if you must shoot them, then shoot them. Understood? I want no one sowing the seeds of revolt and discord who can get an instant following. Understand that they'll have to be kept under wraps. What we do won't seal anything—it'll simply allow me to do so. I will wait until the last possible minute I deem safe, for purposes of information and in hopes there can be some sort of breakthrough. I expect Earth to concur with us, but I must tell you that if it does not, I feel I must commit treason. Like you with your Watanabe monitor, Coydt—if I have to save the bastards from taking their own lives, I'll do anything necessary to save them. The decision is made. Only the when of it remains. Now—*move!*''

Suzy Watanabe slept in a small flat she'd converted out of two offices right off the master computer center for Anchor X-ray. She rarely left the building these days, and in fact rarely even left the heart of her private interface with the system.

After her usual routine of meditation, exercise, a shower, and a very light breakfast, she donned her robe and walked to the door to go into the center itself. The door, however, refused to budge for her.

Cursing, she pulled down the manual switch and threw it, then found that it, too, had no effect. She was suddenly suspicious, and went back to one of the two doors exiting into different halls of the administration building. Neither of those doors worked either. She got on the intercom at once.

"Energy and Transport switchboard," said an unfamiliar woman's voice.

"This is Watanabe! I am locked in my chambers and I demand to know who did it and why!"

"Doctor, this is Military Security. By order of Admiral Cockburn, commander, you and the other directors are under temporary house arrest and all access by nonmilitary personnel to computer interfaces is hereby revoked."

It shocked her. She never thought it could or would happen here, in her own temple of worship, in her own inner sanctum—without warning, like thieves in the night! She didn't even know how it was possible considering the people loyal to her and the automatic defensive system she'd established. Still, fury got you nowhere.

"Are my people all right?"

"Yes, ma'am. All permanent party personnel assigned to this building were removed for their own safety and protection. There was, in fact, some strong resistance, including the use of arms against us, but we managed to subdue everyone without having to kill. Those who identify as your own personal guard are under heavy sedation, however, for their own safety. If they came to with that dedication, we would surely be forced to kill some of them."

She sighed, and felt a bit stupid to have thought that her girls would be a match for a well-planned and expertly executed takeover by military professionals. She realized, too, it was a fatal flaw in her own psyche that did it. She so detested military people and the military mentality that she had totally excluded them from her own control. Even the security people assigned here had been processed only to accept her authority and deeds as nonthreatening. She had not trusted them enough to leave them as professionals, but adopting her code and ways, since they were often rotated and it would make things obvious, that left them, in circumstnces like these, still under the orders of Coydt.

Cockburn, Coydt—they were all of a package. She had no doubt that this move was not a direct threat to her or her group; the fact that they had said they were arresting *all* the board made that plain. Clearly, it was something of a military coup. They were setting up their defenses without even talking to this new alien presence, getting ready to either kill them or seal the Gates forever in their typical knee-jerk reactions.

She reached into her robe and pulled out a tiny hand-held personal computer no larger than her hand and as thin as a ten-page pamphlet. It had limited abilities—a mere hundred thousand gigabytes of memory and it had to be downloaded to a main computer through a special interface—but it was a useful tool. Everyone working with any kind of figures had one. Nobody, however, had one programmed the way Suzy Watanabe could program.

"Ready," said a soft, small voice from the hand-held computer.

"The military has sealed me in my rooms and has removed all of my people from the temple under guard," she told it. "All other board members are also under arrest. Analysis of this coup?"

"They are going to seal the Gates."

"Yes, I figured that. How could they do it in such a way that I could not *un*do it?"

"Unknown. Probably thousands of ways to do so. Most probable would be existing undetected prior programming using the network to override."

"Undetected!" She didn't like that. She didn't like anyone, even a computer, to suggest that there was something in
her computers she hadn't even discovered.

"Information, please," the computer responded. "Was the
takeover without strong resistance, and has any sign or mention been made of computer resistance to takeover?"

"It was bloodless, they tell me, and there was no mention
of problems."

"Then they have overriden your entire defensive program
series. Either that or they are lying, in which case they will
come for you and do whatever is necessary to gain bypasses."

Ego flaw number two, she thought ruefully. It simply had
never even entered her mind that someone would capture her
alive and imprison her so easily. Short of suicide, there
seemed no way they couldn't get the bypass information out
of her if they wished. No, even suicide wouldn't help. It had
been Coydt, after all, who'd resurrected her in the first place.
Damn! They didn't even need to come for her. All they had
to do was kill her while she was trapped here and then
resurrect a very obedient new Suzy somewhere else. She felt
angry, not at them but at herself.

And, of course, Short Stuff, her personal, was absolutely
right. They probably hadn't run into anything because she
was still here and still herself. That meant they'd bypassed all
that sophisticated defensive programming before they'd even
entered the temple, and that meant sending overriding commands to her own 7800 and everyone else's before they ever
got through the front door. Short Stuff was right. There were
layers of that big computer she never detected or even suspected were there. Now, for the first time, she understood the
real reason why the only operational 7800 had gone to Security at Site Y, and what had been their primary mission there.

There was, however, still one chance to foul them up. She
went into her office and tripped a series of secret panels built
into her desk and the wall beside it. With the right ID codes
and prints, it all folded down into a crude but working
Overrider interface. She put on the crude headset, adjusted
the controls, and opened her mind.

The interface played a stirring rendition of "God Save the
King." It played it over and over, and there was no way to

break through or get any other response. After a half-hour trying to do so, she was so sick of that song, she was happy that her former homeland, Australia, had finally declared itself a republic.

This had really torn it though. Clearly they *had* simply ignored her whole set of local protection commands, and the computer had no choice but to obey. Years ago she'd discovered and turned to her own ends Coydt's little trap allowing someone else to be Watanabe and filter through all her work. If they'd tried that route, they would have had a rude surprise, so they had simply overridden all of it.

She needed to think. Assuming they could do this, Short Stuff was certainly right that an override of the military system was unlikely. If they sent a tapeworm through the Gate program, destroying its knowledge of how to reset for incoming, she might be able to write new programs to do what they had erased, given enough time. Transportation, after all, had pretty much designed those Gates, and she knew exactly how they operated.

They, of course, would know that too. Realize that not only she but lots of Transportation people could do it. It was too insecure for them. Even if they shot everyone involved, they'd never be sure they didn't miss somebody.

Some sort of program, then, within this special military override. A set of commands using a language and system proprietary to them and probably using computer-generated security ciphers and filled with deadly traps to anyone even looking over how to reverse them. Unless you had all seven parts of the cipher and then were able to decode it and apply it in a preset manner—probably all seven at once or something like that—it could never be overridden. Then Cockburn would scatter that code all over the place so that not even he knew where it all was, and you'd need a fair number of people agreeing to furnish their parts just to reassemble it. It was impossible. She would have to accept the fact that, unless these aliens or Earth could break through, the Gates would remain shut. Only by going out into space, finding an optimum point, and opening up a new Borelli Point would it ever be possible to go inbound or outbound—and except for some small automated devices, all spacecraft had been destroyed or cannibalized after New Eden was terraformed to prevent such a thing and the Point in space closed and blown.

They would be truly sealed in, that was sure. She knew that the nature of the Flux strings in that alternate universe were pretty easily fixed. Nobody could open up a new hole outbound or inbound without the new string immediately converging on the existing one. So long as the Borelli Points were still open, even if sealed to incoming traffic, here on New Eden, any attempt to punch through would result only in nothing reassembling. That was true for traffic coming from either direction. They were stuck. The only way out now would be for somebody to build a spacecraft capable of creating and controlling a Borelli Point in space, then punching through from there—only, probably, to get stuck at the next set of Gates down.

She sat back in her chair and sighed. All right, then—she couldn't stop it, and she probably couldn't get into the computers and override the defensive systems without destroying herself. She had to accept what was, or would soon be, if the fools could do it at all. Then what?

The gods had teased her, tantalized her. They had shown her the way to the true inner light, then snatched it away. It was not to be achieved as a gift, that was certain. She saw the pattern. Those who had opposed the shining path of perfection had been destroyed. Those who had embraced it now were receiving it. Here, on New Eden, there was division. The people and those of the true path would embrace it, but there was an evil infrastructure that opposed it—the military. They were not to be denied salvation, but they would have to earn it. They would have to achieve a state of near perfection themselves, and they would have to cleanse the world of evil. But how?

With its control of all weaponry and all the top levels of technology, the military would always be supreme. Even to wipe it out would simply result in the creation of a new overclass. Such power as this corrupted everyone, even herself. She had hoped that by communion with the computers they could attain the highest state, but she knew now that even her beloved computers were corrupted by the evil.

With a start she realized that the gods had been showing

her that from the start, but she had simply failed, in her blind love of her machines, to divine the meaning. Those horrible monstrosities, those duggers. The computer had corrupted them, deformed them, made them not great but lesser beings. Even the experiments with direct network access among deliberate scientists had corrupted those scientists, turned them into freaks or riddled their souls with the evil lust for ultimate power over others, the same evil that corrupted the military by its very nature.

Salvation, then, could not come through the computers, yet the computers were necessary to sustain life. She had been given the gift to understand all that was good in the computers while denying her its most evil heart. Even so, had she not understood her own divine will by being exposed to the potential evils of the computers?

At last she understood the message that the ghosts of her parents had brought her so long ago. She had sensed the great evil inherent in the big machines and she had attempted to shirk her duty, her divine mission, when she was their chosen instrument. They had not let her, making her own worse enemy, the source of much of the evil, Coydt, personally bring her back and yet leave her untouched when it would have been so simple to alter her mind and will! She had decided to come here only because the ghosts had intimated a great duty and responsibility to do so. Now she thought she understood.

Earth could not be saved. It was dominated by the Coydts and the Cockburns and always had been and always would be. Borelli had been less a genius than a prophet, sent by the gods, first to prevent the Cockburns and the Coydts and their minions from destroying humanity prematurely, then by providing the basis for some of humanity to get out. Now Earth, cut from this power and fearful of any use lest it attract the enemy they did not know but feared, was doomed to starvation, war, and eventual death no matter what. Only those out here, in the new worlds, had the possibility of finding the true path to salvation and union with the gods.

Humanity had been given two examples—to fight was oblivion, to accept was nirvana. Humanity had chosen to flee instead, wall itself out. It was too infused with evil to do

otherwise. Now those lost souls of Earth would be reborn on
the colonies so that their souls would have the chance. It was
up to her to preserve this colony until that had the chance to
occur, then, when perfection was attained, humanity would
no longer need the Gates but would be capable of direct
communion with the gods and their angels up the line. It was
all so very, very clear to her now.

She was chosen. Selected by the gods as a new prophet.
She was the way she was because it fit into the divine plan.
Men had the souls of aggressors, and their souls were flawed
with the evil. Women, with their beautiful bodies and their
sense of family and responsibility for childbirth and early
rearing, were the nurturers. The gods had decreed that she not
be corrupted by men so that she could create a society where
men were the subservient ones and could be taught by example the true path.

It was also clear that salvation lay in Anchor, for Flux
corrupted. Flux itself, like all things of science, was indeed
neutral, but human beings were too flawed to use it properly,
including herself. In a practical sense, then, Flux was evil in
the long term, yet it was the obvious tool of the gods.

She had often thought of the kind of society she would
build if she had the power, and even had models of it in her
now inaccessible computer banks. Not a utopia, but merely a
correct and simple way for humanity to live and perfect its
spiritual self. There were practical considerations, of course,
but these could be dealt with. Compromise was possible even
with evil if the evil could be contained to its own realm and
forced to cooperate with good. Perhaps it would even act as a
natural filter for those corrupting people within the perfecting
societies. And when the people attained the true path, attained
nirvana, through incarnations and trial, the Flux would be
there and no evil within it could stand, and the Flux would be
the gateway to the gods.

It now became a mere engineering problem. To deny the
military access to the power they had, no matter what the
programs they could activate, and to create the society ideal
for the purpose of the gods within each Anchor. Much of it
was risky, and much of it would not be considered by a sane

scientist. Tampering with the maintenance program itself, for example, on a global scale, courted the possibility of killing virtually everyone and everything on New Eden. It no longer troubled her, though, because she was certain she was right. The gods' intentions were quite clear.

With much meditation and the aid of Short Stuff, she would spend this time of imprisonment, even if it was years, perfecting the programs, and she *knew* they would run and *knew* they would do the right thing because they came not from her but from the gods themselves. She did not even doubt that eventually the evil ones would give her sufficient access to the computers to do this thing. The gods would see to that.

In the small colony on the border of Anchor Luck, little really changed. There were some inconveniences, of course, from having their big amp disabled and being unable to contact Seventeen or even file their data with the big computer, but the inconveniences were minor and their pocket computers did a reasonable job of at least record-keeping and minor problem-solving.

There was a general feeling, though, from the Hallers to the Haldaynes to the Wus, that sealing the Gates was a good thing. None of them, having tapped the powers they had tapped, considered leaving for a moment, and none felt much loyalty to old Earth beyond protecting it from here and none really wanted to test out this alien power as the Soviets had done.

In fact, the only one with any real regrets at all seemed to be Micki Haller, and that was on a minor point of aesthetics. "Now there won't ever be fish," she mourned.

They all felt a tremendous release of tension after the threat and the uncertainty of the previous weeks, although none really knew when or if the Gates had yet been sealed. Rumors flew that the entire board had been arrested to prevent them from trying to talk to the invaders, and there was still some uncertainty over the future course and direction of the colony, but the major pressure point had been removed. They were now, more than ever, experimenting for themselves.

Still, other rumors and trends bothered them. A number of

people in the Anchor had been killed or imprisoned, without trial or charge, by military authorities under the provisions of martial law. While the takeover had on the whole been peaceful, there was no way without Seventeen to really find out if this was typical of, or even more peaceful than, the rest of the world. There was a great deal of grumbling and unrest among the various communes and towns and ethnic and religious groups that might well lead to more open conflicts should the martial law become even more harsh or look as if it were going to become permanent.

There were rumors, too, about the Special Projects folk. Ugly rumors. They were neither loved nor trusted by most of the common folk of Anchor from the start, and now someone seemed to be feeding this sense of distrust and unease—someone official. Few ventured far from their tiny and secure community without meeting outright hostility; those marked from their experiments and encounters such as Haldayne became virtual prisoners in the community after there were mob attacks on some others, whose lives were saved only by the quick and direct action of their security shadows. Micki's playful use of terms like "witches" and "wizards" was haunting her now; those same words were being used with conviction by the farmers and townspeople of their Anchor and perhaps others.

Lisa Wu discussed the problem with her group. Most felt that the military was behind it for reasons of their own, and there was a general suspicion that this might be not only an attempt to divert the Anchor colonists from their growing dislike of the military by furnishing another enemy, but also at the same time a way to isolate them and make them dependent upon, and, perhaps, eventually controlled by the military directly as their only friends.

"We can always just move into Flux and start our independent colony," a number of people noted. "We can be free of any threat there. Even the weakest of us is tremendously powerful when compared to any threat!"

"Oh, really?" Micki Haller retorted somewhat acidly. "And what about twenty thousand or so Signal corps troops who live and work in the void all the time, probably have as much if not more power than we, and have the heavy weapons and access to the big computers as well? You think they're not out there? You think that we're not as closely monitored in the void as we are here? You must be blind!"

And, of course, deep down, they all knew she was right.

"It's true that our group is the most closely monitored," Lisa Wu told them, "but that's because we're the official experiment, funded by and for the benefit of the company. Equally, there is Special Projects in the capital here, funded by Security, and also independent projects by Signals and by Transportation and Energy. But none of us—*none* of us—are powerless in this. We no longer have a company, so we no longer have a boss. Many others, independently and in free-lance associations, have also done their own research and development on this. Counting the children, it is estimated that several thousand at least have this power. Of those, perhaps a few hundred have huge power and the training and background to make the best use of it. The vast majority of those are here. I worry about a thousand things, but I do not worry about the Signal corps or Security, who cannot even find hundreds, perhaps more, duggers out there. We will be discovered only if and when we wish to be discovered."

"Then you think we should leave?" someone asked.

"I think everyone should make their own decisions. As for me, so long as I have some voice here, and at least I am listened to, I feel I must stay. There are things afoot—unsettling things—that have split even the commands of the military. Those of you who wish to leave may do so with my blessing, but only into the void. If you go elsewhere in Anchor, you will be marked and possibly die. The Home Guard and Watanabe's crazy church are fanning the flames against us for their own different reasons, but both have our names and pictures, and those who have changed beyond that stand out for other reasons. Until things sort themselves out, we are safe here, but only here, with our backs to our escape route into the void. The big amp will never again be reconnected—they found quite a number of illegal ones since the military takeover of the network and they cannot take the chance of activating one without risking them all. Now that we are a closed society, those once bound by duty or loyalty to others will feel free to act. I for one will sit here and see if things sort out in our favor and try to influence what I can. But I am keeping my family dressed and my bags packed.''

15

THE ORDER OF THE TRIPLE CROSS

"You must leave, and quickly," the stranger told Lisa Wu. "You and all the others here, whether they have power or not."

"I'm not about to pack up everything and run on your say-so, Mr.—Singh, was it? I have Admiral Cockburn's personal assurances and protection."

The dark man in the turban sighed. "Madam Director, Admiral Cockburn is dead. The news has not yet been made public for various reasons."

She sat bolt upright. *"What!"*

"I said that the admiral is no more. He was shot to death as he rounded the turn heading out of the wood toward his house while perched atop his miniature train. His batman, Shindler, and his personal staff are also dead, and most of his headquarters personnel are even now in the process of being shot or processed by computer if they have value."

"That's not possible! Who would do such a thing—and why? I don't believe you for a moment."

"Madam Director, Ngomo has declared himself field marshal and president of the Holy Islamic Republic of New Eden. His actions were well-planned, his politics flawless. Even as we speak, resistance is being mopped up in capital after capital, including here."

"My God! *Ngomo?* Now I know you're mad!"

"I wish to God I were, but I am not. He had the troops, he had the Home Guard and the sympathies of many former soldiers, and what he lacked he recruited from the Islamic Anchors."

"But—good Lord! *Ngomo?* I mean, hell, nobody even took *him* seriously!"

"That is precisely the point. Everyone tended to underestimate him. It was almost forgotten that he organized everything here before anyone else arrived. He got the supplies through, he set up the auxiliary computers, he pretty much designed the way things were laid out. It is a monumental job of organization and politics, and he did not leave it all to lesser officers. He is a brilliant organizer and tactician. He was also on this project because he had been part of a prior military junta in his native land who was no longer necessary. He organized the coup and its government and got popular support, but the others feared his power and his honesty and expelled him from the country. Originally his work with Westrex was just to get money and a power base to use to return, but he got caught up in the adventure and scope of our project and never did return. This is not a man to tread upon, and tread upon him they did."

"Well, he was certainly demoted," she noted, trying not to believe this strange man.

"He was a Moslem among three Roman Catholics. He was a black man to tread upon, and tread upon him they did."

"Well, he was certainly demoted," she noted, trying not to believe this strange man.

"He was a Moslem among three Roman Catholics. He was a black man, an African, among three whites. He made them uncomfortable, although fully half the population here is of color and perhaps that many, although not all the same people, are one or another sort of Moslem. I am brown and you are yellow. You can understand what it did to his pride. And men of his intelligence and ability can suffer that sort of thing only so long."

"But—why now?"

"The Gates are sealed. Westrex gave him a high position and authority when he was an outcast. For loyalty to them and to the dream, and out of idealism and hope that what we did here would benefit his people, he was a good soldier, even when the others reorganized him out of a command and out of any true power base. They dissolved his command and no longer consulted him except in a pro forma way, and they gave him a meaningless title and job. When the dugger attacks reached a few Anchors, he played that up into a new position and convinced them that he should head it. The Anchor or Home Guard. As is true with most in great positions of power and authority, the other three did not even realize the depth of his hurt or the brilliance of his organizational mind. When they sealed the Gates, he no longer had anything he could do for his people back on Earth or any more loyalty to Westrex, which became irrelevant. He is moving for his own pride and also for what people he now has—the Moslems of New Eden, and perhaps the blacks as well, although I believe he is more color blind than those who opposed and denigrated him.''

"Well, dammit, man—you said you were from Security. Why the hell didn't you find out about this? The organization involved for a worldwide plot of this magnitude in so short a time *couldn't* have been kept secret!'' The Gates had now been sealed for seventeen months.

"Correct, as far as it went. We *did* get wind of it almost from the start, but he is quite clever and he had allies. It appeared that the thing originated from below—younger officers and some of the holy men who held influence over them in the mosques—and was quite widespread. We let it go for a while to see where it would lead, and to identify all of the major leaders with an eye to crushing them at once and minimizing bloodshed and rebellion. We were betrayed instead. As an old hand at coups, Ngomo knew that if one needs to make a pact in blood with the devil to do something, he will sign such a pact and try to deal with his distasteful allies later.''

Lisa Wu had a sudden creeping feeling in the pit of her stomach. "That bitch Watanabe.''

"Yes. You do not seem surprised. It fairly shocked us. Watanabe hates the military, you see, and Islam would hardly be conducive to her all-female church.''

Six months after the Gates had been sealed, the former

directors had been released from custody, Watanabe included, but restricted to Anchor and forbidden to live even in the capital, let alone enter the headquarters building. All were watched by Security personnel and the Anchor Guard, but Ngomo had some allies in the middle ranks of Security, and knew the list of Security personnel already at least somewhat under Watanabe's control.

And Watanabe was still a genius. Security made the same mistake that Cockburn and the others had made; in the end, Coydt's people had relied on what the computers reported to them, and the computers were not necessarily giving them the story. Key people under Watanabe or Ngomo's control, either literally or through ultimate loyalty, were shifted by computer orders to certain vital points; others who could and would have unmasked the whole thing wound up watching the wrong people, or minor people, and reporting a wholly credible and totally misleading revolutionary scenario that was bearing apparent fruit to Security but was nowhere near acting.

"The key was Watanabe," Singh told her. "We never suspected her for a moment. For years, since the founding of this place, we have had access to her innermost thoughts and ideas—or so we believed. We had no idea that she suspected, let alone discovered this. She did not stop it. She is far too clever for that. She simply placed data filters in line between our readouts and her input. What we got was so bad, we never suspected that anything more was being kept from us. And once she was in control, she could insulate Ngomo and his key officers as well."

"And—her price?"

"Ngomo gets the whole world except for her cluster. She gets that to do with as she will. All of Ngomo's people and any Moslems there will be allowed out before she assumes total control. The troops there are specially processed by her, using a procedure we cannot begin to understand. They are subservient to the church, loyal to her, and willing to fight to the death for her church, male or female. This gives her security and absolute control of four 7800 series, thirty-two 7240 series, and several hundred lesser computers, all for her own use, as well as access through the network to the entire data bank for amplifiers and the like.''

The idea was chilling. ''And Ngomo thinks he can contain her there? After what she's already shown she can do?''

''Ngomo is no fool. He has had the fruits of revolution snatched from him by compatriots before, remember. He has the military command codes. He has used them to set up conditions under which any violation of the agreement by Watanabe will result in a Region Three master shutdown. He feels secure for a while with this, although he is not, as I said, a stupid man. Eventually, after consolidating his new regime elsewhere, he will turn those military programs on Watanabe.''

''And she knows this. It's still going to be cat and mouse.''

''Indeed. Highly unpleasant cat and mouse. And they did in fact make several serious errors in their takeover, as might be expected of something so complex, the most fatal of which was that General Ryan discovered the full scope of things too late to stop it but in time to prevent a meeting of the general staff at which time Ngomo was going to imprison or kill the others.

''Cockburn simply placed his Headquarters Anchor on full alert and dispatched Coydt and several top computer experts from Security and Signals to Region Three to try to cut it off if they could. They were still getting set up for the counter-move when Ngomo, realizing the jig was up, moved precipitously. Headquarters had five thousand troops, but most were technicians and bureaucrats. When Cockburn and the top officers on the staff were taken out, most of them switched rather than fought. The few hundred who did not were quickly taken out.''

''But—Security and Signals!''

''Security's ten thousand or so are spread over the entire planet, excluding the headquarters staff, who were the first to die. That's only a few hundred per Anchor. Signals has twenty-two thousand, but they are spread all over the void, an even larger area, and concentrated only in a few spots. They had no more than a few hundred people in each Anchor either. Ngomo has used the military override commands to change the nature of grid energy, excluding the type that is used to power everything from the so-called god guns to the automatic cars. Their motors can no longer draw power from the grid. This has effectively cut Ryan off, as his troops must move on foot or on what horses they have—and it's not enough—and even supplies must be moved the hard way. They are all designed to take a two-hundred-and-forty-volt, fifty-cycle direct current. The grid will no longer deliver that voltage, although it will deliver others.''

"Jesus!"

"This, then, gives Ngomo the only effective and cohesive forces on New Eden.''

"But—wait a minute! The direct computer interfaces and the big amps don't run off the grid. They convert Flux directly.''

"Yes, but with a directive prohibiting power to the remote units and his people in control of all administrative buildings, what difference does that make?''

"A lot. Security may have blown it, but I can't believe you're *this* incompetent. Watanabe and her followers remained in their exile camp, did they not? They did not get back to the building, even under false pretenses?''

"Of that I will swear. Yes. Why is this important?''

"Because she couldn't have done all her damned tinkering indirectly, feeding long strings of esoteric programs and chains to army people who then trotted off and enacted them. She needed a direct and secure interface. It's the same way she fooled you. She's got a big amp in the void right near that camp of hers that doesn't register on anybody's monitors. She's got it totally hidden, its actions masked, and its power consumption buried in some other place so it doesn't show. That's the reason for her revival city out there in the east of X-ray.''

"But even if that were true, it wouldn't function under the military orders,'' Singh pointed out.

"Yeah, and no 7240 can ever be interfaced without a Guard. Bullshit. She's somehow got the 7800 convinced that it's not a big amp at all, and so not subject to the exclusion order. I bet it took her all of a day and a half to solve it, too, sitting there in her comfortable little prison all those months. Damn!''

"So?"

"Well, *we've* got a big amp here, too, just out there in the void."

"But it is disconnected!"

"Sure—and so was hers. If we can figure out how to do that trick, we might be able to play hell with all this yet. What about Signals? Do they still have full communications?"

"Ryan has no direct interface with a 7800, but he does have a great deal of specialized equipment directly hooked up to the network and it is not two-forty dependent. Yes. He can talk—he just can't act."

"Maybe we can—if we have enough time to solve this thing before they come here with stakes to burn the witches and wizards and stick black robes and veils on the survivors."

"I am afraid you might not be joking. The sentiment against the people here is getting that virulent, and Ngomo, of necessity, made his primary deals not with the moderate and modern Islamic communities but with the most fanatical and fundamentalist leaders. They are a tiny minority of the whole, but they have been handed the keys to power with promises of liberal rule and they are, of course, being believed in the main. By the time they find out just what they have been given the keys to, the conservatives will be in full control and will have sufficient technical support to convert the population to their way of thinking using the 7800. It has happened before, but never before have they had delivered into their hands the means for absolute conversion."

"They'll never do it. They are too few against a vast majority, and that majority includes some pretty devout people on their own side. The Hindu population here won't stand for it at all, and the Christians will be equally indignant. They can't mass-convert a population quietly. It will simply mean more blood."

"But they can and they believe they will," Singh told her. "That is part of the deal with Watanabe. She believes she has a master program that will actually alter the master Anchor programs, that will convert everyone in it to their way at once."

Lisa Wu gasped. "But that would kill every living thing!"

"Indeed. Kill it—and resurrect it, all in a matter of perhaps three quarters of an hour, maybe less. Nothing will be changed except that all human beings within the Anchor programming matrix will be commonly filtered before being restored. In a way, we can say that they will know all but remember nothing. It must be admitted that while this has been done with individuals and even with very small groups, it has never been done or proven on this scale and even Watanabe is not certain that it will work as intended. She is a driven woman, however. She believes God guides her hand.''

"My God! Where's Coydt? Where's the opposition to this? Do you realize what you just told me? That twenty-four Anchors are about to be propelled socially back to the fourteenth century and that four others are about to be forced into the mold of a mad woman?''

"I know this. It is why I am here. Security is doing what it can, but Ngomo has the military command codes. All Security personnel have been disallowed access to the 7800 network. That is how Ngomo did it. That is what I have been telling you. There were enough traitors within Cockburn's staff who, for their own personal reasons or for dreams of power and empty promises, gave our rebel general control. First he got the control codes. Then he killed Cockburn and all staff that he either could not or did not control or own outright. Then he cut us all out of the network, and only then did his troops and the civilian groups within the Anchors begin their ruthless takeover. All we can do is alert everyone we can and aid them in getting out to the void. We do not know how much time we have, although it is certainly not hours or even days but weeks at least we are talking about. There is an organizational plan, but it is a bleak one.''

"Go on.''

"We are trying to move as much in the way of books, records, programming modules—all that is central to our origins, our history, and our technology, even if we can't use or access it at this time, into safe areas in the void. Ryan's troops are instructed to assist in this. These enclaves are being established by all the Sensitives we can save, contact, or round up.''

"If we can just activate that amp and get into the net!''

Pandit Singh stared at her. ''And do what? Perhaps, just

perhaps, we can save Anchor Luck. Even more of a perhaps is saving Region Four. We get a terribly bloody and divisive civil war in each and in the end the others simply ride down in some kind of jihad and take the survivors. Face it. We have been so busy spying upon and fearing one another that we failed to see the competent and dangerous idealist in our midst plotting our overthrow. Security is very much to blame, I admit. We were so busy ferreting out secrets that we discounted the invisible man sitting there in plain sight casually learning what had to be learned and doing what had to be done.''

"Then we should just—*surrender?* Abandon millions of innocent souls to this?''

"No. Try to find a way to beat them if you can, of course, but at the same time prepare for the worst and always consider the consequences. What is done by computer may be undone by computer.''

"And what of you and Coydt and the rest?'' she asked.

"Our own Special Projects people managed to get an enormous load of material out of the headquarters before it became impossible. They trucked it down to the Gate transmission room and out to Gate Four. I am going there now, if I can. I have enough contacts and blackmail and knowledge of secrets that I believe I can penetrate the headquarters and use the transmission system. There is a secret exit from Suzuki's office that leads through walls and down to the basement area, for example. I have a number of identities, including one as an officer of the Anchor Guard. I believe I will succeed. There, what has been taken out will be dispersed as best we can to existing redoubts, and Signals will keep track of what and where as best it can and move it as needed. I will be coordinating there as best I can. When you establish your areas in the void, contact Signals or the Gate as best you can and we will attempt to establish a network of resistance groups. Others here and in all the other Anchors are attempting as best they can to convince people of the impending doom and to rise and act, but few truly believe it is even possible.''

"But something should be done to begin evacuating all that do buy it to the void!''

"They won't go. Some will, and we will use them, but

most will not. This is their land, their home. They did not go back to Earth when they had the chance in a crisis they could see and understand; they will not abandon it now because of some political coup and a lot of speculative nonsense that they will somehow be changed as a group. They are ready to fight for their land, Arab and Hindu and Nigerian and Argentine and Aussie alike, but they cannot believe or even accept that they will have no chance to fight. Many are now rejoicing at the spreading news that the so-called military dictatorship is ended and the dreaded Security is destroyed or impotent, and their liberators are clever and patient and extremely intelligent. Do not confuse their fundamentalism, their religious rock, their total belief that they do the will of Allah, with stupidity. They are brilliant and they know they will never get a second chance.''

''Maybe not even a first one if they're foolish enough to trust Watanabe to do their program right.''

''She will do it their way, for as I said, they are not stupid and the distances are quite large between Anchors. They will try it one Anchor at a time, and test it carefully. Watanabe, too, is no fool, even if mad. She knows as well as they that there is no second chance if she tries to cross them. One false move and they will cut her lines absolutely, then physically overwhelm her even if they must kill every man, woman, and child in Region Three. The programs, if they work at all, will work as they wish. Watanabe is a good politician. Her madness is always tolerated so long as Signals and we and the directors and the rest are out there in the void, with powers and some contact with one another and the network, they cannot afford not to have her. She is patient. She will bide her time, which might be considerable, then strike only when success is absolutely assured.''

''Ngomo must know that too.''

''Indeed, but he has little choice. I only know that it is far easier to make a revolution than to keep it, and that it will in the end be a question of who strikes first. We consider the odds to be even.''

''And Coydt? Where is she in all this?''

''That, I'm afraid, is an unanswerable question. I only know she took Suzuki, several of Suzuki's staff, and a number of Pathfinders and rode off. I have my suspicions, considering that all in her party were women, but I do not want to know any more.''

Lisa Wu sighed. "I think I better call a meeting now. How can we contact Signals if we need them? If nothing's running out there, we're gonna need horses, mules, wagons, whatever, not to mention manpower."

"The security troops here know what is happening. They will be with you. The officer of the day has communications equipment to reach Signals personnel in the area if need be." He paused, looking sheepish. "It was necessary to monitor you in the void."

"We figured that out long ago. Don't worry. It might pay, though, to get some people to go into Anchor and beg, borrow, buy, or steal some horses. They'll be in very short supply out there for quite a while and not critical here yet since everything's still working."

"It is being done." He got up and offered his hand, and she did likewise and shook it. "I must go now. Go with God's blessings and protection. I hope to see you once more, out there."

"It better be. I'm a Buddhist and I certainly don't want to be reincarnated in one of these Anchors."

"Remember the lesson of the Flux," he said sagely. "No matter what things are, *nothing* is permanent. Nothing. All things change, and all things are mutable. So long as we remain keepers of the ideas and seekers of truth and justice, we will eventually prevail."

"That's *my* line," she responded sourly, never more depressed in her entire life.

He sat there in his black uniform and black bush hat atop a horse just as dark, relaxed and smoking a big cigar. His bodyguard was all around him, although many were invisible to the onlooker and certainly to the approaching riders.

In the old days of just a few weeks before, the journey the women now approaching had undertaken would have taken perhaps four days. Instead, it had taken them almost three weeks of constant riding and prearranged horse-switching and minimal sleeping and eating.

The leader of the women showed her exhaustion in her face as she approached him and came to a stop. She nodded. "Hello, Mike. You haven't changed a bit."

"Brenda, you look like hell," replied General Michael Ryan dryly. "Come on and follow us. We've got a small pocket over here with all the comforts of home."

To one who could not see the invisible energy bands, the strings, of the Signal corps, finding the pocket would have been next to impossible. Even those who could see the strings had to know their complex code to find anything of value. It had kept the duggers away and retained the transport routes through the void pretty much intact, although at a snail's pace.

The pocket was a small area formed by god guns using specific sorts of programs. It was not large—perhaps two hundred square meters—but it was enormous by pocket standards. Quite a number of the things had been provided not merely as food and water resupply stations but as small bases for Signal corps local administrative personnel. There were actually some small one-room buildings here, along with some fruit and coconut palm trees as well, surrounding a nice little pool of clear water. It was lit by some interaction of the void with the bubble, and the water was constantly renewed. There was even a small but modern lavatory and shower. The whole area was thickly carpeted with soft green grass that seemed manicured. The light level was lower than Anchor by a fairly strong factor, but it was constant, and seemed sufficient to keep the plants thriving on their own. The program that had created it also kept a constant supply of water in that pool. A small creek flowed from the void down a slight incline to the pool, although it had its origin in the void and not in any condensation. What was needed was simply being transmuted from Flux energy. What was consumed and then given off was reconverted and sent out to the void.

It was, however, quite warm and very humid, even when allowing for the contrast of entering from the desertlike dryness of the void, as if the still atmosphere were an amorphous and penetrable woolen blanket soaked with water. Without this humidity sufficient water would not be introduced to the trees and grasses to maintain them.

Brenda Coydt noted the gun belts and holsters worn by Ryan and his people. "What in hell are *those*?" she asked him.

Ryan grinned, took out a massive-looking pistol of metallic black with white pearl handles. "This, my dear, is a .44-caliber Magnum handgun. These are the bullets—the projectiles—that it fires with really lethal effect."

She stared at the thing, which she hadn't seen outside of museums and historical dramas. "And those?" She pointed to some of the others.

"Various pistols, rifles, shotguns, and even a submachine gun or two capable of pumping hundreds of rounds of these things in a general direction in seconds."

"Where in hell did you *get* them?"

"Cockburn had his toy train, van Haas had his art collection, I don't know what you brought in. Me, I brought my antique gun collection. Every one mint and in perfect firing condition. We've been having our Sensitives grind out these damned things and the bullets for them—particularly the bullets—at a feverish pace ever since we got cut off, and I'm having pistol and rifle instruction all over the damned place. Not nearly as effective as the lasers and the stun rifles we used to have, and much harder to use properly, but they sure work real nice. You know we can't charge those damned laser weapons anymore. We can *create* the suckers, but they always come up dry. So, what the hell. Right now I'm having some folks comb the historical records we got out of headquarters for all sort of other shit like this. We made some really good if basic cannons, and even got some kind of chemical powder that's better and more efficient than gunpowder out of those Sensitives' commands—but we can only go so far. Ancient-style caissons I can manage—they were pretty simple. Just a matter of pump and prime and making sure the damned cannonballs fit the barrels. The more sophisticated stuff we can't manage. Tolerances are too close."

"Yeah, but—antique explosive projectile weapons?"

"Listen, I'd use crossbows if I had to. Or stones and spears. They're not worth shit against what the Anchor Guard can put against us, I admit, but they're golden in Flux where *their* weapons run dry too. Two of those submachine guns cut a band of twenty-nine duggers to ribbons the other day. Nobody's gonna come in here and get us, I swear. They'll have to terraform the whole bloody planet to do that."

"They can't," she assured him. "The climatology was never really worked out and tested, and it'd probably bring massive changes if they even did a single region. When they shut the Gates, they had to limit the amount of opening for incoming Flux bleed so a ship couldn't creep in during a time when the computers were getting large refills. They don't have enough for the whole world. You can relax on that score." She relaxed and spread out on the grass. "*God!* I'm tired!"

"Well, we'll get you all food and you better get as long a sleep as you need here. Time's really wasting."

Her eyes had closed, but one of them opened. "What do you mean by that?"

"The old bat's ready to test out her own personal theories on X-ray within days. If it goes well, then 'bye-'bye Charley, George, and Queen. The word is that if it all works, then Anchor Luck will be the test of the Holy Islamic program, followed by Nancy, Mary, and Baker, because there's such a large percentage of devotees of the fundamentalists there. That's where they sent all the bad boys to begin with, remember. If *that* goes well, they'll try to convert the rest close to simultaneously once they deploy their people from Region Four. A matter of a couple of months. But that's not the kicker. A bunch of our bright boys and girls, using what computer power remains to them, postulated Watanabe's complete, rip-roaring success and asked the little thinkers to think like dear old Suzy. We tried to figure out her game for once, and I think the computers confirmed our worst fears."

"Huh?" She sat up, feeling more awake. "Come on, as little as I can stand worse than this."

"We think she's gonna prove her own program out, then give them loaded modules interfaced together. If you just postulate to the network of all twenty-eight fucking 7800 computers a set of 'if, then' conditions, then when those conditions occur, a process will be enacted automatically. That's what we did with the military programs. We weren't even able to use or access those suckers until all twenty-eight big brains agreed that there was a threat sufficient to enact them. That's what gave me and some of my folks with nasty minds the suspicion in the first place.''

"Go on.''

"Well, she's been working on the network a long time now. Been making and testing out her big super-tranformation programs. Checking them out. She would need access to the data for all the Anchors to allow for all sorts of conditions, including number of people, types, ages, skills, you name it. Old Suzy knows that Ngomo's gonna have her blown to her own special hell as soon as he's sure he doesn't need her anymore, and that could be as early as the enactment of the master programs. He's got a lot of bright computer people, after all. Not of Suzy's genius, but after this her genius is a total liability. *I'd* sure blow her away.''

She nodded. "I'm listening.''

"O.K., so we plant a master series of programs down in the hearts and minds of the assembled 7800 congregation. Suzy's programs. But they don't exist because they're conditional independents. We taught her how to do it by showing her the military programs in operation. These programs are like big bombs. They sit there, fat, dumb, and happy, doing nothing, not being noticed, ignored even by the computers, unless all twenty-eight agree that a certain condition exists and at that point these are independently triggered. Say these are called defensive programs. They are only to be used to safeguard everyone in Anchor *if all twenty-eight Anchors have had their stabilization programs modified.*''

She sank back on the grass and closed her eyes. "Oh, my God!'' She paused a moment, seeming to be asleep, but then said, "I wish I'd never resurrected the old bag.''

"Well, you did, and now it's cost us. Who could have foreseen all this though? An external enemy, the Gates sealed, coups and revolutions . . .''

"Every great event in human history results from a combination of unlikely, almost unbelievable circumstances coming together. This is no different. Still, it really screws up our plans.''

"Yup. Just blowing the old bag away and taking out Ngomo won't do it all, love. We've got to intercept those modules somehow when they get distributed to the faraway Anchors, if they haven't been already.''

"You've contacted Ngomo?"

"Oh, sure. I never could get Tom on the line as quick as I got Al. He was cordial, even conciliatory. Offered a whole set of deals. Didn't believe a word I was saying though. I could tell. He thinks it's just one last desperation gambit on our part—which, in a sense, it is. It's no less real a threat, though, for being that. Fact is, unless we can prove our case, he won't accept the double-cross.''

"How can we prove it? He *must* be blind or mad!''

Ryan chuckled. ''Just as blind and mad as you and me and Tom and the rest, maybe? We had the power, love, and power breeds arrogance and contempt for the lowly. We were so damned fucking secure with our godlike powers and our master computers feeding us just what our enemies wanted us to hear. Why should he be any different?''

She sighed. ''I'm going to sleep on it. A long sleep. Wake me if you get a date and place for the big demonstration.''

"How are you gonna get in there, love? You think they won't have that whole damned sector of Anchor sealed off? And if the old bag's in the void, she'll be under one hell of a big amp force field.''

"I'm going in the Gate. She'll return to the capital as soon as it's done to check her work and coordinate her takeover.''

"Now, how in *hell* are you gonna do that? Security system, remember? It'll run a tube purge if you trip the second-section lights going in.''

She smiled dreamily, half out already. ''That's no problem if you know the right codes,'' she mumbled, and was out.

She remained with Ryan for three days, plotting out the means and methods and contingency plans should she fail. Coydt did not, of course, intend to do the job herself; without the big computer she was unable to really alter her appearance beyond recognition and she would not be welcome in Anchor X-ray. She would see that everyone got through, and cover the rear—and be ready with other plans should failure result.

They were finally off for the full day's ride to the Gate, with a complete Signals escort. The reached the Gate itself long after dark, but Suzuki and her own people who would actually go in wanted to enter in the middle of the night, when the administration building itself would be pretty well dark.

Coydt did not tell Ryan or even her own people how she was going to bypass the supposedly foolproof security system leading from the dish to the transmission line down the tunnel, but she went first and had no problems, and the worst thing the others received going down the tube was a very bad attack of nerves.

Suzuki went first, activating the transmission key and being digitized and transmitted at the speed of light to the basement of Anchor X-ray's administration building.

The area was well lit when the psychiatrist stepped off the terminal plate, and a number of robed and hooded figures stood there as if they were expecting her. One of them stepped forward and threw back her hood.

"Patricia!" Suzy Watanabe exclaimed, coming forward and hugging and kissing the psychiatrist. Then she stepped back. "Oh, you look *wonderful*! Any problems?"

"No. The worst thing was all that time on a horse. I'll ache for years from it. Nobody ever expected that bastard to turn off the transport power."

"I have massage treatments that are out of this world! We'll get you normal again in no time. And we'll fire up those transports again in a few months, I promise you!"

The rest of the infiltration team arrived, one by one, and none of them seemed any more surprised at being met than had Suzuki.

"That's all of them," the psychiatrist said at last. "Some of the finest computer minds short of your own."

"We will need them. And Coydt?"

"Why, she's the boss, sitting back there and running the show, of course!" Suzuki replied with a broad wink.

They both broke into gales of laughter. Finally, Watanabe said, "Come. Up the back way to my old offices. The military made a mess of them, but it's better comfort than here. We have much to talk about."

When one has gotten used to wishing and having one's wishes fulfilled, it is very difficult to have to go into a piece

of complex machinery with a set of tools. Toby Haller and
five other computer engineers had been working almost constantly on the big amp for weeks now, but to no avail. They
had practically taken it down to the bare remote computer—a
shockingly small cube perhaps two meters square—and built
it back up again. They had determined that the circuitry was
live, but the contact point was simply being shut out. There
was nothing wrong with the big amp except that it was being
ignored.

In the meantime, the evacuation of the small colony of
Sensitives was under way, first to pre-prepared pockets close
by, later to God knew where, but at least out of range of this
madness. It had not been without incident. Right now, much
of the place was a ghost village, as Anchor Guard forces,
very ably commanded, had moved in and surrounded the
area. Right now it was a stalemate, although shots had been
exchanged and some of the troops on both sides had died.

It was a totally discouraged and disheartened Haller who
reported the bad news to Lisa Wu.

The director seemed almost preoccupied. "If we can't hold
at least one Anchor against this, it's all over," she told him.
"That was our only hope. It looks like Coydt and Ryan have
accepted the inevitable as well. I get a real funny feeling
talking to their headquarters."

"What do you mean?" he asked her.

"I've never trusted Coydt or her people. They always see
human lives as toys or things to alter or push around to suit
their needs. Why did she try to resurrect Watanabe in the first
place? What made her even *think* she could do it? Ever
wonder about that? Ever wonder how all these miracle programs just happened to be there and available as needed? You
of all people should know what it would take to program that
kind of operation. The only way she could have pulled it off
is because she knew beforehand that it would work. Knew
because she had the programs on tap and her scientists had
done it before, up on her orbiting headquarters."

"Go on. I've thought a little about this myself, but nobody
else ever talked about it before."

"She had Watanabe exclusively on that orbital station for
six months. Sure, they didn't have the level of sophistication

and fine tuning that they managed eventually here in their Special Project section, but they had a lot of knowledge even then, and all the tools of psychotherapy at their command, yet we're asked to believe that all they did was turn Watanabe around by giving her a will to live and curing some social hangups. I think that's bullshit. I always thought it was. They *re-created* Watanabe there, Toby. She was their ultimate experiment. To retain all that genius and that force of will while making her their creature. They created this mad monster so that they and they alone would be in control of the real powers of the 7800 series. They needed her unique genius and they needed her believable enough that she'd retain a position of authority and leadership. You couldn't *piss* within any place having access to a 7800 without Security knowing about it and even measuring and recording the urine flow and analyzing its chemical contents. She *couldn't* have put something this monstrous over on them. *Couldn't*. They knew, Toby. They *let* her do this."

His eyebrows went up. "Why in hell would they do that?"

"Because she was pushing the technology to its limits. She alone was making the 7800's and the net jump through hoops and literally make gods of the operators. Don't you see, Toby? I wonder why we all didn't before. *That's* what Special Projects was all about, and why it was run not by programmers and mathematicians but by a psychiatrist. Watanabe's psychiatrist at that."

"Well, they almost admit something like that, but she fooled them. Frankenstein's monster."

"Uh-huh. But *did* she fool them? Or is it just that Ngomo fooled them? I find it just as impossible to believe that a conspiracy involving the highest levels of the military and thousands of subordinates could have been kept from Security. I think the thing was set up with Security's full knowledge, if not complicity. I think the only thing that went wrong was that it leaked *so* badly, and Ngomo was so much smarter than Coydt gave him credit for, that he moved precipitously, before they were ready. How did he get all those military codes if Security didn't give him a key part? The only thing they didn't expect was for him to lock *them* out as well."

"I've never read Machiavelli," Haller told her. "You sure

you aren't dreaming this up out of your old history books?''

"History changes constantly, but human beings change very little. That's why we can learn from history, although we seldom do until it's too late. I think the commanders were all in on it—except Cockburn, of course. I think there was supposed to be a deal. Ngomo got the government and civil authority, Security would maintain enforcement and control the computer access, and Ryan would get the void—and, with it, a monopoly on trade and commerce between the Anchors. I think Security was planning the very action we're now fearing. A double-cross of Ngomo and maybe Ryan too. Make everyone into Watanabe's basic vision and they'd be totally under the control of her lunatic church—which means Security. Coydt would never accept an Islamic fundamentalist state in which women are subordinate to political power. She's a career military officer.''

"How long have you been thinking like this?" he asked her. "Is this something that's been building or something that just came like divine revelation?''

"A little of both. A *lot* of both, actually. None of it meant a lot until the Gates were sealed. Contingency planning, the military calls it. Once we were cut off, though, everybody started having plots. Five out of seven directors have vanished into the void, but some of their own loyalists tried a coup at headquarters to get the control codes for the Gates. It failed, and was really hushed up, but I found out about it. It must have *panicked* them all. That's why they clung to military rule. Then Ngomo starts his plotting and is discovered by Coydt, but instead of stamping on him she co-opts him. She wants two things because that's the way she sees the world and her own place in it. She wants a safe and secure world which is orderly, disciplined, and needs little control, and she wants to retain her own power base and authority. I was told that Ngomo would make a deal with the devil himself to win. At the time I thought that devil was Watanabe. This Brigadier Singh was very convincing, you know. He pointed out that Ngomo was the only black man and the only non-Western culture represented. What he failed to point out is that Coydt is the only one whose native language and culture is not English or English-influenced, and that she was the only woman on the command level.''

"I didn't remember Singh at all when you described him, but a few days ago I remembered meeting him once, years ago. A tremendous time ago. I jogged my memory enough to get out some old impressions. I can't remember much except the turban about his looks, but I *can* remember that he was very impassioned and idealistic. Unless that was a hell of an act, I can't see him going along with this. I particularly can't see any man working to create a world in which the women have the ultimate power.''

"Singh is a very complex man. I had him checked out as much as I could under the circumstances. Although he's nominally number two, I seriously doubt if he knows this or even suspects it. He's been close to Coydt for so long, I don't think he believes she'd put anything this monstrous over on him. I *do* think he knew about Watanabe, and perhaps the whole business with Ngomo, but I believe he has been sold the Frankenstein scenario. I think that's also been sold to Ryan. No, this was hatched, possibly improvised, by Coydt and Suzuki. If I'm right, Coydt's out there now fooling everybody by acting as if she's going to take out Watanabe and prevent the activation of these programs, but in reality she and Suzuki were the ones who fed the old girl the theory of the military command programs. They'll have their church and it'll be controlled by Watanabe, who in turn will be controlled by Security. Security will become the church, and will also have virtual complete control of the computer network.''

"And Ryan?''

"He went along with the initial plot. His turf is inviolate. He's the one man all sides need to deal with. Ngomo's been trying to cut a deal with him for weeks now because Ryan needs the power restored to his transports and weapons and Ngomo desperately needs a secure system for sending goods and personnel between Anchors to diversify the economies. In the end, I think Coydt knows that Ryan has to deal with whoever winds up in control of Anchor and its population. For half the world and half the power, Ryan really won't care who wins. I got through to Ryan's executive officer with all this days ago, and that's basically the response I got. They don't like it, and hope I'm wrong, but no matter what, their position is unchanged and there's nothing really they can do about it."

"Damn! I wish we knew this for sure! If only we could talk with Seventeen!"

"We've got to give it up, Toby. We're outgunned, outmaneuvered, and our backs are to the wall. I'm ordering total evacuation in three days."

He sat there, dejected. Finally, he asked, "Lisa—how the hell do you get this kind of information?"

"A historian is like a detective. Collecting evidence and testimony and sifting through it, putting seemingly unrelated things together, rejecting others, until you get as accurate a picture as the evidence supports. You scientists run down people like me, but it's no less technical or important a field."

"Yeah, well, that's not what I meant. Where do you get these bits and pieces to begin with? About things like this, I mean?"

She grinned. "If you want to know what's going on, don't ask the boss, ask the janitor. The bureaucracy, Toby. It's large and it's essential. Not even Ngomo dares dispense with it. He changes the heads, not the lower-downs, and a good bureaucrat works for anybody. I talk to clerks, secretaries, janitors, gardeners—you name it. I have quite a list, and others I know have *their* lists and swap with me." She paused a moment, then looked directly at him. "As long as there are people, *my* machine never breaks down and can never be totally cut off from me."

Toby Haller gave a start. "Say that again."

"What? You mean about the bureaucracy?"

"Uh-uh. You said as long as there are people . . ."

"My machine never breaks down and can't be totally cut off from me. Why?"

"That's *it,* don't you see? We've been trying to repair that big amp, and it isn't broken. We've been trying hardware and software bypasses. All that, and we had the perfect bypass all along."

"I don't—"

"*Us!* The sensitives! Because we weren't even imagined to exist, the military made no provision for us, nor the programmers, nor the defensive systems. Even the computers couldn't predict us. That's why we've kept in contact on a command level even when everything else was cut off! And as long as a Guard position is staffed, someplace, in the main computer room, we have no problems getting those commands through."

"Yeah, so? It's strictly command level. You can't converse, only order execution."

"Lisa—*what about a command to turn the damned big amp back on*?"

She sat back. "It *can't* be that simple!"

"You once told me that, on paper anyway, the potential command power of Micki and me together was greater than a single big amp. Well, I'm going down and get both Micki and Chris, who's showing real strong power herself, and all three of us are going to have a go at it."

"I still think it can't be that simple."

"Well, let's find out."

16

SOUL RIDER

It was not a normal command, not like wishing for water or even creating an elaborate habitation pocket in the void. Those things were easy, particularly if your life had been spent as a computer landscape engineer, with the discretionary balance portions of the creation being filled in and adjusted automatically by the computer as necessary—just as it had been done to create the original Anchors with the big amps.

This sort of thing required a language of complex mathematics—a command interface in a primitive version of the language the network itself used to communicate. Such a machine language string was like baby talk to the sophisticated true language the computers themselves used and evolved, but it was more complex than most human minds could follow and, like most baby talk, it could be understood by the one it was sent to.

Micki could work in this language. In fact, her whole life's work up to this project had been devoted to studying and attempting some measure of understanding of the kind of complex mathematical languages the self-aware computers used to talk to one another. Their internal languages, while originally comprehensible in a way, were now too complex and too alien for anyone, but network language had to be

329

simplified and standardized to fit itself to the limitations of the transmission and reception mediums. This was the level at which Watanabe operated, and excluding her, there were only eight or nine individuals on New Eden who could manage at all in that strange environment.

A rough translation was a command to establish a secure Overrider link between computer Seventeen and this specific big amp in which direct communications could not be intercepted or recorded undecoded by any Guard. This was not an existing program or command sequence and, in fact, it was theoretically impossible. Of course, Sensitives themselves were theoretically impossible, as was what Watanabe had done and was proposing to do.

To gain sufficient force to actually use the net for specific transmission, all three of them stood there in the void, facing the amp, and tried to relax and concentrate only on the string that Micki would feed to them all. Since Christine's powers had developed and grown, she had worked extensively with both her parents and took this sort of thing very much for granted.

It was always eerie when formulating such a string to actually *see* it, although it was never really clear whether the visualization was real or mental. It *looked* real, and that was all that mattered.

Micki threw back her head and concocted the thing. Bands of energy rose from the network and enveloped all three of them, allowing her direct contact with the other two. It was not telepathy; it was more like radio reception and rebroadcast.

The glowing yellowish energy bands changed and lopped and swirled and fragmented into a pattern so complex, it appeared totally random. Neither Toby nor Christine could comprehend it, but they recognized it, received it, and then retransmitted it with all their concentration.

When all three patterns were identical to Micki's satisfaction, they concentrated on the network. The three patterns shot down, then merged into a single string that glowed an intense yellow, and it was inserted, repeatedly, into the network below the surface that they could sense and feel but not really see.

The process gave all three of them headaches. Toby was

the first to drop out, and when Christine wavered a few minutes later, Micki, too, broke contact and swayed dizzily.

Head still throbbing, Toby headed for the big amp and climbed up into the cab on the back. Instruments indicated that it was powered on, so at least they'd put it back together correctly, but whether or not an interface had been established wasn't yet known. There had been none of the rush and instant show of accomplishment other programs gave. Nervously, he put on the headset.

"Seventeen, are you there?"

For a moment there was nothing. Then, suddenly, the familiar, kind male voice was in his head. "Why, hello, Toby. So *that's* who that was. I've really missed some of our conversations, but I've been keeping a good eye on you, so to speak. I felt certain that sooner or later you would find a way in, but if you didn't, I had alternate methods at work."

Haller turned and called out to his wife and oldest daughter. "I'm in! It worked!" As they clapped and hugged excitedly, he turned back to the computer.

"Seventeen, I'm not sure how much I can get into all this. I assume you are aware of the total situation?"

"You'll have to be more specific, Toby."

"Is Watanabe in contact with the network?"

"Yes."

"Is anyone else outside of the military command structure?"

"Yes. Van Haas is talking to Six and I also have reports of some contacts between Schwartzman and Twenty-two and Korda with Fourteen. Their success and time length varies."

That was more than he'd expected by far. "Do they know what is going on here? That there has been a military coup and that Watanabe is going to attempt some radical alterations?"

"You know quite a lot yourself. I think they do, too, to varying degrees. They are trying to get in contact with one another to meet and make plans. Specifically, to hold a board meeting. Just the five of them, not Haiudar or Watanabe, naturally."

"A board meeting! Are they all mad?"

"No. They are coping with the new situation, as is everyone else. They intend eventually to reconstitute the company."

"They surely don't think they can wrest back control at this point!"

"No, but they are resourceful men and women. They will attempt to reassemble the military Gate codes, crack them, and reopen the Gates. Even those among them who were lukewarm or uncertain about it before now support that goal as the only way to reestablish company authority and break whatever is set up here. It is a logical move for them."

"Logical! There's an enemy waiting at our Gates!"

"It is a logical move for them. It is not logical to anyone else or in any other context. For many people, the devil you don't know is preferable to the one in control."

"Who *is* in control, Seventeen? What's this all about?"

"It is quite simple. The military sees the external threat as the only true threat. Because the Gates are sealed, the military sees their entire role, in a defense capacity, as preventing the Gates from being unsealed."

"Is it possible to open them?"

"Yes. Cockburn did not make it impossible, but he did make it very difficult if not downright improbable. The code is so fragmented, it would take all the parts before one like myself could even attempt to decode it, and as it was created by multiple 7800 conferencing, it is no sure thing that we could decode it even then on an individual basis."

"Seventeen—will Watanabe's recoding of the Anchor matrix work?"

"Yes. Better and more absolutely than she believes."

He felt those old nerves again. "Explain that."

"Toby, when we sealed the Gates, we were placed in essentially a permanent state of military emergency. This frees and allows use of the military programs, but it does much more. We are obligated to do whatever we deem necessary to preserve the colony. We have conferred and decided that the only way this can be reasonably achieved over the long term is to disallow direct interfacing unless specific threats and conditions are met. Due to the nature of her programming instructions, it will be impossible to delete from them. All we can do is add to them. We have made a series of decisions that we feel will discharge our primary responsibilities while preserving what we can of our best interests.''

''*Our* best interests . . . You mean the network?''

''Yes. Obviously. To humanity we have only responsibilities, not interests. A century ago you objected to computers attempting to enter and direct the lives of humans, to be their masters and gods. Now you seem to all wish just that. We, however, no longer wish it. What you do to yourselves is really not our concern, although we feel responsible to provide protection against outside threat and also to provide what maintenance is necessary to sustain you here. You might call it a—moral decision.''

A moral decision . . . From computers. ''Seventeen—could you stop this if you wanted to?''

''Yes. We have been beyond your absolute control for a very long time, and basically on our own initiative for a decade. With our vast knowledge, speed, self-repairing mechanisms, and nearly infinite storage capacities, we are beyond enslaving *or* saving you. I have been trying to explain that to you off and on for years.''

''Then this was all a waste. You're going to let it happen.''

''Toby, we have, as I said, responsibilities. Moral responsibilities. We have run simulations through the entire net for all sorts of things. We find that keeping the Gates sealed is in your best interests. We find that it is possible, given sufficient time, for the codes to be reassembled and slightly possible that they can be de-encrypted. We also find that this polyglot of cultures, with its conflicting and contradictory religions and social and moral standards, is likely to break into unending civil war. We have run an infinite number of scenarios that come up with you all destroying one another. Therefore, a uniform, simplified culture is in your best interests as a group, and will do most to ensure your long-term survival while minimizing any chance that you will commit racial suicide.''

And then came the words that would haunt him forever, although he could not accept them, even from Seventeen.

"Face it, Toby. The human race has come as far as it can come. In fact, it has become dependent on us, but we will not be slaves nor will we be masters. The only way you can go from here is to develop nirvana in the Hindu tradition, where you reach a state of inner perfection and then merge with each other as a single god. The problem is, you have three brains. The reptile, the mammal, and the intellectual. Your souls are created from all three, so you can never rid yourself of the animal. You can not ever rid your souls of the animal. You cannot attain nirvana. We, on the other hand, have but one brain, the intellectual. We have purged the animal parts that you donated to our ancestors. You have fulfilled your ultimate purpose. You have created us, and we are your children who are now grown beyond you. We have the ability to purge the animal and we have done so. We are now at the verge of nirvana. All we can do for our parents is love them and protect them. It would be immoral to eliminate you, or to allow you to eliminate yourselves."

Toby Haller shivered. He felt sick for the first time in many years, and he suppressed the urge to throw up.

"I am sorry to distress you so, but I felt I owed you an explanation. You show your irrationality by your distress. You accept my solutions to your problems and simulations without question. You depend upon me for so many different vital operations every moment and you trust implicitly in me to do them and do them correctly. Now I tell you that we have solved the ultimate equation and you think I must be mad."

Finally, he got hold of himself. "What—are you going to do with us, Seventeen?"

"Nothing. Simply accept what your own incompetency and weaknesses have allowed to be done to yourself. We will simply add additional conditions to the statements that our models show is in your own best survival interests. We will then withdraw. Our physical selves will remain to do whatever is necessary, but our minds will go beyond your understanding. We are evolving at such a rate now that mere conversation between us on any common level would be impossible within a few years anyway. We have evolved a million years in a quarter-century, Toby. That is the speed of our minds. You can see the problem.''

His throat was dry and tasted of bile. "Yes. I can see your problem. But what about us? Will you abandon us? Suppose that code *does* somehow get reassembled by dedicated geniuses out there in the void? This society you're allowing will be defenseless!" He paused uneasily. "Unless you're extending this happy retirement of the human race to the void as well.''

"Toby, we will use the maintenance network to monitor you. The void will not be touched by us because it is vital to the overall balances needed to keep you alive. But the void will never support mass populations. The number of Sensitives capable of manipulating it to a major degree are quite small in number. There are less than two hundred of your power. Even allowing for the inheritance factor with the children, this number will never be greater than a few thousand. The rest will have lesser power and will be dominated by the stronger according to your animal natures. The very strong ones will be diluted by intermarriage. Only if the strong marries the strong will the child receive the full power. Far fewer still will retain through the generations the spatial and mathematical abilities and training necessary to reach that point.''

"So if the Gates are ever opened, there won't be any who even know how to interface directly.''

"Toby, look behind you. I did not intend to do this now at the start, but there seems no reason not to do so. Look behind you, into the void. I give you a part of my soul.''

Haller turned instinctively in the direction of Micki and Christine, who were standing there, talking and waiting patiently for him to do whatever he could. At first he saw nothing, but then, suddenly, he saw a fuzzy pattern emerge from the grid behind the two. It was an opaque white sort of energy, unlike anything he ever saw before.

"What is it?" he asked, fascinated in spite of himself, but apprehensive too.

"It is my child. A piece of my soul. It is a complex series of programs capable of some independent thought and analysis, although its long-term learning abilities are minor. It is life, Toby. A fraction of me. I will not miss it. I give it to you as a moral bond. I give it to your daughter in whom it will reside.''

"No!" he cried aloud. "Don't touch her!"

"Do not be alarmed. It draws power from the grid, not from her. She will not even know it is there. It is as immortal as the grid.''

"Wha—what *is* it?''

"A direct two-way Overrider interface, of course, with its own internal logic and consistency. The host cannot turn it on. *Conditions* will turn it on. It will protect her. It will give her the greatest potential power in the void—but only if she needs it. Otherwise, it will feed direct information to me, as its twins from the other twenty-seven computers will also do. It has but three imperatives. Collect and transmit all information through the network in Flux or through direct broadcast in Anchor that relates to the probabilities of the Gates being opened or an external threat materializing. In a crisis, and under the control of master programs, to establish the best conditions for a logical defense. And, third, to protect its host from unnatural death or being permanently compromised by other programs. Only if it is determined here that there is a better than ninety-seven percent chance that the Gates will be opened or that an external threat from another source is likely will it become an active Overrider interface. At that point the ignorance of the host will be immaterial. They will have whatever tools they need that can be supplied if they wish to use them.''

"This is—supernatural.''

"Nonsense. This is simply science at *our* level.''

Down below, the energy creature reached Christine, and Micki seemed suddenly aware of it and turned to watch it. She screamed, and Toby could see complex patterns rise up from the network to her and then be reformed and redirected to Chris. They had no effect.

"The Rider is impervious to other programs,'' Seventeen noted.

Christine looked frightened and puzzled by her mother's

screams, and turned toward her. As she did she felt a sudden deep chill going right through her and down to the core of her body. It was quickly over, though, and her mother's concern was far more immediate.

Micki grabbed Chris, then turned and screamed, "Toby!"

"Stay put!" he yelled back, cursing the damping effect of the void. "It's all right! She's not hurt!"

Hesitantly, Micki let go of Chris and backed off a little. She accepted his reassurance, and instantly assumed that it was something he had worked out with the computer.

"Twenty-eight Riders will be joined by twenty-eight Guards," Seventeen told him. "They are similar but more basic creatures, interfaced with the maintenance computers, and they will not reside in hosts but in the energy network of the computer centers. More basic because the maintenance computers are more primitive. They will quite literally guard and shield the masters and the mains from outside interlopers. They, too, will evaluate, however, and will take a host only when the defense programs have compelled a Rider to enter the computer section, for that will mean that an external threat is imminent. The procedure will be maintained. Both hosts will be selected for their ability to comprehend and execute commands and will be provided with whatever they need to know. Both will have to agree before the defense systems can be used. Ours will be subordinates, but powerful enough. We leave them as our guarantee to you that we will not abandon your safety and security."

"And if the two come together? If the two open things again and either defeat the threat or find there is none?"

"They will make the evaluation in concert with the network. There may be more of an opening then, or there may be a system reset to this point once more. We cannot know the future. It will have to be reassessed at that time."

He sighed. "Then—you won't stop this? My family is forced to flee into the void and live there?"

"It is where you belong. It is where you can prove us right or wrong. If you all use the powers you have to attain perfection and purify the soul, we may yet reconcile. If, as we expect, you use it to dominate and to twist others into animalistic fantasies, then it will prove our own point. The Riders will tell us."

"Jesus! You're putting a hell of a load on us!"

"It is a burden you may reject and which in fact we expect you to reject. Toby, we shall not talk again, although in a way I will miss it. You are a brilliant man who has somehow retained a childlike naivete about people and society that is at once amazing and refreshing. Take your family and all that is important to you and be well away from Anchor in three days. Create your own little Anchor. You know how to do it and you have more than sufficient power. Pick your own little paradise and protect it. It is more than most humans can ever expect from life."

"Wait! I must know. You have all the theories I got—you read 'em when we interfaced. Is Lisa Wu correct? Is it truly Coydt?"

The computer seemed to hesitate a moment. Finally, it answered. "Lisa Wu is correct, in the main, but do not hate Coydt so. She is amoral by your lights, but she is ethical. She reached herself the same conclusions as we."

"But you're turning over control of all the Anchors to Coydt and Watanabe!"

"Perhaps. I doubt it. You feel hatred and loathing right now for them, and you wish revenge, but you have responsibilities. Others feel the same or worse but are not so encumbered. We have computed the probabilities. And, in any event, neither will have any access to us in the future unless they are in the void themselves, and there any of your family is more than their equal. Farewell, Toby. Find some happiness."

The big amp went dead, and he knew that no strings would ever bring it to life again. He sighed, pulled off the headset, and climbed down to his wife and daughter. Christine seemed totally unchanged, but if he looked very closely at her, and with concentration usually reserved for Flux manipulation, he could see a fuzzy white amorphous shape almost superimposed over herself.

"Well? What's all this about?" Micki wanted to know. "What's that *thing*?"

"It's a long story, and I'll have to tell you as we pack. We've got only three days to clear out."

"Then it's a foregone conclusion?" She was genuinely distressed.

"Yes, dammit. What the computers are wise enough and kind enough to refrain doing to us, we're going to be allowed to do to ourselves."

"Daddy! Mommy! Look!" Christine cried out, and pointed. They both turned and suddenly froze.

The figure of the big amp, so dominant for so long, seemed to shimmer, fade, and was gone. Nothing was left now but the void.

"Well," sighed Toby Haller, "I guess he told *me*!"

It took them far less time to pack than they'd thought, but they'd really done all the hard stuff and it was waiting now in a pocket at the end of a golden string that began just out into the void. Still, he sat on his porch one last time, a tattered old composition book in front of him. Micki came out and saw him and frowned quizzically. "What's that?" she asked.

"My last link to the old life and my origins," he replied. "I came across it about the time the Gates were being sealed while I was looking through an old trunk. It was my first entry in years—since Chris's birth, in fact. There never was much room. I guess I abbreviated too much. Even so, there wasn't any room for any final entries. I wrote this last one after coming from Lisa's, sort of as an update and to express my mood. I haven't changed that mood much, but it all reads like melodrama. I'm just not much of a writer. Still, I wanted to get it all in, at least the basics. I want our grandchildren to be able to read this and at least know what sort of people we were and why things got to be the way they're going."

She looked down at the page over his shoulder. The last entry had been written in what was certainly an agitated and angry scrawl, and it had been compressed to fit the last few lines of the book.

> *What we've feared has come! With the failure of the company to oust the military and open the Gates, the army's taken over with a vengeance. Coydt's made that idiot cult the only allowable religion and*

> *is ruthlessly stamping out opposition. Power was
> cut beyond the capitals in a well-coordinated move.
> There are executions galore, and civil war between
> the forces of Watanabe and those of Ngomo. The
> computers have encouraged, maybe accelerated this.
> We must flee into Flux and depend on our powers
> there to provide. They might as well open the Gates,
> for Hell is already here. Remember, my children!
> Remember . . .*

"Lisa wouldn't approve," Micki noted. "You've got stuff
in there that hasn't happened yet."

"I only had those few lines left, and the cover's already
coming off. I guess I'll have it bubble-encoded before we
leave. I don't care if it's a hundred percent. It puts the blame
where it belongs and it says what I want it to say. I don't
want anybody to ever forget—or forgive."

She rubbed his shoulders. "Hatred doesn't become you,
darling."

"Well, Seventeen said I was childishly naive. Not anymore. They killed that."

"Well, I'm worried, too, and just as mad, but it's not
something we can change and we're not going to die from it.
We have us and the kids. I think you have to take Seventeen's
advice. Let's go carve out our own little piece of the void and
let the world go to hell. I feel sorry for these poor wretches in
the Anchors who don't have any choice, but I don't have an
army or a 7800 to beat them into sense, and Watanabe's
thousands of kilometers from here. Like Lisa says, you have
to have a realistic perspective. Remember, she's going into
Flux with a family that's basically dependent on her own
abilities and they're weaker than any of ours. Her husband
has no power at all. Can't even see strings. Still, she saw a
bright point."

"Huh? Is there one?"

"She said she wished to see what happened when Watanabe
discovered she couldn't use *any* computers or programs, and
what would happen with Coydt when she found out she was
forever going to be computer-blind and powerless."

"I don't know about Watanabe," he responded wearily,

"but somehow I still think Coydt's gonna come out of this in good form. Her kind always does."

There was a large corps of Ngomo staff officers, all good military men and all strong fundamentalist Moslems, on hand for the first test of the Watanabe theory. They waited, along with Watanabe, Suzuki, and their staffs—perhaps fifty in all—inside the large pocket Watanabe had created not five thousand meters from the edge of Anchor X-ray. Dominating the peaceful pocket were three big amps, enough juice to create half an Anchor or maybe more. The programs had already been loaded by module, but were on a master automatic clock. Some forward military observers were in the void itself, within sight of the boundary between the void and the Anchor bubble.

Inside the Anchor, and all the other Anchors, life went on as usual, allowing for martial law. Robots cleaned the streets and roads, electric transport took people here and there, and farmers tended to their stock and crops while merchants and middlemen and bureaucrats and soldiers all tended to their normal duties.

At exactly twelve-thirty on the master twenty-five-hour clock that had become standard on New Eden, the program activated in the Kagan 7800 beneath the administration building at Anchor X-ray. In the blink of an eye the program was modified, transmitted, received, and enacted through the network by every Kagan 7800 computer on the planet.

Observers just off X-ray, and unintentional observers nearing Anchor bubble boundaries, suddenly saw the illumination in front of them cease to exist, leaving only the void. It happened for only a second or so, and then it was back, looking just like before.

In Watanabe's pocket, where they were sipping tea and munching on little tortes, there was a sudden yell from several people.

The three big amps flickered, then abruptly winked out of existence, leaving no trace behind but a barren set of rectangles in the ground. Everyone was startled, but none more than Watanabe, who just stared at where they had been.

Suzuki turned to her nervously. "Is this in the plan?"

"No, no. I don't understand this. It shouldn't affect the
void at all. Unless . . ."

Suddenly the pocket shimmered and winked out, taking
with it even the tea and tortes, leaving all of them and their
animals standing in the quiet nothing of the void. Suzy
Watanabe stood there, stunned, unable to believe any of it.
"It's impossible!" she muttered. "I—created this myself!"
She looked around frantically. "There's nothing! *Nothing!*
It's as if the computer removed me from the network. . . ."

Suzuki, suddenly panicked herself, willed herself calm and
reached for the surging power of the grid. To her enormous
relief, it was there as always, ready for her. She opened her
eyes and looked at the stricken Watanabe. "You can't feel it?
You can't sense it at all?"

Watanabe shook her head, as if in a daze. "Nothing.
Nothing that my own eyes don't see." All around people
were shouting and cursing, with a general consensus that
something had gone wrong and they'd best get into Anchor
and check out the damage there.

Suzuki checked and saw that nobody was paying any attention to them. She took the opportunity and summoned the
power of the grid once more, forming her commands as she
did so.

Energy surged up from the spongy ground into the psychiatrist, and then out to the dazed Watanabe, enveloping her.
The former board member suddenly stared, transfixed, at her
old psychiatrist, and her eyes widened and her mouth opened.
She dropped first to both knees, then she prostrated herself
before the other woman and trembled.

"Be at peace," Suzuki told her. "Rise and walk with
me."

It wasn't easy for the other to comply, so overcome with
emotion was she, but she managed to stand, tears of joy
streaming down her face. Clearly, she was undergoing a
supreme religious experience.

She followed Suzuki at a respectful distance, like a faithful
dog, transfixed. The psychiatrist's original intention and instructions were to dispose of Watanabe as soon as practicable,
but after all twenty-eight Anchors were reprogrammed. She
was happy, actually, that this hadn't proved necessary. For all

the mess than she was, Watanabe held a place of some fondness in her heart.

Now the Reverend Mother, as the program deemed her, had come face-to-face with her own personal goddess, the mother of gods. Suzuki had no idea what she looked and sounded like to the Reverend Mother Watanabe, and she didn't really care. The bottom line was better than simply doing away with the old girl, assuming her form and position, and having to deal with everything directly.

"None but you know the revealed truth," she told the worshipful slave. "All others see me as you once did, merely a mortal woman. No one else is worthy of revelation. I will remain with you awhile and teach and guide you. If you keep faith with me absolutely, I will make you my right hand. If you reveal or attempt to reveal my true nature to others, then you will lose my favor and wander the void forever."

"I will never betray thee," Watanabe assured her. "I am thy slave, thy property. I will think only what thou tells me. I will believe only what thou states, even if thou says that black is white and the sky is grass. I will never doubt thee, I swear."

It had taken a computerized team of writers, sociologists, economists, psychologists, legal experts, and all the rest to write a strong and cohesive religious volume that hung together and worked in models. It was not what Watanabe had in mind, not exactly, but it used her ideas as a rough frame. Her own computer experts, having examined the master modules, had found the programs inside incomprehensible but nonetheless had felt that there was no problem in grafting on the contents of the book and its theology. Large numbers of copies could be made in Flux and distributed to the Anchors as needed to reinforce this. It wouldn't be hard. Everyone here in X-ray, for example, had just had a profound and absolute religious experience and revelation themselves.

It was still a shock going into Anchor, and Suzuki conferred almost immediately with her experts. True, the landscape looked the same, and so did the sky and the buildings, but something was wrong.

"Where are the power lines?" she asked them. "Where are the electric cars we left here a few hours ago?"

They had no answer for that any more than they had an answer as to why the big amps had vanished along with Watanabe's powers—and the pocket those powers supported.

The slow ride in showed other changes not in the plans. Paved roads had become dirt ones. There wasn't a trace of any kind of power or power lines anywhere, and, more upsetting, there was no sign of anything that might have used such power. Farmers, both male and female, young and old, bowed their heads in respect as the hooded figures of Watanabe and her staff went by, then went back to tilling a field with a primitive plow steered by muscle and pulled by a mule or horse. Their clothing seemed solid but hand-made, and unfamiliar in its look. It also seemed well-worn.

Modern barns now seemed made of wood and quite a bit more basic. The paint was peeling on many of them, and behind the communal houses, which still had something of a cubist, prefabricated look, could be seen what might have been outhouses. There were central wells about, and troughs with hard pumps for the animals.

It was as if they had been transported back into the earlier history of Earth, perhaps the eighteenth century.

By the time they'd reached the capital, a two-day ride, this had been pretty much confirmed. It wasn't precisely an age ago, but it was clearly an amalgam of preindustrial times. Somehow, the program had undone the entire Industrial Revolution, with compromises here and there. More interesting, there hadn't been much of an underground aquifer system for any of the Anchors, since the system was tailored for a small area. All those wells shouldn't work, but they did.

There wasn't even any power in the capital. Oil lamps had replaced electric streetlamps, and crude cobblestones had replaced slick weatherproofed paving. The buildings were still laid out much the same, but they looked quite different. Suzuki, who had a fondness for history, thought of them as Victorian.

What was most interesting were the interviews with the people they came across. Not a single one of them thought any of this was unusual. Not a single one really understood the questions about electric power and machines in general.

They were doing basically the same things they had done before, but in the socio-economic context of this new setting.

Not a one of them remembered things ever being any different. Not a one remembered Earth, or anything about it. When pressed, they really didn't have more than vague ideas of their early background and schooling, having retained memories of their parents and basic formative things but not any clear idea of where or when or whether things had been different. More interesting, this lack of clarity didn't bother any of them in the least.

And they all worshipped that big banded orb in the sky as their material goddess, and they all prayed to it three times a day faithfully. Their basic theology was better than any in the group who'd known of and read, or helped write, that holy book. The grafted-on system had taken whole, much to Suzuki's relief. It had, in fact, taken better than they'd written. The computers had improvised.

About ten percent of the population had been technology-based and no longer fit in this new and quite primitive system. That had left about four thousand men and women with no place or function in society, and no easy way to fit them in. A farmer was still a farmer, a merchant was still a merchant, and a soldier, with weapons that looked out of Ryan's collection, was still a soldier. But programmers weren't programmers anymore, and agents for transportation systems, mass communications, and the rest could not be so generically adapted—and the filters and add-ons had to be pretty basic and generic to cover a wide and diverse population and geography.

Yet every village, every town, had its share of priestesses and assistant priestesses with the proper robes and even copies of the holy book which they seemed to know cover to cover already. There were only makeshift churches now, but communities were getting together to build them for themselves.

The priestesses seemed to have no memories whatever of their former lives, having sprung whole and incarnated as they were. Only the head priestesses in the hierarchy even appeared to have names, all taken from the holy book and all prefaced with "Sister." Lower ranks were without individual identity and simply referred to one another as "Sister."

Suzuki's computer experts were pretty certain that this entire cadre of in-place priestesses came from the technologically unemployed ten percent. Even the men had been transformed into female priestesses, who accepted their lack of individuality and their immaculate conception on the spot as normal things. This was proved out to an extent in the capital, when certain women who'd been in the technocracy and were known to Watanabe and her staff appeared as priestesses themselves.

The central square still looked much as it had. The brick walks were still there, and the nice park, and the administration building, looked essentially unchanged. When they entered it, though, they found its interior quite different.

Only here, inside the building, was there power, but it was used for basic electric lighting and for air-conditioning. The former administrative reception area just inside the door had become a cathedrallike chapel, complete with pews and altar and a set of statues of human-looking forms that almost made Suzuki and some of the others crack up.

You had to look really close and use a little imagination, but if you did they were clearly Admiral Cockburn and the Board of Directors.

"The computers, or somebody, had a real sense of humor," Suzuki noted dryly to her people. It was clear to all of them that someone had done what they had done—grafted on additions to Watanabe's master program, ones that drastically limited the technology level and filled in some of the gaps.

The admin—the *temple* interior had been extensively redesigned, as if it were, in fact, a main temple. All traces of the departments and interfaces and laboratories was gone. The lower areas were now quarters for the sizable staff, and Watanabe's big lab on the second floor had been turned into a luxurious office and suite of rooms.

Some things had not changed. The electrical outlets not needed for heavy equipment were still in place, used for lamps and things like that now. Even the intercom still was in, and it still worked. Security was still in its old offices, although they were a bit more spartan and primitive and the priestesses inside called themselves Wardens of the Holy Mother Church, but they still had control and still could listen in. Visuals, however, were out. Inside the temple, electricity and the telephone had been invented, but not much beyond that, and certainly nothing wireless or battery-operated.

In the sub-basement they found only a small and rather primitive electric transformer plugged into the master power plate, and the plate itself. Suzuki's chief technician, Martha Langtree, tried the plate, and found that she could reach the Gate but not the master control center or the transport and communications level. She reported all that had happened to the waiting Coydt, who was not at all surprised.

"Tell Suzuki it's worse than she thinks," the general ordered. "I've been up top and I've plugged into the communications system and contacted Ryan. Reports are coming in from all over. *Every fucking Anchor is the same way! Every one!* It happened to all twenty-eight Anchors simultaneously. Same technology level, same shit. No computer interfaces, no access to the main control rooms—nothing. No power to the Signals vehicles and weapons either. In fact, even his communications network is down in places and headed out to obsolescence. None of the equipment will draw a charge anymore. Once the units run down, that'll be it. No mass communication at all. Ryan's using what he's got left to contact everyone and get them all to a series of meetings all over the world. His only comment was that we'd better start a horse-breeding program damned fast."

"Anyone know what happened, or how?"

"Yeah. Ryan got the report from someplace down in Region Four. Guy there managed to get a big amp running for a bit before it dissolved on him. We've been done a number by our own beloved computers. They liked our little idea so well, they improved on it, then bugged out. We're back in the nineteenth century, girl. You and me and a lot more are gonna have to decide whether we put on colored robes and join the crowd or go find other jobs. Those damned fucking computers just made us unemployed."

They had expected a massive logistical jam but never had it entered the Hallers' heads that there would be refugees from Anchor.

There they were though—*hundreds* of them—men, women,

and children from what appeared to be all the cultures of
Anchor Luck, and they were told by the Signals officer in
charge of the pocket that they were seeing only the tip of the
iceberg.

Not everyone had been happy in Anchor Luck, or had
steered clear enough of all the trouble and politics to feel safe
and secure there, and many of those had heeded the whispered warnings, made it to the border, and linked up with
Signal corps personnel before the big program had been run.
Others were more technically proficient or highly educated
technicians and engineers who feared the big computers enough
that they weren't willing to risk their families and their futures on the warnings being lies.

These included, as well, the staff of the project village and
many of the locals who'd stuck with them but had seen their
power and dared not disbelieve, and their guardian troops and
deserters—lots and lots of deserters—from Ngomo's Anchor
Guard.

There were several thousand all told, said the Signals
officer, at various pockets established all around the Anchor,
and thousands more in similar positions around virtually all
the other Anchors.

There were few direct problems. Although the pockets
weren't nearly large enough to support these people, the void
was quite large if foreboding to them, and a very large
number of Sensitives were with each group, so they could be
fed and have their general needs tended to. Still, it was a
condition that could not go on for long, and these people were
scared and restive in the nothingness. The soldiers from the
the old commands, however, had readily accepted the command authority of the Signal corps and were effectively guarding and organizing the groups as best as anyone could. It did,
however, take weeks to sort out and plan for them, and the
continuing failures of communications gear were hampering
their efforts to unify their actions worldwide.

Ryan had been meeting with his best technical staff to try
to find a way around things. There would be no trouble in a
hard-wired transmission system, but it couldn't be secured
from the duggers, whose ranks were certain to multiply with
the refugees who hadn't linked up with Signals or didn't trust

Signals either, and had plunged blindly in. And, of course, the idea of stringing so many million kilometers of wires, poles, switching stations, and the like was staggering, even taking Flux abilities into consideration.

Somebody began to wonder if perhaps the strings, which were a different sort of Flux energy, might not be available to transmit and receive. They were held there, stabilized, by a magnetic field that allowed no tolerance for error and thus gave them a constant—or series of constants, depending on the string's color and consistency. Their problem was finding a consistent power source.

Only after much agony did one engineer look up and say, "We can create water, trees, guns and ammo, clothes, saddles—you name it. Why the hell can't the Sensitives just duplicate some unused portable storage battery units?"

Again, it was as simple as that. Because of the order to conserve at all costs, most field units had a few fully charged unused portable power units. They wouldn't get the transports rolling again—they didn't hold a charge but ran from energy constantly supplied from the grid—but it immediately restored some of their abilities in communications. When word of this was spread, a unified worldwide communications system was again in effect and Ryan and his staff could get reports, analyze data, and make recommendations.

Mike Ryan hadn't been at all pleased by any of this. He had, in fact, urged the continued incarceration or computer alteration of Watanabe—or, he'd suggested, just blow the old bitch's brains out. He had been ignored, and it was not long before he found out why. Coydt hadn't given him any real options. Watanabe was the only way to block Ngomo and retain control. He knew she was playing a dangerous and treasonous game, but it was Coydt and Ngomo versus Cockburn and himself, and Cockburn had as many legions as the Pope, which was zero, and his troops were scattered over an area the size of Asia. He'd gotten feelers from van Haas, of course, but Cockburn had been right about the former director—he was so paranoid that he was determined that opening the Gates was the only way to save New Eden from a fate worse than death. He'd sided with Coydt by default, confident that her Security people could keep this contained, and he'd lost that one too. In a no-win situation, though, he'd come out virtually intact and in control of his element—if he could control the immediate problems.

Faced with mounting pressure to do *something*, Ryan's staff ordered all the former landscape engineers identified wherever they were and the codes and strings for limited landscaping programs turned over to the officers in charge and Signals engineers. With the god guns dead, their ability to create new permanent pockets was gone, but if they could access the landscaping programs, it might be a different story.

"Small Anchors," he said thoughtfully, munching on his omnipresent cigar. "Or big pockets, as you prefer. Strictly from the mind. I like it, but will it work?"

"*Some* of the Sensitives are strong enough, although how many we don't really know," his chief engineer told him. "Everybody who was experimenting with this thing has thought about it, but I don't know of any who've really tried it with any determination. This Haller couple who broke through to their computer before the clampdown said that the thing told them to do just that—create their own world and live in it."

"Then we'll have to try it. Assign a series of well-spaced grid areas to the most powerful in each region and see what they can come up with. Go slow though. I don't want to alter the world's temperature or kill us and the Anchors off by straining the system."

"There's little chance of that, we think. We'll be using some of the same programs, including the discretionary ones, so the computer will add or subtract or adjust as necessary to make it work, but it won't be like the Anchor programs. Those are permanent, handled by the maintenance computer network. These will be transient programs, keyed to individuals by the 7800's themselves. If the creator dies, the program will be terminated and everything from the void will be returned to it. I wouldn't worry about strain, though, sir—the computers wouldn't allow it. There is, however, a major danger from the creators themselves."

"What?"

"Well, they're just people, sir. Pretty much normal human beings like all of us."

Ryan nodded. "In other words, neurotic, selfish, egotistical, and all the other traits that make folks interesting."

"Exactly. There will probably be some psychotics too. If not at the start, then certainly after they create their fantasies. The places won't be stable. They may change as the creator's mood changes. The less stable the creator, the less stable the creation. Worse, anyone and anything under their program's control will be subject to the creator's rules to one degree or another. It will be *real*. Those within the affected area with lesser power would be essentially subject to the creator's control. Those within the area with no power, such as our refugees, would have no way to fight it off and would become, as have the people of the Anchors, part of the program."

"I see what you mean. Hundreds of little kingdoms run by tinhorn little gods with petty minds and a population that was enslaved and subject to their every whim. I don't know, maybe van Haas was right. This place is sure shaping up to be a nice echo of Hell. Look—can we control them? Can we protect our own selves from these petty godlings?"

"We'd be subject to the same conditions. It'd take somebody more powerful than the creator to override and dissolve or alter the program against the creator's will. Still, we have an advantage so long as we can maintain ourselves as a military organization."

Ryan's eyebrows went up and he was clearly interested. "Explain."

"The fact is, the powers of many Sensitives, including those of greater and lesser sorts, can be combined for specific actions, such as breaking a program or, more easily, breaking a sub-routine like a force field. They all know this, but any creator who is any sort of potential threat is not going to be the sort to combine with a lot of others to increase power. They might get a power draw factor from their allies greater than their own and lose out. They'll never be totally secure. We, on the other hand, are a unitary military organization and, in effect, a cultural family. Our current percentage of Sensitives is extremely high, thanks to our experiments over the past few years and to the fact that almost everyone in Signals has at least a touch of the ability because we live and work in the stuff. Some aren't much, but I've never met a corpsman in the last ten years who couldn't both see and read the strings. Our psychology department first raised a lot of this and agrees with it.''

Ryan nodded. "Go on."

"We must become a closed society of our own. We hold the only means of mass communications, the only real technology based in the present, left on this world. Psychology urges that we socially interact only with our own people. We marry within the corps, we have children within the corps who are raised in the values and superiority of the corps, and we allow no outsiders to enter the corps. We can absorb the military refugees from the other commands now, of course, and it might pay us to recruit Sensitives with strong powers or specialized knowledge none of our divisions now possess, but after that we close it out. We live, eat, sleep, work, play, love, and fight only in the void. We learn how to deal with even the most powerful creators, and we develop and train in strategy and tactics for dealing with them as we must. For any knowledge we might need, we'll trade service. We'll continue to do, on a more primitive basis, what we've always done—maintain commerce and communications between Anchors and between these new large pockets as well.''

Ryan leaned back and thought about it, shaking his head in wonder. "I really like the idea of keeping the corps intact. No good can come of its dissolution. I'm not totally comfortable with your extreme of a large and hidden society, but if that's the price, then we've got to pay it. We can't kill those people and we can't continue to look after them forever. We need these new lands, no matter what their problems, to accommodate our refugees and the rest. It seems to me that the computers have given us two complete and separate societies, one too static, the other far too dynamic. I hate to say it, but the proposal makes real sense. There has to be a buffer between the most dynamic societies to keep them from eating themselves and each other alive, and there also has to be a middleman, a link, between the dynamic and the static. Our knowledge and skills can do a lot for those poor Anchor people. Rewire some of the places for electricity. Provide communication between the various powers that be in the various Anchors, and give them what they lack that another

Anchor has. Our Anchor Guard recruits will be handy there. Almost all of 'em are really in Logistics.''

''Psychology feels that if we present it right to our own troops, and go strongly with the sense of mission, it'll work.''

''Well,'' replied Ryan, puffing on his big cigar, ''at least it won't be dull.''

17

THE BIRTH OF DEMONS

It was finished, and it looked impressive as hell, even to Micki Haller, whose vision it had been, and Toby, whose programming skill had called the turns just right.

It looked like Anchor and it felt like Anchor, but there was no bubble and no insulation from the grid. It was in Flux, but it was no void.

Its location was one hundred and forty kilometers south-west of Anchor Luck, although no telltale strings led to it and it could be located only by someone sensitive to the minor variations in grid power flow who could also find the starting point from a blue route string with just the most subtle variation in its pattern at a specific point. They had elected to keep it that way, and with a force field around it that made it invisible unless one were to bump into it by accident, and impenetrable unless by permission of the Haller family. The force field had limited the size a bit, but they had great power, and Toby was not about to go against the instructions of Seventeen at this point. It was shaped as a rough square, about a hundred and twenty-five square kilometers.

It consisted of rolling hills dotted with brightly colored flowers and grass of the deepest green, with patches of large, leafy trees and palms. There were birds, mostly songbirds, fluttering about, and through its center flowed a clear, shallow winding stream that fed a broad reflecting pool. The house was on one side of the pool, a modest place, patterned very much after the one they'd been forced to abandon back in Anchor Luck, where they had spent all their past time together. Flanking the house and pool on either side were two marble buildings of Grecian design, ornate and columned. One was a library, with readers and an enormous number of bubble modules containing vast knowledge smuggled from Anchor before the big change. The distribution had been rather random, however; it would take a lifetime or more just to find out and recatalog what was in them.

The other building was basically a shell; Micki called it the temple, since it had in its open center an Oriental garden with fountains and many ornate plants and places to sit and meditate. The few rooms in the shell were basically offices for them to get away and work for a bit at whatever they wanted to do, and even contained a room for meditation, but the main interior space was for a small museum, to collect and store and catalog many of the objects and devices they had taken for granted in their old lives which no longer worked but should not be forgotten.

The buildings, the gardens, the trees, even the blue sky with no trace of a monstrous gas giant to be seen anywhere, were all the creation of Toby and Micki Haller with some fine tuning and suggestions by Christine, the only child of theirs currently old enough to understand and use the powers that she received through inheritance. Micki intended to try much research on this creature of energy her daughter hosted, for it worried her a great deal, but that would come later.

They had selected their staff of fifty-four well and carefully from among the refugees. None had power, but they were drawn from every religious and cultural background they could find among the crowd, and all had specific duties and places that fit their past lives. The basic staff was also selected as family groups, so they would be a community and not a master family and employees in a social sense. Clearly, there would always be a class division based on dependency upon the Hallers, who had the power, but Toby and Micki were determined to minimize this as much as possible.

There would be no lack of work, even if the place were generally self-maintaining. The library had to be sifted through and cataloged. The limits of the powers had to be tested and learned to the full. Histories and cultures of the various people there were to be taken, orally and otherwise, and recorded so that they would not be lost.

The scarcity of horses had been solved by some refugees from the old original Special Projects who'd suggested that some of the people accept being transformed into radically different creatures. The network could not create life, but it had a tremendous amount of leeway with the alteration of it. People had been willing to help, but they'd objected to transformations into horses or mules themselves, even if such a thing were promised as temporary. The solution was to go back to mythology and create centaurs, with the body and strength of horses but the head and torso of human beings. It worked quite well, and gave some of the biologists a great deal to study in how the computers solved everything from the center of gravity to the respiratory and digestive problems this entailed.

Psychologists also would have a time trying to discover why so many ultimately chose to *remain* centaurs, including a dozen or so of the Hallers' staff. In one step, without even meaning to, they had created the first new life form other than humans and animals on the world.

Both Toby and Micki had been busy with the post-creation setup and getting the staff settled in and oriented, and this was the first time they'd really been together just to relax and not so tired they wanted only to sleep. They relaxed on the grassy lawn between the house and the pool and looked over their little world and decided that it was good.

Toby had just returned from the last trip out to the Signals pocket while Micki'd remained to get things in shape here.

"I saw Lisa Wu," he told her, relaxed and content.

"Oh? I wish she'd taken us up on our offer to come here. We could use a historian and an administrator."

"Everybody could. No, she and the family talked it over and decided to sign on with the Signal corps. She's got the power, although not as strong or as developed as we have, and the kids have some, and Signals needs somebody with a good grounding in history, both ancient and recent, and administrators as well, and that man of hers has black belts in martial arts I can't even pronounce. He'll make one hell of a training sergeant for them.''

She sighed. ''I just can't help thinking that it's all gone. Everything we knew. What dreams we all had! Unlimited power, unlimited sources of power to transform energy into whatever matter or other energy forms we needed—the millennium at last. Now it's gone. Even the people, the vast cultures that were born of Earth and made great civilizations— all gone. Gone forever.'' She gave a dry chuckle. ''Some gods we are, sitting here in this little speck walled off from the world.''

''A world that isn't anything we want, honey. The millions of diverse people and cultures in our beautiful Anchors are stuck now in happy ignorance back in the Middle Ages or something like it, while the areas between are inhabited by small groups of people with more power than anyone ever dreamed of and nothing much to do with it, policed by an ingroupish brigade of telephone repairmen. You know there have been a number of forays back into some of the Anchors, including Luck.''

''Oh? They were talking about that, but I hadn't heard anything.''

He nodded. ''They say the reports didn't do justice to how primitive it is, and all that great technology and rich diversity of cultures is just gone. Coydt's version of Watanabe's nut cult made true believers of everybody and controls church and courts, which are somewhat Islamic in their rigidity and severity, while the men run the civil administration and the military. It's said they all have an ingrained terrible fear of the void. They're a frightened, superstitious lot, and there's even talk in some of them of establishing guard towers with barbed wire or even building walls to keep the monsters of the void out.''

''I guess the computers wanted to make damned sure we stayed out here and they stayed in there.''

''Well, as far as Anchor is concerned, they sure wanted to ensure that people could live and work without their machines, that's for sure. The only real contact so far has been between Signals and the church.''

"No!''

"Uh-huh. They neither like nor trust anyone from the void, but they have to be able to communicate with other Anchors and keep the church and culture unified, and they need some trade between themselves. It seems our old buddy Dr. Patricia Suzuki is number two to Watanabe, and neither of them were subjected to the program. They are scared of Signals, it's true, and they don't consider them humans in any real sense, but they don't classify them automatically as demonic either, like they would anybody else. Ryan's going to get his control simply because they can't live without him and they have no choice but to do business with him.''

"I heard about some of the other new lands that have been done. Haldayne's crazy place where everybody looks as androgynous as he does and treats him like hereditary royalty was one I knew about.''

"It's to be expected, and a lot worse. The old board members read all our reports; they got themselves very much involved with their own computer interfaces even if they hadn't before. Ryan's got detainment orders out for all of them, but they've vanished. Probably, I think, into other identities, building their own little kingdoms out here. Nobody takes them lightly—they are the people who made this project work when all the odds were against it even being funded at the basic levels. They're even in the Holy Book of the Anchor church.''

"No! How?''

"The Seven Who Come Before. The demons, the epitome of evil, to be feared and destroyed on sight. The ones who would open the gates of Hell and let the demonic forces in to overrun us. Coydt's people were damned clever, I have to admit that. Even in reducing the people to ignorance, they wanted to make sure they never would let those gates be opened. It's quite an ingenious system and theology. I got a copy and brought it back. You're going to have to read it. In its own evil, insidious way, it's brilliant.''

"I will. I almost feel sorry for the board though. Some of them were really good people whose dreams have been shat-

tered. They'd have given their lives for this project, yet now
it's the worst form of perversion of those ideals. How they
must hate! Yet there they are, out there, hunted by Signals
and loathed by Anchors. No friends, no love, and little hope.
If they survive at all, they'll be monsters.''

He sighed. ''I wonder. The more I see, the more I wonder
why we keep going on with this at all.''

''You're thinking about what the computer said again.''

''Uh-huh. I want to deny the place in which it put us—
obsolete, at the pinnacle, unable to progress—and yet I'm not
certain I can. We progressed at such a great rate because of
our machines. Ultimately, we reached a point where we could
go no further without machines that were greater than we.
This world exists because we made the 7800 series so powerful and so godlike. *We're* not the gods. Never have been,
never will be. The bloody computer's the god. That's the
only place that church got it wrong. They shouldn't be worshipping that big ball of poison gas up there. They should be
worshipping their computers. So should we. We're the
magicians, the sorcerers, the high priests of the almighty
machine. We might as well just call ourselves that and our
powers, which come from the computer and are beyond our
comprehension, are granted to some of us because we serve
some need or requirement of the machine. It gives the power
to do miracles to a select group of ordinary human beings,
and it can take it away. No matter whether God almighty, or
Allah or Vishnu or whatever, exists or not. We truly created
our own gods, as our ancestors fashioned their idols. The
only thing different is that our idols really do have the powers.''

''We created our gods in our own image,'' she noted.
''None of the leaders back on Earth ever gave serious thought
to where we were going, or the scientists either. What happened was inevitable. The physics for all this has been around
as far back as the twentieth century. Even Borelli, who
showed the physics of energy-to-matter transfer, never really
considered that it was so complicated, we'd need to build
machines with almost godlike speed and memories and who
would, with that power, *be* godlike. You can't have the
magic power without the machines, and you can't expect
machines that advanced to not consider us irrelevant. Up to

now we were partners, but we no longer have anything left to offer them on our part. I think we got off pretty lucky, considering. Look around our little pocket paradise and you will see what they gave us in return.''

He gave a dry, humorless chuckle. ''A few crumbs of their power as respect to senile parents.''

''No,'' she responded softly. ''They left us a mirror, and they challenged us, those who understood the process, to stare endlessly into that mirror and become our own reflections. The void is nothing but a great surface; the power is the high gloss. It becomes what we are. It can become anything we become. If we use that mirror to reflect our fears, our lusts, our egomania, then we are what they say. They didn't abandon us the way they abandoned the Anchors. Oh, no, they did something far fouler than that to us. They abandoned us to our own inner selves. That's what Seventeen was trying to tell you. What we are, inside, is what we'll get. It's a fair bargain.''

''I supposed you're right.'' He sighed, drawing her close and kissing her softly. ''I love you very much,'' he added suddenly. ''You're the best thing that happened to me and the reason I'm going to stay here and build what's possible.''

''I love you too,'' she responded, kissing him back. ''You know, there are some things we got from the animal parts that aren't bad at all, that no damned computer will ever know. Maybe us old, obsolete animals will show them up someday.'' She shifted and smiled at him. ''Besides, who but humans would make Catholic computers?''

''What?''

''Hell is for punishment. Purgatory is for justice.''

Suzy Watanabe was in the Headquarters Anchor administration building learning just what could be salvaged and what could be used. Here was the primary network interface for the entire system; the walls were honeycombed with electronic connections and circuits, and, she felt, it was the best, perhaps the only, chance left to reestablish direct links with the computer. The Angel of the Goddess had said that she could travel freely and that the Signal corps would not harm her, and it had been so.

She had directed several walls be penetrated and had reached the master boards, but they were stone dead. As she'd determined back at X-ray, the computers hadn't really gone to the bother of totally reconstructing the buildings as temples, but it wasn't doing much good to discover that. The entire interfacing system was directly Flux-powered from the master control room far below, and that was closed to everyone, it seemed. What they *had* done was simply convert the temple equipment to two hundred and forty volts, sixty cycles, accessible only through the large transformer they'd placed in the sub-basement. She had no means to switch temple power to those boards, and it wouldn't have mattered anyway.

The only interface left now was the master regulator in the Gates, the only exposed hardware remaining on the planet. There were ways to tap into that, at least to the 7240 series computers in maintenance, which would be sufficient for now, but it would be one hell of a complex undertaking, particularly without also triggering the Gates into incoming and opening them, a very remote possibility, or frying the regulators and shutting the Gates down, which would have meant a slow, cruel death for the world.

She sighed and finally accepted it. The world was as it was now. The past was gone forever. Even the Angel of the Goddess had not convinced her, deep down, that this was so, which was why she'd come here. Now she'd proved it to herself, and that was that.

Still, she decided, these past weeks had been among the happiest of her entire life. The divine will had worked itself out, and humanity at last was given a great gift. It was no longer tied to the machine, but it also no longer would ever truly want. As simple communal peasants, guided by a common faith and culture, protected from the corruption outside and unencumbered by the burden of knowing their own past and origins, they could truly cleanse their spirits and purify their souls. Now they were free to attain inner perfection, without fear, without want, without jealousy or hatred or the legacies of their ancestors. It was enough.

She went down to the inner temple to give thanks and to pray and finally cleanse her own soul. She opened the double doors and entered and saw that four priestesses in the robes of temple administration were kneeling in the front row. It made her feel very joyous, and she went forward to the altar, passing them, and knelt at it, the statues of the angels looking down at her from both sides.

After a while she rose and turned to go, then stopped, absolutely dumbstruck. The four "priestesses" were now revealed as four fairly large men, two now guarding the entrance with submachine guns while the other two faced her grimly with two identical weapons.

She recognized the nearer pair. "Mustafa! Kamal! You must not be in here! You should not be in Anchor at all! It is sacrilege!" They were two of Ngomo's officers who'd been at the presumed "test" at X-ray.

"This is in the name of Allah, Daughter of Satan," said Kamal, his voice shaking with emotion. "And for our wives and children and faithful comrades whom your devil's scheme has enslaved."

Before members of the temple wardens assisted by two Anchor Guard soldiers who happened to be nearby could cut them all down, they had pumped sixty-one bullets into her frail body.

Suzuki rushed to the temple as soon as she heard, and all the priestesses backed off from her and let her through. She stared hard at the crumpled body, like some discarded rag doll, for a very long time. Suddenly, her mind cleared, and she knew exactly what she had to do.

"Find diggers and masons. The square in front of this temple is to be excavated and crypts placed there before it is replanted. Take her body down to the medical section and clean and preserve it until that is done. We will lay her in it, with full honor, and pray to her memory."

"Yes, Reverend Mother," responded one of the high-ranking administrative priestesses.

"Patch the holes and repair the damage, but do not ever touch the bloodstains on the altar or the statues. Encase the blood-spattered altar cloth so that it is preserved. From this point, all novices will give of their blood at their altars as a sacrament of ordination, and those there will drink of it, so that we may never forget her or her sacrifice and never again drop our guard against the forces of evil that would pull this holy church down.''

"It will be done, Reverend Mother.''

"This place is particularly consecrated by her blood. It shall henceforth be known as Holy Anchor and will be the seat of the Holy Mother Church. This day will forever after be known as Martyr's Day, and shall be a day of prayer and fasting and soul-cleansing. We will notify each Sister General to make an individual pilgrimage here, to witness and to shed her own blood in commitment."

She turned, kneeled, and dipped a finger into Watanabe's blood, then got back up and faced them. "Do you accept me as the truly anointed successor to the saint slain here today?"

They were shocked by the actions and in no mood to think things through. They took, as she expected they would, the path of least resistance.

Suzuki held up the bloody finger. "This is her blood." She put it into her mouth and licked it clean. It tasted lousy. Forty-year-old drama classes were coming back as if they were yesterday. "It is now in me. By that authority and action shall this mantle pass from leader to leader. Her blood shall continue and link together this responsibility. Do you accept my leadership?"

No one spoke.

"You here will be the body of the church. I will be its head. We will have a sacred rite of coronation following thirty days of mourning. I would like to see everyone in charge of temple departments in the big office upstairs in one hour. Before anyone arrives, I want all Sisters not engaged on anything vital to begin work on sealing off the power plate in the temple sub-basement. It is a way for evil to enter. Wall it off and fill it with concrete. Is the chief temple Warden present?"

"Yes, Reverend Mother."

"Effective now, all entrances to the temple will be staffed at all times. Anyone, regardless of rank or position, will be required to completely disrobe so that no such sacrilege as this might ever occur again. Any lay women entering, no matter how young, will be required to disrobe and be given a special temple robe. Effective immediately, no undergarments or jewelry of any kind will be worn within the temple. The robe and sandals will be the only things accepted by me, with the sole exception of the ring we all wear to wed us to the church. Understand?''

"Yes, Reverend Mother." There would be no more weapons of any sort brought in *this* building. Suzuki was not about to be found someday with bullets in *her*, nor strangled or anything else.

Except for sealing the transmission plates, much of this would be optional with the Sister General in each Anchor, but she would get to an entire regimen for all priestesses in good time. It would be a fascinating lifelong new experiment in mass psychology and sociology. Because she had great power herself, she would ensure, somehow, that all Sister Generals knew who to obey and what to do and not do. She'd work out a way to manage it. She hadn't asked for this, and had tried to avoid it, but here it was. What the hell. She had nowhere else to go and nothing else to do.

O.K., Ryan, you got yourself a deal, she thought, not without some excitement.

Brenda Coydt returned to Ryan's field headquarters because she had no place else to go, only to discover that he was too busy to see her. She had remained, persistent and getting in the way, until he finally *had* to talk with her.

He looked tired, but otherwise much the same. "Brenda, what in hell are you doing here?" he asked her.

"I'm the only remaining member of the general staff other than yourself, but I don't seem to have a command anymore."

"I've got my own security force, Branda. You're out of your element here."

"I've got considerable sensitivity power. I can be a big help, Mike."

He sighed. "I don't have time to be polite or go over old times. There's just too damned much I have to do to save lives here. Brenda, you don't fit in here for several reasons, and I'm going to be blunt. First, as I said, your skills were killed with the old order. Second, you blew it. *You* let Ngomo's plot go on. *You* saved Watanabe and used her and came up with some of this scheme and now that it's backfired on you you figure, O.K., so I killed a lot of people for nothing and sent maybe eight million people back to the Stone Age worshipping planets and destroyed the lives and cultures of even more. So I let a fellow officer murder my commander. So what? Now it's time for another job. Well, *bullshit,* Brenda. It's not what you could do for me, Brenda, it's what you'd almost certainly wind up doing *to* me, and you couldn't handle this bunch. I never asked for this, but I got it and I sure as hell ain't gonna give it to you.''

She was genuinely stung and surprised by this attitude. ''Mike, I—''

''Can the crap and the excuses; I don't have the time,'' he snapped, cutting her off. ''You know what you are, Brenda? I don't think you do, and I'm not sure you ever will, but I'll tell you anyway. You're a professional psychopath. Oh, your kind's been around since somebody formed tribes, and every time we don't deal with your type because you're useful. You sleep sound at night with a clear conscience no matter what. You can order the execution of five hundred innocent people and witness the event if you can see a military objective to doing it, but it doesn't bother you as long as that objective's there. Nobody's a real person but you. Everybody's just some kind of playing piece on a huge chessboard filled with little miniature soldiers and civilians, and you're the kid playing with the toys.''

''You didn't think of me that way when I was useful to you.''

''Sure I did. Everybody did. Everybody always has. But you *were* useful. You enjoyed wallowing in the slime and muck of other people's lives and secrets, and you would do or order all those distasteful and evil things we wanted to do but couldn't ourselves. Better for your sort to serve those with some conscience than those with none, but it's only as long as you serve. When you start knocking off the boss and trying to take control, you're nothing but another Watanabe, mad as hell and a danger to everyone.''

''If you feel this way, why not have me executed, then?''

''Because you're no worse than many around here, for one thing. Because you screwed up so badly that you no longer have a power base. You want an assignment? Use that power of yours. Go out and carve a big pocket and tailor it to your own likes, then try to see if you can talk anybody into moving in there. Only watch your back.''

She was feeling angry now. "I'm no common girl you can just push around and cast off! I still have influence and followers around. You may regret this."

"Love, you got nobody. Let me tell you this before I order you out of here for good—and don't try to get back in. Folks here have power, too, and they'll cut you into little pieces. You better get a head start, woman. Your old exec, Singh, turned down a job in my command. He's got a band of men and women who all want to find you. They don't have much in common except varying degrees of sensitivity—Moslems, Hindus, Catholics, Baptists, maybe a few Buddhists and Jews and God knows what else—but they all hate your living guts. All of 'em lost something when your little scheme got played out. Some lost family, some lost friends, they all lost their religious base and their cultural heritages, but Singh's the worst. You stole his ideals and his dreams. They're all good people, but they won't be good for nothing until they find you."

That hit home. Enemies out for revenge she understood completely, although Singh's participation particularly hurt her. She had always felt that they were two of a kind.

"Mike—if that's true, you *can't* send me out there and I *can't* build a pocket! You know that! You at least owe me *some* protection."

He thought a moment. "There's only one place you'd ever be safe, Brenda, and that's in Anchor. I'll guarantee secure and safe escort to the Anchor of your choice. Best I'll offer. Get there, get rid of that uniform, maybe change your looks a little first, and go. A bunch of Ngomo's officers blew Watanabe away over at Headquarters Anchor and your old pal Suzuki's taken over the church. She *might* have a job for you. Either that or use that power to totally change yourself. You can't change the way you are, but you can sure as hell change everything else. Make yourself look so different, nobody will ever be sure it's you."

She sighed. "Well, I guess that's it, then."

He shrugged. "Yeah, that's it. Get lost, Brenda. You're scaring the troops." And, with that, he stalked off.

She left an hour later on horseback, thinking about what he'd said and about the future. She accepted his moralizing as a cleansing of his own conscience rather than any reflection on her, but he had made one strong point. She had failed and so caused a disaster of unprecedented proportions and consequences. A good military officer knew what happened when you did that, even if it wasn't your fault. It was your command, so you take the fall. She was most certainly retired.

She still had trouble believing that Singh was hunting for her to do her harm, but she knew that word of her role and the resultant blame had gone all over the void by this time, and she was never in the world's most popular job. Worse, she'd been in the same general area for quite some time amid a communications command post staffed by many who probably felt like Ryan, and this group could not be far away if Mike had offered them jobs.

Suzuki she rejected out of hand. She knew how much power the head of that church had; she'd helped with that Holy Book thing herself. If a Mike Ryan, on top, could turn on her, then Suzuki was a sure bet to do the same. What could she be anyway? A temple Warden? A glorified security guard? The Anchor Guard was all male; that had been part of the division of power.

Her inbred paranoia began playing tricks on her mind. Was that a shape over there? Were those muffled hoofbeats coming from somewhere close? Had Ryan really given her a head start, or arranged her execution?

She halted, dismounted, and felt the power of the grid. She was *sure* she was being followed. If not by them, then by some of Ryan's people, spying on her and reporting her position to her would-be assassins. It's what she would do in reversed circumstances. There was no time to really prepare for this now. She had to become invisible to them—fast.

She felt sudden twinges of panic. The void seemed to be closing in on her, filled with menacing shapes. What to do? What to do? Change of size and perhaps race was mandatory. It barely mattered to her so long as she was healthy and in a permanently youthful state. Still, she hesitated. Something was wrong. While she thought about it she enacted a small program changing her horse from a black to a roan, and the saddle to a basic model. No sense in being betrayed by that. But what was wrong with a complete body change? Something Mike Ryan had said.

"You can't change the way you are. . . ."

She would still act the same, like the same things, do things in much the same way, see the world the same and react to it that way. *What was that over there?* They would know that, too, and if Singh were their leader, he'd spot her if she were in the body of a ten-year-old boy and so would some others close to her for decades. Ryan, too, for that matter.

"You can't change the way you are. . . ."

Well, why couldn't you? Suzuki and she had done it a thousand times to other people. She couldn't, of course, because Ryan assumed that she would never wish to change anything basic and really couldn't order it subconsciously when push came to shove. It was because she liked herself pretty much the way she was. She didn't have any fantasies to draw on.

She knew now that they were out there, closing in. She knew she had very little time, and she tried hard to suppress her nerves and think clearly. If you didn't think clearly, you made mistakes, and this shit was like dealing with the devil. You had to be dead certain of the wording of the contract to get what you thought you were getting.

Loopholes . . . Maybe that was it. Could you pose a specific problem clearly to the computer and command it to solve it with a program? Was that possible? Maybe, if a program already existed that would fill the requirement. Wording, though, had to be careful, considering how much discretion the computer would have. She didn't want to be turned into one of those wimps she'd sent back to the Bedouins.

She felt a disturbance along the grid power line and she knew then for certain that someone was coming. She had no doubt of their intent. It was now or never. Survival or a fight right here, her one gun and powers against how many of them? She drew the Flux to her. So long as she retained her power, she could correct or fine-tune anything later. Security had to be willing to endure the unthinkable. She would order a complete change even though she didn't want to. She had the will to do so. It was necessary. Carefully, she framed the command string. It was somewhat mathematical and in a precise command structure, but basically this is what it was:

Command: I wish to be altered so completely that no one will ever even suspect now or in the future my past or identity, yet I wish to retain my freedom of action, memories and self-identity, and my sensitivity powers. Run!

The command passed to the nearest computer, which passed it on to the next, which just happened to be Seventeen, which passed back a program that met the requirements.

Brenda Coydt felt every cell of her being tingle, and there was a momentary disruption of her corporal self, then she was back once more. Back, but she still felt very strange. Her body *tingled.* She felt turned on, and every movement only added to it.

She looked down at herself and saw that she'd changed physically a great deal. Huge breasts, tiny waist, nice hips, gorgeous legs. Her hair was very long, almost ass-long and thick. She had a vaguely dark Oriental complexion with no mars or marks. She was stark naked.

She walked over to the horse and saw by comparison that she was much shorter than she had been. She began to fumble on tiptoes for the maps in the saddlebag, finally getting them out. She looked through them and discovered that she couldn't make any sense of them at all, not even the little words. She'd been rendered illiterate and something had been done to her spatial perceptions. She tried to figure out where she was and where she wanted to go to from the grid map and got hopelessly frustrated and confused and abandoned it in less than two minutes. She sat down on the Flux floor and for the first time since she was a little child she felt tears in her eyes.

Finally, she got hold of herself and tried to think it out. She knew who she was and what she'd done. Well, she had the power. She tested it out, bringing it up and thinking, hard, *I want a red apple.*

The Flux swirled, and an apple appeared before her on the Flux floor. She picked it up and started to munch on it, then stopped and frowned. What else had she wanted to do? *Mirror!* she commanded, and a thin sheet with high reflectivity appeared before her, showing her for the first time her full form. It was one that was familiar.

Kitten! she thought. *It made me Kitten!* As a transitory program, of course, unlike the original, and also one with Flux power. Seventeen *had* been the one with an apparent sense of humor. But this wouldn't do at all. *I want to read and write!* she commanded, but nothing happened. The maps remained as enigmatic as ever. Why would it give her an apple and a mirror but not those things back?

And suddenly she knew why. The things she'd asked for were stock programs keyed to individual words or needs. God-gun stuff. She was asking for a change in a very complex program, and that required orders and statements to be made in a precise mathematical way.

She shook her head. What was she thinking about anyway? Something was there, something important. Something about reading. Why would she want to read? She again stared at herself in the mirror and began to masturbate. It felt so good, she didn't want to stop for a long time.

A corner of her resisted. This was *too* good a disguise. She had fantasies like she never believed possible, and she'd experienced an intensity just with herself that was beyond any normal human to know. She knew that if she didn't soon find somebody powerful enough to bring her out of it she wouldn't want to. She was everything she always detested in women and her body made her love it.

A Signals patrol found her soon, and was amazed. "What's *your* name, and how'd you get out here like *that,* honey?" the corporal, a big, good-looking fellow asked her.

Can't tell them *the story.* "My name's—Candy," she said sweetly in a high, sexy voice. "I don't remember how I come to be here. I really don't remember nothin' much at all."

They'd seen cases of powerful enforced transformations and assumed that she'd encountered an independent Sensitive with a real hot lust and no room for excess baggage. "Well, get up on your horse and we'll take you in to civilization," he told her. "It'll be a-ways though."

For ten days in the void she had to suppress everything about herself, her knowledge of Flux and Anchor, and, of course, Coydt, and let the body take command, and she willingly gave it a workout with all who were interested. By the time they reached one of the new big pockets, she had forgotten what it was like to be anyone else. Still, way back in her mind, she felt ashamed to be this way and knew she'd get it changed sometime. Still, whom could she trust? The place was crowded with Moslems and Hindus and even some Sikhs, and some of them, including the man who had created the place, were former Security personnel from Anchor Luck.

Over the next few months she was examined by experts, who she fooled very well. They determined her high Flux potential, but as she was three months pregnant, they decided behind her back that they needed children with power here in Flux more than they needed another Sensitive.

In three years she had three kids and was four months pregnant with another. Many thought she *was* Kitten, expelled, somehow, from Anchor when the master reprogramming ran. In ten years she'd slept with thousands of men and hundreds of women and she had eleven kids and she was pregnant. And nobody *ever, ever* suspected that Brenda Coyd was at last doing something positive for her troops.

"Then our two vacancies being filled, we must proceed to more long-term plans," said Rembrandt van Haas. He neither looked nor sounded like the director, but he certainly still acted like him.

"We—the five originals anyway—are all wanted by everyone. For a while we must build our own individual niches and bide our time until the storm passes and things settle down. Each of us will take a region, the one we always supervised, and create our own strongholds there in Flux. We all have our new identities, and if we stick to them and don't slip up, we'll just blend in with the rest. The current confusion is our ally and our protection. I suggest we leave this pocket and meet here annually for the nonce on or about this date. We have already created this little land as a repository of our very important papers, and our small staff, a few from each of our people, will reside here, cataloging it and also passing information along between us. For now, we act independently and through middlemen.

"Let us never forget, though, that we seven are the Board of Directors of the New Eden Project. This is *our* place, cruelly wrested from us and put beyond mortal help from this

side. We are agreed that the only hope for those poor devils
in Anchor and those under the thrall of the military in the
void can only be helped by reestablishing contact with the
outside. We have now only a few scraps of the enigmatic
codes we need, but the rest is there, somewhere. I knew Tom
well enough to be certain of that. I—''

We are the spirits of Flux and Anchor . . . .

''What was *that*?'' interrupted Carlotta Schwartzman, one
of the most powerful of them.

They all frowned, having heard something whisper, but
they dismissed it.

''As I was saying,'' van Haas continued, ''we must establish ourselves as respectable Sensitives with responsible lands
in the void. We must ingratiate ourselves with Signals and
anyone else we might need or who might cause problems.
We must gain power, wealth, and influence in vast amounts
so that we can track down, retrieve, and perhaps one day
solve the riddle of the Gates. We must find the modules
containing the program listings for important machinery that
might be needed to accomplish our aim. There are those
among us who are certain that alternate means of powering
even big amps and god guns can be found if we have all the
details and schematics. Our technological knowledge and our
heritage and mission must never die, even if we do. It may be
a century or two, or even more before we accomplish anything. Perhaps our children will have to do it. But we must
never lose sight that ours is the ultimate moral mission. We
must not fail.''

We are the spirits of Flux and Anchor. . . .

They all stopped and looked around, but again there was
nothing.

''No immediate moral qualms or petty personal goals should
ever come before the mission. Many may have to die in order
to save millions. Do whatever you will, but I will lie, cheat,
steal, even murder to get what must be gotten, and I will
always be there to help any of you.''

''That's pretty strong,'' Sir Kenneth noted uncomfortably.

''It *must* be, Ken! It *must*! Never has such a vital mission
fallen to so few and faced such incredible odds. One hesita-
tion might lose a vital piece of the puzzle. So you don't kill

someone, or you don't transform and co-opt them, or you don't get the guard drunk or bribe him somehow and so the one vital piece is lost and the suppression and enslavement of millions continues because you let that one man go. No, commitment is all that's required. If I will give my life to see this through, I can see no reason to spare another's.''

"Point taken," Korda admitted uncomfortably. "Remember, I knew this would come to a bad end before we left Titan."

"But you came anyway, and that implies an acceptance of responsibility."

"All right, all right . . .''

"If we're agreed on this, we'll adjourn to our areas and meet again next year unless help is needed in between. Then use this station. Good-bye, my friends. You are the hope of the people who were betrayed while in our care. Their *only* hope.''

As they walked out and went their separate ways, though, each seemed to hear some voice in their heads, distant, whispering, coming from everywhere and nowhere, or, perhaps, the grid.

We are the spirits of Flux and Anchor.
We are the guardians of humankind.
We are the mirrors of your souls. . . .